RICH KIDS

RICH KIDS

Robert Westbrook

A BIRCH LANE PRESS BOOK
Published by Carol Publishing Group

A Birch Lane Press Book
Published by Carol Publishing Group
Birch Lane Press is a registered trademark of Carol Communications, Inc.

Editorial Offices: 600 Madison Avenue, New York, N.Y. 10022
Sales & Distribution Offices: 120 Enterprise Avenue, Secaucus, N.J. 07094

In Canada: Canadian Manda Group, P.O. Box 920, Station U, Toronto, Ontario M82 5P9

Queries regarding rights and permission should be addressed to Carol Publishing Group,
600 Madison Avenue, New York, N.Y. 10022

Carol Publishing Group books are available at special discounts for bulk purchases, for
sales promotions, fund raising, or educational purposes. Special editions can be created to
specifications. For details, contact: Special Sales Department, Carol Publishing Group,
120 Enterprise Avenue, Secaucus, N.J. 07094

Manufactured in the United States of America
10 9 8 7 6 5 4 3 2 1

Library of Congress Cataloging-in-Publication Data

Westbrook, Robert.
      Rich kids : a novel / by Robert Westbrook.
         p.   cm.
      "A Birch Lane Press book."
      ISBN 1–55972–106–5
      I. Title.
   PS3573.E827R5   1992
   813'.54—dc20   91-47056
                                                 CIP

For my own kids, with love
Loam, Gabriel, and Torello

Part One

1

I was only the piano player, penniless except for a small amount of greenery and silver in my tip jar.

I sat at the black baby grand beneath a hanging fern in the big picture window of the restaurant. My fingers noodled over the ivories and I stared half hypnotized out the window into the summer twilight. It had been a hot day, just beginning to cool, and the people going by on the main street looked heat-whipped, wrung-out, ready to sit down and collapse over a beer. Young women walked by in blue-jean cutoffs, bare legs and midriffs on parade. Some of them smiled at me. Sex was in the air with the coming of night, a distant promise of paradise.

I was playing an improvised version of the Pachelbel Canon in D, stolen from George Winston, but with a few touches of my own—a lot of blue notes thrown in, flat thirds and fifths, and a slow swing bass so it would sound like people making love rather than like people praying in church. I was good at making music sound like sex. Kismet came over, the world's clumsiest waitress, and right in the middle of the Canon in D she started telling me all about how another waitress had just stolen her pasta primavera from the kitchen. People tend to confide in piano players.

"The bitch just took it, Jonno! Took my order! I mean, does she think I'm a natural victim or what?"

"You gotta fight for your pasta, sweetheart," I told her, not missing a note.

"Well, I was tempted . . . I was *really* tempted to tell Heather to take the primavera and stick it up her ass. The shiitake mushrooms, the sundried tomatoes, the works . . . *up your ass, bitch!*"

For Kismet's benefit, I changed from the Canon in D to an old Nancy Sinatra song, "These Boots Are Made for Walking." My repertoire is really extremely varied, nearly schizophrenic. Unfortunately, Kismet was twenty years old, too young to pick up on such far-reaching musical allusions. She went on at some length about how Heather always stole her food and one of these days she, Kismet, was really going to work up her nerve to do something about it. Unfortunately, Heather had a lot more clout in the restaurant—she was fucking the manager, whereas Kismet was only fucking me. Life in the carnal kitchen was not always easy, not always kind.

"God, she's *looking* at me now! What am I going to tell her?"

"Who?"

"The pasta primavera lady. Look, she's sitting by herself at table fifteen. She's been waiting for her dinner for forty-five minutes."

I glanced up from my ivories to table fifteen. I saw an attractive lady, early to mid-thirties, sitting by herself, dressed in a comfortable but no-nonsense beige skirt and white blouse. She seemed self-contained, not a bit self-conscious about sitting alone; she wasn't even pretending to read a book. And Kismet was right— the lady was looking at both of us with undisguised interest. I guess she was wondering what her waitress was doing chatting with the piano player when her pasta primavera was so tragically overdue.

"She has that lean and hungry look," I said. "Give her another basket of bread and blame everything on the kitchen. If that doesn't work, remind her there are people starving in Ethiopia and she's lucky she has dinner coming at all."

"Oh, Jonno! I just *let* Heather steal my food and I didn't say a thing! My problem is I'm not aggressive enough."

"Honey, maybe that's not a problem. In fact, maybe this planet has too many aggressive people on it already and what we need here are more sweet gentle darlings like you."

I could have gone on like this, in 4/4 tempo for some time, but Geoff the manager came over with his angry pink face. "What the hell are you doing?" he hissed at Kismet in that special restaurant undertone managers use on waitresses when customers aren't around to hear. "You have an order in the kitchen getting cold!"

Kismet blushed with shame and grief and hurried off toward the kitchen. She was so klutzy she accidentally kicked the leg of a chair on which a fat lady was sitting, trying to drink ice tea. The ice tea dribbled down the fat lady's chin onto her blouse and Kismet stopped, full of incoherent apologies.

"You know, I really gotta fire that cunt," mused Geoff the manager.

"She goes, I go," I told him, switching to Chopin.

"You're kidding!"

"Nope," I told him.

"Jesus Christ!" he muttered, and hurried off to help the fat lady wipe herself. Kismet fled into the kitchen, narrowly avoiding a disastrous collision with the dessert cart. I sure got a kick out of Kismet. Basically, she was the only person I could even half tolerate in this place. Kismet was long of leg and blond of hair, quite a pretty girl who was into horses and health food and cheerful sex. She was a lot younger than I was, born of weed-wacky parents in the early seventies, a seriously hippie-dippie pair who gave their other kids names like Frodo, Maya Moon, Sunshine, and Sinsemilla. Kismet's parents had seven kids all in all and provided for them quite nicely on a fifty-acre marijuana plantation in Mendocino. I joke about this, but Kismet probably had survived her childhood much better than I had survived mine.

The story of our love affair would not exactly inspire grand opera. A few weeks after I had drifted this way and got myself a job as piano player in the restaurant, Kismet worked up the nerve to invite me for dinner one night at her place. She lived in a converted tack room among the redwoods on a big ranch twenty miles out of town in the hills above the Pacific Ocean, receiving free rent in exchange for taking care of some horses. She was a terrible cook, she burned the chicken and managed to drop the salad on the way to the table, but her clumsiness moved me in some mysterious way. So I stayed with Kismet in her narrow loft that had windows overlooking a small meadow. Owls hooted from the branches of the big redwood trees as we made love; in the morning I saw a family of deer in the meadow and Kismet brought me coffee in bed. This first evening had occurred three months before, and I was still there. I guess it was an improvement over sleeping in my car, which was the way I had been living before I met her.

Such is the history of my love affair with the world's klutziest waitress. If it was love, it was a low-rent variety with few commitments. We got on pretty well, except for the times she told me all her childhood secrets and then expected me to gush forth with mine in return. She couldn't understand why I was not more forthcoming. "Let's live in the present," I said. When pressed hard, I said my parents ran a hardware store in the San Fernando Valley, for it had always been a fantasy of mine to come from a background that was "normal." Basically, I found Kismet about as interesting as a loaf of white bread, but I think I would have killed anyone who harmed her.

So I was the piano player and Kismet was the waitress, and outside the window I watched the light fade from the exhausted sky and the cars and people hurry down the street. The name of the town was Petaluma. It was a community in Northern California an hour or so above San Francisco which had once described itself as "The Chicken Capital of the World," though these days the chickens were long gone, replaced by shopping malls and little houses lining the freeway. The restaurant-bar in which I played was called the Eggery, bearing witness, I suppose, to the town's noble past. The Eggery was full of new wood trying hard to look old and atmospheric, the sort of place you could buy a T-shirt from the bartender that said: I GOT LAID AT THE EGGERY. Already, the place was filling up with a singles crowd, guys and girls in tight stone-washed jeans with blow-dried hairdos, looking to get into some sort of omelette for the night.

Once upon a time I had been a rich kid, but now I was just a working man paying off the debts of the past. It wasn't easy. I worked a double shift. Later in the evening, I would leave the baby grand in the window and join the band onstage, step behind my old Yamaha mama, my trusty DX-7 synthesizer, and commence to play the pop songs that so delicately lubricated the ritual of love, allowing chromosome Z to ask chromosome Y for a dance. It was humble work, but someone had to do it.

2

The mid-thirties lady sitting by herself at table fifteen was about to change my life. Not that I knew it yet. Like a lot of things, it caught me unawares.

After Kismet pointed her out to me, I found myself glancing at the lady from time to time, watching her in a peripheral sort of way as I played the piano. She was handsome enough, I suppose, but no great beauty, a woman with pleasant features and brown hair cut in a simple feathery style that looked as if she didn't like to bother with it too much. She had a natural way about her that was attractive. She was sexy even, in a trim mid-thirties manner that was frankly a relief from the young self-conscious chickens normally at roost in the Eggery. But I think what made me notice her was the fact that she appeared to be so out of place there. She didn't seem either the right age or type to be found in a California-cuisine fern bar cum piano player in Petaluma.

The lady eventually got her pasta primavera. I watched nervously as Kismet served it to her, relieved to see it end up on the table rather than on the lady's lap. With Kismet as your waitress, you always had to keep your fingers crossed. But there was more. Kismet produced a three-foot-tall pepper mill, offering to grind fresh pepper over the lady's pasta. A few weeks earlier Kismet had let go a mighty sneeze into someone's salad while using this same device, but this night she did the grind just right, with a flourish and a graceful turn of her pretty wrist.

I was beginning to relax, but then Kismet tucked the pepper mill under her right arm like a baton and spun about with military precision . . . neatly knocking two wine glasses off table fourteen behind her. Oh, my poor Kismet, Queen of Klutz! The couple at table fourteen were definitely not amused, particularly since the white wine left a stain on the man's trousers which made it appear as if he had just peed in his pants. The guy was mortified. I think he was about to get really nasty, but then the thirtysomething lady at table fifteen intervened. She managed to calm him down, turned the thing into a joke, saying it was her fault for wanting the pepper in the first place. She even treated the angry couple to fresh glasses of chardonnay to replace the house rotgut they had been drinking. I liked her for that. It showed some class.

So I started playing for the lady at table fifteen, trying to think of tunes she might like. I do that sometimes, pick out a person in the crowd and play for them alone. I started going through some theater tunes, Kurt Weill, Gershwin, Rodgers and Hart. Some of the tunes were fairly obscure, nothing you would hear today on the radio by a long shot. But I sensed from the way she tapped the table in time to the rhythm that the lady was familiar with the music. I appreciated this. Playing piano in Petaluma, ex-chicken capital of the world, can be a real desert. Most people you meet don't know shit from Shinola about the great old songs.

And then a few minutes later I looked over at her table and the lady was gone. Just like that. Nothing but an empty coffee cup, a white tablecloth full of crumbs, and a tip tray with some assorted bills and coins scattered about. I felt obscurely let down.

Somewhere between nine and nine-thirty the Eggery transformed itself from a mere restaurant into a mating factory. I closed up the baby grand and Kismet brought me a plate of rice and veggies before I could order something suicidal like a greasy burger and fries. I ate and then joined the band onstage. Halfway through the first set I saw her again, the lady from table fifteen. Only now she was sitting at the bar talking with Jimbo the bartender, and they were both looking straight at me. I had the definite impression the mystery lady was asking Jimbo all sorts of questions about me, and suddenly this was not so much fun anymore. My initial feeling of liking this lady changed abruptly into a growing unease. I was a man who liked his privacy.

I tried to tell myself I was wrong, but the lady kept staring at me onstage. This was beginning to get unnerving. The band and I were playing a Stones tune, "Brown Sugar," doing it with a Latin beat, which left the dancers slightly confused, but, what the hell, we were being creative. I stood behind my Yamaha DX-7 moving to the groove and letting my fingers dance across the keys. Sometimes, when I was really inspired, I would play with my nose and my tongue just to get fancy, and even with other extremities I will not mention—but this was only the first set, after all, and you have to let the evening build to such climactic acts of abandonment.

The last song of the first set was the Doors' "Light My Fire," and I could usually play the whole intense Ray Manzarek organ solo note for note, which brought the house down. But tonight the mystery lady was blowing my concentration to hell; her eyes never left me and it was beginning to drive me nuts. Halfway though the solo, I actually forgot what key I was in, and had to improvise through some pretty weird shit, using a chromatic run straight out of Bartok to get back on course before passing the solo on to Goofy George on the guitar.

"We'll be taking a short break now," said Chris, our lead singer, breathing into the microphone. Chris thought he was very sexy the way he did this, his "FM voice," as he put it. "Our name is Foreplay and we'll be here in fabulous Petaluma next weekend, and the weekend after that too . . . so tell your friends, and come GET . . . IT . . . ON!"

There was lackluster applause, and most of the audience forgot about us instantaneously and were busy meeting new and interesting people of the opposite sex.

"You fucked up your solo," said Chris, turning his accusing eyes my way. Besides being lead singer, he was also head honcho of the band.

"I was only trying something new," I said. "Atonality can be extremely hip."

"Let's just stick with what works," Chris replied. Poor guy, he was probably imagining an agent from a record company might be

out there among all the lustful singles and we'd blow our big
chance. He wandered off stage, and I was starting to do the same
when the woman from table fifteen finally made her move and
came my way.

"Jonathan Sangor?" she asked.

"C'est moi," I answered suavely, but I was on my guard. No one
in Petaluma ever called me anything other than my nickname,
Jonno. She smiled at me, a big wide-open smile like there was
some joke between us, though what the joke was I sure didn't
know.

"I'm Myra Fisher," said the lady, offering a businesslike hand-
shake. "I guess you know I've been watching you all evening. Can
we sit down and talk?"

"Sure," I said. I followed her to one of the back tables, and I
couldn't help but notice that Myra Fisher had a nice rear end
which did an intriguing little samba as she made her way across
the room. Frankly, I hate it how I thought about sex all the time,
but there it is. I was an animal.

She sat down and faced me over a bowl of miniature pretzels
which we both ignored. Her eyes were hazel. There was something
appealing about Myra Fisher, I thought. Tough and sexy and com-
petent.

"Well, you're quite the mystery man around here, Jonno. I've
been asking around, and no one knows a thing about you. You just
drifted into town one day, a phantom piano player."

"Well, the music's what's important," I said carefully. "Who
gives a shit about the player?"

"Oh, I do. Players fascinate me, and you're good, Jonno. Really
good. The bartender said he thought you came from the San Fernando Valley somewhere, that your parents owned a hardware
store down there. He said he thought you studied at Juilliard, but
he wasn't really sure."

"Does it matter?"

"Sure it matters. Your parents didn't own a hardware store,
Jonno, and you didn't study at Juilliard."

"No?" I tried to smile, but I didn't like this a bit.

"Your sister Zoe taught you to play the piano, and your father
. . . well, I guess I can understand why you'd keep him a secret.

I'm sure it's to your credit you tried to make your way in life without him."

I studied my fingernails trying to mask how suddenly naked I felt. "Let me guess ... you're a talent scout from a big record company come to take me back to my rightful place in the Big Time?"

"Guess again."

"You're a cop."

Myra smiled prettily. Then she reached into her large handbag and pulled out a six-pointed star and a laminated piece of ID with her photograph on it, identifying her as Detective Sergeant Myra Fisher, Special Investigations Unit, Los Angeles County Sheriff's Department. I passed back her ID and for a moment our fingers touched.

"Myra, I gotta tell you, I'm disappointed. Here I was thinking this was the start of something new and wonderful."

She laughed girlishly and didn't look like a cop at all. "Oh, Jonno!" she chided. "You know, you're really too good for Petaluma. Even if I'm not a talent scout, I have to tell you, a player like you should be in Los Angeles or New York."

"Maybe even Paris or Timbuktu," I agreed. "But what do you want from me, Myra?"

Her smile disappeared. "You don't know why I'm here?"

I shook my head.

"Shit," she said. And suddenly she *did* look like a cop. "This is my least favorite part of the job." Sergeant Myra Fisher reached into her handbag again and surprised me by bringing out that week's copy of *Time*. She opened the magazine, searched for a page, and then handed it to me. The page she showed me was the "Milestones" section. I had to read it twice:

DIED. Alexander Sangor, 69, in a fatal fire in the bedroom of his Hollywood Hills home; the cause of the blaze is under investigation by the Los Angeles County Arson Squad. Founder of the Sangor Agency, which still represents many of Hollywood's top stars, in 1969 Alexander Sangor became legendary CEO of Everest Pictures, bringing that studio an unparalleled string of big box office hits throughout the 70's and 80's. Sangor is survived by his fifth wife, Trisha, 24, and six children: Ragnar,

45; David, 39; Carl, 38; Zoe, 37; Jonathan, 36; and Opera Sangor, 15, the well-known star of the hit TV Sit-Com, *Life in the Fast Lane*.

It was strange to find us all there in black and white, the rich and celebrated Sangor family. I couldn't take in my father's death all at once. I found myself struck by irrelevant thoughts, like how David, Carl, Zoe, and I were each one year apart in age and how strange this might seem to someone who didn't know the complexities of Dad's different affairs with different women. I wondered about "Trisha, 24," a stepmother I had never met, and if *Time* always gave the age of the grieving widow, or if this was merely part of their usual bitchery. And most of all, I wondered about Dad dying in "a fatal fire in the bedroom of his Hollywood Hills home." This was the thing that made it a little hard for me to breathe.

Sergeant Fisher was studying me in silence as I read the article. She didn't speak until I laid the magazine neatly on the table.

"When's the last time you saw your father?"

"*Saw* him? . . . I think it was six, seven years ago, in Greece. I was living there for a while."

"You get around, Jonno."

"I had a flat in Athens with an Italian contessa . . . but that's a long story. We were walking through the Plaka one day and all of the sudden I saw a film crew—and there was Dad. He was standing by an arc light. I couldn't believe running into him like that halfway around the world."

"Were you glad to see him?"

"Hell, no. I did the instinctive thing. I ran for cover. I kinda shielded my face with my hand and guided my Italian contessa and our French poodle toward a bottle of retsina up the street."

The lady cop nodded as if this were perfectly understandable. "You had a problem with your father?"

I shrugged. "No problem, really. I loved him and hated him, probably just like any normal son. Mostly I just had to get out on my own. Live my own life."

"It must be tough growing up with so much money," said Myra with only a trace of sarcasm. I didn't bother to answer. Statements like this were part of the reason I had hidden my past so many years.

I tried to form my next question. It took great physical dexterity to get out: "So my father's death . . . the fire . . . it was accidental?"

Myra broke down and took a handful of miniature pretzels from the bowl on our table. "God, I have no willpower," she complained. Then she looked at me and spoke in a very different tone: "Okay, Jonno, I'm not going to play with you. Your father was murdered. Frankly, we've been keeping this kinda quiet to avoid all the razzmatazz from the press, but we're sure of it now."

"But how can you be sure? A fire . . ."

"Your father had his head bashed in before the bedroom was deliberately torched with a homemade bomb. There was so much damage to the room it took us a few days for our investigators and the coroner to piece everything together, which is part of the reason the media haven't gotten hold of this yet. But they will, of course, and then God help us all. It was a very angry kind of crime," she added. "Very angry and very sensational."

I took a handful of pretzels too, hoping Kismet wouldn't see.

Myra smiled. "But you'll never guess what the murder weapon was!"

I stared at her. "An ice pick maybe?"

"Jonno! You're not listening. I said your father had his head bashed in."

"Maybe a big ice pick. Maybe a goddamn *gigantic* ice pick," I said.

She narrowed her hazel eyes at me. "Your father was killed with his Oscar. First time I ever heard of anyone bashed over the head with an Academy Award. Best Picture for 1972."

Despite myself, I laughed. Myra kept staring at me. I suppose good children aren't supposed to laugh when they find out how their father was murdered.

"It's poetic justice," I tried to explain. "That fucking Oscar was everything to my dad. It's the reason the rest of us were miserable. . . . It's the reason for everything, I guess. Funny it should have killed him."

"Funny, indeed," said the lady cop looking me right in the eye. I was beginning to see where this conversation was leading.

"Maybe it was a burglar," I said hopefully, knowing it was not.

"Sorry. It was someone who knew the house too well. The security alarm had been turned off from inside."

"Maybe someone forgot to turn it on? All that high-tech stuff can be a big pain in the ass."

"Jonno, tell me something. When did you actually talk with your father last? Did he ever phone you?"

"Maybe eight or nine months ago. He phoned me in Hawaii to invite me to his most recent wedding. I'm not sure how he found me there, unless it was Albert, our butler. I always send Albert a Christmas card, you see."

"But you didn't go to the wedding?"

"You kidding? I've seen all the stepmothers I ever care to in one lifetime."

"What were you doing in Hawaii?"

"What does anyone do in Hawaii? Working on my suntan. Learning how to mix a perfect mai tai. Commingling with the beach bunnies."

I tried to flash my devil-may-care rock 'n' roll smile, but it came out pretty sick. Frankly, I hoped Sergeant Fisher wouldn't delve too far into my Hawaiian interlude, because at the time in question I was getting ready to captain a forty-five-foot sailing yacht from Hilo to the Northern California coast, with a hold full of Hawaiian buds. I would have made a bundle on this trip, but a Coast Guard cutter started coming after me twenty-five miles off Bodega Bay in California. I ducked into a fog bank, dumped my cargo overboard, and arrived home broke. Such is the story of my life.

Kismet came by with her cocktail tray, surprised to find me deep in a tête-à-tête with the lady from table fifteen. In a tentative voice, she asked if we would like anything. "Coffee, please," said Sergeant Myra Fisher. "A double shot of gold tequila," said I, "with a wedge of lime and a shaker of salt." Probably it was the request for salt which disturbed Kismet so.

"Sweetie," she said softly, leaning close to my left ear. "Should you really be doing alcohol when you're working?"

"Sweetie," I told her right back, "I'll *do* alcohol any fucking time I want." I was on edge and I'm afraid I snapped at her, which wasn't fair. Kismet, after all, knew I had had my problems with "substance abuse," and she was only trying to be helpful.

"Jonno . . ."

"Get me the goddamn drink, Kismet. I mean, are you the fucking waitress, or what?"

Kismet was really hurt. I could see it in her eyes and the way she sulked her way back toward the bar, letting her cocktail tray hang limply at her side.

I felt terrible, I really did. My father was murdered, my cover was blown, I was sharing a table with one shrewd cop, and I had just unloaded my misery and tension on probably the one person who was on my side.

"That's your girlfriend, I guess," said Sergeant Fisher. I couldn't imagine how she could tell.

"We've been together a few months," I admitted.

"Isn't she a little young for you?"

"Sure," I said. "But what the hell? A mature woman would probably find me ridiculous."

She laughed. "Oh, I don't know. Especially now you're so rich."

"Myra! You're looking at someone who makes about eighty dollars on a good night when people are generous with the tip jar. I *used* to be rich, Myra. Past tense. And I'm glad of it."

"Then I'm sorry to be the one to tell you that you're about to inherit a bundle. And much as I like listening to you play the piano, this is the moment I also need to say you don't have to answer any of my questions. In fact, maybe you might want to have a lawyer present. Frankly, I think you should."

"Oh, Jesus," I sighed. "Have we come to this already, Myra? Our relationship has barely begun and already we're talking lawyers!"

"Well, I warned you," she shrugged. "Anyway, this is the big question. kind of a cliché, I guess. Where were you on the night of the murder? We're talking about last Wednesday, August twenty-eighth, a little after midnight."

"Actually, Myra, generally I turn into a pumpkin around midnight."

"Sure, but what I want to know is did you leave a glass slipper behind?"

I laughed, but I was stalling for time. Unfortunately, almost any other Wednesday night in the past few months I would have been good for an alibi, but on this particular Wednesday, the previous Wednesday, I had no alibi at all. I was relieved when Kismet came back with her tray of drinks. She served coffee to Myra while studiously avoiding eye contact with me. Then she slammed down a salt shaker, a small plate of lime wedges, and a double shot of tequila so hard that half of the tequila splashed onto my lap.

"Why don't you just put this on my tab, dear," I told her.

"Why don't you stick it up your ass," said my Kismet, storming off. I was proud of her that she was learning to express her anger so well.

I knew I had worse things to worry about than a squabble with my girlfriend. I downed what was left of the tequila in one fast gulp. For a moment my entire body breathed fire, which settled down into a mellow glow. Detective Sergeant Myra Fisher from the L.A. County Sheriff's Special Investigations Unit was watching me.

"So let's get back to last Wednesday night, pumpkin. Maybe you were here in Petaluma playing for your adoring fans? Maybe you were in bed with your girlfriend? Tell me, Jonno, and that'll take care of it."

I wanted to laugh, cry, and run like hell. "Look, I have a problem. I went camping for a few days . . . by myself."

"No Kismet?"

"Maybe you can understand this. Sometimes I need to get away from everybody and everything. It's like my life depends upon it. I have to hole up and brood about things someplace where no one knows me."

"Sure, I can understand that, Jonno. You're talking about the serious blues here. Don't you think cops get the blues? Just tell me where you went."

"Well, that's the problem. I left on Monday afternoon. I thought I was going to drive to Reno and stay in some motel and drink and gamble for a couple of days. But by the time I got up into the mountains I changed my mind. I decided the hell with Reno, and I drove down Highway 395, down along the eastern edge of the Sierras toward Bishop. I pulled up some dirt road and lived out of my car for three days. I got back here Friday afternoon in time for the weekend gig."

"Sort of a lost week, huh?" suggested Myra cheerfully. "Well, you sure picked a bad time for it, Jonno. Bishop is only a few hours from Los Angeles and you could have zipped down there easy to murder your old man. Did anyone witness your little camping trip?"

I shook my head. "A few kids came up the road one night to drink beer. It was dark and they avoided me, and I sure as hell avoided them."

"Well, that's too bad," Myra said. She seemed unhappy for me, like she really wished she could help me find a better alibi. Then she brightened. "Did you and Kismet have a fight? Is that what set you off on this little journey of self-discovery?"

"No. Does it matter?"

"Well, a fight would show this was a spontaneous thing, taking off for a few days. Nothing premeditated, if you see what I mean."

I saw what she meant. "I told Kismet I was feeling confused about my direction in life. I didn't know whether I wanted to be Mozart or Mick Jagger or maybe nobody at all. It was her idea that maybe I should go off into the woods and meditate. She's really very understanding about stuff like that. I was supposed to be communing with nature and letting the Great Spirit guide me. Unfortunately the only spirit I found was tequila."

Myra grinned. "I hate the woods myself. I always get bugs in my sleeping bag and twigs in my underpants. Well, I sure wish you had a better alibi, Jonno. But maybe we can find someone at a gas station, or a store where you stopped. Someone who saw you. We'll look, you know. We'll send some people up around Bishop with your photograph and ask around. So maybe it'll turn out okay for you. *If* you're telling the truth." She smiled apologetically. "Well, *someone* murdered your father, Jonno. Maybe it was you."

I had a strange sense I had dreamed this somewhere or that we were both reciting lines that had been prewritten. I didn't feel entirely real. I wished I had another shot of tequila, but I didn't want to appear to be quite that desperate.

"Let's drop the alibi question for the time being," Myra said. "There's something else I wanted to ask you about. It's about the fire, Jonno. Like I said, someone torched your father's bedroom with a homemade bomb and it's a miracle the whole house didn't burn down, the entire neighborhood, for that matter. I think maybe we're dealing with an arsonist here."

"Yes, I can see that. An arsonist," I said. My mouth was so dry

I could not swallow. Myra seemed to be looking at me from a great distance.

"Now," Myra said, "the thing is, *you're* an arsonist, Jonno." She spoke in quite a conversational manner. "Actually, you burned down your boarding school when you were sixteen. You were even institutionalized for a while."

Now I could hear my heartbeat throbbing in my ears. I concentrated on trying to look as sane and normal as anyone else in this thieving, homicidal world.

"Look, just for the record—I didn't burn down the *entire* school, okay?—just one teeny little dorm. And I wasn't crazy. My father put me in the institution as part of a deal where the school wouldn't press charges. He also endowed a new library so the whole thing wouldn't go on my record. It's amazing what money can do. In fact, I'm surprised you found out about it, Myra."

She didn't take the cue and tell me how she learned about my brief career as a teenage arsonist. Right then she was giving me a very serious and deeply sympathetic look, like some of the psychiatrists I used to see back when I had money. "But *why* did you set fire to your dorm?"

"Maybe I was sick of algebra. Maybe I wanted a vacation."

"I'm serious, Jonno."

I shrugged and told her the truth: "Maybe it was the only way I had of getting my father's attention."

She nodded slowly. She was a very understanding cop, this Sergeant Myra Fisher. "Your father must have been a very busy man."

"Busy is hardly the word for it. Try possessed. He was always out there looking for that Academy Award that was going to kill him one day. I mean, this was a guy who at any given moment might be making three movies at once, getting a divorce, juggling a few mistresses, and all the time plotting how to take over a neighboring studio. What time did he have for children?"

"You sound bitter."

"Bitter?" I said. "Bitter! Anyway, to get back to why I set fire to my boarding school. I should admit I *did* have a certain fascination with matches. I was curious to see how one very small match could touch a curtain, and the little flame would grow and spread from the curtain, up the wall and out the room, and before you knew it . . . maybe the whole world would be on fire, Myra. That's what fascinated me. There seemed such a lot of dormant power in a single match."

"I see," said Sergeant Fisher.

"No you don't. I was starved for power. That's one of the problems about being a rich kid. It's always your parents who have the power—lots and lots of power—but never you. I mean, most people I met didn't even bother to learn my name. I was only Alexander Sangor's son. *He* had a name. I was nothing but a piece of shit."

"I see," said Sergeant Fisher.

"Look, I like talking to you, and I'm trying to be honest, but you shouldn't use this against me. I'm all right now, Myra. I don't set things on fire anymore, I worked it out. I was just a kid. A very unhappy little rich kid. I've come a long way since then, even if I only look to you like a broken-down piano player in a dive. It may be humble, but at least it's my life and my career." I smiled at her crazily. "Look, I'm the success story in my family, Myra. I got out from under."

From the way she was looking at me, I didn't think she believed me. I thought she was about to say something horribly perceptive, but that's when I was saved by rock 'n' roll. The guys from the band were drifting onstage again and it was time to cut the interview short.

"Look, we gotta play music now," I told Myra. "The boss gets upset if we take long breaks. I'm a working man these days. I can't afford to lose the job."

"I'll wait," she said pleasantly. "I believe I've covered everything, but maybe I'll think of a few more questions."

I went to the bar and ordered another quick shot of tequila from Jimbo the bartender. My hands were shaking. Jimbo was a young stud, good-looking, a real self-absorbed asshole. He didn't even notice my fragile condition, but sidled over and started telling me all about his latest conquest; the gory details of how he finally fucked Heather the waitress—fucked her all night long and in every conceivable position—and now he had to keep it a big secret from her boyfriend, Geoff the manager, or maybe he'd lose his job. It made me sick to listen to him, but I didn't say anything because I thought I might need another drink sometime soon. Up onstage, Chris was giving me hand signals to get my ass up there behind my DX-7. I gestured toward the bathroom and indicated I had to take a pee. Even great art like ours had to obey the whims of nature.

I went toward the men's room, but on a sudden impulse I didn't stop there, but went down the hall into the kitchen and out the backdoor into the alley. Two Mexican dishwashers were emptying garbage into a big green metal bin. The smell was terrible, rotting garbage against the moist California night, but I inhaled great greedy gulps of the outside air, filling my lungs with freedom. I had never been so relieved in my life as I was then to escape the Eggery. I knew with a deep and utter certainty that I'd sooner blow my brains out than go inside to play the hit parade for Sergeant Fisher.

"Hey-ya, Jonno, how's the man with the magic fingers?" came a soft flirtatious voice. I turned and saw Heather smoking a cigarette, leaning against the wall of the restaurant near the backdoor. This was the very Heather who had stolen Kismet's pasta primavera. I was filled with an indescribable rage. Her cigarette glowed in the dark as she sucked on it. Heather had long black hair and a hard face and a hard body. She was sexy in a way, but I didn't like her. She'd been putting the make on me for months.

"Listen to me good," I told her. "If I ever hear of you taking Kismet's food again I'm going to tell Geoff you're screwing around with everyone who works here. For starters I'm going to tell him how you fucked Jimbo last night."

Heather's eyebrows raised about half an inch. "You're kidding," she said.

"Hell, if I am. And you'll be out of this restaurant on your goddamn ass, honeybuns. So don't you ever . . . don't *ever* take Kismet's food from the kitchen again. Do you understand me?"

"Hey, no big deal," she said, stamping out her cigarette. "Nothing to get a hard-on about."

She spun around and was gone. The two Mexican dishwashers were looking at me like I was some kind of lunatic gringo, and they were probably right. I guess this was my parting gift to Kismet: Heather would leave her alone. Maybe. It sure as hell wasn't much. I wished I could have given her more, but I didn't have anything more to give.

So I ran. I was a coward, I guess. I'd been running from things all my life. I ran down the alley to my car, my rusty old '65 Buick LeSabre, that was parked on the street. Not daring to look behind me, I fired up the engine and drove down East Washington Boulevard to the freeway, where I headed south.

At first I told myself I didn't know where I was headed. But I knew. I was going home.

3

And so the prodigal son returned. I drove all night, making the journey back from rags to riches in a little over eight hours, traveling down Interstate 5 through the great empty heart of California, a hard straight road where the miles clicked by on the odometer, marked only by occasional island clusters of service stations and fast-food restaurants glowing in the darkness alongside the freeway.

I was feeling lonely and there was something impersonal about the freeway at night that made me think of death. When I was young, my sister Zoe sometimes sang old Negro spirituals for me in a clear alto voice that made everything all right, no matter what else was happening in our family. I started thinking about Zoe, which was always a big mistake. I found myself singing one of the songs she taught me, beating time with the palm of my hand against the steering wheel:

> *Rock my soul in the bosom of Abraham,*
> *Rock my soul in the bosom of Abraham!*
> *Rock my soul in the bosom of Abraham,*
> *Oh, rock my soul!*

This is the most comforting song I knew. I could almost hear Zoe's voice taking the high part, singing so angelically pure with that crazy schoolgirl French-British accent of hers that came from being raised in Paris. Zoe had the most lovely voice I'd ever known. Thinking about her I found there were tears streaming down my face. It had been at least a decade since my last cry, and I thought I'd better get off the freeway. I pulled into a rest stop, surrounded by great diesel trucks and station wagons full of sleeping children, and I cried a hemorrhage of grief without end.

It was a good, all-purpose cry. It covered my father's death and my own fucked-up life and my brothers and sisters, and even klutzy Kismet whom I had left behind. When the tears stopped I felt peaceful as a baby. Lingering over the last hiccoughs and snivels, my head seemed to clear. I realized it had been a big mistake to run away from the lady cop in Petaluma. There would be hell to pay for this misdeed, but meanwhile it sure felt good to be away from there.

I stayed in the rest stop a long time, unable to go back, unwilling to go forward. It was comforting to be nowhere. I began to wonder which of my brothers and sisters had bludgeoned our father to death and then set fire to the house. That it was one of us, I had not the slightest doubt. Fire was the clue. Fire ran through my family history like the leitmotiv of a Wagnerian opera.

Eeny, meany, miney, moe, I thought, *Is it Carl, Rags, Opera, David, or Zoe?*

I guess we were not very nice children. We were spoiled and desperately unhappy and very arrogant, which is not a winning combination. Being rich kids, I don't suppose anyone will feel a whole lot of pity for us . . . but I do. Sometimes late at night, driving down inhospitable freeways, I can feel very sorry for us indeed.

It was funny, but I could remember the first match I ever lit: I must have been six or seven years old and I was trying to light my father's cigarette. All of us kids used to gather around him and it was a game we would play to see which one of us might light his cigarette first. *Whoosh!* Three or four or five little matches held up so optimistically, like candles in church looking to find favor with God; we all loved our father and wanted to serve him. But he was in and out of our lives like some mythical figure you stopped believing in after a while.

"Here, Dad! Here! Use my match! . . . No, mine! Mine!"

All of us pressing ever closer around him with our lit matches. I remember he laughed: *"Hey, don't set me on fire, my little darlings!"*

But that's exactly what one of us little darlings had finally done.

Talking to Myra had jarred loose some memories. Like the time my father took me out to the expensive restaurant in Ojai after I had set fire to my boarding school. I was sixteen years old and it's one of the few times I recall having been alone with him. Just him and me, no transatlantic calls coming over the wire, no other kids squealing for his time, even the great movie empire left unrun. I guess this was the best part of setting fire to my school: My father actually came for me, rescuing me from the infirmary where I had been kept a virtual prisoner awaiting his arrival. He came like a god, deus ex machina—his machina being a gleaming black limousine—and he took charge of everything, issuing quiet, self-confident orders to the headmaster and school psychiatrist. People believed in my father and did as he told them.

It seems a little crazy to me now: Here I'd set fire to my dorm and my father comes and takes me out to an expensive dinner at the very best restaurant around, the elegant old Ojai Valley Inn. We sat across the table from each other separated by crisp white linen and a candle in a glass chimney.

I think he was uncomfortable in this role of concerned parent. He put a cigarette into his mouth and I automatically lit the match for him. It flared for a brief phosphorescent instant, revealing his strangely handsome face, a face that was not really handsome except that thinking made it so. If you looked closely you would notice his eyes were too deeply inset, his face too long and angular. But mostly you didn't see these things, you took him as he wanted to be taken, for my dad was an illusionary man, the creation of his own imagination and he willed himself to be handsome. I used to think it was only his hair that gave him away. It had a goofy way of sticking up in certain places, making him look a little like a hick from Nebraska, which was exactly what he had been originally, before he reinvented himself and came to Hollywood as one smooth son of a bitch.

"Why'd you do it, Jonno?" he asked finally. Just like Sergeant Myra Fisher years later. "Just tell me why."

"Well . . ."

"You know it's wrong, don't you? You just can't go around burning things down, Jonno . . . no matter how you feel."

I lowered my eyes in shame, following the line of my father's silk necktie. I always loved the way he dressed. Tonight he wore a dark Italian suit of raw silk and one of his custom shirts with French cuffs. He looked just right. I knew I would never look as good in clothes as he did. My fingers played unhappily with his pack of cigarettes, Pall Malls in a crinkly red package with a Latin inscription on the front and a fake coat of arms.

"Can I have one, Dad?"

"A cigarette? You *smoke*, Jonno?" My father gave me what he hoped was a stern look. It was on my lips to say, Well, not usually tobacco, Dad. But I was in enough trouble already. My father suddenly smiled: "Well, you're sixteen. I started at twelve, I guess."

So he pushed the red crinkly package my way and I lit up. *Whoosh* went the match and my smoke joined his. For a moment it looked like a wispy dragon hovering overhead, and then the dragon drifted out the window toward the darkened golf course.

"Just tell me *why*, Jonno. Are you unhappy? Is it a girl? I know I've been busy, son. Maybe I haven't had a chance to talk to you about things as much as a father should . . ."

"It's a girl," I told him.

"Hell, wouldn't you know! Are you in love—is that it?"

"Yes, Father."

"Are you fucking her?"

"Yes, Father."

"Jesus, you're using a rubber I hope!"

"Well, sometimes," I lied.

"Is she pregnant?"

"No, no . . . it's not that."

"Then what's the problem, for chrissake?"

"It's over," I told him. "That's the problem. She doesn't want anything more to do with me." Actually this was a simplification.

The problem more accurately stated was that the whole thing had started in the first place.

"Jesus, you want me to talk to her parents? Do they *know* who we are? Maybe I could arrange a private screening at the studio, something that will impress them."

I tried to keep a straight face. "I don't think that'll help, Dad."

"Jonno, let me tell you a secret. *Everyone's* impressed by Hollywood, though there are some of these sour intellectuals in places like New York who *pretend* not to be. The goddamn Pope in Rome, Jonno. If I offered him the right part in the right picture, he would be on the first plane to the Coast, I swear to God."

"Dad, I'm not trying to make a movie," I reminded him. "I'm trying to make a girl."

"And she doesn't want you? Well, well . . . young love," said my father with a vague shake of his head. He had to smile a little. A chip off the old block, sort of thing. Then he got very serious.

"Look, Jonno, I hate to see you not get what you want. There are lots of girls in the world. I can see now I should have been talking to you about this sooner. Men like us—powerful men—we can have our pick. But it's important to keep your cool. There's nothing worse, son, *nothing*, than a guy who's pussy whipped. What I'm trying to tell you is go ahead, enjoy the pleasures of the world, but keep your eyes on the prize."

"But what's the prize, Dad? That's what I'm trying to figure out."

"It's whatever you want, Jonno. Anything at all. Now here's what I'm going to do about this girl thing. There are a lot of actresses that come in and out of my office—starlets, you know. They're older than you, maybe twenty-one, twenty-two. These young ladies have their priorities straight, they know which end is up, believe me. I think they can teach you a few things, Jonno, so you can put the sex thing in the proper perspective."

"Jesus, you're going to *give* me a starlet?"

"I'm only going to *loan* her to you, Jonno. She won't really be yours until *you* own a studio one day. You understand that? And it's on condition you don't burn down any more schools. You're going to have to promise me that. Does that sound fair to you?"

I had to admit, this sounded fair. My dad had a certain cat-who-swallowed-the-canary look on his face he sometimes got when he pulled off a difficult deal. Parenthood might be an alien concept to him, but he was on his own home turf now. "I guess this is the tough part, son. You're going to have to make up your mind. You have to decide what you want. A blonde, brunette, or redhead?"

I puffed on my Pall Mall and let out a thin stream of smoke. "This is a very tough decision," I told him.

"Life is tough," he told me. "And victory belongs to those who are unafraid."

I stared at him. I knew this was crazy, that in normal families fathers did not offer their sons such things as aspiring young starlets. "I want all three," I said at least. "I want the blonde, the brunette, *and* the redhead."

My father was staring back at me like he'd never really seen me before. I met his stare and did not blink. I knew if I blinked he'd never have any love or respect for me again, not ever.

After a long time, he asked in a very deadpan voice: "So tell me, Jonno, do you want them one at a time? Or all three together?"

"First one at a time, and *then* all together."

Dad broke up slowly. First he grinned, then he laughed, and in a moment he was slapping the table in sheer exuberance that he had a son who was as big a bastard as himself. "Not bad! Not fucking bad! But you went just a little too far, son. A good negotiator's got to know when to quit."

"What do you mean?"

"What I mean is you get them one at a time, you son of a bitch! What a nerve you have! Anyway, all at once those ladies would fucking eat you up!"

I was giddy with his praise and comraderie. He kept smiling at me and shaking his head. "You know, I do believe I've just seen the future of Hollywood, and it has your name on it, son. Your goddamn name in lights!"

My dad ordered a bottle of champagne from the headwaiter and two glasses. The headwaiter momentarily seemed on the verge of asking my age, but then he glanced quickly at my father and decided he'd better not.

He brought the champagne, Moët & Chandon on ice. My dad and I had three glasses each, toasting first to blondes, then brunettes, and finally redheads. And that's how he punished me for setting fire to my expensive boarding school in Ojai.

I drove through the night. The flat straight emptiness of Interstate 5 ends abruptly at the Grapevine, a stretch of road a hundred miles north of Los Angeles which climbs into the brown dusty mountains that contain the L.A. basin. God put these mountains here so that his lost angels might breathe smog. What I like best about air pollution is what it can do for an ordinary sunrise: Poof! It's like the sun is a big torch, lighting a sky full of gasoline. Coming into the L.A. basin over the Grapevine, I watched the glory of an orange dawn exploding to the east. The traffic became slow with the morning commute. Los Angeles came at me, mile after mile, a growing behemoth until at last I was in the thick of it, feeling like an insect returning to the hive.

I was coming home. The dawn filled me with a burst of restless energy. I started getting wild ideas about how I might investigate my father's murder myself, discover which of my darling brothers and sisters was a patricidal maniac, turn him or her over to the attractive Sergeant Fisher, and I could walk away free, possibly even with a small inheritance. It seemed to me I would have an easier time solving this case than the police because I knew all the deep dark secrets. The more I thought about this, the more it seemed exactly what I had to do to clear my own name.

But meanwhile, cruising down the highway to truth, I encountered my first major obstacle as a detective of family crimes. My gas gauge was down to the one-quarter mark and I had exactly thirty-four cents in my pocket after filling up in Coalinga at three in the morning and buying a candy bar. This was not the first time I had set out on a journey with high hopes and few resources.

By the time I left the freeway near UCLA, I was running on sheer optimism. I drove the final few miles to Beverly Hills, hoping the empty gas tank could squeeze out a few more teardrops of energy to get me home. Near the Beverly Hills Hotel, there was a small explosion toward the front end of my car. I discovered I had a flat tire, my left front, but there was no spare in the trunk so I drove on it anyway, wobbling up Coldwater Canyon at five miles an hour, hoping I wouldn't be pulled over by the cops.

Coldwater Canyon goes up into the hills behind the Beverly

Hills Hotel, winding its way past seriously rich mansions protected behind high walls, houses so somber and heavy with wealth they look like bank vaults or department stores. I think the only people who can afford to live here anymore are ex-dictators from Third World countries who have looted the national treasury and have fled to the land of dreams to avoid various firing squads.

My house—the house of my childhood—was beyond the northern edge of Beverly Hills, up toward the top of Mulholland. At a little past eight in the morning, I pulled into a stately driveway and came to a stop at a familiar wrought-iron gate. I left my engine running, afraid the Buick might not start again if I turned it off, and walked to the speaker mounted near the gate.

My bowels rumbled at the thought of being home. After driving all night, I felt nauseous and had trouble standing upright. For a moment, I hesitated. I wasn't at all certain what my reception would be here. I rang the buzzer. "Yes?" came the familiar voice of Albert, butler-handyman and general lifelong counselor to the Sangor family.

"Albert, it's me, Jonno. Let me in."

"Jonno!" he cried.

From the sound of his voice, there seemed at least one person glad to see me. In a moment I heard the electric whir of the big iron gate swinging open. I returned hastily to my car and drove on my bad tire, limping up the long drive. When I saw the gate close behind me, I felt my whole body relax. I loved this house; I hated this house; but every muscle and nerve of me knew it for the security of home.

I parked alongside a creamy Jaguar convertible and a sleek Mercedes convertible. When I turned off the ignition, the Buick shuddered and sputtered to silence. I stepped outside to look at my past.

It was an old house, old and rambling and full of wood, with flowering vines growing up the sides. If you can imagine a sort of Deep South version of the White House, moved from Washington, DC, to Hollywood, that would be my family home. The house was painted white, with four very pretentious columns holding up the two-story façade. They were architecturally useless, but served to tell the world we were rich. From where I stood, I could not see any signs of the fatal fire, but that would be around the back in

the eastern wing. In fact, everything was weirdly peaceful, untouched by time or violence.

The house had a pretentious French name, as houses like these
tend to: La Chanson d'Or. The Sangors and their Golden Song.
The pun didn't quite work and it was all invented anyway, since
my father's name at birth was Sangwolovitch, not Sangor, and our
ancestral home was no more real than the fake colonnades in front.

While I stood gaping at the old house, weak in the knees, exhausted from the long drive and no sleep, Albert came out the big
front door and into the driveway. He stopped, and for a moment
I could see how I must look in his eyes: I was unshaved, my hair
long and wild, my face still streaked with dried tears.

"Albert, you old fuck, you look *great!*" I cried. And he *did* look
great too, though he was quite an old man now, with tufts of white
hair around the dome of his shiny bald head. No one had ever
treated Albert like a butler—not ever—and old as he was, he was
dressed in jeans, sandals, and a quietly-loud Hawaiian shirt. When
my father found him, thirty-five years before, he was trying to
make a living as a character actor in B-movies, but playing our
butler turned out to be the role of his life.

He hugged me, and for a moment—with my head on his shoulder—I nearly started crying again.

"We'll have to get you cleaned up," he said gently. "The police
have been here looking for you."

"Has my father been . . . you know, been buried yet?"

"There's going to be a memorial service in the next week or so.
You'll learn all about it at the family meeting this afternoon."

"Family meeting?" I repeated dubiously. "Jesus, I don't think
so, Albert. I've been gone a hell of a long time."

"Gone but not forgotten, Jonno. Welcome home."

Albert took my arm and guided me gently into the shadows of
the big old house.

"I suggest breakfast, bath, and bed. In that order. When you're
rested, we can sort things out."

He seemed happy to take charge of me again after all those
years, and I was glad to let him. We were in the foyer beneath a
heavy crystal chandelier, with the large curving staircase sweeping
up to the second floor with its Gone-With-the-Wind bravado. I
heard a sound and turned to my left. Coming out of the library

was a very lovely young woman I had never seen before. She appeared to be a rich man's woman, as carefully tended as a formal garden. She had delicate features, large dark eyes, a smooth oval face, and closely cut dark hair that seemed to emphasize the fawn-like quality of her pretty face. She was dressed in a simple but elegant white shift which managed to be simultaneously chaste and suggestive. Just as I was wondering who the hell she could be, the answer hit me and brought a twisted smile to my lips.

"You must be Jonno," said the beautiful girl, with grave politeness.

"Mom," I said, shaking hands with my twenty-four-year-old stepmother. I must say, it was a thrill to discover I wasn't really an orphan after all.

4

We sat in the sun room smiling at each other, my new stepmother and I. It was the dance of strangers, sizing each other up.

"Now how long have you been away, Jonno?"

"Sixteen years," I said.

"Your father was hurt you didn't write or call."

"Often I was in strange far-off places," I told her. "Places so strange and far-off they hardly even had post offices and telephones."

She didn't know what to make of me and I felt unsettled being home, exhausted from the long drive. The sun room was a converted porch at the rear of the house, an informal spot that had been the creation of an earlier stepmother, the French actress Michelle Cordell, who had been Mrs. Alexander Sangor the Third. The room had bright furniture, many potted plants, and a big sliding-glass door that opened onto the flagstone terrace and the swimming pool. For me, this house was full of too many mothers who had come and gone. From where I sat, I could just make out the wet bar at the far end of the pool, a small marble counter with four wicker stools standing in the open between two palm trees. This little setting was the creation of the American actress Corina

Norman—Mrs. Alexander Sangor the Second—who happened to be my *real* mother, and who never liked to be more than an arm's length away from the nearest gin and tonic.

Meanwhile, Trisha St. Amant Sangor, my twenty-four-year-old stepmother—Mrs. Alexander the Fifth—started telling me about the night my father died.

"It's so absolutely ghastly. I still can't believe it happened. Thank God Albert woke up and smelled smoke, otherwise the entire house might have gone. *The entire house!*" she emphasized. Real estate, I sensed, was an important consideration for Trisha St. Amant Sangor.

"What time did this happen?"

"Albert called 911 at 12:18. Last Wednesday night, you know. The fire department was here in minutes, but your father was already dead, of course. Some horrid person had hit him over the head."

"Offed by his Oscar," I said thoughtfully. "You know, Trisha, life has some strange endings."

She lowered her eyes delicately. I had a feeling I wasn't the stepson of her dreams: unshaved, unwashed, uncouth, and twelve years her senior. But she was making a noble effort. There was a question I was dying to ask her—a very obvious question—but it was hard to put into words, even for someone as tactless as myself.

"Trisha, you'll have to pardon my curiosity. But just exactly where were *you* on the night Dad was bludgeoned to death in your bedroom?"

She gazed at me without expression. "I was at the beach house. Your father had been so busy lately, I thought it best to get out of his way."

Oh-ho! thought I. Not many months into the marriage and she was sleeping at the beach house already. I had seen this movie before. Other stepmothers, other marriages, seeking their inevitable way toward divorce.

"I like the air at Malibu," she explained.

"Don't we all," I agreed.

"For me it's especially important to be able to breathe, and the town has gotten so bad lately. I do a lot of running on the beach. Sometimes five miles a day. It's how I stay in shape. Are you a runner, Jonno?"

"Sure," I confided. "I've run from everything, all my life."

"That's not so terribly funny," she said.

I shrugged my shoulders and sat back in my yellow chair in the sun room feeling the dead weight of years. Everywhere I looked, I saw memories. To tell the truth, I was glad Trisha St. Amant Sangor was a stranger to me. She was the only thing there in that big tomb of a house to which I had no past connection.

"The cops think it was one of us," I mentioned. "The immediate family or an intimate acquaintance, sort of thing. You see, the burglar alarm had been turned off from inside. . . ."

"The damn thing didn't work, that's all," Trisha exploded, and I was surprised to see she was angry. "The crushing irony of all this is we pay five hundred dollars a month to a private security company and they absolutely guarantee—*guarantee!*—to have their people here within two minutes of any break-in. But it's a complete myth, of course. The problem, Jonno, is you can barely find anyone who speaks English around here. When they should be working, they're off taking a siesta!"

"So you think the Mexicans did it?"

"Jonno, I adore Mexicans, I really do—they're such a sweet people. But they're the main reason nothing quite works right in this town anymore. And as for your father's death, well obviously it was some poor crackhead from the ghetto. He sees a big house and thinks he'll never have to work again! The police can't protect us from these people, and so they turn around and absolutely feel they must blame one of us. It's their revenge, you see, because we're rich. . . ."

Her words washed over me. Trisha was so pretty it took my breath away, but she was as brittle as a porcelain doll. She didn't even speak like a young woman, but had the class prejudices of someone much older. That was money for you. It made you old before your time. I hadn't thought I could get any more depressed, but I became so, second by second. I seemed to be slipping deeper into the yellow chair until I was afraid it might wrap around my body and suffocate me.

"Well, Jonno—at least you're home now," she said, changing the subject, trying to be as bright and cheerful as the furniture. "What do you plan to do with yourself?"

"Survive," I told her. "That's the plan, anyway."

She succeeded in pasting a false smile on her face. I sensed she could walk over dead men with that smile. The room glowed with morning sunshine. The young Mrs. Alexander the Fifth sat in her sunny yellow armchair, her little feet tucked daintily under her body, gazing at me with a polite curiosity that was beginning to show signs of strain. She had perfectly glossed nails, I noticed. Perfect skin. A perfect figure. In fact, it was beginning to annoy me a little, all this perfection. I almost longed for a pimple somewhere. This was not beauty so much as a hard glossy shell—like her nails—designed for maximum survival in Southern California.

"Why don't you tell me about my father's last few hours," I suggested, surprised to discover I was curious. Maybe the old man had some final epiphany in which all of life's mysteries became wonderfully clear.

She tilted her head prettily to one side. "From what I gather, there was nothing unusual. He ate dinner at Morton's."

"Morton who?"

"It's a restaurant," she said, very deadpan. "An extremely *fashionable* restaurant."

"Ah, yes, *that* Morton," I said, trying to be impressed.

Trisha didn't seem happy. Knowing who people were, and which restaurants were chic, was what Hollywood was all about. My ignorance was a kind of anarchy attacking the very foundation of Tinsel Town.

"He had dinner with a producer who was going to do a few M-O-W's for him . . . Movies of the Week," she added when she saw my blank stare.

"Dad was into television?"

"Your father was into everything. After Morton's, he went to Westwood where there was a sneak preview of his new movie, a big sci-fi thriller that came in fifteen million over budget. Alex wasn't happy. He thought it moved too slow, and I gather the questionnaires filled out by the target audience came back sixty-eight percent negative. So he went down the street to Hamburger Hamlet afterward with the director and the editor and they talked about changing the ending. Then he came back here, around eleven o'clock, according to Albert, who was just going to bed. Your father made a few phone calls and then went to bed himself. And that's the whole story."

"Who did he call?"

"The police tell me the last call he made was to London. He fired some director who was just starting a picture there."

"He fired a director at eleven o'clock at night? Jesus!"

"It was early morning in London," Trisha reminded me. I guess this made it all right.

I grinned. "Well, well . . . it seems Dad went down doing what he did best. Wheeling and dealing all the way. Sort of reminds me of a captain of a sinking ship."

"Your father was a very successful man," said Trisha solemnly.

"And isn't success a marvelous thing? I guess you were pretty lucky you spent that particular night in Malibu. Those Chicano crackheads might have turned you into quite a sad enchilada, my dear."

"That's not funny, Jonno."

"No, I guess not. I'm on edge being home after all this time. You'll have to forgive me, Trisha."

"Do you want to see where your father was murdered?" she asked.

This wasn't exactly my idea of a good time, but I said sure, I was dying to see where my father was murdered. Trisha led the way out of the sun room, past the living room into the foyer, and up the great curving staircase to the bedrooms.

"I'm sure Dah-veed's going to be so thrilled to see you!" she chattered as we climbed to the second floor. She pronounced my brother David's name in the French manner he always preferred. "Dah-veed talks about you all the time, you know. Honestly, you're like a myth in this family, Jonno."

"So what's old Dah-veed up to these days?" I asked. "As a kid I was never sure if he'd end up as a child molester or the president of a bank."

"Don't you know? He married Christina Dorn. They have a fabulous three-point-two-million-dollar home in Bel Air and two adorable children."

"Who's Christina Dorn?"

"*Who's* Christina Dorn?" Apparently I had committed a new faux pas. We had reached the top landing and my stepmother turned to me in disbelief. "Christina Dorn, my dear, is the hottest thing on television. She plays Laura in 'Chesapeake Bay.'"

"Isn't that a little far from Bel Air and the two adorable children?"

"My *God*, Jonno. It's a series! It's filmed right here in Hollywood, of course."

"Of course," I said. Actually I wasn't paying a whole lot of attention to her, and I didn't give a flying fuck who David had married. We had arrived at an intensely familiar part of the house. The children's wing was off to the left of where we stood—I could almost see the door to my old bedroom—but Trisha led the way down the hall to the right, to where the adults had lived their separate lives of marriage and divorce, occasionally stopping by the children's wing to say goodnight, always on their way out, always wrapped in furs and splendid clothing and smelling of exotic perfumes.

"You know about Dah-veed's job, of course?"

"Let me guess. He's living off his wife?"

"Honestly, Jonno! Dah-veed's the head of the studio."

"Which studio?"

"Everest Pictures, of course. What other studio *is* there in this family?"

"But that's Dad's studio," I objected.

"Not for the past year it wasn't. Dah-veed took over after your father left."

I was starting to get a queasy feeling in my stomach. Approaching the master bedroom, I began to smell the cold remnants of fire, the heavy acrid smell of burnt wood. At the end of the hall was a door, which Trisha opened so that we could enter. I remember my father's bedroom as a large and wonderful place, painted a very pale green, with comfortably opulent furniture of an art deco style, and airy windows looking out upon the backyard grounds. Stepmothers came and went, but the bedroom remained, a magical place to which we children were occasionally invited.

Fire had changed all that. Today there was nothing but a charred shell, with water-soaked furniture from the firemen's hoses, and broken windows. The great emperor-sized bed was a ruined tangle of blackened springs. I stared in fascination at the spot where my father had been incinerated.

"It's sad, isn't it, what fire can do? I've already received some estimates of how much it's going to cost to have this repaired. Thank God for the insurance."

I didn't say a thing. I was finding it more unsettling than I thought.

"Anyway, about the studio . . . it was a real coup d'état," said Trisha, while we both stared at the burned bed. "Alex had a few flops and Dah-veed was able to convince the board of directors the studio needed someone younger at the helm."

"Dad must have been furious."

"Actually, Alex was quite impressed at how cleverly Dah-veed pulled it off. And it turned out to be a blessing in disguise. Cal-Star gave Alex a deal as head of their entire operation with a guaranteed salary of three million dollars a year. They even built a lovely office for him in Beverly Hills. It's designed like an Italian palazzo, you know. And since Alex still owned forty-eight percent of the stock back at Everest, he really ended up with the best of everything."

"Well, well," I said. I have to admit to some culture shock, moving from Petaluma to Babylon in a single night. In Hollywood you could win by losing, if you played it right, as long as you didn't lose all the way.

I felt dizzy and sick to my stomach. This blackened room of death was a lot to take after a night of no sleep, and I was afraid I might pass out. I tried not to breathe the acrid air. I began to imagine I could smell the sweet sickly aroma of burnt flesh. My father's flesh. It was sweet and sour, actually, a sort of human barbecue. My legs could barely hold me. The room was burning hot, but my forehead was cold as ice.

"You wouldn't think a mattress could burn so fast," said Trisha vaguely, staring into the blackened springs. It was like we were watching television together. Neither of us could take our eyes from the fatal spot. "Actually, there wasn't a whole lot left of your father. Just a few charred bones. And the gold in his teeth. . . ."

"Well, it will spare the expense . . ." I began. For a moment I could not finish, but I forced myself: "It will spare the expense of a cremation."

Trisha was staring at me. I knew I was going to faint, but I was proud of myself I was going down with a tasteless joke. I might not have grown up to be rich and famous, but I sure had developed a fine gallows humor.

I fainted forward into the blackened springs of my father's funeral pyre. The last thing I remember, Trisha was standing over me, prodding me delicately with her foot, and saying from a very great distance: "I *knew* I shouldn't have married someone with grown children. . . ."

5

"Wake up, Jonno," came a voice in the darkness. It was my old butler, Albert. "You're a mess, you terrible boy. I hope you know that."

I rubbed my eyes, feeling groggy as hell. I found myself in the bedroom of my childhood, in the northeast second-story corner of the rambling old house. The narrow bed in which I lay was more than familiar. I knew every creak and crack of it. It had once been my virginal springboard into the world of imagination, from which I had passed many a steamy adolescent hour dreaming of delicious girl-flesh.

Albert was walking about, pulling open the curtains to let in a blinding white afternoon. He was wearing a gray apron over his jeans and Hawaiian shirt, which made him look at least *slightly* like a real butler.

"Yes, a fucking mess," he mused solemnly. "When did you sleep last, Jonno? Who's been taking care of you, I wonder?"

"I've been taking care of myself."

"Sure you have. That's why you're in such *fabulous* shape."

"So how's your love life, you old fart?" I countered, knowing exactly where *his* weak spot was.

40

"You dare ask? I was seeing this lovely boy, but the bastard threw me over for a horrid little tart from Tarzana. It was really quite sad to be so mistaken about someone."

I grinned. Albert was an outrageous old fag and I could banter with him all day. But he wasn't in a bantering mood. "The police say the murderer left the house through your bedroom window, Jonno. Rather a rude thing to do, don't you agree?"

"*My* window? How do they know?"

"He—or is it she?—apparently clobbered your father to death and then came in here, climbed down the oak tree to the ground, and hiked up the old horse trail behind the house that you kids used to play on, up to Mulholland where an automobile was conveniently waiting. The police found various clues, I imagine—who knows what exactly?—I presume the ground was disturbed in some suitable way. Maybe the idiot left a trail of bread crumbs."

While Albert was speaking I found myself staring at the gnarly old oak tree whose branches rose to my second-story window from the ground. When I was a kid, this tree had often provided a convenient escape route from the house to the world of trouble below. I had often bragged I could get up and down in thirty seconds flat. This murder was pressing very, very close to me.

"And the fire . . ."

"The fire didn't start until after the murderer was well away. Apparently there was some sort of incendiary device left behind on a timer. But the police aren't giving out a lot of information on that."

I sat up in bed to discover I was wearing underpants and nothing else. I guess Albert had undressed me and put me to bed. The sights and smells of my old bedroom were hitting me in waves, a fairly heavy dose of déjà vu. I looked around to see a host of familiar objects: the wooden dresser where I used to hide cigarettes, the desk at which I did my homework, the psychedelic rock posters on the walls. Everything was so familiar that it seemed for a moment my entire adult life was nothing but a bad dream, a thing of shadow and little substance, caused by a very large case of indigestion.

As I looked around, I realized there was something bothering me about my bedroom. At first I couldn't put my finger on it. Then I figured it out.

"Jesus, Albert. My bedroom looks *exactly* like I left it sixteen years ago."

"And why not? It's always been here waiting for you, Jonno. Someone had to make sure this bizarre family didn't *completely* self-destruct."

"*You* kept my room like this?"

"Who else?"

I didn't know what to say. The whole thing seemed a little weird, actually. "So where are my clothes?"

"In the garbage, where they belong. I have some of your father's things here. I've let out the pants while you were sleeping, and I think they'll fit."

Albert pointed to a pair of tan slacks and a blue oxford shirt folded neatly on a chair. On the floor nearby were two brown leather loafers shined to a high gloss, and a pair of beige socks.

"I had to send out to Neiman-Marcus for the loafers," he said. "I trust you haven't totally *shrunk* from malnourishment and your feet are still at least *vaguely* size ten."

"Albert, for chrissake, get me my jeans and sneakers from the damn garbage," I told him firmly. But Albert had never been the kind of butler you could order around.

"Listen to me, silly boy, the big family powwow starts in forty-five minutes. There's going to be a very important man present by the name of Arnold Weinstein. He's the chairman of the board of Everest Pictures, and I want you to make a good impression."

"Hell with that," I told him. "Being the black sheep of the family means I can go easy on the good impressions. After all, why fuck with my image?"

Albert gave me his sternest look. "Jonno, get your spoiled ass into the shower. You will find shampoo and shaving gear and everything you need. I'm going to give you a haircut when you emerge, and see if I can turn you from a frog back into a prince."

I swore a little, I whined, I whimpered, and in the end, I did exactly as he told me. In my family, Albert has always been the voice of God. Even my father did as he said.

I remember as a kid wishing I had a butler like my friends' families had, instead of a mincing old queer like Albert. But I must admit, it was nice to hear his voice again. Actually, he was the only member of my family with whom I had kept even vaguely in touch over the years. Three years after I left home, at the age of twenty-three, Albert managed to find me where I was living at the time on the island of Bali. Albert was on his yearly vacation, and we had dinner together at a small seaside restaurant, Albert with his current young man, and me with my current harem, which consisted, at that particular moment, of two blond Swedish girls from Stockholm who were out to see the world.

The evening was not a great success. Albert's young man and my two Swedish girls hated each other on sight. But from that time on, I fulfilled a solemn promise to keep Albert informed of my current address, and I had even sent him strange and disjointed letters from time to time, from strange and disjointed places. So I was a wanderer and an exile, but somehow it had been important to know that Albert remained in California, my sole connection with the past.

I showered, shaved, and walked back into the bedroom with a towel around my waist. Albert positioned me in a chair in the center of the room. There was a sheet in his hand, and on a nearby dresser, two pairs of scissors, a comb, and a blow dryer had been set out with surgical neatness.

"Hey, Albert," I said uneasily. "Do you think you can lend me a hundred bucks or so? I hate to ask, but to tell the truth, I arrived here with like twenty-five cents in my pocket and I have to buy a new tire for the Buick."

I knew it was an indication of how low I had fallen, hitting up the old family butler for money. But Albert only chuckled and continued to cut my hair.

"You don't need to borrow money, my dear boy. Don't you realize how your life has changed? You're filthy rich now, a disgusting capitalist muckamuck, and you'd better get used to it."

I laughed uneasily. "Sure!" I said. Sergeant Myra Fisher had also said something about me inheriting a bundle, but I couldn't take it seriously. When Albert didn't comment further, I prodded: "You know damn well I'm not expecting Dad to have left me anything. I was the family fuckup."

"You have it *all* wrong as usual, Jonno," said Albert in a distracted manner, studying my sideburns. "As it happens, you're the principal heir."

"Don't fuck with me. I may look tough, but I'm emotionally fragile."

"Be quiet and listen, Jonno. I've seen your father's will, and this is how the pie gets divided. Your new stepmother, Trisha, gets a half million. Andrea Ames, your *last* stepmother, gets a half million. The rest of your brothers and sisters—Rags, Carl, David, Opera, Zoe—they each have equal shares in your father's remaining personal assets, including this house, the house in Malibu, the duplex in Manhattan and all the cash in the various CD's and money market funds, all of which comes to about thirteen, fourteen million dollars."

"So what about me?"

"You're left out of the split, Jonno."

"Well, what did I tell you? What the hell is there left for me to inherit?"

"The studio," he said simply.

"The *what?*"

"That's right. You are about to become the principal stockholder of Everest Pictures."

I had a good laugh. "Jesus, Albert, you scared the shit out of me for a moment. The way I understand it, Dad was fired from Everest in some power play featuring my swell brother, David."

"Oh, he was. Quite true. The government was threatening an antitrust suit, and the SEC was at his throat. You must understand, your father at that particular moment was majority shareholder at Everest, and at Cal-Star International, *and* he was orchestrating a raid against Fox as well. This was the late-eighties, my dear, and everyone was trying to gobble up everyone else, floating all kinds of lovely junk bonds to finance their moves. Most of it was legal, at least, but some of the financing was, well, a bit *too* creative."

"Albert, high finance is total gobbledygook to me. Can't you get to the point?"

"The point is, your father was forced into a strategic retreat. He retired as CEO of Everest and reduced his stock holdings there to forty-eight percent. That's what you've inherited, Jonno, forty-eight percent of Everest Pictures."

I had to stand up and pace about my old bedroom to fully absorb this news. "But why me? What the hell do *I* know about movie studios? Jesus, why didn't Dad leave me something simple, like the beach house at Malibu? I *know* how to surf."

Albert had quite a smirk playing across his lips. I think he considered this a very big joke that I would now have to grow up and take on some heavy responsibility. Personally, I did not share his enthusiasm.

"Well?" I demanded. "Why not Carl or David or Rags? Or even Opera? Or Zoe, for that matter?"

This last name was a little experimental. To say her name aloud in this room, in this house, I had to work my mouth hard. Albert gave me a wary look.

"It's quite simple," he said. "Your brother Carl's a bloody socialist and would probably give away the whole kit and caboodle to the poor. Opera's far too young and flaky. David's a miserable little twat your father never could stand. And as for Zoe, well . . ."

"What about Zoe?" I asked sharply. Albert left his thought about her dangling, pursing his lips in deep thought.

"I think your father found Zoe a bit unpredictable," he said carefully.

I laughed, maybe a bit too wildly. "Unpredictable! I love it! But you've left out Rags."

"Rags is ill. Didn't you know?"

"What's wrong with him?"

"I think I'll let him tell you. You'll be seeing him this afternoon. As for the studio, you were always the heir, Jonno. *Always.*"

"Come on!"

"I'm serious. Your father thought you had the necessary balls for the job, if you would only grow up a little. I must say, he was rather impressed when you sailed that silly yacht full of marijuana all by yourself from Hawaii to California. He said a boy who could do that, could swim with the sharks in Hollywood."

"Wait a minute! How the hell did he find out about *that*?"

"I used to let him read the letters you wrote me. I hope you don't mind, Jonno. It was an act of mercy."

"But I never wrote you about my dope-smuggling adventure! Albert, what's going on here?"

"Well, my dear," said Albert slowly, "You're not going to like this."

I waited, glaring at him.

"Actually, we had a team of private detectives keeping an eye on you, starting about seven years ago. Your father decided he wanted to know who you were, and what you were doing with your life. Perhaps he was trying to decide if he would leave you the studio or not."

Albert was right. I didn't like this. "So how much is this bloody studio actually worth?" I asked grumpily.

"Whatever anybody will pay for it. Right now there's a Texas oil man who's making feelers at $56.30 a share. That would bring the total price of Everest Pictures to about a billion dollars."

"And my share . . ."

"You own forty-eight percent. Figure it out for yourself."

I was quiet a few minutes, trying to count on my fingers, and not making very much progress getting to a billion. Beyond a thousand bucks, money gets pretty abstract for me.

"Four hundred and eighty million dollars!" I said at last, staggered. Albert had to hold the tan slacks up for me to step into. At this point, I would have stepped into a space suit without knowing the difference. There was a dazed look in my eyes. "Four hundred and eighty *million* dollars!"

"*If* you sell to the Texan. And frankly, I do not advise that at all. You don't need money, Jonno, nearly as much as you need a job."

"You want me to *run* the studio?"

"I want you to finish getting dressed."

This was all beyond me. I was frankly gaga. I had no idea my father was quite so rich. I knew the story, of course, of how Dad got his first big break, making the important move from agent to studio executive: In 1968, Everest Pictures produced a low-budget movie about a carnivorous bat that became the first major blockbuster of modern times. As it happened, my father—as head of the Sangor Agency—represented almost everybody except the bat: the two stars, as well as the director, the screenwriter, and the man who had written the novel. My dad's commission added up to an incredible fifteen million dollars. More incredible still, he told Everest they wouldn't need to pay him a penny of this money in cash. Instead, he would take his commission in previously unregistered company stock, as well as in a job as vice president in charge of production, with an option to personally produce two pictures a year. The rest was history, as they say.

"Wait a minute, Albert. You keep saying I own this goddamn movie studio, but actually I only own forty-eight percent. That's very nice and all, but I can't exactly call the shots, now can I? I mean, what if I want to do a remake of *Cleopatra* as a musical in drag? I'll have to get permission from the other fifty-two percent."

"Relax," said Albert smiling. "As it happens, *I* own three percent, which gives us all the majority we need."

"*You* own three percent!" I cried in astonishment. "Good God!"

He shrugged modestly. "Well, over the years I took my annual bonus in stock options. Last year, when your father was forced to disinvest down to forty-eight percent, he was able to increase my stock holdings so that together we would still have control. It's a very long story, Jonno. . . ."

"But David . . ."

"Jonno, your brother David only *thinks* he ousted your father. Actually, he played right into your father's hands. Believe me, there are deals within deals here. But right now, you need to get your ass down to that meeting with your lovely siblings and the chairman of the board."

"But Albert, this is incredible!" I said. And then a new thought struck me: "Jesus! Does David know I'm getting the studio?"

"Yes he does. And look out for David, Jonno. He's going to be coming for you, and he's very, very dangerous."

I was dressed and ready to go, but in all the excitement of finding myself heir to possible millions, I had momentarily forgotten Detective Sergeant Myra Fisher of Special Investigations.

"This is really swell, Albert, but what about the cops? Unfortunately, the chances are someone in this family is a mad killer and right now the best suspect happens to be me."

"Did you kill your father, Jonno?"

"Of course not."

"Then relax, and get out of here."

"But who *did* it, for chrissake? You know all the deep dark secrets in this family. So tell me."

"Maybe the butler did it," said Albert, his hand on the back of my neck, pushing me toward the door.

He smiled, but the funny thing was, for a moment there I almost believed him.

6

I nearly died with laughter when I saw my older half brother David who I used to hate so much when we were kids.

He had a ponytail now, just a short little thing bobbing over his collar, and he also had a fashionable three days of stubble on his chin to show how laid back he was. I suppose this was David's idea of how an up-to-date CEO of a movie studio should look, though never in my wildest dreams had I imagined he would grow up and pretend to be hip.

"Jonno! . . . My God, it's been a long time! What is it now? Fifteen? Twenty years?"

"Sixteen years," I said. My brother David gave me a bear hug and we stared at each other with silly grins on our faces. He was dressed in a nice double-breasted charcoal-gray suit that was fashionably formless and seemed to be made from the very softest hair of some poor exploited creature. Worms, I believe. David had gained weight since I had seen him last. It was as if he were a balloon that time had inflated to twice its original size, stretching and distorting the features I once knew.

And oh, that ponytail! I had to restrain myself from giving it a good hard yank!

The big family powwow was held in an outbuilding we generally referred to as "the meditation studio." This was an octagonal redwood structure built in a pseudo-Japanese style at a far end of our property. Like the sun room, the meditation studio was the creation of Michelle Cordell—Mrs. Alexander the Third—an avant-garde French actress who had been popular in a certain kind of black-and-white film in the sixties, a film in which she inevitably, at some point in the story, appeared gloriously nude. Despite her fabulous looks, Michelle's career never really took hold in mainstream Hollywood, and so she had a lot of time to sit around the house, smoke dope from morning to night, and dream up such things as octagonal meditation studios built in a pseudo-Japanese manner.

There must have been twenty or thirty people gathered for the family meeting. I had a sense of a lot of half-familiar faces swirling and surging around me. I had no idea who most of these people were. Lawyers, consultants, and sycophants of the family, I presumed. Wives, mistresses, and sexually significant others. Everyone looked rich and successful at whatever it was they did. I was standing with David when a young girl I had never seen before threw her arms around my neck and called me her long lost brother.

"Jonno!" cried the strange girl. "Don't you know who I am? I'm your sister, Opera!"

"Opera! Hey, that's fantastic!" I cried. We grinned and cooed at each other. My little sister had reddish-blond hair and rather lovely pale skin. She looked pretty damn grown-up for fifteen. She was dressed in a slinky gold-colored dress which showed a lot of leg and shoulder. I had seen photographs of her from time to time, once on the cover of *TV Guide*, but I had never met her, since I had left home a year before she was born. I'm sure it wasn't easy bearing a name like Opera Sangor, but then, she had been born at a moment in history when parents had felt it their absolute duty to be fiendishly original at their children's expense.

She seemed glad to meet an errant big brother. "Oh, Jonathan! You were always an absolute myth to me. I mean, whenever I did anything bad, got caught smoking cigarettes or something, everyone always said, 'If you don't watch out, you're going to end up just like your brother Jonathan!' "

"What a recommendation," I said, with a wink at David.

"Our kid sister's going to be a big, big star," said David. "Have you been watching her in 'Life in the Fast Lane'?"

"Sure," I lied.

"Bet you don't," said Opera.

David started telling me about a movie Opera had been all set to make with Dad. It was about a teenage girl who saves a killer whale from her uncle's fishing net, and then the whale and the girl end up becoming fabulous friends. In Hollywood, writers get paid enormous sums of money to come up with ideas like this.

"The first environmentally conscious teen movie," David assured me happily.

"But Dad was trying to screw me on the price," Opera added. "Can you believe it? My own father!"

"Well, Dad always was better at making deals than having children," I remarked.

"I'm taking over the production personally," David confided, lowering his voice. "We're hoping to start production in the Bahamas next spring."

I tried to appear interested in all the details. David and Opera talked shop a little, arguing over the working title for the film. Opera wanted to call the thing *My Best Friend*, but David had his heart set on *Teen Whale*. No one asked my opinion, so I kept my mouth shut.

Being a celebrity, Opera was much in demand. After a while, someone I didn't recognize hauled her off to another part of the room. This left me stranded with my brother David.

"Quite a kid," David said. "She's going to be a bigger star than your mother and my mother put together."

"Let's just hope she comes to a better end," I remarked.

David laughed. "So, Jonno, I hear you've become a musician. Albert's been telling me you play piano in some little town up north. Santa Rosa?"

"Petaluma," I told him.

"Never heard of it. Must *really* be small," he grinned. "Me, I've been slaving away all these years, Jonno. Making movies. Taking care of business. So how long do you plan to be around?"

"Well, I don't know. Maybe I'll stick around awhile, get involved in the family business—make some movies."

"But, Jonno, for a free spirit like you, you'd probably find it incredibly boring having to show up at an office every morning."

"Is that what movie making is? Showing up at an office?"

"Sure, it is," he assured me. "You know, Jonno, Dad was the last of a dying breed around here. These days, movie making is just like any other business. It's all cost analysis, market surveys, lawyers, and accountants. Dull, dull, dull. I doubt if it would be very enjoyable for a piano player."

I grinned right back at him. "I'm sure you're right, Davey. But since Dad left me the studio, I feel I owe it to him to give the business a try. Don't you think so, Davey? For Dad's sake, I mean."

Davey was a name he used to hate back in the old days, and we were getting back to the old days fast.

"So you think you're going to inherit the studio?"

"I *know* I'm going to inherit the studio," I said. "It's in the will. In black and white."

"Oh, Jonno, you've become such a country bumpkin! In this town, there's *nothing* black and white about the law. It's the person who has the most creative lawyer who wins! Why, there are smart guys in this town who could take that studio from you just like *that*," he said. And he snapped his fingers in front of my face to show how easy it would be to take Everest Pictures away from me. "Just like that," he said again.

When we were kids, this would be the moment we might start taking swings at one another, but since we were sophisticated adults, we pretended to regard one another with bemused interest. I escaped from David by saying I was in need of some liquid refreshment.

I walked across the room to a little bar where Albert and Trisha were handing out hors d'oeuvres and drinks. I found myself with a canapé in one hand and a scotch and water in the other. I downed the scotch and water, and immediately took another.

"Go slow with the scotch, please," said Albert softly but succinctly into my left ear. "And don't let David bait you. He *wants* you to get angry and show everybody what a marvelous lunatic you can be. Just keep your cool, Jonno."

"I'm cool, I'm cool," I assured him.

I felt an arm around my shoulder, and heard a voice in my ear: "You haven't changed a bit, you crazy fuck."

God, it was my older brother Carl! Only now he was a gaunt middle-aged man with thin sandy hair and round, rimless glasses balanced on his nose, the kind of glasses John Lennon used to wear. He looked like some undernourished nineteenth-century poet, but he had always looked like that, even as a kid.

I let out a loud cowboy yell and threw my arms around Carl with maybe too much gusto, spilling part of my drink. I had always looked up to Carl in a big way, and relied on his moral judgments.

"How are you doing, Jonno? Keeping the flames of truth alive?"

"Just keeping alive, bro. How about you?"

"I'm hanging in there. Sometimes by a thread, but what the hell!"

Our little sister Opera waved at us from across the room, thrilled to see such a happy family reunion in progress. And then two men with short gray hair and tennis-court tans gathered around her like Indians circling a wagon train. Being a successful child actress did not look like my idea of fun.

"Cute kid, our little sister," I said to Carl.

"Yeah, she's cute as a python. She had her first abortion at thirteen. By fourteen she was heavy into booze and cocaine, but she's over that now. She's been sober for nearly a month. Did Opera tell you about her new BMW?"

"Isn't she too young to drive?"

"That's the point, Jonno. Unfortunately, that small fact didn't stop her from going out and buying a forty-seven-thousand-dollar silver Beamer convertible complete with cellular phone and FAX machine. She keeps it in her mother's circular driveway and goes round and round the fountain."

"Well, I guess she's earned a few toys."

"It's fucking nuts, Jonno. And it breaks my heart to see that bright, funny fifteen-year-old child being exploited by a bunch of greedy bastards who don't give a shit about her except how much money she can bring in. I mean, what's she going to be like at twenty? This exploitation of children makes me sick."

"What's her mother say about it?"

"Andrea Ames? What the hell would *she* care? Opera's become her meal ticket for the rest of her life. Most of the time she's off traveling in Europe. I think she's in Paris now. Opera's being raised by servants, for chrissake!"

"Sounds familiar," I told him.

"Yeah," he said gloomily. "You'd think people would learn, but they never do."

My brother Carl had always been upset by all the injustice and wicked ways of the world. He was the first utopian socialist I had ever known, maybe the *only* utopian socialist in all of Coldwater Canyon. When he was a kid, Carl spent his time planning the redistribution of the world's wealth so that families like ours would be driven out of their cushy mansions and forced to work honestly with their hands.

"So, what are you doing with yourself these days?" I asked him.

He sighed and shook his head in a deprecating manner. "Well, I've started a shelter for the homeless, Jonno. Jesus, I *had* to do something. I was able to take over an old building near Hollywood Boulevard. I offer beds, food, showers, counseling, a day-care center for the children. Most of all, I'm trying to get the homeless organized into a political voice. Man, the poor people in this country break my heart. And George Bush is even worse than Ronald Reagan. . . ."

Carl launched forth into a tirade about current politics. I wasn't really surprised that after all these years this should be the first thing he chose to discuss with me: cuts in social programs, unfair tax breaks for the rich, and how the only liberals left in this country seemed to be a few Hollywood celebrities who earned millions of dollars a year. As I watched him talk I could see his face had been molded by all the anger inside. He looked pinched and sour and his complexion was sallow.

"You'll have to come down to the shelter, Jonno, see what I'm trying to do," he said.

"Sure," I told him.

"You should get involved. That's always been your problem, Jonno. You'll never be happy until you learn to live for other people than yourself."

"Are you happy, Carl?"

He stared at me almost angrily through his John Lennon glasses, his lips pinched and drawn. And suddenly he laughed and gave me another big hug, neatly avoiding my question. "Son of a bitch, it's good to see you, Jonno! We'll have to get drunk one of these nights. Oh Jesus, look who's here!"

Carl was staring over my shoulder at a shriveled little man in a wheelchair who was being pushed our way by a young giant with blond hair. With a shock, I realized the man in the wheelchair was my oldest brother.

"My God, that's . . ."

"Yeah, it's Rags," said Carl. "Didn't you know he was sick?"

"Well, Albert said something. My God, what's he got?"

"AIDS!" cried Rags merrily, coming to a stop in his wheelchair. "Can you believe it? I *finally* came out of the fucking closet, and what happens? I get the disease of the century! How's that for justice?"

I really didn't know what to say. I tried to smile, but honestly, it scared me to look at him. Disease had ravaged Rags's body so that what was left of him reminded me a little too much of E.T. before he went home. His body was so insubstantial it looked like it could blow away in the wind.

"Oh, this is my friend, Keith," said Rags, introducing the blond giant behind him. Keith was as healthy looking as Rags was sick, and about twenty years younger. Keith glared at us in an unfriendly way, as though we were somehow responsible for his friend's condition. And maybe we were in a way.

"So the gang's all here," said Rags. "Except for Zoe. Where the hell is Zoe?"

"Tibet," said David, joining our group. He was with the two gray-haired men who had taken Opera away, and my new stepmother Trisha. Opera came up alongside of me and took my arm possessively.

"Jonno, I think you'd better meet Arnold Weinstein, chairman of the board of Everest Pictures," David said. "And Buddy Templeton, Dad's lawyer."

"Nice to meet you," said the two men. To me they looked nearly identical. I wasn't certain which one was the chairman of the board, which one the lawyer, and frankly I didn't much care either way.

"Well, Jonno, we're going to have to do some serious talking," said one of the men. "Maybe you should drop by the studio Monday morning."

"Oh, and then you can come on my set!" Opera cried. "I'll introduce you to all my friends!"

"Zoe really should be here," said Rags frowning, interrupting us from his wheelchair. Since he was sick, we all looked to him with silly polite expressions on our faces. "Did anyone try to phone her? I mean, *someone* should phone her, don't you think?"

"For chrissake, you can't get *through* to Tibet by telephone," David said impatiently. For a Hollywood person, being inaccessible by telephone was an unthinkable offense. "I sent a telegram to the poste restante in Lhasa, but who knows if it'll reach her?"

"But what's she *doing* in Tibet?" Rags asked, almost irritably. "She should be here with her family at a time like this."

"I heard she was studying in a monastery," David said. "Tantric yoga or something. You know Zoe."

"It's a lamasery," I corrected.

"Whatever," David said with a grin. "I bet she's giving those Buddhist monks some wet dreams they'll never forget!"

I felt a wave of heat pass through my body. I couldn't bear to hear David talk about Zoe like that. Then one of the gray-haired men, I think it was the chairman of the board, began talking about Zoe too, how she was so beautiful and how when she was young he had always urged Dad to give her a screen test. Then Trisha started talking about a trip she had made to Japan and how horribly expensive and crowded everything was. I think this was supposed to be vaguely related to Zoe being in Tibet, more or less the same part of the world, give or take a few thousand miles. There were seven or eight of us standing around in a circle, with Rags in his wheelchair at the center, and it was one of those group conversations that went off in aimless directions and kept arriving at dead ends. I couldn't stand it. I slipped backward out of the circle and began to make my way to the bar.

Someone tapped me on the arm. It was David, who had managed to follow me.

"Listen, Jonno, I thought I'd better warn you about Sergeant Myra Fisher. An attractive lady for a cop, don't you think? Unfortunately, I had to tell her about how you burned down your prep school and got put into an institution for a while afterward. I hope you don't mind, Jonno. I mean, I knew she would come across the information sooner or later and it seemed kinder for someone in the family to tell her about it first."

"That was very kind of you indeed," I told him. "I was wondering how she found out."

"Don't mention it. You know, Jonno," he said, lowering his voice to a confidential whisper, "I hate to tell you this, but there's a law that says a person is not allowed to profit by his crime. What I'm trying to say is that if you happened to get convicted of Dad's murder—I mean, if the evidence just *happened* to point that way—you wouldn't get diddleyshit out of the estate. No studio, nothing."

I shrugged. "Well, I've never been all that materialistic, Davey. Other things concern me more."

"But I just wonder," David said, "what the cops are going to make of a guy who's an itinerant piano player and has a history of violence and mental illness and setting things on fire? Frankly, if I were you I'd make a run for it. You might end up very happy in a place like Paraguay. Hell, you could play piano in a whorehouse or something. It could be just the thing for you."

I decided I was going to have to slug him after all, just for old times' sake. He smiled at me, winked, and I smiled back. Then I felt a kind of roar in my ear and my fist slammed into David's nose and he fell backward and all around me people were screaming. David lay on the floor and his nose was a bloody pulp. I had an idea I might kick him in the balls while he was down, but all of a sudden there were three people pulling me away from him—Albert, Carl, and Opera.

I was breathing hard, but still smiling, grinning like crazy. "It's nothing," I said. "Just a little family squabble."

"Oh, I think my nose is broken!" David said in a very nasal voice. There was blood all over his shirt. Trisha started screaming.

"Someone call 911! . . . We got to stop the bleeding! . . . Get some ice quick! . . ."

Everyone seemed to be talking at once and running about trying to do something about David's damn nose. Everyone except Rags in his wheelchair, who sat there shaking his head and saying how crazy this family was.

I turned and made my way blindly out the door, not stopping, not looking behind me. Outside, I took a deep breath of air, but it seemed close with cloying Southern California foliage and brought no relief.

And then I felt a cool soft hand upon my sleeve. I thought for a moment it was my little sister Opera. But I turned and nearly had a heart attack. It was my big sister Zoe.

7

Zoe was standing so close it took my breath away. She was inspecting me with the profound cat-like attention Zoe always gave everything. She had wonderful big dark violet-and-green-flecked eyes. She was still the most beautiful woman I'd ever seen.

There was a smile on her lips that was half sad. "Oh, Jonno!" she said, "I was watching you through the window. Hasn't anything changed after all these years?"

"I guess not," I told her, looking at her hard.

It's a funny thing about Zoe, when she was thirteen, she could have passed for twenty. Now, she was thirty-seven and she still remained that perfect and radiant twenty, as though all her life had been lived under some magic spell. Carl, who was better educated than I was, once described her as pure Botticelli. She was definitely Venus on the clamshell standing at the morning mists of time, a Renaissance, rather than a Hollywood, blonde. Little cherubs might well blow their horns at the sight of her. I always had.

Her hair was still a dark rich honey-blond, thick and long as she wore it as a child, held at the nape of her neck by a simple tortoise-shell clip. She was wearing tight faded jeans and some shirt of

58

coarse peasant cotton that was the color of dark blood. Despite the casual clothing, she appeared as excruciatingly elegant as always. It was the way she held herself, like a dancer waiting for a private orchestra to begin to play.

All I could do was stare at her, and she stared back at me. When I finally spoke, my voice quavered only a little. "Everyone said you were in Tibet."

"I've been back two weeks, but I wasn't ready to see the family yet. I came to arrange a show of my photographs at a gallery here."

"Two weeks?" I had to laugh because suddenly I realized there was an even better suspect for the murder of Alexander Sangor than me. Zoe just kept staring at me with her beautiful innocent and wicked eyes. She made my legs feel like Jell-O.

Then Albert came out of the studio.

"Jonno, you *can't* run away this time," he started to say, and then he saw who was with me and he stopped cold. "Oh, shit," he said slowly. But Zoe and I hardly heard him.

"Well, Jonno, did you think about me sometimes?" she asked softly. "I thought about *you*."

That's when I got mad. *Think about her?* Every moment of my adult life I'd been haunted by the long reach of my sister Zoe's terrible beauty. She had destroyed me, she had turned me into a wandering shadow. Zoe was the reason for everything, and God help me, I loved her just as much as I had ever loved her before.

It was just too crazy. I had to get away. So I turned with a careless shrug of my shoulders and started walking down the path, forcing myself not to run.

"Jonno, come back here!" called Albert.

"Let him go," I heard Zoe tell him, her voice soft and sad. And so I went, over a small Japanese bridge from the meditation studio and along a gravel path through the woods. And when I knew they couldn't see me, I did what I had learned to do so well the past sixteen years, I ran. I set my feet in motion and went bounding over the path toward the house with the leaves of the trees slapping against my face. It was just too crazy. I ran as if the hounds of hell were on my heels.

I was done with the past, but the past was not done with me. I ran to the front of the house and there came a new surprise. Detective Sergeant Myra Fisher was standing in the driveway beside an unmarked late-model car that could only be an official vehicle. She had a companion, a grim-faced man wearing a checkered sports coat with impenetrable dark glasses balanced on his nose.

"Jonathan Sangor," said the man in a mournful voice. "We would like you to come to the station with us."

"We should warn you that anything you say can, and will, be used against you in a court of law," intoned Sergeant Fisher. "You have the right to remain silent, you have the right . . ."

They were surprised when I laughed. "Just *take* me," I said, "and let's leave the bullshit for later."

They didn't seem to understand how good they looked to me at just this moment, that jail seemed a thousand times better than another moment spent with my family in this rich and terrible house.

Part Two

I used to think that having money was like being marooned on an island, a very pleasant island with lots of pretty palm trees and an emerald-green ocean all around that was able to protect you from every hard reality of life except maybe disease, heartbreak, insanity, and death.

We children were only the flotsam and jetsam, the wreckage that got left behind, washed up on shore by very tricky currents. The adults made their brief strategic alliances, furthered their careers, and sailed on. Frankly it wasn't all that easy being a rich kid. People smile when I tell them that and say, "Oh, sure." But I'm here to testify to our pain.

I should begin this story with my father.

Before he reinvented himself, my father's name was Alexander Sangwolovitch, and he had been born of Polish immigrants who had come to America to improve their lot. Alexander was raised on a small farm outside of Omaha, Nebraska, where his father grew corn, a fact which was unfortunately unearthed by a snide writer for the *New York Times* many years later when reviewing one of Dad's movies. It could not have been smooth sailing being a child of destiny growing up in the corn belt in the midst of the Great

Depression. Alexander's father was a heavy drinker, brutal to his family when drunk; his mother a weepy ex-schoolteacher who introduced Alex to the world of books . . . books that provided a magic window to a world beyond the dreary farm, a world of escape.

I've only seen one photograph of my father as an adolescent in Nebraska. I think he burned the rest. In the photo, Alex is wearing clothes that appear too small for him and there is a brooding, uncomfortable expression on his face, as though he were keeping his legs crossed tightly so he wouldn't pee his pants. His eyes seem to be looking inward, plotting and planning his escape, dreaming his way out of his present discomfort. But maybe it's hindsight to see all these things in a single grainy black-and-white photograph from 1935. In a sense, the most remarkable thing about Alexander Sangwolovitch was that there was nothing apparently remarkable about him at all.

When Alex was fifteen, his mother died and he was left alone with his alcoholic father. This is the moment Alex chose to work like hell at school and in his spare time read every book he could get his hands on. The world should pay particular attention to silent and unhappy children with books hidden beneath their pillows, but of course it seldom does.

Now comes a magical transformation. Somehow this Nebraska farm boy spent a year after graduating high school where he did little but study and read novels and half starve to death. At the end of this year he won a full scholarship to Princeton University. Don't ask me how he did it. I think the motivating force for Princeton came from reading F. Scott Fitzgerald and my father's own romantic yearning for wealth and grace and beautiful people who did not have dirt beneath their fingernails. My father simply reinvented himself as completely as a butterfly stepping out of a cocoon.

I've seen plenty of photographs from my father's stint in the Ivy League, for this was a well-recorded epoch in his life: gone is the dark brooding look, replaced by an endless smile, a bright and confident Alexander Sangwolovitch—already called Sangor as a nickname by his friends—laughing and beaming at the camera at football games, at dances, from sailboats, and lawn chairs, and the wealthy homes of his new friends. God knows what my father told these people about his background. I'm sure he made up something entertaining and did a real song and dance to get by. Thus, the humble beginnings of showmanship, the torturous convulsions of a person seeking acceptance and applause.

Alexander Sangwolovitch graduated from Princeton in 1943, and saw the end of World War II in the tail end of a bomber over the Pacific. I've always envied those who fought in this war, and returned home with such a clear conscience and uncomplicated desire to make tons of money and succeed in the world. My father saw just enough of the war to transform himself into a hero, and I'm sure he cut a very handsome figure as he came marching back to New York City and shed his uniform for a gray flannel suit.

At this point, he must have asked himself exactly how he would make his fortune. At college, he had flirted with the notion of becoming a novelist à la F. Scott. But shooting down Jap planes, and being shot at in return, cut a young man's folly short and forced him to look at life with a survivor's instincts. Alex knew his limitations, and he made a wise decision: He liked books, he liked money, he liked hanging out with the best people. So, voilà, he would become a literary agent! It was as simple as that, and within a month after his discharge he landed a job at the prestigious Madison Avenue literary agency of Sturgess and Wattleby. Alexander Sangor, as he was now officially known, was on his way. An attractive young man, smart and aggressive, he was soon mixing with the glamorous celebrities of New York.

His new job included reading the unsolicited manuscripts sent in by literary hopefuls. Each day the mail brought Sturgess and Wattleby a score of novels, autobiographies, and books on strange subjects from insects to mating rituals among the wealthy of Manhattan. It was Alex's job to glance through these manuscripts— perhaps read the first chapter—and then return the pages with a polite note of refusal. However, one morning in February of 1946, my father received a submission in the mail that was to change his life.

It was a novel called *Flowers on a Grave* by an author who signed himself I. M. Lambert. The story concerned three generations of an eccentric New Orleans family, following their loves, deaths, marriages, and careers. From the first paragraph, Alex knew he had come across a real find. "My God, a southern *Bud-*

denbrooks!" he cried, for even then Alexander Sangor had developed that most-Hollywood instinct of comparing a thing to something else, preferably a *successful* something else. Alex took the manuscript home, read all night, and in the morning he wrote a note to I. M. Lambert on Sturgess and Wattleby stationery to the author's address in New Orleans:

Dear Mr. Lambert,
    I very much enjoyed your novel, *Flowers on a Grave*, and I think we might be able to find a publisher for you. Why don't you give me a call? Or better yet, if you can pop up to New York, we'll discuss this further, preferably over a nice bottle of beaujolais?

Yours Sincerely,
Alexander Sangor

A week later, a young woman arrived in his office. She had windswept red hair, a clear complexion, and a look of poetic bedazzlement in her deep green eyes. She had a bewitching figure, and it didn't hurt a bit that she had a charming Southern drawl.

"How may I help you?" my father asked.

"I believe I'm ready for that bottle of beaujolais," said the passionate redhead, offering her pale, elegant hand. My father was soon to understand that this was I. M. Lambert—Miss Isabelle Marietta Lambert—author of the novel he had so admired, and that she had just left her suitcase at Grand Central Station, and was thrilled to be making her first pilgrimage to New York.

Oh, how he must have chortled at the sight of this beautiful young lady writer appearing at his desk. It was like the rabbit coming to the wolf and asking to be escorted to dinner! Cunningly, Alex whisked I. M. Lambert out of Sturgess and Wattleby's before she might meet any of the more senior staff, and he took her to lunch at a bistro in Greenwich Village. This was a clever move. Isabelle was no dummy, but as I have said, this was her first trip to New York, and she had grown up in the deep South with a literary and poetic image of Greenwich Village as a kind of mecca for a writer's soul. The handsome young literary agent praised her first novel over a very nice beaujolais nouveau. They clinked glasses and toasted her success. My father briefly excused himself from the table, called his office to say he was sick and would not be able to return that afternoon, and then he spent the rest of the afternoon, and the evening, showing Isabelle Marietta Lambert the sights of New York.

Before they knew it, before she could even discover that Alex Sangor was a *very* junior member of Sturgess and Wattleby, they were in bed and in love. It was a passion born of mutual self-advantage. Isabelle and Alex did not know this yet, but they were suffering from a syndrome I would call "Hollywood love," that is, love for richer and better, and for the duration of success, and until something even more advantageous comes along. "Hollywood love" is real. I'm sure Isabelle and Alex felt all the right kinds of hot flashes, in all the right places. But it is the kind of love that mysteriously evaporates the moment the circumstances of mutual self-advantage disappear.

However, for the time being, life was a fairy tale for the young couple. So what was there not to love? Within two weeks, *Flowers on a Grave* had been bought by Scribner's with a $100,000 advance—a huge sum for an author in those days—and my father was the new golden boy at Sturgess and Wattleby's, with a new office and a huge raise. Six weeks after they met, Alexander and Isabelle were married in a civil ceremony in upstate New York. (Yes, quick marriages are also a notable feature of "Hollywood love," a sure giveaway, in fact.) Approximately eight months after the marriage, on December 4, 1946, my brother Ragnar L. Sangor was born at the Lenox Hill Hospital in Manhattan. The three of them—Alex, Isabelle, and Rags—settled into an old brownstone on Bank Street in Greenwich Village, and if they had been clever, there they would have remained.

But the wind was blowing from the West. *Flowers on a Grave* was published in 1947 and was a huge critical and commercial success. So why not try Hollywood? Why not more money, more fame, more bedazzlement—more everything?

Alex made his first trip to the Coast in the spring of '47 and he managed to engineer the movie sale in a way that changed the way books were sold to studios forevermore. Up to this time, scrupulous literary agents from Sturgess and Wattleby's gave a book to one studio at a time and waited politely for an answer. Alex invented a new formula: He gave *Flowers on a Grave* to two studios at once, Columbia and Fox. He set a bidding war in motion, and then he turned around, fucked over everyone he had been dealing with to this point, and closed the deal with MGM at an even greater price. And all this done with exquisite Princeton manners, and wearing the very best clothes. Hollywood was impressed with Alexander Sangor. He was clearly their kind of cowboy.

Isabelle was hired to write the screenplay at twenty-five hundred dollars a week, and Alex joined the Beverly Hills office of Star Creations, Inc., an agency which did not represent authors and books, but rather actors and actresses; motion pictures, in fact. Alex bought his first California home on North Palm Drive in the flats of Beverly Hills, he had baby Rags and his nanny flown in from New York, and the Hollywood days had begun.

Now here we run into a problem: Hollywood is fertile ground for some people, but for others, it causes them to mysteriously self-destruct. Why this is so, it is hard to say. My father had the knack, he had the killer instinct. Within a few years he was one of the most successful agents in town, representing some of the most successful stars. But Isabelle Lambert did *not* have the knack. She grew restive and unhappy and neurotic in the Southern California sun.

Poor Isabelle. . . . I always believed I would have liked her better than my other stepmothers. She was not happy being a Hollywood writer, and Hollywood, in return, did not like her, for the industry is wary of arrogant novelists from the East who have arty values and want to keep their novels just the way they wrote them.

Flowers on a Grave was a great success as a book, but a dismal failure as a movie. Isabelle retreated into herself and began a long angry novel about race relations in the South. The story concerned a white woman who has an affair with a black man, and then gives birth out of wedlock to a nice milk-chocolate kid who was supposed to be the hope of the future.

Oh, my father tried to warn her! He told her America was not ready for milk-chocolate children, but she ignored him. She was very angry. Angry with Hollywood. Angry with herself for going there. Angry with success for being such a disappointment. She threw her book at the American public like a slap in the face, and it was published to a mute and embarrassed reception in the fall of 1950.

Alas, the year 1950 was not to be remembered for its tolerance of bleeding-heart liberals who looked to milk chocolate as the hope of the future. Isabelle's new book had an unfortunate title—*Red Is the Color of My True Love's Blood*—which referred not to politics, but to the fact that Negroes and Caucasians supposedly have a similar fluid flowing in their veins. For Senator Joe McCarthy, however, *red* could only mean one thing, and it was not long before Isabelle Lambert found herself unable to work in California, or even to find a new publisher in New York. In 1951, she was brought up before the dreaded House Un-American Activities Committee, and when she refused to testify—invoking the First Amendment rather than the Fifth—she was given a six-month jail sentence for contempt of court, and reviled everywhere as a communist and an enemy of freedom.

Now, I hope you do not imagine my father was there in the courtroom holding her hand. Mysteriously, his love faltered just as I. M. Lambert's star began to fade. He found a new love. It was during his wife's trial, in fact, that Alex began a hot and tempestuous affair with his most successful client of the moment, a fabulously sexpot actress, the "it" girl of 1951—Corina Norman, a woman who was destined to be my mother.

After her six months in jail, Isabelle was released, and she returned not to Hollywood, but to New Orleans. She was determined to get back to her roots. She wrote Alex and requested only that he put their son Rags on a train with his nanny to New Orleans, but Alex refused. Isabelle took the matter to court, but Alex hired a clever lawyer to plead that a proven communist sympathizer—a white woman who, in fact, advocated sexual relations with black men—was clearly unfit to be a mother. The judge, who was up for reelection, agreed. He granted permanent custody of Rags to my father, and by extension, to my father's new wife-to-be, the actress Corina Norman.

Isabelle reacted in a most unfortunate way. She opened the window of her New Orleans hotel, stepped out onto the ledge, cried "Fuck you!" three times in the general direction of California, and then she jumped to her death on the hard sidewalk eleven stories below.

Personally, if I had been her, I would have bought a gun, caught a plane to the Coast, and shot my father's balls off. But then, I guess, I wouldn't be here with such an interesting story to tell.

9

My older brother Carl was born on March 18, 1953, a memento of the hot romance between Alexander Sangor and Corina Norman, the "it" girl of 1951, who was still going strong two years later. The affair had begun in a secluded bungalow at the Beverly Hills Hotel, but by the time of Carl's birth, my father and Corina were suitably married and had moved together into the big house on Coldwater Canyon. Just to be cute, they named the house La Chansón d'Or. I guess they wanted to show the world that the Sangor family was not interested in songs of mere brass or silver. At the time, of course, it was considered quite the thing for people who were trying to reinvent themselves to elevate the stature of their home with a pretentious European-sounding name. La Chanson d'Or, I should mention, stood between Casa Monte Carlo to the west and Quail Ridge Manor to the east.

Corina Norman, the first songbird of La Chanson d'Or, was a raven-haired beauty with heavy breasts and a sultry mouth. She had lips as red as cherries and a face that was a perfect valentine. According to her official studio bio, Corina Norman grew up in Raleigh, North Carolina, where her parents ran a small dance studio. Unofficially, she hailed from a lot further south than Raleigh—

San Juan, Puerto Rico, to be exact—where she had been born with the name Maria Rodriguez. Her parents owned no studio, small or otherwise—but they *were* dancers, performing the cha-cha and rumba for tourists at a local hotel.

When Corina was twelve, her mother ran off with a businessman from Argentina. This left my grandfather without a dance partner, and, being an enterprising person, he promptly auctioned off his daughter's virginity and used the proceeds to bring them both to California, land of opportunity. Unfortunately I never met my grandfather Rodriguez, though I sometimes feel the cunning of his dark blood flowing through my veins. He was killed in a knife fight in San Bernadino in 1949 and buried under his new California name, Bill Norman. At least he lived long enough to see his daughter become a big movie star, though I don't believe she ever gave him a dime.

I was born on December 18, 1955, and by this time Corina Norman's career was already on the skids due to a public taste for a new kind of heroine, in a new kind of film. I think Carl would agree when I say our mother was not exactly the mother of one's dreams. In fact, she was hardly a mother at all, except for a few minutes here and there in various photo opportunities, where she smiled into the camera with Rags and Carl on either side of her, and me—the baby—generally on her lap. The moment the photographer was finished, she'd brush us off like flies and return us into the care of our butler, Albert. To tell the truth, I was never entirely certain she even remembered our names. She often got us mixed up or referred to us generically as "the little animals." Our big crime was being born and ruining her beautiful figure. In fact, when she was drunk, which was often, she used to scream that we were the reason for her sagging tits and wrecked career.

So there we were, born into this life with a big mark against us. We grew up with our big half brother Rags in our lovely house, La Chanson d'Or, and we cried, laughed, and pooped in our diapers like babies everywhere. Carl and I were luckier than Rags. Our mother merely despised us in an offhand manner, but toward Rags she could be truly vicious. I guess the reason for this was that even if Carl and I had ruined Mom's figure, at least we were "hers." Rags, on the other hand, had issued forth from "that commie slut," which was the phrase Corina generally employed to describe her predecessor, Isabelle Lambert.

"You stupid boy! Can't you ever do anything right?" This was the old refrain. My mother glowered at Rags with her scornful Spanish eyes. She insulted him in a thousand ways. When Dad wasn't around, she could get really nasty: "You little shit, why don't you do us all a favor and jump out a window like your mother? . . . Stupid boy, if you were any uglier we'd have to put a paper bag over your head!"

Her harsh humor always sounded as if she were translating from the gutter Spanish of her childhood. I remember once Rags was sunbathing by the pool, lying on his stomach on the warm pavement, and he let out a scream of pain. My mother had just walked by and deliberately burned the bottom of his foot with the end of her cigarette. "You little shit," she said as she passed by. "You stupid horrible ugly little shit!"

I guess this couldn't have done wonders for Rags's self-esteem. But the funny thing about Rags, the terrible thing, was he took all this abuse with a smile. He tried to pretend it was all a big joke. Corina would tell him he was a spastic little fuck and Rags would just stand there grinning, staring modestly at the floor and shaking his head like he was pleased with the attention. When the insults grew in venom, the grin erupted into a goofy laugh, a really nerdy chuckle that would start deep in his throat and end up way high in the nose. Generally, it was this goofy laugh that drove Corina over the edge. She'd yell some final operatic epithet and storm off in search of gin, unable to take it anymore. I guess Corina Norman felt sorry for herself. It wasn't easy being a rich and beautiful movie star saddled with such imperfect children.

As for us children, somehow we survived and imagined this was how every family behaved. We kids stuck together. We had our world and the adults had theirs, and rarely the twain did meet. Our father was gone most of the time, and our mother was a seldom-seen being who slept until noon, and avoided us as best she could, which was easy in such a big house. Fortunately, we had our butler, Albert, whom we adored, and we had two and a half acres of overgrown land, a thousand places to play and hide. Despite its hokey name, and despite our parents, La Chanson d'Or was a great place to be a kid. There were attics and basements, nooks and crannies, and rooms upstairs where the adults never ventured. La Chanson d'Or was an entire universe enclosed from the outside world by high walls, and behind the protection of these walls we thrived like hot-house flowers.

I'm almost ashamed to say this, given how things eventually turned out, but I was actually a reasonably happy child, at least up until the time I was twelve years old. I remember long sunshiny days, and peeing in the swimming pool, and fantastic gun battles staged between Rags, Carl, and me over the sprawling Coldwater Canyon estate. Rags was almost exactly ten years older than I, and eight years older than Carl. He was a pudgy, sly child with thin dark hair, pimples, thick eyeglasses, and a very wacky sense of humor. I didn't realize at the time how rare it was for an older brother to spend so much time with his younger half siblings. I thought he was the best thing on earth, I hated my mother for torturing him, and it didn't occur to me until years later that Rags might have some big problems which kept him from the company of people his own age.

When I was six, Rags was sixteen—and a very magical thing happened: Rags got his driver's license, and my father gave him a car, a cute little MG convertible, fire-engine red. For Carl and me, this was the best thing that could ever happen. Rags now had the means to take us to all kinds of interesting places, and we started going everywhere, generally at speeds well in excess of the legal limit. But what the hell, Dad always paid the tickets and squared things with the cops. We must have gone down to Disneyland at least once a week, and to the old Pacific Ocean Park in Santa Monica. We saw movies galore and went to all the beaches, and sometimes we even went on camping trips. Rags was the perfect older brother. He taught us how to drive, how to smoke cigarettes, and how to masturbate.

This last skill, of course, I had come upon myself, being an inventive child. But to tell the truth (and this is a little embarrassing to admit), I got the whole thing slightly wrong: I used to lie on my bed face *forward* on my stomach, with my hands groping downward to the pleasure between my legs. Rags turned me around, so to speak. The three of us then proceeded with ritualized circle jerks, meeting for this solemn purpose in all kinds of places: the changing room by the pool, the woods where the meditation studio was built, and our various bedrooms. Rags supplied vivid erotic images to jerk off to, describing fabulous sexual encounters with his various girlfriends. Carl and I naturally took his stories to be gospel truth. We heard all about sex in automobiles, in speed-boats, in airplanes, even on rooftops. Rags had a very inventive mind, and when I grew up, I often thought that if sex really *had* been as interesting as Rags described it, probably none of the world's lesser business would ever get done.

Another thing Rags did was teach Carl and me a litany of swear words, and for months at a time whenever we'd meet, we would repeat an elaborate exchange, almost like a secret code between us: "Twat did you say? Scum again . . . I cunt hear you." Really obnoxious, of course, unless you happened to be an eight-, or nine-, or maybe even a ten-year-old boy.

But of course Rags was *not* eight or nine or ten. He was eighteen, nineteen, and even twenty during the heyday of our circle-jerk orgies. I guess some people might have a problem with the fact that Rags was older than we were, raise an eyebrow or two. And yet our group sex was really extremely innocent in its steamy brotherly way. I've always thought that Rags was not so much a child molester, as simply a child. He was one of us, mentally, more our age than a young adult.

We were all kids together, marooned on the island of La Chanson d'Or.

So time passed in the sleepy manner of childhood. There were good days and bad days. Sometimes Corina decided we were miserable brats for making noise and waking her before noon, and she would punish us in various ways. Albert, whom we loved, started to be gone much of the time, traveling with my father as his valet, and because of this my father hired a maid from Germany to take charge of the household. Her name was Gretchen Krieger and we kids really hated her. Basically, she was an indentured servant, although everyone was very careful not to call her that of course. Dad paid her plane fare to the land of plenty, and in return she would remain our all-purpose slave for five years, and after that he would sponsor her for U.S. citizenship.

Gretchen was in her early twenties and she had long black hair that was generally held up in a tight bun on the nape of her neck.

As a child, I felt there was something frightening about Gretchen Krieger.   Her hair was pulled back so tight it almost seemed to stretch the features of her face. She had the palest, most sunless skin I had ever seen. About once a week she told us her great saga, how she had escaped from East Germany over the Berlin Wall, and how a person must work very hard to be someone in this world. I realize now that Gretchen hadn't crossed the Berlin Wall and the Atlantic Ocean for nothing. She had big plans for her new life in California, but I guess we children did not make it easy for her. There were all sorts of things we detested about her, small and large. She had hairy underarms, for example, which Carl, Rags, and I thought was really gross. Even worse, she was extremely nosy and interfering with our lives, and she seemed to take it as her moral duty to act as a parental authority in the vacuum left by our parents.

Once Gretchen walked in upon one of our brotherly circle jerks, and there was hell to pay. At the time, I doubted if Gretchen had ever even *seen* a penis before, much less three at one time. I thought she was going to have a heart attack. She screamed at us for quite a while, and told us our hair was going to fall out, and we would get warts on the palms of our hands, and one day we would all have idiot children. And then she reported the incident to our father, who unfortunately was just back from the Cannes Film Festival. Dad gave us a suitable lecture, and for some time Rags was not allowed to take us anywhere. In an attempt to give us something better to do with our hands, my father arranged for me to take piano lessons and for Carl to study the violin. I'm not certain how this was supposed to reform our characters, since it has always been my experience that musicians are the horniest people I know. Secretly, I rather enjoyed learning to play the piano, but Carl and I got even with Gretchen for causing us so much trouble by putting a dead squirrel in her bed. And we got in trouble for this too, and were not allowed to go to Disneyland for an entire month.

Well, that was tough, of course, a real drag. Gretchen was definitely a big cloud on our horizon. But the worst thing that happened to us in those early days of my childhood came about six months later and it concerned my mother, Corina Norman.

I must have been about nine years old. I was asleep one night in my bed when I was awakened by the thud of someone falling on my floor. I heard a voice say, "Fucking hell!" I opened my eyes and my bedroom was dark, but I could see the glow of a cigarette and my mother's face. She had just fallen on the floor and was trying to stand up again. The cigarette was dangling out of her mouth and she had a bottle of something in one hand.

"Fucking hell!" she said again, struggling to her feet, swaying in the dark. I had no idea what had brought my mother staggering to my room in the middle of the night, but I closed my eyes hoping she would go away. I believed that as long as I pretended to be asleep she couldn't harm me. Then she sat down heavily on my bed and the strangest thing occurred: She put her arms around me and started sobbing and saying soft incoherent things in Spanish. I felt her wet tears against my neck and I was overwhelmed by the smell of her cigarette breath and gin. "Oh, no one cares about poor Corina," she moaned, switching to English. "Poor lonely Corina." Instinctively I became the world's soundest sleeper, not moving a muscle.

After a while she stood up from my bed and I heard her take a drink from the bottle. "My children don't care . . . ungrateful animals! . . . maybe Carl," she said, and she staggered out of my room.

When she was gone, I got up quietly from my bed and went to my door. I could see her down the hall with the cigarette still dangling from her mouth and the bottle in one hand. She opened Carl's door and went into his room. I wondered if I should go help him in some way, but to tell the truth I was scared to death of my mother, especially when she was so drunk. I told myself I was only nine and Carl was older, he was eleven. There are times like this when you convince yourself everything is all right, but deep inside you know it's not all right at all.

So I got back in bed. In those days I had a very comforting fantasy world I could retreat to, a running serial in which I was always the hero and did fabulous things and in return received incredible amounts of love and adulation. I could switch this fantasy on and off when things got tough, and on this particular night I tuned out my mother's visit and fell asleep again quickly in the midst of a great adventure.

I woke up later. It was still dark. I heard a terrible scream from down the hall and I smelled something strange in the room. It was smoke. Outside there were sirens and people moving about on the lawn. I thought this was awfully exciting and I jumped out of bed and opened the bedroom door to the hall. But as soon as I opened the door, clouds of smoke came billowing into my room, smoke so thick I couldn't breathe or see. Then I heard a second scream from down the hall, and I knew it was my brother Carl.

It was all so overwhelming that I started crying and choking on the smoke all at once. I tried to get back to my bed but I couldn't see a thing. And then two strong arms grabbed hold of me and a wet washcloth was pressed over my face. It was Albert. I don't know what he was doing home at the time, because my father was in London, but I was sure glad he was there when I needed him. Albert picked me up in his arms and carried me away. Over his shoulder I could see angry bursts of flame coming from Carl's room. I never saw Albert move so fast before. He carried me downstairs, out the front door, and dropped me onto the lawn next to Rags. Then he tried to go back inside for Carl, but a fireman stopped him.

Everything seemed to be happening at once. There were hoses and fire engines and people rushing about, and even an ambulance had arrived in our driveway with the siren screaming. Albert, Gretchen, Rags, and I waited together in silence on the front lawn while the firemen went inside for Carl. Then a tall man in a hat and a black raincoat and boots came rushing out with Carl in his arms wrapped in a blanket. I didn't even know if Carl was alive. He seemed black all over, like a piece of chicken I had once seen left on the barbecue too long. He was put in the ambulance, and the ambulance turned on its siren again and rushed off down the driveway, leaving the rest of us staring at the sad glow of tail lights.

And that's when I saw my mother, sitting on a lawn chair with a glass of something in her hand. Eventually, the official cause of the fire was said to be an electrical malfunction, but I knew my mother had somehow caused it. She must have dropped her cigarette on Carl's bed when she made her nocturnal visit, and then staggered back to the safety of her own room. There's an old saying that God protects drunks and little children, but in this instance He seemed to let the little children fend for themselves. I don't know. I guess anything could have happened in there. Carl never spoke about it, not even when he was older and I asked him, and I doubt if my mother even remembered being in his room.

"Isn't this just swell?" she said gloomily, standing in front of our burning house. "The photographers are going to come and I look like shit."

I really hated her at just that moment. I remember wishing she had burned to death in the house. Carl was in the hospital for nearly three months. He had second- and third-degree burns over most of his body, but at least his face was spared. They gave him skin grafts and just about everything money could buy, and eventually he looked pretty good as long as you didn't look at him too closely in a swim suit.

So that was the first Sangor family fire. Fortunately, kids have an amazing ability to forget. Life went on and I remember mostly sunny days. Then, when I was twelve years old everything changed and I soon learned what real trouble could be. It all started when I discovered a hole in the fence to the estate of a great mansion where a movie star lived next door. And on that same fateful day, I met my half sister Zoe.

10

I guess there had been trouble brewing for some time among the adults. In 1966, my mother was hired to play the lead in a biblical epic to be filmed on location in Italy. She was to play a pagan Roman princess who falls in love with a Christian slave and eventually they get married and become more or less proper Episcopalians. Probably you've even seen this movie, but not starring my mother because she was fired after three weeks of shooting for showing up each morning at Cinecittà, the studio outside of Rome, bleary-eyed drunk. The film was supposed to be Corina Norman's comeback picture, but she only came back to Hollywood, drinking more than ever. Up to this point, my mother had been able to convince the gossip columnists that her semiretirement was due to her love for her children and her great desire not to miss a single precious hour of their formative years. But now the truth was all over town: Corina was a failure!

Of course, in Hollywood the word failure is something not even to be whispered in polite society. My mother was suddenly a social pariah, and my father had already switched horses in midstream, switched women, that is, though none of us knew this yet.

News of the adult world filtered down only occasionally to the children's quarters. Our mother certainly told us nothing, and, in general, we were not much interested in the rise and fall of great studios, or marriages and divorces, and the constant flux of careers—the events beyond the high wrought-iron gate of La Chanson d'Or. Occasionally, when he was home, our father would stop into the children's wing and hold forth for twenty minutes or so, telling us about some great new success in his career. Dad loved to gloat about his victories, and he wanted us to idolize him, which we did, of course. He was always the distant and golden god who made our lives possible.

I remember he would come into one of our rooms—usually Rags's room, since it was the largest—and sit in the big rocking chair, loosen his tie, and raise a cigarette to his lips. Right away Carl, Rags, and I would scurry about looking for a match: Oh, the honor of being allowed to light my father's cigarette! And the glorious smell of tobacco lingering in our bedrooms long after he himself had departed—to New York, London, Paris, Rome, mythical places—leaving behind only a little smoke.

"Well, my darlings," he would say—for he always called us his darlings—"I made tons of moola for us today."

And we would hang all over him and say things like, "Cool, Dad! . . . How'd you do it, Dad?" And he'd narrow his eyes and tell us some thrilling saga of manipulation and high finance, and how he had managed to screw MGM or Paramount, Warner Brothers or Fox, getting the bastards to pay twice as much for one of his stars as they intended. We loved it. We thought our dad could do anything. The only thing we held against him was that the visits were too few, too brief.

It was on one of these visits to the children's wing, on a late summer day in August of 1967, that we learned of the big domestic changes that were in store for us. My father sat down in Rags's rocking chair and he did not look quite as jaunty as usual.

"Well, my darlings, I know you've been wondering where your mother is."

"Isn't she in her bedroom taking a nap?" Carl asked. "Nap" was the basic code word in our family for falling-down drunk.

"Carl, your mother has been gone for nearly six weeks," said our father solemnly. Carl, Rags, and I glanced at each other. We realized the house had seemed more quiet than usual, but we had not particularly noticed her absence.

Dad scowled. I think for a moment he must have found it strange our mother could have been missing for six weeks and none of us would notice, even in such a large house as La Chanson d'Or. "I certainly wish I had more time at home," he faltered. "It's the price of success to be gone so often. Anyway, my darlings, some- times in the lives of adults . . . well, people get a divorce. And that's what your mother and I have been doing the last six weeks. As a matter of fact, she's been in Nevada where these things are a little faster, and she's met a nice man there who owns a big Las Vegas casino."

"But, Dad, aren't we ever going to see her again?" Carl asked. I believe he was the only one of us who seemed even slightly perturbed by our mother's sudden exit from our lives. Rags, for his part, was positively grinning ear to ear.

My father cleared his throat. Actually, Corina Norman had no desire to see the children again ever, and she had gladly given custody of us to our father. We learned later she was about to marry mobster Jackie "Spats" Guardino, who was thrilled to have a once-famous actress as part of his entourage—but he certainly didn't want children either, just a sultry siren at his side. Hoping to spare our feelings, Dad mumbled a few things about how our mother would certainly send for us after "things settled down a bit."

"And now there's something else," Dad said, and I noticed that for the first time in my memory he didn't seen entirely comfort- able. "I've been seeing a very nice girl for some time now. For quite a *long* time, as a matter of fact. She's a famous actress in Europe," he added brightly, as if fame made everything all right. We stared at him dumbly. "Well, I don't expect you to understand this until you're older, my darlings. I certainly loved your mother very much . . . and *your* mother too, Rags. But marriage can be confining, and, as you know, I've had to spend a lot of time in Europe, and a man can become lonely . . . and when you boys grow up, I think you'll discover that if a man has, well . . . a certain stature in the world then it's possible for him to . . . well, keep a mistress."

I'm sure my mouth was hanging wide open. But my dad had not finished telling us amazing things, not by a long shot.

"And now that your mother and I have come to the parting of ways, it's finally possible for Michelle and me to be together. . . . What I'm trying to tell you, my darlings, is that you are about to have a new mother."

"Good God, *already*?" Rags asked.

"Actually, we're going to be married next week—we'll have a big party. . . . Won't that be fun? And I have another surprise for you as well!"

"My God, what?" Carl, who seemed to think this was enough surprises for one day, asked in some alarm.

"You're going to have a new brother. And a sister too."

"*A sister!*" we all breathed in unison. Being a family of boys, this seemed a terrible and wonderful thing. I was already vaguely wondering if she would join us in our circle jerks, and what this might be like, to masturbate with a girl around.

The news of our enlarged family left us all feeling stunned, particularly since we learned this big change was effective immediately. Our dad had waited until the very last moment to tell us the news, and now our new mother and siblings were flying in from Paris and would be arriving that very afternoon. I couldn't absorb it all at once.

Really, it took me a number of years to appreciate the full extent of Dad's great deception, that our new brother and sister were actual blood relations. They were Dad's children just like Rags, Carl, and I were, and he had been keeping this separate family in Paris, in an apartment near the Luxembourg Gardens, and living a double life since way back in the days of Isabelle Lambert. In fact, Dad had met Michelle Cordell sixteen years earlier when she was just a very pretty girl, and he had become her protector and helped her along the thorny path of an acting career, and had even resided at the apartment near the Luxembourg Gardens during his prolonged stays in France. Now that Michelle Cordell had finally become a big star, Dad wanted to marry her: She was valuable to him, whereas Corina Norman was not.

So Dad smiled like crazy. After he had managed the hard part and broken the big news, he was feeling pretty good about himself.

And why not? This was a guy who emerged from the ashes of every relationship in complete victory.

"I can't tell you how glad I am this is all out in the open, my darlings," he said, and he gave us each a big hug, and told us he loved us more than anything in the world, and he got out of there fast. When Dad left, Rags, Carl, and I looked at each other without a word.

"Well, at least she's a looker," said Rags at last, referring to our new mother. He seemed to know something about her.

"So what's she like?" Carl asked grumpily. "Does she drink too much? Is she intelligent?"

"I can only tell you she has great tits," said Rags with a knowing smile. "She takes off her clothes a lot. They do that, you know, in French movies. It's considered normal over there."

"Do you think she'll walk around *our* house naked?" I wondered.

"Probably," said Rags. "French people don't think anything about it."

"Hell with it, let's play catch," I suggested. To tell the truth, I was tired of thinking about new mothers and brothers and sisters and just wanted to be a kid again. But Rags and Carl seemed more upset by the changes than I was, maybe because they were older and understood it more—Rags was twenty-one and Carl was four-teen. They weren't in any mood for a ball game. "Hell with it," I said again, and I left them to their own devices and went out into the backyard with a baseball bat and softball.

I was in a funky, dissolute mood. I was nearly twelve years old. I didn't understand the changes that were coming down, but I knew vaguely that something momentous had happened. Bored with myself, I began to throw the ball up into the air and hit it with the bat, aiming at the trunk of a maple tree about fifteen feet away. I was never great at baseball. Half the time I missed the damn ball, swinging away impotently at the empty air. But today, for some reason, I really connected. With a crack, I sent a line drive sailing hard beyond the maple tree, over a stretch of lawn, and into the tall shrubbery that divided our property from the house next door. Impressed with my skill, I jogged toward the bushes to find my softball.

This was not the first time we kids had lost a ball in this partic-ular shrubbery. I crawled on my hands and knees into the hedge, where there was enough space for a small body to enter if one kept low and near the roots. I came—as I had often come before— to a wooden picket fence which marked the beginning of the next property, Casa Monte Carlo. In a moment I saw the ball. It had somehow slipped through the fence and was sitting a few inches into the next yard, resting in a spot of sunlight in an alien flower bed. I uttered a few curses. We had never been able to figure out a way into this yard, and I was afraid my baseball was lost to me.

But I didn't give up right away. I crawled on my stomach with branches scraping against my back until I was completely enclosed in the hedge. There was something cool and secret inside this shrubbery. I found I liked being here, away from the eyes of the world. I sat for a moment, and tried to solve the puzzle before my eyes: The slats of the fence had spaces about one inch wide, through which I could see my softball.

But the ball, which must have slipped through these slats, was nearly three inches in diameter. So how could the larger ball slip through the smaller opening, I wondered. What was one to make of this essential mystery? With some uncertainty, I tried to reach through the slats. To my surprise, a portion of the fence moved aside easily with my hand, lifting up like a trap door. The fence here was rotten, and apparently the baseball had hit this spot and traveled on through. I did likewise. I crawled after the ball into the next yard.

I had no idea who lived next door in Casa Monte Carlo, or what I would find here. This may sound strange, but the estate was not visible either from our property or from Coldwater Canyon Boulevard, and in the wealthy areas of West Los Angeles, each house is an island, and people go out of their way to avoid any knowledge of their neighbors.

I felt I should turn back but now that I was there my curiosity was awakened. I picked up my baseball and found myself in a secluded oval of grass, with a neat gravel path around it that was lined with carefully planted flowers. At the far end of the oval was a life-size bronze statue of a naked woman with one arm stretched up to the sky. The statue was green with age, and I later learned it was a Rodin.

I was intrigued. This was a perfect little park, both elegant and serene. Careful not to make any noise, I walked on the grass alongside the gravel path. I came to the shaded arch of a grape arbor through which I could see a small fountain beyond. I had never seen a formally landscaped garden before. Oh, we had some flower beds at our house, and some nice lawn in the front and in the back around the pool, but particularly at this time—before my new French stepmother—our grounds were fairly wild. The property next door, however, was beautifully landscaped and everything seemed much grander and more elegant than where I lived.

So I wandered on. I passed through the grape arbor toward the fountain, and from this point I could see a portion of the house itself, a huge salmon-pink Mediterranean villa, with stucco walls and a roof of slanting red tiles. From where I stood, I could also see a tennis court and a swimming pool that seemed to be shaped like a small lagoon. And then, to my horror, I suddenly heard the scuffling sound of footsteps coming my way along the gravel path. I ducked back into the hedge behind me, hiding my small body inside the thick green foliage. In a moment I heard a booming male voice singing something operatic in a foreign language. Italian, I was to understand later. Then the language changed to English, and the song continued bawdily in an improvised fashion: "Oh, sit on my face and open your legs . . . And then turn around and give me some head!"

I heard a silvery feminine laugh, and in a moment a man and woman came into my view through the hedge. I was astonished. I recognized the man immediately as Marco Mallory, the famous movie star who always played romantic swashbuckling roles in movies where he would swing down from chandeliers with a sword in hand and rescue beautiful women from impossible situations.

For me, at not quite twelve years old, Marco Mallory was my image of a perfect human being, and he looked even more impressive in real life: vast shoulders, glossy black hair, a face that seemed carved out of stone. He was wearing a shimmering silk oriental robe, but the lady walking next to him—to my great surprise—was wearing nothing at all. Or rather, to be more accurate, she was wearing pink high-heeled slippers, false eyelashes, a great deal of makeup, and her red hair was coiffured in a kind of elaborate beehive hairdo. She was perfectly elegant and proper, except for the fact that between her earrings and slippers there was nothing but unadorned flesh. I could not help but observe that she was not a natural redhead.

I had never seen an actual naked lady before, but I was to see something more astonishing still. Marco Mallory sat down on a small concrete bench along the gravel path, and the lady knelt in front of him and opened his splendid oriental robe. The famous movie star was wearing nothing underneath, and the perfectly coiffured woman calmly took his erect penis in her mouth and began to suck up and down on it like it was some kind of hard candy.

I had heard Rags talk about such things, of course, but I didn't *really* think people actually did them. I stayed very still, afraid I might cough or sneeze, for they were barely a dozen feet away from where I was hiding. In a few minutes, Marco Mallory gave a great sigh and the lady stepped back with something milky running down her chin.

"Ah, my sweet flower!" came the booming bass voice. "If only you had two tongues, rather than one!"

With a laugh, the happy couple stood up and strolled back down the path, and out of my sight. I waited in the hedge for nearly fifteen minutes, not daring to move. Finally, when I had not heard any sounds for some time, I scampered out of my hiding spot and ran as fast as I could past the fountain, past the bronze statue of the naked woman, and over the formal oval of lawn to the spot in my fence which would take me home.

I crawled through the opening so fast I tore the back of my T-shirt on a branch, and I came out into the safety of my backyard with my face covered with dirt.

My God, did *I* ever have something to tell Rags and Carl! I ran toward the house, through the backdoor, into the kitchen, and I was making my way through the dining room into the central foyer to go upstairs, when I stopped in further astonishment on this most astonishing day. Before me, wearing a pleated skirt and knee socks and a simple blouse, was the hallucinatory loveliness of my new sister, Zoe.

11

The first time I ever saw Zoe, she was standing in the open doorway of our house, a suitcase in hand, with her mother behind her. I wouldn't want anyone to think I fell in love with my sister on first sight. Actually, it took perhaps twenty, possibly even thirty, seconds. At the end of that interval, my life had been changed forever.

In those twenty to thirty seconds, Zoe emerged upon my consciousness slowly, like an image appearing on photographic paper in the dark. At first I was struck only by her face and figure. But then I saw something else. She was perilously close to tears, gazing up with large and frightened eyes at the grand staircase of our house, her lower lip slightly trembling as she seemed to contemplate what life might have in store for her here in barbaric California.

This is the moment I fell in love with Zoe; I was lured by her looks, but captured by her heart-breaking vulnerability. I certainly had no experience with girls—much less, girls who were about to cry—but looking at Zoe, I seemed to feel what she was feeling, what it must be like to arrive a stranger in this strange house, and I found myself filled with an overwhelming urge to protect and comfort her.

Physically, Zoe and her mother—the French actress, Michelle Cordell—were extremely alike, a bigger version and a smaller version of the same theme. They had the same thick, luxuriant dark-blond hair which they wore long and straight, according to the fashion of 1967. As far as I could tell, neither mother nor daughter wore makeup. Their skin was pale and clear. Their eyes were flecked with many shades of greens and blues and gold; they had high, almost Slavic cheekbones, and despite their blond hair, they had an air of foreignness to Southern California. Zoe was thirteen and her mother thirty-four, but they might have been sisters. Without doubt, they were the two most beautiful women I had ever seen.

Zoe was a little more than a year older than I was, but for me she was a woman. I could hardly believe this was to be my new sister, and that, furthermore, she would be living in a bedroom very close to my own. I nearly swooned. To tell the truth, I was already in a state of erotic palpitation from what I had witnessed in the garden next door, and seeing Zoe so soon afterward threatened to throw me over the edge.

Zoe's big sad eyes slowly swung my way, and for a moment she looked at me, the little boy who was staring at her. Unfortunately, I knew all too well what she saw: a grubby little kid, not quite twelve, with a torn T-shirt and a dirty face. I hope I've made it sufficiently clear that there was nothing at all sensitive or refined about me. I was a nasty little boy at an obnoxious age, who talked mostly about boogers and farts, tits 'n' ass, baseball and cars. Never before had I found myself particularly lacking, but in one brief glance from my new sister, I felt my whole world destroyed. I saw myself as she saw me, and I had a sudden longing to raise myself up from the preadolescent slime into the clean ethereal reaches where I imagined my sister lived.

All this happened in a moment. Zoe simply looked at me, shattered my life, and then lowered her eyes in defeat, as if there could be no hope for her in such a house with such a little brother. I was aware of a limousine behind the mother and daughter, framed by the open doorway, and my father and Albert taking luggage from the trunk. I continued to stare shamelessly at Zoe. She was like an angel come down from heaven. Beauty to make you weep. And then a figure stepped out from behind this perfect mother and daughter, a boy with a round, freckly face and a wicked little grin. It was my new brother David, and paradise was abruptly lost.

Rags and Carl had come down the stairs and were staring at the new members of our family with the same incredulity as I. My father appeared in the doorway and began to make introductions.

"Rags, Carl, Jonno—this is Michelle . . . Dah-veed . . . and Zoe."

Martians and Earthmen could not have been more awkward meeting one another than my brothers and I were with these exotic Parisians. David was fifteen—a year older than Carl, three years older than me—but he was a big boy, tall for his age and overweight. He shook hands with Rags and Carl, nodded at me in an offhand way, and began his relationship with my family speaking French, which sounded like a lot of nasal gibberish in my ear. When David received nothing but dumb stares in return, he switched to an ironic and perfect English, amused that these natives of Southern California were not terribly cultivated.

"Hey, what kind of name is Dah-*veed*?" I challenged, trying to hold my own. I didn't like him from the start; I tried to imply that maybe only some kind of pervert would have a name like his.

"It is a French pronunciation. But you can call me David, if it is simpler for you."

"I don't care one way or another," I assured him. I returned his ironic smile with a deep glower. Dah-veed put a protective arm around his younger sister Zoe. I *really* hated that.

Our new stepmother went around and gave each of us a hug and a kiss on each cheek. Michelle Cordell smelled awfully good, of a spicy substance I was eventually to recognize as patchouli oil, and her manner was both motherly and flirtatious. From the beginning, I was inclined to like my new French stepmother. Later I discovered that much of her easygoing nature was due to the fact she was almost always stoned on hashish. But frankly, this was an improvement over my last mother, my *real* mother, who was always drunk.

So we all said hello and shook hands. For the briefest instant I even held Zoe's hand in my own. It seemed cold and smooth as marble. She disengaged quickly, as though my hand were somehow sticky and unclean. I wanted to tell her that I adored her, that I would wash if necessary, and that if she needed anything,

absolutely *anything* . . . but there was luggage to be brought in
from the driveway, and the house to be inspected, and we were
soon separated.

The house was topsy-turvy all that day. And indeed, life never
again settled down to its previous patterns. Carl, Rags, and I each
retreated to our separate bedrooms, none of us really knowing
what to do with ourselves. From what I heard the adults say, Rags
was to be moved into one of the guest rooms downstairs, and his
old bedroom would be given to David. As for Zoe, she would get
the large bedroom in the children's wing that we had been using
as a game room and a place to store our toys. As it happened, this
room was directly next to my own. But until it was remodeled for
her, Zoe would sleep in the second guest room downstairs.

I found myself pacing aimlessly to and fro in my bedroom. I
took a shower and washed my hair, and I stared into my bathroom
mirror for the longest time, running a comb through my hair and
trying to imagine if Zoe could possibly find me attractive. I decided
she could not. I hated the way I looked: I had black hair, olive
skin, and rather limp brown eyes with long eyelashes. I looked
like a goddamn girl—and not just any girl. As it happened, I looked
almost exactly like my ex-mother, the sultry Corina Norman.

I was screwing up my face trying to look hard and masculine
when Carl came bursting into my room with a huge art book under
his arm.

"I found it! Jonno, you really *must* look at this!"

Carl put the book down on my bed and it fell open to quite an
amazing sight. It was a painting of my new sister Zoe standing
stark naked on a big clamshell with a bunch of angels looking on
from the corners. In the painting, Zoe's hair was a bit longer than
it was in real life, so long it modestly hid some of the parts I was
dying to see.

"Well, what do you think?" Carl was asking me. "Is it her, or
what?"

"Jesus," I said. "Jesus H. Christ!"

"This is Botticelli's *Birth of Venus*," Carl told me, and for the
rest of my life I would always identify Zoe with that painting. Not
that she was exactly like it. To tell the truth, Zoe was prettier and
not quite so plump, and yet there was something about the painting, a mood maybe, an essence that was entirely and utterly Zoe.

Carl was staring at the book in rapture. For a moment I thought, this is swell, Carl knows how I feel about her and he's showing his support. But then my heart sank when I realized Carl's rapture had nothing to do with me. *He* was in love with her himself!

I guess I'd better describe Carl as a kid, because he was not at all like me. At the age of fourteen he somehow looked like a funny old man, almost like he looks today. There were no visible signs of his burns, but he tended to wear long-sleeve shirts with the buttons done up to the top. He didn't have the John Lennon glasses yet. But he had the John Lennon look: aesthetically reedy, the starved poet, the intellectual wise guy.

He was as different from me as night and day, and different from Rags too. I don't know how he got to be like he was. He was unpopular at his school, a very right-wing anti-Semitic private school in the Valley, a place called the Harvard School. He was the kind of kid who dared stand alone. He read a lot, listened to jazz and classical music, and despised pretty much everything about Southern California. He was a bit of a cultural snob, the way smart kids can be who are unhappy with their real surroundings.

The Sunday *New York Times* was delivered to our house each week, and that city became Carl's intellectual mecca. San Francisco had some pull on his affections, but New York was the place to which his soul aspired. Not long after he had been burned in the fire, he decided he was a socialist revolutionary, and at the age of fourteen, he had managed to discover the beat poets. He used to read aloud to me people like Kenneth Patchen, Lawrence Ferlinghetti, and Allen Ginsberg. What I'm trying to say is that Carl was sensitive, poetic, and intellectual. I knew without a doubt that an elevated creature like Zoe would prefer Carl to a fart 'n' booger man like me. In fact, I had lost the race before it had even begun.

"It's her, isn't it?" he kept saying, gazing longingly at the Botticelli. I'd never seen him glow like that before, like he was lit up from inside.

"Sure it is," I told him. "Only Zoe's hair isn't so long. And we don't have a whole lot of angels flying overhead. But other than that, it's just like her."

I don't think he even heard me. I guess for a lonely poetic kid like Carl, Zoe was a dream come true. I kept very quiet and didn't let on that I felt the same way about her myself. I knew he deserved her, whereas I did not.

Carl blabbered on a bit about how maybe Zoe was more medieval than Italian renaissance. He could imagine her walking barefoot in some Gothic cathedral, poor guy, her dainty feet against the cool stone. Or maybe dancing around a maypole in some green and virginal field. Carl eventually left me, wandering off in a self-induced daze of romantic fervor. After he left, I sat on my bed and felt miserable.

Rags stopped into my room for a moment and asked if I wanted to go to the beach with him and "check out the babes," as he put it. I said, "Fuck the babes," and Rags gave me a funny look. A very sad look, as a matter of fact, I realize now, all these years later, this was a big day for him too: He had lost us, Carl and me. Our threesome would never be the same. Zoe's arrival had changed everything.

"Fucking hell!" I said when Rags was gone. I couldn't remember ever having felt this weird before. And then I happened to glance out my bedroom window and saw the cause of my discomfort. There was Zoe herself walking slowly across the lawn toward the swimming pool. She stood for a moment with her back to me, staring down into the turquoise water. All of a sudden I saw her shoulders convulse in a very major sob. I knew she was crying even though I couldn't see the tears. Then she turned and ran blindly past the pool house toward the protection of the woods.

I didn't hesitate. I climbed out my window onto a thick branch of the oak tree that grew up to the second floor. This was an old trick of mine, and something I was proud of. I was like a monkey in those days, and in a moment I had scurried down the tree onto the ground below, and set off into the woods to spy upon Zoe. I didn't exactly think about what I was doing. I simply couldn't help myself.

Zoe was following a small path I knew well, one that led to the creek bed where my new French stepmother would soon build a meditation studio. I took a shortcut through the woods and came up from the side to find Zoe standing thoughtfully by the edge of the bank. She was dressed as I had last seen her, in a white blouse, pleated skirt, loafers, and knee socks. I could not help but notice that she had magnificent knees; mysterious girl's knees that made you try to imagine the various wonders a few inches up. I wasn't sure if she was still crying, but then, in a moment, I heard a heart-wrenching sob escape her breast. Her pain was too much for me to bear. I stepped out from my tree and approached her.

"Hey, are you okay?" I asked, feeling very stupid. I mean, *of course* she wasn't okay or she wouldn't be standing in the woods crying. Zoe uttered a small gasp of surprise, glancing at me in terror.

"I didn't mean to scare you. It's just, I saw you come out here . . ."

"Please go away! Please leave me alone!" she cried.

"Sure," I said. "Okay, fine." But I was not going anywhere; I just stared at her like some kind of mongoloid idiot, not able to think of a single word of comfort I might offer to this beautiful, alien creature. And then it came to me, the one thing in my life I might offer her, the one thing that was not nasty or gross.

"Hey, look . . . would you like to hear me play the piano? I mean, I've been taking lessons a year and a half. I can play the 'Moonlight Sonata' by Ludwig van Beethoven."

Zoe was staring at me like she couldn't quite comprehend who I was, or what I was saying. She shook her head violently. "I can't. . . . Please just go away!"

Her voice back then had an even stronger French/British accent than it does today. I really got a kick out of the way she spoke. I could have listened to her all day.

"Please, I just want to be alone. . . . The 'Moonlight Sonata' you say? Well, all right then," she announced, abruptly changing her mind. "There is actually a piano in this house?"

I assured Zoe that yes, indeed, there was an actual piano in the house, a black baby grand in the living room.

"And your name is John?" she asked severely.

"Jonathan. Jonno, really. But actually, you can call me anything you want. I'm twelve," I lied, adding a few months to my age.

Zoe followed me back along the path toward the house, and I tried my best to make conversation. "You'll like California, I bet. We've got plenty of sunshine, but I guess you know that already. But I gotta warn you, it *does* rain in the winter."

When she didn't answer, I shut up, leaving well enough alone. Already, it was a miracle she was following me to the piano and I didn't want to reverse my luck. When we got to the living room, I sat on the shiny black bench before the piano, while Zoe sat cross-legged nearby on the floor. This position revealed more than her knees, even a few inches of porcelain-smooth thigh. My nasty little-boy eyes darted nervously from the piano to the mysteries of girl-flesh, trying not to be obvious.

"All right, play for me," she challenged. So I played. In the year and a half since I had been forced into piano lessons, I had made some progress. The first movement of the "Moonlight Sonata" is extremely easy. It is a piece for beginners. But I found it mysterious and lovely and calmer than the waters of our swimming pool on a full-moon summer night. I played the movement melodramatically, louder than it should be, but full of an emotion I did not completely understand. All the time I played, I felt Zoe's eyes carefully watching me, and this made me play more dramatically still. In fact, I think I ended up playing that first movement louder and more melodramatically than it has ever been played before or since. I mean, the way I played the thing Beethoven could have renamed it "Appassionata."

When I came to the end, I realized Zoe had moved up from the floor and was standing looking over my shoulder at the sheet music.

"Can you play the second and third movements?" she asked.

I shook my head.

"Would you like to hear me play them for you?"

I nodded, and I let Zoe take my place on the bench, while I stood behind her, not particularly astonished that she could play because I imagined Zoe could do anything. Now, as everyone knows who has studied the piano, the first movement of the 'Moonlight Sonata' is pretty easy, but the second and third movements are decidedly not. Zoe played through the stately second movement, and I was impressed. But when she hit the fast third movement, I could hardly believe my ears—for this movement is pure Beethoven, a torrent of fast-moving notes, and Zoe's fingers were flying over the keys. I mean, my new sister was a goddamn virtuoso!

I listened with my head bowed. I was hearing music straight from heaven. Zoe played the piano as if she had stolen fire from the gods. When she was finished, I could not find words to say what I felt, so I remained in quiet agitation.

"So there it is," said Zoe, closing the sheet music. "Do you want to be able to play the piano well, Jonno?"

I nodded. "Oh, yes!" I said. She turned around on the bench and scowled at me. "Perhaps you think it is easy to play the piano well," she said severely. "It isn't. It is very hard. If you want to learn to play, you must give yourself to it completely. You must practice many hours every day. You can't fuck off."

This really surprised me; I hadn't expected Zoe to be the sort of person to say "fuck off." But I loved the way she said it, with her elegant French/British schoolgirl voice. In fact, I had never really heard "fuck off" sound quite so splendid until I had heard it uttered in her patrician tones.

"Let me see your hands," she demanded, and I held out my hands for inspection. Zoe took one hand and then the other, pulling and examining each and every finger. I loved to be touched by her.

"Well, you have nice hands, Jonno. You have long fingers. Look, you see, your fingers are longer than mine." And she held her palms against mine, and all our fingers touched and my heart was beating so fast I thought I was going to faint.

Zoe stood up from the bench, and she was staring at me now with great intensity. "Tell me, for I must know the *absolute* truth. How badly do you want to play the piano, Jonno?"

"Oh, real bad," I told her. "So incredibly bad, I mean, I can hardly even *talk* about it."

"Will you do exactly what I tell you? Will you put yourself entirely in my hands?"

"Oh, yes!"

"Do you promise? Do you cross your heart and hope to die?"

"I hope to die, Zoe. If ever I let you down."

She smiled gravely. I had never met a human being quite so intense as my new sister Zoe, and I was giddy with having given myself to her. It felt a little like jumping off a cliff. "Then I will be your teacher," she said at last. "I will expect you to practice three hours every day, and the first time you miss a day I will stop your lessons forever. Do you understand? I am only interested in serious people, Jonno."

"Hey, you are looking at a serious person," I assured her. "Incredibly, almost *unbelievably*, serious."

She laughed. It was a shy, funny little laugh, and her eyes brimmed with mischief and brightness. I had never seen Zoe laugh before, and I liked it as much as I liked everything else about her. "Oh, I don't think you are serious, Jonno. I think you are the joker in the deck. But we will see."

We saw all right. Our lessons began right then and there. Zoe sat down with me on the piano bench and showed me the fingerings and intervals for all the diatonic scales going around the circle of fifths, and she explained the circle of fifths as well, and how it was the organizing principle for all Western music. And after that she showed me the three different minor scales and how they had evolved from medieval modes. My head was spinning with all the new information and with the fear that she would find me stupid and stop being my teacher. Carl came down into the living room while she was giving me my lesson, and for a few minutes he hovered over our shoulders.

"Hey, this is wonderful!" he said. "Maybe you can give me violin lessons?"

"I don't play the violin," said Zoe without even looking at him, and after a moment, I realized Carl had wandered off. To tell the truth, I didn't even pause to feel bad about him, though I knew he must have been wounded. I only thought about Zoe and the music she was teaching me and the fact that we were sitting so close together on the piano bench our hips were touching. And it was wonderful. I could smell the sweet fragrance of her skin and I felt I could practice the piano about a hundred hours a day as long as she never left my side.

"All right, that's it for now," she said at last. "Do you have any cigarette papers?"

"What?"

"Cigarette papers. Well, it doesn't matter. I have a pipe. Let's get stoned."

At this point I was beyond surprise, and I would have done anything Zoe might have suggested to me, including throwing myself off a tall building. As it was, the year was 1967, Timothy Leary was telling an eager world to turn-on and tune-out, and Zoe had stolen some hashish from her mother's stash. Lord, my new sister was an innocent and sinful angel! We took her paraphernalia, pipe and matches, back out to the woods, where we sat by the creek bed beneath a willow tree, and Zoe took me to paradise with her.

The hashish gave boldness and poetry to my tongue. I told my angelic sister I loved her, and she laughed at me. Over the years, I was to get used to this laughter—for this was to be only the first time I would declare my love, and only the first of many times she would laugh at me—and hashish, too, would be the first of our vices, but certainly not the last.

12

For the next few months, life was busy at our home on Coldwater Canyon. The house was full of carpenters and decorators in the day, and celebrities and trendy Hollywood hotshots at night, for our new French stepmother turned out to be a fashionable, up-to-date sort of person, and she liked to entertain. To handle all this traffic, two more servants were added to the domestic staff: a cheerfully overweight black woman, Dinah, who came in during the day to do general cleaning—she worked under the strict supervision of Gretchen—and a jaunty Filipino chauffeur, who went by the name of Speedo. Speedo was a crazy little guy, small and wiry as a jockey, and his face had a yellow complexion that fascinated me. He lived in a room above the garage near Albert, and smoked foul little cigars, though not when he drove my parents' limousine.

And so there we were: five kids, two adults, four servants, two cats, and an Afghan dog that my stepmother brought from Paris; a Rolls, a Cadillac limousine, a red MG, and a little cream-colored Mercedes sports car my stepmother liked to dash around in. La Chanson d'Or had turned into a very busy, chic little household. The biggest change since the days of my real mother was that for

99

the first few months after their marriage, my father and Michelle were often home in the evening, and for a while, at least, we actually *saw* them.

It was, as I keep saying, 1967, and the youth movement with its attendant rock culture had come to Hollywood. Suddenly even people like Otto Preminger were wearing Nehru jackets and giving interviews to the press in which they described their experiments with LSD. Hollywood did not create the new youth styles of the sixties, but it was quick to react when it realized there was money to be made. All at once, even "movie" was a nonword—now people discussed "films," or better yet, "cinema"—and the most hard-boiled cigar-smoking producer let his hair grow a bit longer and began to pretend that making money wasn't everything.

Michelle Cordell, as you might imagine, was very hip and part of the new sixties scene. Being a French actress with a proclivity to appear au naturel guaranteed her place among the avant garde. She had friends who were British rock stars, and she was irreverent, brash, and sexy. And she had absolutely the right kind of legs for a miniskirt. As for Dad, he entered the Age of Aquarius by letting his hair grow down over his ears and collar; he sported a bushy new mustache and wore paisley shirts and horrible bell-bottom trousers. I should mention that the Age of Aquarius did not cost him a penny. He began to represent rock stars as well as movie stars (with his new wife he had social access to both worlds), and he was now making millions of dollars every year.

For us kids, our home had become a psychedelic funhouse. We became used to the sounds of Ravi Shankar, the Beatles, and the Stones thundering on the stereo downstairs, and the aroma of incense, marijuana, and patchouli oil drifting upward to the second floor. It is such a vastly more conservative time now that it is hard to remember how, in the late sixties, people were convinced they *should* take drugs, even if they didn't want to, because dope got you in a closer groove with "reality." In this stoned age—with a fog upon L.A., so to speak—even my father was forced to smoke an occasional joint at a party or two, to prove he was young and hip enough for his ten percent. Probably Dad hated being high since he was the sort of person who always needed to be in control. But in Hollywood, if you don't stay up with what's currently in style, you might as well put your head in an oven and turn on the gas.

And so it was weird having the adults around so much, but at least they were pretty out of it most of the time, so it wasn't too bad. During the frequent parties, I would often make a brief foray downstairs and return to the children's quarters with a stolen bottle of champagne. Carl and I and Zoe would fill our toothbrush glasses with Moët & Chandon, sit on the shingled roof outside Zoe's bedroom window, light up a joint, and discuss philosophy. Or rather, Carl and Zoe discussed philosophy, for I was not really bright in that way, and I would mainly listen.

It was a funny thing about Carl. After that first afternoon when he had rushed into my bedroom with his tongue hanging out over *The Birth of Venus*, his passion seemed to cool. At least he no longer shared his feelings with me, and I soon convinced myself he wasn't a rival at all. I came to believe his interest in Zoe was only intellectual, broadly poetic in some elevated manner a very carnal person like myself could barely understand. He was fascinated by Zoe—and who can blame him? But I thought it was because here, at last, was someone on his own mental level, someone he could talk to.

And talk they did, hour after hour. As I've mentioned, Carl had become a devout socialist and he spent many evenings trying to convince Zoe that private property was the source of all evil in the world, and that rich families like ours should be stripped of all our wealth and sent to work in factories. Zoe, I should mention, was incredibly knowledgeable herself, and read serious literature in both French and English. She agreed with Carl up to a point; the present distribution of wealth was clearly unfair. But Zoe had an innate love of aristocracy, and was not willing to accept a completely proletarian world, particularly when it came to such things as "cinema" and "art."

"You're an elitist!" Carl insisted.

Zoe reiterated, "If you reduce everything to the common man, then you will have common art and common music. You'll be left with something about as interesting as American TV," said Zoe.

"No, no. American television is *totally* a product of capitalism. In the new society, workers will *love* the ballet and opera. They will joyfully read great books."

Zoe and Carl were so smart it really blew me away. I loved to hear them go on and on. Occasionally, I would feed the fires of conversation by zipping downstairs to steal another bottle of champagne, or a joint from an ashtray—crawling cunningly behind sofas and chairs, looking up miniskirts—and retreating upstairs like a stealthy shadow.

"Just a minute, young man!" cried Gretchen one time, catching me in the act, holding me by the scruff of my neck. "What do we have here? Drugs and alcohol? Aren't you ashamed of yourself?"

"It's not for me, honest!" I lied. And then I made up a real whopper: "It's just I'm so upset seeing my parents doing this stuff, I want to flush it down the toilet."

She smiled sarcastically. "What a good boy, Jonno! But still, I think I must bring this to your father's attention. He will be grateful to me for being so watchful over his children, yah?"

"No, come on, Gretchen. *Please!*"

I couldn't dissuade her and she hauled me back toward the living room where she disturbed a dozen Hollywood celebrities, two rock stars, a very hip Yogi from India, and one famous Italian film director.

"Mr. Sangor, may I speak with you, please. It is about your son, Jonno."

Dad was trying to close a deal with the Italian film director and he gestured to Michelle to go see what was wrong. My stepmother was on the sofa near the big stone fireplace and I got a real shock when I saw who was with her. It was Marco Mallory, the movie star from next door, sitting calmly by her side. He looked at me and I blushed from head to toe, and then his gaze traveled to Gretchen.

"Well, well, a domestic crisis," said Marco, his eyes still on Gretchen.

"Let me see what's the matter, Marco," said my stepmother, and she stood up and came over to where I was standing. Gretchen explained what I had done in a real kiss-ass sort of voice, like she was only trying to help, but Michelle howled with laughter when she saw me with a bottle of Moët & Chandon in one hand, and a very fat joint in the other.

"Jonno! Jonno!" she cried, giving me a big hug. "You must not smoke marijuana and drink alcohol at the same time. It will make you impotent when you try to make love to the girls! And then where will you be?"

I had not yet managed to make love to anyone, and so I took this remark very much to heart.

"What if the *girl* is stoned and drunk?" I asked seriously. "Can I make love then?"

"Then you may do whatever you want with her, mon cher, as long as she has said yes," said my stepmother, kissing me on both cheeks. She sent me back upstairs with a very playful warning to behave myself. It was the damndest thing: Just before I headed back to the children's quarters I caught a glimpse of Marco Mallory standing with Gretchen. She was offering him a canapé and he was staring with unconcealed interest at her tits. What was so strange about this was that Gretchen didn't *have* any tits, at least as far as I was concerned. She had the figure of a boy, and I couldn't for the life of me imagine how my favorite swashbuckling movie star could take the slightest interest in her.

"Allez! Allez!" cried Michelle, seeing me linger on the stairs, and I ran up the final flight back to where things were at least slightly easier to understand. I should mention that I had managed to retain possession of the joint and the bottle of Moët & Chandon.

I'm not saying life was always a party in those days. There was David to contend with, and there was school. And there was also the matter of unrequited love.

The school situation was like this. Zoe and I were in the eighth grade and seventh grade respectively at a very artsy-craftsy private school on a hilltop in Bel Air, called the Bel Air School, just so no one would think we were being bused to East Los Angeles or anything. As for David and Carl, they were in the tenth grade and ninth grade at the Harvard School, which was an Episcopalian military school for young men on the other side of Coldwater Canyon in the Valley. The Harvard School was a rigorous place, designed to create young Republicans of firm character, and academically it was supposed to be the best private high school in Los Angeles. A lot of non-Jewish movie people sent their kids there, or people who at least pretended not to be Jewish, for the place was definitely anti-Semitic. Maybe it's changed now, but back then the school had only one Jew, a poor tortured child by the name of Aaron Berger, and one utopian socialist, a poor tortured child by the name of Carl Sangor. Carl got into fights nearly every day, coming home from school with a bloody lip or nose and his uniform all torn. At lunchtime, the seniors would take turns putting him and Aaron Berger into a garbage can and rolling them down the steep hill from the senior quad to the drill field. This was the sort of education that was supposed to build men of character. David, I should say, did great at the Harvard School; within six months he had become an altar boy in the chapel and a sergeant in the cadet corps. He could clean an M-1 rifle, recite Julius Caesar in Latin, and beat up any commie faggot (including Carl) who opposed the current U.S. struggle for democracy in Vietnam.

Rags, by the way, was now twenty-one years old and had settled into his starting position at the Sangor Agency, which had once been Star Creations, Inc., but was now completely owned by my father. I have to admit that Rags was a real fuckup with no ambition at all, and certainly no desire to grow up. People got used to him at the Sangor Agency as the kid who generally put whoopee cushions on people's chairs, screwed up the mail distribution, and provided buttered popcorn at the screenings of clients' movies in the company's private projection room. But what could you do with him? He was the boss's son.

And so life went on. Each morning, Monday through Friday, Rags drove his little red MG convertible to Dad's offices on North Canon Drive in Beverly Hills, while a school bus came to whisk Zoe and me off to Bel Air, and still another bus came to take David and Carl to the Valley. The Bel Air School was a downright silly place, where we were encouraged to call the headmaster "Uncle Scottie" and the headmaster's wife "Auntie Beth." Each morning the entire school began the day by standing on our Bel Air hilltop, stretching our arms outward toward Catalina Island, and reciting a poem entitled "The Exaltation to the Dawn." You probably get the picture of what this school was like. At least it was a gentle place, unlike the Harvard School where people like me tended to get beat up. And at least I was with Zoe.

Unfortunately, my relationship with Zoe had not progressed very far, despite the fact we got stoned together and our piano lessons were continuing full steam ahead. At school, Zoe totally ignored me, and if I tried to sit next to her at lunch, she would tell me to go away. Worst of all, at home she often treated me in a horribly maternal way. And I can assure you, maternal was not what I had in mind with Zoe. To give you an example, she wouldn't even let me smoke dope with her until *after* I had done my homework and piano practice, and, in general, she treated me as if I were a sweet, but basically annoying little boy.

At school, I managed to keep a pretty good eye on Zoe most of the time. I was always aware, for instance, that if it was 11:20 in the morning, and I was stuck in social studies, Zoe would be about thirty-two yards away, in classroom 8C, studying algebra. At lunch, even though she would not let me sit with her, I kept an eye on her from across the room, noting who she sat with and what she ate.

Unfortunately, Zoe was extremely popular. She was a quiet, thoughtful girl—never loud and silly like the other popular girls— but there was something about her that drew, alas, not only people, but specifically, *boys*. Older boys. Rich, handsome, popular boys who drove cars. Boys who were as slick as polished marble and filled me with an all-consuming jealousy that was like walking around with a burst appendix.

I used to watch Zoe in the lunchroom with these boys circling around her, all of them doing their mating dance. It was revolting to watch. Tenth graders, eleventh graders, even a senior boy named Brian Dearborn who drove a Porsche to school every day. Sometimes I imagined myself swinging down from a chandelier in the middle of the lunchroom, sword in hand, fighting off Zoe's suitors, lopping off a few testicles, and carrying off my beautiful prize; she and I on a big white stallion heading toward the woods, just the sort of thing my next-door neighbor Marco Mallory might do in one of his movies.

By December, Zoe was actually "going steady" with one of these revolting boys, an absurdly handsome, but shallow, eleventh grader named Skip Johnson. What a name, for chrissake! I mean, how can you even take *seriously* someone with a name like Skip Johnson? I was sick with despair. He even took her out on weekends, Friday and Saturday nights during which I sat desolately watching the clock, and waiting for the sound of the car that would bring Zoe home.

But my watching and waiting eventually paid off. One day not long before Christmas vacation, I was in the boys' locker room changing for P.E. when I heard two boys in the next aisle discussing my sister. Fortunately, they could not see me. It was Skip Johnson talking to the loathsome Brian Dearborn, and I almost stopped breathing so I could hear them properly.

Brian said: "Come on, tell me the truth. Does Zoe put out, or what?"

Skip: "I wish. You'd think with a bod like that she'd want to share it with the male race, or something."

Brian: "Have you finger-fucked her?"

Skip: "You kidding? I can't even get her bra off. I think maybe the bitch is frigid."

That was it. The two boys wandered off with their tennis rackets to the court. I was left behind, dizzy with anger and jealousy. *Finger-fucked her . . . frigid!* I had to reach out to my locker for support. I forced myself to keep breathing slowly and not do anything rash like kill someone. Be cool and collected, I told myself. Bide your fucking time!

And two nights later I had my big chance. Zoe said I could smoke a pipeful of hash with her on the roof before bedtime, and Carl was too busy rereading *Das Kapital* to join us.

"Jonno, I need to speak with you," she said. "You've got to stop following me about at school."

"I'm *not* following you. I mean, where the hell am I? Fucking *nowhere*. I don't even sit near you on the bus."

"But you're always looking at me. Honestly, Jonno, I'm flattered, but it's like you're breathing down my neck."

I took a hit on the hash pipe. "Okay," I said bitterly, "I won't breathe down your neck anymore. All right? I won't even protect you against all those jerks you call boyfriends."

"Skip is *not* a jerk," she told me mildly. "You simply don't understand him."

"Yeah? Well, you know what *I* heard him say to Brian Dearborn in the locker room two days ago? He said you're frigid, for chrissake. I swear to God."

Zoe put down the pipe and regarded me closely with that look of hers that seemed to pass through skin and bones.

"I think you're not telling the truth, Jonno. And this kind of jealousy, you know, it doesn't really suit you."

"Yeah? Well, you're the one who's wrong, Zoe. Those guys are jerks. I don't know what you see in them anyway. I heard Brian ask Skip if he had finger-fucked you, and Skip said no, you were a frigid bitch, and he hadn't even been able to get your bra off yet."

"He said *that*?"

"I swear to God! And if you were *my* girlfriend, I'd never talk about you to anyone that way."

Zoe narrowed her eyes. I'd never seen her angry before, but now her body was rigid with fury. She wouldn't say any more about it, and in a few moments after we had finished the pipe, Zoe told me I should go to my room.

I was repentant now that I saw I had hurt her. I would never do anything to hurt Zoe.

"Look, I'm sorry. I didn't mean to . . ."

"Just go to your room, Jonno. Forget about it."

But the next day at lunch, Zoe was not sitting next to Skip Johnson. And I never saw her sit next to Skip or Brian Dearborn again.

I had triumphed. If I kept on my toes, I thought, maybe, just maybe, I could kill off all of Zoe's suitors, one by one. And then, when I was the last man on earth, maybe she'd have me. Frankly, I was not optimistic, but a guy has got to have a plan.

13

I've had a few decades now to think about Zoe, and try to understand her. And believe me, I've needed the time. Today I know there are women in the world more beautiful, brighter, more talented, more of everything, I suppose. But what Zoe had, was a kind of vitality that made it hard to take your eyes off her. She was very changeable. You never entirely knew where you stood with her. Some days she was incredibly vivacious, other days sullen and brooding, but there always seemed to be a fire raging inside of her, and it was this fire with which I was burned.

At Christmas, something happened that was to have some consequence in our lives. My father gave Zoe a good 35mm camera, a Nikon. He also had a darkroom built for her in what had once been a walk-in closet on the ground floor. Apparently she had asked Santa Claus for this exact present. She had learned about photography in Paris from one of her mother's friends, a famous fashion photographer, and she now decided it was time to capture her world on film.

From the moment on Christmas day that Zoe first laid eyes on her new darkroom, she set to work with the single-minded determination that characterized everything she did. All that vacation, she photographed everything in sight: houses, trees, animals, and each member of our family—even me. Her black-and-white photographs had a starkly realistic quality. They said, simply: This is tree. This is Jonathan. Zoe had a way of going straight to the heart of things.

I'm sure you won't be surprised to learn that I too developed a sudden and passionate interest in photography. Before long I convinced Zoe to teach me how to do the basic grunt work of the darkroom, removing the film from the metal canisters, setting up the various chemical baths, and so on. I was looking for any excuse to be with her. As it turned out, I was also a great help, since she was going through vast quantities of film, and now she could concentrate on the more creative side of the process, mainly, playing with the enlarger and experimenting with different ways to print.

Naturally, I was happy as a clam to spend so much time with my half sister in the small darkroom, both of us lit so strangely by the red safelight. She discouraged conversation. In fact, she forbade it, unless I had a technical question about the proper temperature of a chemical rinse, or something of that nature. It was alright with me. We spent silent hours together, and I was always thrilled to see Zoe make the images appear, like magic, on sheets of photographic paper that she held beneath the sharp-smelling liquids on a tray. What I liked best about Zoe's new obsession with photography—next to just being with her, of course—was that it temporarily stalled her interest in boys. Perhaps she was feeling burned by the Skip Johnson episode. Whatever the reason, she now spent her Friday and Saturday nights where I could safely keep an eye on her, in the darkroom.

Sometimes, Zoe let me follow her around on her photographic surveys of the neighborhood, her Nikon in hand. I was allowed to carry her camera bag, full of different lenses and extra film, as well as the tripod she used for certain shots. I watched her photograph houses, cars, birds sitting on branches, gardeners mowing a lawn, all the details of ordinary life. Sometimes she seemed positively indiscriminate, as if she was hungry to fill her universe with people and things and could never quite get enough.

"Zoe, that's a really *ugly* car," I told her once when she was immortalizing a servant's battered old Ford in a neighboring driveway.

"That's the point," she said. "Now we've captured its ugliness forever. Now it's *my* ugly car, don't you see?"

Zoe was probably way ahead of her time. One day, she hit me with a request which literally knocked my socks off. "Jonno," she announced quite matter-of-factly, "I've decided I want to photograph you in the nude."

I wasn't sure I heard her right. I was so nervous I got the whole thing backward. "You mean *you'll* be nude?"

She laughed at me. Probably it had never occurred to her that anyone could be quite as stupid as her twelve-year-old half brother. "No, *you'll* be the naked one, of course. Good God, Jonno, what good would it be for the photographer to be nude?"

I could have told her what good it would be, but I thought I'd better not.

"You mean, you want me to take my clothes off?"

"My dear, you're not going to be modest are you? I mean, that would really be *too* boring," she assured me. "After all, there are literally billions of people in the world, and each one of them either has a penis or a vagina, so it's not such a very big thing."

I tried to explain that it *was* a big thing to me, but Zoe wouldn't hear a word of it. "Jonno, I'm only trying to get to the absolute naked truth of things. I want an unclothed universe. And you're my assistant, and you happen to be a boy, and you absolutely *have* to help me."

"You won't, uh, show the pictures around at school, or anything?" I asked nervously.

"Good lord, no. But if it bothers you, I'll simply find someone else."

She had me there. If I didn't do it, there were probably all kinds of jerks à la Skip Johnson who would gladly volunteer. I certainly did not want Zoe to be photographing any strange boys but me, and so at last I agreed. It was a quiet Saturday afternoon in February—everyone had gone off in different directions for the day— and Zoe marched me into my bedroom and locked the door behind us. Frankly, I felt like I was about to be lined up in front of a firing squad and shot.

"Zoe, while I'm totally for artistic expression, I really don't know about this. . . ."

"Don't be such a baby! Just *do* it, for chrissake. You can undress in the bathroom and come out with a towel around your waist if it makes you feel better."

Zoe loaded her camera while I disappeared into my bathroom with a long sigh. At twelve years old, I was a very scrawny kid, but I had made some bumbling progress into puberty. I had, in fact, about a quarter inch of pubic hair, of which I was both extremely proud and embarrassed. The idea that Zoe was about to witness this patch of fuzz first hand, left me numb with fear and breathless with anticipation.

I came back into my bedroom with a lonely towel around my waist and such a look of terror on my face that Zoe took one glance at me and laughed.

"God, Jonno, I'm not going to eat you!"

I wanted to tell her that if she ate me, it would probably be a lot easier to take than just standing there. She removed my towel and threw it casually across the floor. "Hmm," she said thoughtfully, "You're circumcised."

"Well, they do that here . . . even to genitals . . . I mean, gentiles."

Boy, was I nervous!

"Jonno," she said, "Just *relax*."

I tried to relax. For the sake of photographic art, I sat naked at my desk while Zoe snapped off a roll of film. The idea, I suppose, was to see a *real* seventh grader doing his homework. I think if I could have stepped out of my skin, she would have preferred that, in order to get to all the blood and muscle beneath social pretense.

After the shots at the desk, Zoe wanted me to stand by my bed looking out the window to the backyard. This is when trouble started. Despite every command my brain sent urgently to the lower part of my body, my penis began to engorge slowly with blood until it stood stiffly at a forty-five-degree angle to my body.

"Jonno, this isn't funny. Think about something else, like arithmetic, or brussels sprouts."

"Zoe, I'm *trying*—I swear to God. But I just don't have any control over it."

"No control over it?" She seemed to find this scientifically interesting, and she moved closer to the object under discussion, snapping one picture after another.

"What a strange looking thing," she said vaguely. "It's really *not* particularly pretty, is it? But I suppose it has a certain primitive power."

I was more than hard. To tell the truth, I was about to explode. "Look, if you're curious, you can . . . well, *touch* it," I told her breathlessly.

You can't blame a guy for trying, but my sister shot me a stern and disapproving look. "I think it's time you put your clothes on, Jonno. Maybe you should run around the block, or take a cold shower, or something."

Zoe packed up her camera and unlocked the door to my room. But before she left, she turned my way and I saw a very sly smile light up the corners of her angelic Botticelli mouth.

Oh, she knew what she was doing to me alright!

14

So that's how it all began. It wasn't such a big deal, really, but when I try to find the exact moment things got crazy in my life, I'd have to point to that set of photographs of me in my birthday suit. Not that anything happened right away. In fact, I soon forgot the excruciating embarrassment of standing cum boner in front of my half sister, and within a few days I felt quite proud of myself, like I was a bold and daring fellow. But what neither Zoe nor I counted on was that while moments quickly pass, photographs last more or less forever, and this particularly cheesy session might come back to haunt us in a big way.

It was around this time that my stepmother, Michelle, flew off to Brazil for two months to make a film in Rio de Janeiro, and my father flew off in another direction, to London, where a project of his was about to go into production—the film starring the giant mechanical bat that was to become the first blockbuster of modern times, and catapult my father from the mere president of a talent agency to the vice president of a major studio. With so much at stake, Dad cheerfully abandoned his new wife and family, and set up housekeeping in a suite of rooms at the Connaught Hotel, bringing Albert along to look after him.

There was a sense of general relief in the children's quarters to have the house to ourselves once again. We were certainly back in familiar territory, left on our own with servants to take care of us. Only now our circle had expanded from three to five, to include Zoe and David.

I haven't said much about David yet. Frankly, I have an urge to skip over him, he was such an ass-kissing son of a bitch. Just to give you an idea, from the moment he entered our household, David spoke fluent German to Gretchen, for chrissake. And he didn't even do it in a halfway cool manner, but with a horrible smirk on his face that the rest of us hated. He had learned German from spending much of his childhood in a fancy boarding school in a German-speaking part of Switzerland, and Gretchen, of course, really ate it up. In fact, David soon became her pet, and she was constantly comparing how good he was to how bad we were.

Gretchen had worked out a set of culinary punishments in an attempt to maintain some control over us. It was pretty gross, really. She served us dinners like brussels sprouts and cow tongue when we were bad, and filet mignon and french fries when we were good. Needless to say, we ate a lot more tongue than filet mignon, and the tongue often ended up in strange places, in various people's shoes and trousers, for instance, or sticking out of the mailbox to greet the mailman when he arrived.

So, okay, we were bad children. But you have to visualize the five of us, with Rags at the head of the table, sitting around a very formal dinner setting beneath a crystal chandelier, and Gretchen appearing from the kitchen with an enormous cow's tongue surrounded by parsley on a silver platter.

"Here you are, children. Something very healthful tonight."

Oh, we snickered and made disgusting jokes, all of us except David, that is. As soon as Gretchen's back was turned, brussels sprouts started to fly across the room. "You're so immature!" David would tell us. "In Europe, sophisticated people eat all kinds of things. . . ."

"How about eyeballs?" Carl might interrupt.

"Or big dicks!" I might add, with the vast wit and dinner-table sophistication of a twelve year old.

When Gretchen returned to the dining room, David would

speak to her in German, telling her all the nasty things we had done. As a result, David was the only one who ever got to eat dessert. Sometimes, as a very special favor, she would make him his very own apple strudel, which was a kind of disgustingly rich German pastry.

And so it was natural, I suppose, that we should hate him. In these dinner-table wars, Rags was the worst of us, though he was twenty-two now and should have known better. He did things like put actual dog shit on the serving tray to return to the kitchen, something even *I* found disgusting. And Zoe was the best of us. She laughed at most of our jokes, the vaguely clean ones at least. I always felt she was on our side, rather than on David's. But she didn't play any part in the general mischief. Really, I had the impression it was the same to Zoe whether she ate tongue or brown rice or nothing at all.

David was always on the lookout for new material he could use against us. Sometime in the spring, he found out about the marijuana plants Carl and I had started in pots on a seldom-used terrace near the children's wing on the second floor. He told Gretchen about it, and one day Carl and I returned from school to find our plants were gone.

Carl and I were really pissed. We had our revenge by sneaking into David's room and blowing our noses long and hard onto his pillow, and then placing the pillow neatly back under his bedspread in the hope he would not notice what awaited him until his cheek touched the alien snot and goo.

David had his revenge for *that*, and this is when the big trouble began. I remember it was a spring day, a Sunday near the end of the school year, and the weather was already hot with a premature hint of summer. Dad was still in England, but Michelle was back from making her film in Brazil. Zoe and I went to the Catholic church in Beverly Hills because she had recently decided she was a Roman Catholic, and if Zoe was a Roman Catholic, I sure as hell was going to be one too.

In church she wore a white dress and a funny little round hat, and she had the most angelic expression on her face of pure yearning for goodness. Frankly, I spent most of the mass just watching her. I loved to see her on her knees praying, her eyes tightly closed, praying so hard it scared me a little because I didn't know what it was Zoe was asking from God. I think she loved the mystery of the mass and the music and the incense and Jesus looking down at us with his sad mild face from the cross. No one else in our family gave a fuck about religion, but Speedo was assigned to drive us back and forth in the limousine and sometimes Zoe and I smoked a little dope on the way home from church. Back at the house, we'd play Mozart sonatas for each other on the piano, and maybe a little Bach, and it was really a very nice way to spend the day.

But on this particular Sunday we arrived home at La Chanson d'Or and I knew right away something was wrong. Michelle met us in the foyer looking greatly pissed, and she and Zoe exchanged a volley of fast words in French that I didn't understand.

"Wait in your room, please, Jonno," said my stepmother, switching to English. "I want to speak first to Zoe, then I will speak with you."

I was mystified. I waited on the edge of my bed for the next ten minutes wondering what could be happening. Finally Zoe appeared, flushed, her cheeks stained with angry tears.

"What's happened?" I asked in alarm.

"Oh, it's so stupid! My mother got hold of those photographs. She wants to talk with you now."

To tell the truth, I did not immediately understand which photographs she was referring to, since Zoe had taken thousands all in all since Christmas, and it was now nearly three months since I had posed for her au naturel.

"Do you mean . . ."

"Yes, you and your damn erection! Jonno, this is really your fault."

"*My* fault!"

"I wasn't trying to be pornographic, as you know. I was only trying to be truthful."

"But how . . ."

"David, naturally. He went through my drawers and found the photographs. He gave them to Gretchen, and *she* felt it was her absolute moral duty, I suppose, to turn them over to my mother."

"That fuckhead!" I cried. "But I thought people took off their clothes all the time in French movies. I mean, what's she so upset about?"

"Jonno, even in French movies they haven't quite progressed as far as erections. Look, go down and speak with her. I tried to tell her it was utterly innocent. Maybe she'll listen to you."

I was shattered. Not only was I furious at David, but now I was in the embarrassing position of having to explain my well-photographed erection to my French stepmother, who I really did not know *that* well. She was waiting for me in my father's den, a room lined with shelves of books and scripts. She was sitting behind a desk trying to look stern.

"Jonno! What *am* I going to do with you?"

"I know it looks bad," I agreed. "But it was really . . . I mean, it was like . . ."

"Like what, mon cher?"

"Well, like I was an *object*. You see, Zoe had been taking pictures of cars and houses and things like that, and she just . . . well, wanted a naked kid. What can I tell you? We did it for art."

Michelle cocked a very French eyebrow at me. I imagine she had seen quite a few things in her lifetime done for "art." She came around from behind the desk and made me sit down next to her on an uncomfortable little love seat, so we could have an intimate tête-à-tête about this photography business. I should mention that my stepmother was wearing jeans so tight you could see the indenture of her crotch, as well as a white knit tank top that managed to show a few inches of bare stomach, bellybutton, and the exact outline of her breasts and nipples. She looked so much like Zoe it frightened me a bit. And yet, I didn't like the way she looked at all. Her blond hair seemed to spill chaotically over her shoulders, like she had just gotten out of bed. To tell the truth, there was something a bit sluttish and slovenly about Michelle Cordell, which was certainly *not* true about her daughter. Michelle glanced downward to one of the more explicit eight-by-ten glossy photographs in her hand, and she sighed.

"You seem to have become slightly aroused, Jonno."

The tips of my ears began to glow a hot red. "Well, that was a bit accidental. You see, I was just standing there . . . and Zoe was looking at me . . . and . . ."

"I see," said my stepmother. "Jonno, did Zoe touch you in any way?"

"Oh, no!" *Lord, I wish she had!*

"And did you touch her?"

I shook my head mournfully.

"And she remained fully clothed?"

I nodded. Michelle put an arm around my shoulder, and it was strange, but I could feel her right breast against me almost as plainly as if she were wearing nothing at all. I mean, I was being positively nailed by her nipple.

"Well, this is a very difficult question, mon cher. What bothers me is that Zoe is older than you, and I feel she has been, well . . . taking advantage of your innocence. No, let me finish, Jonno. I called your father and he agrees with me that we want you and Zoe to be good friends, but within certain limits. You may not be quite old enough to understand this yet, but I'm afraid Zoe's been playing a rather cruel game with you, and I simply won't tolerate it."

"It's okay with me what she did," I assured her quickly. "Honest. I don't mind a bit."

She laughed at me, and snuggled closer with her nipple pressing into my shoulder. "Oh, Jonno, you don't know how awful we women can be! Especially when we want a man to be attracted to us."

I was getting the picture. Suddenly, young as I was, I knew exactly what was going on. *My stepmother was jealous!* Yes, it's incredible. She was jealous of Zoe. When it got right down to it, Michelle wanted to be the only sexpot in her immediate family circle, and if there were any erections in the vicinity, they should be pointing her way alone. So she rubbed herself against me, and she told me what a bitch her daughter was, and I sat there, and I hated her.

"Now, Jonno, there's one more thing. Your father has decided he would like you to see a psychiatrist for a while. Someone you can talk these things over with."

"A psychiatrist! Merde!" I cried, which was the only French I knew.

"Jonno, all of us should take time out in our busy lives to see a psychiatrist from time to time. It's really a very rewarding experience. A voyage of inner understanding."

My stepmother went on in this vein for a few moments. How I should know myself, that sort of thing. Unfortunately, the problem was that I knew myself too well and knew exactly what I wanted. But I didn't say that. I listened very respectfully as she described the famous child psychiatrist in Beverly Hills I would be seeing once a week, beginning the next Monday. I felt very downtrodden about the whole thing. Half my seventh-grade class at the Bel Air School went to child psychiatrists in Beverly Hills, of course, but I never imagined this calamity would happen to me.

"Can I go now?" I asked.

"Yes, but one more thing. *Someone* has been getting into my dope. I *know* I bought four grams of hashish just last week, and half of it is gone already. Do you know anything about this, Jonno?"

I shook my head, the model of innocence.

"Stealing is a very bad thing, young man," she said ponderously.

"Maybe it's David," I suggested. "I mean, I don't want to rat on him or anything, but I *did* see him sneaking out of your room last week with something in his hand."

"David smokes my hashish?" Michelle asked in some astonishment.

"Oh, yeah. He's a secret stoner. The very worst kind. I mean, he gets stoned alone and probably does weird things to the animals."

At twelve, I tended to go overboard and not to know when to stop. "That'll do, Jonno. I'll speak with him," she said vaguely. I got out of there fast. Poor Michelle probably regretted being a parent at just that moment, and wondered how a perfectly normal sex kitten like herself, who smoked dope from morning to night, could possibly have the misfortune to have children who were also into sex and drugs.

But I had my own problems to think about. I had no sooner closed the door to the den and walked into the living room, than I saw David coming my way from the foyer.

"Hey, it's the pervert!" he said cheerfully.

I didn't waste words. I picked up a floor lamp on my way through the living room, yanking the plug out of the socket, and I swung it at him like a baseball bat. David shouted and warded off the blow with his left arm.

"You're a *crazy* pervert, you know that?"

"You're a rat-fuck-faggot-asshole," I told him. This was my Chaucerian period of English usage. "You scum-shit-twat-licking son of a bitch!"

David, alas, was a lot bigger than I was, even though I had a better command of the English language. He yanked the lamp out of my hands, and when I came at him swinging with my fists, I found myself propelled backward by a hard blow to my chin.

It got a little vague after that. I remember lying on the living-room floor with David sitting on top of me, methodically punching away at my face and ribs. Then I heard women screaming and Zoe and Michelle were pulling David off me. There was a rich taste of blood in my mouth and my ears were ringing.

"He started it, maman," I heard David say to his mother. "He came at me with a lamp. Look at it over there!"

"Mon dieu, I can't take this anymore!" Michelle complained to the room at large. I had a sense she had just smoked a fat joint and parenthood was too, too great a burden. "Why can't you children just . . . just *love* each other?"

I stood up unsteadily and smiled at David. And then without warning, with a high kick worthy of a forty-yard field goal, I kicked David in the balls. He doubled over, screaming in agony, and it took both Michelle and Zoe to pull us apart to avoid any more hostilities.

I was sent to bed without any dinner, and I lay bruised and battered, crying myself to sleep. Sometime later, when it was dark, I woke to a soft knock on the door. It was Zoe, who slipped into my room with a flat box—it was a pizza that Rags had picked up for me.

Zoe sat on the edge of my bed. She was wearing a terrycloth bathrobe, and I could see the edges of a soft cotton nightgown underneath. She looked so good, I actually ended up crying some more. I felt Zoe's gentle hand on my face and head, trying to see if I was hurt.

"Are you all right, Jonno?"

"Sure, I'm okay. I love you, Zoe," I said, feeling I'd best take advantage of this tender moment while it was there.

"I love you too, Jonno," she said. This was worth getting beat-up for. I ate a few slices of the pizza (pepperoni, my favorite) while Zoe sat close by, smelling so sweet and girlishly clean after her bath.

"Oh, look, Jonno!" she said, pointing out my window. "It's a full moon. It's such a warm and lovely night. I wish we could go outside and just disappear into the night! Like moonbeams."

"Well, we *could*, you know. We could climb down the tree," I suggested.

"Really?" Zoe looked dubiously to the branches of the oak tree near my window. "Have you done it before?"

"Sure. I'm a real escape artist, Zoe."

"I think you're more of a con artist," she said. "But wait a minute and I'll get dressed." Zoe left my room and returned a few minutes later dressed in jeans and a black polo shirt, with her camera bag over her shoulder. So I showed her how to make the big escape from the world of grown-ups and authority. We climbed out my window and down the oak tree into the lucid silvery magic of a full-moon night.

And oh, what a night that was!

15

Zoe and I lay on our backs on the hard wooden floor of the meditation studio in the woods, which at this time was only a half-finished octagonal frame, with a skeleton of two-by-fours rising up into the moonlight.

It was a warm night with a soft breeze blowing and a savory smell of new wood all around us. Side by side, we gazed up together at the full moon fat in the sky through the unfinished roof beams. Lazily, without sitting up, Zoe raised her Nikon to her eye and snapped off a few pictures of the moon as it traveled past the branches of a tree into the open sky above the studio.

"Will that really come out?" I asked.

"Mmm . . . fast film, Jonno. Tri-X."

She was always the teacher, even though we had just smoked a monster joint of marijuana laced with fine Moroccan hashish, courtesy of my stepmother, Michelle. I felt totally at peace. For me the world had become gorgeously serene, and I was floating through it with Zoe at my side; the two of us, brother and sister, moving through cosmic space just like the silvery moon.

We didn't speak for a long time, watching the moon move across the sky. I felt Zoe put her cheek against my shoulder.

"Jonno, I've been wanting to talk with you. I really want you to get along better with David," she said at last. Her voice was grave and elegant, cool as the moon, with that lovely French and British accent of hers.

"What you have to understand is David's had a difficult life," she went on. "It was hard for him being illegitimate, always knowing that Alex had another family somewhere, a *real* family far, far away in a mythical place called California."

"You knew about us?" I asked in surprise. I certainly had not known about them.

"Of course we knew! My mother showed us a photograph of you once. All of you. It was in *Life* magazine, I think. You were very little, Jonno, in your mother's arms. Rags and Carl were on either side of your mother, and Alex was standing behind all of you. You were all smiling and looking so rich and happy. A real family, not at all like ours. David hated it so much it bent his soul a little. So, be kind, Jonno. We were only your father's shameful secret."

I had to laugh.

"It's not funny!" she cried, sitting up from my shoulder. "My mother was only someone's mistress and we were bastards. We grew up in your shadow."

"It's not that," I assured her, "I'm only laughing because you imagined *my* family life so wrong! I mean, my mother was a falling-down drunk who like totally hated us, and my father didn't give a shit. He was gone all the time. Why, I bet you saw him as much as I did, maybe even more."

This made Zoe thoughtful. It was weird thinking of her growing up in a strangely parallel family across the ocean. I once saw a movie about a planet that was just like earth, only it was exactly on the other side of the solar system, hidden behind the sun. Somehow this made me think of Zoe with her mother and brother in Paris, and my father flying back and forth between the two worlds.

"Did you hate us?" I asked mournfully, because I suddenly realized this was entirely possible. "Did you hate Carl and Rags and me for being the real kids with the real father?"

"Oh, we were real too," she said softly. And then she added: "No, I didn't hate you, not really. I hated my mother for being so stupid. Alex is such a strong person, but my mother is so very weak, you know. She had to have a man like Alex take care of her, and when Alex was not around, there were other men he did not know about. I hated it that she was such a whore."

"But what about me, Zoe. Did you hate *me*?"

She smiled. "No, I'd better not tell you," she said.

"Come on. Tell me."

"Well, I had a fantasy. You were always the pretty one, Jonno. I saw another photograph of you when you were ten, and I thought you were very good looking, like your mother. Do you know what I imagined? One day I would meet you when we were grown-up, but you would not know I was your sister and you would fall in love with me. And then we would get married, and on our wedding night when we were in bed together . . . no, I can't tell you this, Jonno! It's too embarrassing!"

"Please . . . *please* tell me," I pleaded. I was in agony. "On our wedding night . . . ," I prompted.

Zoe laughed and put her head back on my shoulder. "On our wedding night, I would kill you," she said quite simply, and the way she said it, I believed her. "I would have a knife under my pillow, you see, and I would cut out your heart. Just like that. But frankly I was never sure if I would eat your heart or throw it in the garbage."

I found it a little hard to breathe. Zoe lay quietly on my shoulder, and I wondered if on this imaginary wedding night she would have killed me before or after we made love. This was the big question, somehow a *very* important question, but I was afraid to put it to her outright. The funny thing was, I didn't think I would mind having her cut my heart out, she could eat it or throw it in the garbage as she pleased . . . as long as she let me make love to her just one time first. Just one time! And then, hell, who would even care about living after that?

"But I don't feel that way anymore," she said, making the whole fantasy go up in smoke.

"You don't?"

"No, I don't think I will have to kill you, Jonno. I was wrong, you see. Your life here was as sad as my life in Paris. We both got the shaft."

Somehow this seemed hysterically funny. "That's right, we *both* got the shaft!" I repeated.

"We were both miserable!" she agreed merrily. She giggled, and I giggled too. And suddenly we were both laughing like crazy, because the whole thing was so ridiculous—my father with his two families, going back and forth over the Atlantic Ocean—a big lovely hashish comedy beneath the wonderful fat full moon, and I laughed so hard I nearly peed my pants.

Probably you'd have to be stoned like we were to understand how you can laugh so hard over everything and nothing. "Oh!" we kept saying, trying to catch our breath, as if we were on a roller coaster ride. And then we would look at each other, sputter and splutter, and start laughing all over again. I can't tell you what a free and lovely thing it is to laugh like this, and when we were finally finished, I was surprised to find Zoe actually lying in my arms, her cheek against my chest, her hair tickling my nose just a little, both of us completely at rest. I squeezed her tighter, drawing her to me.

I will always remember this moment. It was completely innocent—she lay in my arms, and we were both as pure as moonshine, brother and sister of the night—and this is how we should have remained. But then something happened. We heard other laughter, not our own, floating through the transparent air from the yard next door. The laughter grew in volume and animation, and was mixed in with a few scattered shrieks of joy.

"Someone's having a party," Zoe said.

Yes, someone was having a party, and I knew who. And I was feeling so relaxed and high I made a big mistake. I told Zoe about our next-door neighbor, the fabulous Marco Mallory.

I told her how my softball had gone through the rotten part of the fence, and had settled in that foreign backyard, and how I crawled after it, and what I saw there. Actually, I tried to be vague about the hard-core details, but Zoe egged me on, asking question after question. She was sitting up now, looking at me intently. She wanted to know everything.

"The lady took his penis in her mouth, you actually *saw* that?"

"Well, I was awfully close, Zoe. I mean, I couldn't *help* but see it."

"And then what happened?"

"Well . . . he came."

"How could you tell? Did he make a sound? Did he close his eyes?"

"*Zoe!* This is getting a little embarrassing."

"But I want to know, Jonno. Anyway, I'm not sure I believe you. Maybe you're making all this up."

"Okay, if you gotta know, I saw a kind of white milky stuff dribbling down her chin. I mean, he really shot a wad."

"How very curious," said Zoe, like some kind of weird anthropology student. "Did you ever go back again into that yard?"

I was becoming sorry I had brought this up, but Zoe was so insistent, I ended up telling her everything. I had gone back several times, in fact, with my heart pounding with fear and anticipation of what I might find. I was drawn there almost against my will. But in all that time, I had not seen another thing, neither Marco Mallory nor any other human being. I had explored the grounds and had even approached the huge sleeping Mediterranean villa, which apparently had been closed for the winter.

Zoe and I listened to the laughter next door. "Maybe they're having an orgy?" she suggested.

I shrugged, though the thought had occurred to me as well. I noticed Zoe's eyes were sparkling in the moonlight.

"Come! Let's go over and have a peek!"

"Zoe, I don't know. I mean, it would be *very* embarrassing if we got caught."

But she had made up her mind. "Aren't you curious?" she asked. "I think it's wonderful to spy on people, don't you?"

She would not be dissuaded. I was particularly worried when she swung the camera bag over her shoulder. I tried to suggest she might be better off leaving her equipment behind, in case we had to make a sudden exit, but Zoe only urged me to show her the hole in the fence where we might crawl through.

The moonlight covered everything with a soft phosphorescent glow. Feeling this was a big mistake, I led the way to the hedge, and then I lowered myself onto my stomach and crawled through. I had a vague hope Zoe would find the crawling part too difficult and give up, but she pushed the camera bag to me, and made her way easily through the opening. On the other side of the fence, we stood up quietly and Zoe went over to the bronze statue of the naked woman in the moonlight.

"Mon dieu, this is a Rodin!" she whispered.

And that's when I learned that this was not any old statue but something that might be found in a museum. I was never surprised at the breadth of Zoe's learning. Music was playing not too far away. It was a Beatles album, *Magical Mystery Tour*, that had come out not many months before. I heard laughter, and then a sound that worried me, a long, low moan.

Zoe now took the lead, walking quietly but decisively over the lawn toward the fountain, and then through the grape arbor to where we could see the big pink Mediterranean villa, which was all lit up tonight with a warm yellow glow. The voices and the music seemed to be coming from the far end of the swimming pool, from inside a red-and-white striped canvas pavilion that had a Tibetan prayer flag flying from the top. The tent was closed on three sides, but open toward the pool, and a glow of flickering candlelight spilled out onto the flagstone.

Zoe lowered herself onto her hands and knees, and indicated I should do the same. We crawled in single file toward the broken green refractions of the pool, whose light sent jagged moving shadows into the palm trees overhead, and we made our way carefully alongside a flower bed. The inside of the canvas pavilion reminded me of a painting of an Arabian harem I had once seen in a book. There were big velvet cushions on the floor, and oriental rugs, and low tables laden with fruit and wine, and a candelabra dripping colored wax. There was even a hookah. But the most incredible thing here was the three people, and what they were doing to each other on the floor.

There were two women and one man, and they were all quite as naked as they were born, except one of the women had some sort of leather belt around her waist. It took me a moment to figure out what was happening. There was one woman in the middle on her elbows and knees, ass up in the air. The second woman with the leather belt was behind her. The leather belt had an artificial penis attached to the front and she was fucking the kneeling woman with this thing from behind. In front of the woman on her hands and knees, the man was reclining against the velvet cushions, leaning back comfortably with his legs spread wide open. The man was Marco Mallory and the woman in the middle was slowly sucking on his penis.

It was quite a tableau, a human sandwich lit by candlelight and the moon and the strange refractions from the green light in the water. The three figures were interconnected and seemed to softly pulsate together in time to the phonograph, which at that moment was playing "All You Need Is Love."

Zoe took her camera out of its case, and screwed a telephoto lens onto the body. When this was in place, she began crawling closer to the canvas pavilion. I tapped her on her back urgently, gesturing, *Let's leave well enough alone!* She smiled at me: *Coward! Come on.*

I couldn't let her go the distance alone. I crawled behind her another dozen feet, and then bumped into her rear end as she abruptly stopped. I came up alongside her and saw exactly what it was that made Zoe pause.

The woman with the leather belt around her waist was none other than our maid, Gretchen Krieger. And the woman in the middle, getting it from front and back, was Zoe's mother, Michelle Cordell.

16

Zoe was staring with a kind of frozen fascination at the tableau of her mother having sex with two people, one at either end, neither of whom happened to be her husband, Alexander Sangor. I became aware that Zoe was clutching my arm, unconsciously digging her nails into my flesh.

"Let's get out of here," I whispered. She shook her head. She looked to me suddenly like a sleepwalker, lost in a dream. I think the three people in the tent were even more stoned than Zoe and I were. They moved in a kind of slow-motion opium dance that seemed to have no beginning or end, as if they were floating somewhere in space and time. After a moment, Zoe raised the camera with its telephoto lens to her eye, and I soon heard the click of the shutter and the whir of the film advancing, again and again. I was afraid the sound would travel to the people in the pavilion, but I guess a bomb could have gone off and they would not have noticed.

I was too frightened to be stimulated by the proximity of sex. I kept hoping Zoe would finish with her photography and we could get the hell out of there. We were both surprised when the three figures changed positions and who was doing what and to whom.

Now it was Marco Mallory who took to the middle on his hands and knees, with Gretchen mounting *him* from behind, and Zoe's mother reclining on the cushions with Marco Mallory's face pressed between her open legs. I was both stunned and embarrassed. It had never occurred to me that a woman might stick a fake penis up a guy's rear end, much less the celebrated rear end of the fabulous movie star, Marco Mallory. Zoe just kept taking pictures, pointing the telephoto lens from one figure to another, sometimes changing focus with her right hand.

God knows how long this went on. After what seemed a very long time, all three figures had something of a group orgasm, moaning and clutching at each other, and then falling over in a heap of flesh onto the cushions. Zoe turned to me and indicated that we could leave now. Even in the cool moonlight I could see her face was burning. Mine certainly was.

We made our way stealthily back around the pool and over the grass to the fountain, then through the grape arbor and past the statue of the naked woman. At last we arrived at our hedge which would lead us back to the safety of home. Zoe handed me the camera and she crawled through first. I pushed the camera through to her, and then I made the journey myself. We stood up in our own familiar backyard, and I found I was still afraid to speak. I began to point us toward the oak tree leading to my bedroom window, but Zoe took my arm and led the way back to the unfinished studio.

"Boy, that was something," I said shakily, trying to see if I could still speak. Zoe turned and put a finger on my lips. Then she took me by the hand and led me back into the studio where we had begun.

She stood on the bare floor and faced me, and, to my astonishment, she lifted her black polo shirt over her head and let it sail softly to the floor. My beautiful sister Zoe was not wearing a bra. Her breasts were full and firm, so very pale in the moonlight. She kept looking into my eyes, but I couldn't read what she was thinking. She kicked off her tennis shoes, and looked away a moment to remove her socks. She stepped out of her jeans and her underpants. She was the way I had imagined she would look without her clothes, only more beautiful still. She stood before me naked, a goddess.

Then, without a word, Zoe came over and undressed me as well, starting with my shirt and ending with my underwear. When I was as naked as she, she put her cool hand around my penis, and pulled me down with her onto the floor. I was about to lie on top of her, when she stopped me with a gesture of her hand. Had she brought me so far only to leave me dangling at the last moment?

"No, Jonno," she whispered. "Not like that."

And then she did something that worried me a little. She turned over onto her hands and knees, facing away from me like a dog in heat, in the exact position we had seen her mother take next door. Zoe waited for me to come into her from behind.

"Zoe . . ."

"It's all right, Jonno. This is the way I want it."

Now I didn't know a thing about psychology, but this seemed somehow wrong, for her to imitate her mother in such a way. I hesitated briefly. I want you to know that. But I was breathless with desire, and to tell the truth, Zoe looked about as good from the rear as she did from the front.

I guess I wasn't the sort of person to pass on such an opportunity, even if in this case opportunity was definitely facing the wrong way.

17

I made a fatal mistake. I thought that just because my body had been inside of her body, Zoe and I would be connected forever, and she would never be a stranger to me again. But I was young and foolish. Probably I was lucky she didn't cut my heart out and throw it in the garbage.

We were lying side by side, nestled like spoons, her back snuggled against my stomach, and my free hand cupping one of her smooth breasts. I had a vague hope we might remain naked like this always. She was so quiet I thought she might be sleeping, but I propped myself up on one elbow and I saw her eyes were open wide, staring into the shadows of the half-finished building. There was something terrifying about her open eyes. It terrified me, because I didn't know what she was thinking, and after everything we had done, she was still a million miles away and more mysterious than she had ever been before.

"That was my first time," I told her, unnecessarily.

"Yes, Jonno."

"Have you ever . . . ever done it before?"

"Yes, Jonno."

I tried not to ask the next question, but it escaped from my lips anyway: "Who with?"

She didn't answer. She lay stone still, and I was afraid to ask again. Finally she moved out from under my arm. She sat up, reached in her camera bag, and found a cigarette to light. Strangely enough, I had never seen Zoe smoke a cigarette before.

"I've been thinking of something," she said.

"Have you?"

"You know, with the pictures I took, we could blackmail them, don't you think? After all, my mother's married and Marco Mallory's supposed to be a big stud. I bet he'd pay a fortune so his public would never learn about how he likes to get fucked up the ass by a lady with a dildo."

I really didn't like to hear Zoe talk like this. But I said: "Hey, blackmail! That's a great idea, Zoe."

"You think so?"

Actually, I didn't think so at all. There was something cold in Zoe's tone that scared me to death. Rags, Carl, and I used to think up crazy schemes like this—plans to rob banks and abduct beautiful girls to hold for ransom, things we'd talk about for hours, but which we knew we'd never carry out. For a few minutes I tried to pretend this was the same kind of bullshit. But I knew Zoe well enough to know she was never reduced to bullshit; Zoe did exactly what she said.

"What do you think he'd pay, Jonno?"

"Well, gee," I said, "I bet he'd pay a thousand dollars for those photographs."

She laughed at me. Cruel laughter. "Jonno! This could ruin his entire career. Don't you see? A thousand dollars is nothing! We could ask *fifty* thousand dollars. Maybe more. But I think we should be reasonable and ask for twenty-five."

"Twenty-five thousand dollars? But Zoe, I mean . . . what do we need with that kind of money? After all, we're rich."

I'll never forget the dark look she gave me, so terrible and full of knowledge. "Oh, my darling brother, don't you understand? It's our *parents* who are rich. *We* don't have a penny."

"But isn't that the same thing?"

She laughed at me again, the same cruel laughter. I don't know how Zoe knew these things, but she was right, of course. There is a world of difference between having wealthy parents and being rich yourself, and God bless the child that's got his own. I learned all this myself years later, but at the moment I really didn't know what the hell Zoe was talking about. I was shocked by her bitter laughter.

"Jonno, we don't have a thing," she told me, "Except perhaps each other."

"I'll always love you, Zoe."

"But will you *help* me? That's what I need to know."

I told her yes, of course. I would help her with anything. But she must have felt my doubt and reservations.

"Lie back," she said. And she spread my legs and knelt before me and this time she carried out the front end of the tableau we had seen so expertly executed next door. I still had a vague feeling this was not right, not like this—not in imitation of her mother— but I was powerless against the pleasure of her mouth.

When it was over, she let me kiss her, and her sweet lips were sticky with my sperm. Oh, Zoe, my darling Zoe! I knew she was in trouble somehow, but I didn't know how to save her. So I said, "Sure, let's blackmail Marco Mallory." What the hell. And we chatted away with a frenetic, crazy energy about how we were going to do it. I could see that Zoe was already giving this fascinating project the same energy and intensity she gave to everything else.

It was a memorable night, all in all. We discussed blackmail and made love until we heard the birds singing on the branches, and the eastern sky became a translucent pale gray with the start of dawn. Then we climbed back up the oak tree to my second-story window—and she left me with a kiss.

I took a shower and listened to the house wake up, and I went downstairs to eat my cornflakes in the sunny breakfast room off the kitchen, and before long the bus was in our driveway ready to carry my love and me to school, me to the seventh grade and Zoe to the eighth.

So that's how it all began. I knew I was in love in a big-time way, but to tell the truth, I wasn't exactly certain if this was heaven, or hell.

Part Three

18

Detective Sergeant Myra Fisher was in my kitchen making up some lunch—a big salad with all kinds of things in it, prawns, Greek olives, red pepper, carrots, and some designer lettuce we had picked up in Beverly Hills. For a cop, she ate a fairly healthy diet. Only the prawns were somewhat chancy. With our coastal waters, they could be radioactive or loaded with industrial waste. But what the hell, sometimes you just had to live dangerously.

"So you went to bed with your sister," said Myra, looking up from the red pepper she was dicing. "Well, it happens, Jonno. The way I see it, there's always a lot of sexual energy lurking around the edges in just about every family. You live so intimately, some-times you share the same bathroom, you see each other naked. Brothers and sisters can't help but be a little curious. At least with Zoe, she was only your half sister."

"You think that makes it okay?"

"What do you think, Jonno?"

Myra had a way of throwing a question back in my direction. In the past week we had become friends but I always had to remind myself she was a cop.

"It wasn't going to bed with her that bothered me," I said. "That

137

was the good part. Frankly I was always grateful I had an older sister around to teach me so much. And Zoe taught me pretty much everything, Myra. She taught me the Exact Right Spot."

"Oh ho!" said Sergeant Fisher, walking from the kitchen with the big salad bowl. She was grinning. "The Exact Right Spot, huh?"

"You bet."

"But guys never know where *that* is. They're always in too much of a hurry. Only gals can find the Exact Right Spot, Jonno."

"If you come over here, Sergeant, I'll show you what I'm talking about."

She laughed. "No way, honey pie. But keep trying. I kinda like it when you're crude."

I guess we had a weird relationship, Myra and I. About a day or two into our friendship, when I was still in the holding cell at the sheriff's station on Santa Monica Boulevard, Myra told me she was gay. Just so I wouldn't get any ideas. She had a live-in lover by the name of Carol, and that's the way it was going to stay. It was strange, but I didn't mind a bit. It was a weight off my shoulders, really. I didn't have to play the game. We could just relax and be friends and give the whole man-woman tango a well-de-served vacation, even though we flirted harmlessly just to stay in practice and we could be fairly obscene with one another.

I liked Myra Fisher, though it was a risky business being friends with a cop when you were the main suspect in a murder investigation. It reminded me a little of a matador having affectionate feelings toward the bull, or vice versa. No matter how you looked at it, we were still in the ring, Myra and I. She held me in jail for forty-eight hours and then she let me go. She said there wasn't enough hard evidence to charge me yet, but they might get around to that at some future time. That was a week ago.

When I got out of jail, I decided to give La Chanson d'Or a wide berth. I wasn't anxious to live under the same roof as my step-mother Trisha, and I had an urge to avoid the ashes of the past. So Albert arranged a small advance from my so-called inheritance and I moved to the Chateau Marmont Hotel, into a big old suite with a kitchenette on the fourth floor overlooking the Sunset Strip.

The Chateau is a wonderfully fake castle nestled up against the Hollywood Hills and it has lots of atmosphere. The architecture is pseudo-Bavarian on the outside and Spanish colonial on the inside

with thick stucco walls and a lobby of polished red tile. Greta
Garbo had lived here once and lots of other old stars too. John
Belushi died here, and when that happened they tripled the prices
because Hollywood is a town very big on its own nostalgia, and
suddenly the Chateau Marmont was no longer an ordinary hotel.
It was a myth.

Myra brought the salad bowl to a small table by the window.
We sat across from each other and looked out upon the swish and
hiss of traffic on Sunset Boulevard below. On the far side of the
street, just so you wouldn't forget you were in Southern California,
there was a towering statue of Bullwinkle, the cartoon moose, and
Rocky the squirrel. I guess every society has its cultural icons.

"So what was it that bothered you?"

"What?"

"You said you weren't bothered about the sex. You were perfectly comfortable being a pervert with your sister Zoe. So what
was it that bothered you, Jonno?" Myra was definitely a sharp
cookie, making us a fine healthy lunch but meanwhile not letting
any questions dangle.

"What bothered me," I said, "was I fell in love. Desperately . . .
eternally . . . passionately . . . the works, Myra. The big banana."

"And you're still in love with her?"

"It's never gone away. You met my girlfriend Kismet up north.
She's a sweet kid but she just isn't Zoe. And that's the story of my
life. I've gone through dozens of relationships, but they always
come up lacking. Every woman I've ever met I've always compared
to my sister, and nothing's ever worked because of it . . . nothing.
Zoe left me an emotional cripple, Myra, and *that's* what bothers
me."

She studied me, chewing on some of our lettuce. "I bet you've
caused a few heartbreaks yourself, my friend."

"I never meant to. Look, every girl I met, I always told her right
at the beginning that I was an emotional cripple, a real son of a
bitch, and let's go to bed, sure . . . but don't get involved."

Myra laughed bitterly and raised her hands toward the fifth
floor. "Will you listen to this guy? Goddamn, I'm glad I'm a dike!"

"Myra, I was being honest."

"What you were being, Jonno, was one hell of a seductive son of a bitch. The lonesome cowboy riding off into the sunset. Don't you know that girls love that shit?"

I shrugged. "I couldn't act any different. I told you, I was still in love with Zoe."

"Jesus, as a cop you hear these stories and it makes you very cynical about the human race. I'm tempted to fly up north and give that poor little Kismet some emotional support."

I grinned at her. "I bet!"

After we were quiet for a minute, grazing through the greens, she said: "So what are you doing now? About your inheritance, I mean?"

"Well, my brother David has hired a whole office building of lawyers. He's filed about a hundred motions saying why he should get the studio instead of me. Right now he's claiming there was a written agreement between him and my father that he would inherit the studio, and this was why he was working for a reduced salary, you see, and was such a loyal employee for so many years."

"Has anyone seen this written agreement?"

"Not that I know of. But that's not stopping David. He's also gone to the SEC since Everest Pictures is a public company, and he's claiming I don't know diddleyshit about the entertainment industry and I'll lose all the stockholders' money. But I guess his main hope is that I'll get convicted of murder so he won't have to deal with me at all."

I paused with a question mark in my voice as to whether Myra was ever going to charge me with my father's murder or not. Frankly I often simply wanted to ask her if I was still her number-one suspect, but it seemed a little rude to discuss professional matters now that we were such good friends.

"So what are you going to do?" she asked.

"What do you mean, what am I going to do?"

"Jesus, Jonno, are you just going to let David steal your inheritance?"

I shrugged. "Hell with it. As far as I'm concerned, owning a movie studio never seemed to bring my father a whole lot of love and joy. Maybe I should just let David have the damn thing."

"Jonathan Sangor," she said angrily, "if you don't get off your lazy butt and fight for what's yours I'll *never* forgive you."

"You won't come and visit me on death row?"

I could tell Myra was exasperated with me. She was about to say something, but then the beeper went off in her handbag.

"Christ, I *hate* that fucking beeper. It makes me feel like a dog on a leash. I gotta use your phone, Jonno."

Myra dialed a number impatiently, spoke to a switchboard operator, got put on hold, and finally reached someone I had a feeling was her boss.

"Yeah . . . I'm with Jonathan Sangor now. . . . Jesus, what's he say? . . . You'd better give me that address. Sure I'll check it out."

"Fuck," she said, slamming down the phone. "I mean, I can never eat a goddamn meal on this job without some asshole lieutenant wanting me to do something. I'm afraid I gotta split, Jonno."

"What's the problem?"

"You'll never guess. Some kid who works in a Chevron station in Brentwood Village says a guy answering your description bought a gallon of unleaded gas in a can a few hours before your dad was killed and your house set on fire."

I played with a prawn, removing some of the shell that had been left on. "This doesn't sound so good," I said. "Is the guy really sure it was me?"

"He identified you from a photograph, Jonno. This puts you about a mile from the scene of the crime on the night of the murder buying a flammable substance. You'd better enjoy life while you can, honey pie. You're not going to find prison life a whole lot of fun."

Myra excused herself and used my bathroom. She left the door open and I could hear her pee. She wasn't real modest.

"Look, I didn't do it, Myra. I didn't kill my father," I called to her in the bathroom. "I wasn't even in Los Angeles then."

"That's what they all say," she called back. "Every goddamn homicidal-maniac-motherfucker I've ever met. They're all innocent, every one." She flushed the toilet for emphasis.

"But I *am* innocent. Honest, I never lie to people who make me lunch."

Myra came out of the bathroom pulling up her underpants. "Then you'd better get your ass in gear and start proving it. Someone's trying to set you up. Hey, do I look okay?"

She was futzing before the mirror on the back of the hall door, smoothing down her skirt. "You look fine," I told her. "What do you mean someone's trying to set me up?"

"Just like I said. Someone's trying to frame you. The gas station attendant in Brentwood is lying and I want to find out why."

"You're just saying that because I'm such a sweet and seductive guy, and deep in your heart you're hoping I'll save you from the arms of lesbos," I said with a leer.

She gave me a scorching look. "Hell with you!" she said. "You wouldn't know *my* Exact Right Spot if it hit you over the head!"

"Then why do you say someone's trying to frame me?"

She grinned. "Because the fire wasn't set with gasoline, asshole. It was set with a small bottle of propane."

"Propane!" I said. "But how?"

"That's an official secret," she said with a smile. And then she surprised me. She gave me a quick kiss on the cheek and hurried out of my hotel suite into the great hard city outside.

19

I was napping when the phone rang. I was on top of my bed fully dressed and I had been having a dream about my father that I couldn't quite remember. Outside the window it seemed to be late afternoon. I struggled toward consciousness and picked up the ringing telephone. Somehow I knew it was her even before I heard her voice.

"Hello?"

"You were asleep," she said.

"I'm awake now," I told her. And I certainly was. It was Zoe.

"I didn't call you before, Jonno. I didn't know if you wanted to see me."

I was silent.

"I understand," she said. "I know why you're hesitant to see me. But I've been worried about you. I can't tell you how relieved I was when the police let you go."

"Zoe, the cops let me go so they could circle around and play with me some more. I think David's helping them along a little, supplying little bits of evidence just in case I don't look guilty enough on my own."

There was a silence and I pictured her, my sister Zoe, some-

143

where on the other side of the telephone wire. Generally, when I fantasized about her throughout these many long years, the image that came to mind was from that first night in the moonlight, Zoe standing in the half-finished meditation studio staring so intently into my eyes, taking off her clothes, one by one, until she stood before me naked.

I stopped my imagination from going any further.

"Jonno," she said, "Let's have dinner. I want to see you." When I didn't answer, she went on. "There's a Japanese restaurant just a block or so west of the Chateau Marmont. It's called Sushi on Sunset. I'll be there at seven. If you come, you come. If you don't, I'll understand."

The phone went dead.

I paced around the room. I stared out my window at Bullwinkle and Rocky. I took a shower. I even watched TV and saw Geraldo Rivera interview victims of incest. When you're in the proper frame of mind, the entire universe is only a mirror of your inner condition.

At about a quarter to seven, I put on a pair of used blue jeans I had picked up in a store on Melrose, as well as a black T-shirt and rubber sandals. In the hall by the elevator I ran into an English rock star whose face I recognized. He was dressed pretty much like I was, but his hair was a lot longer and he was wearing dark glasses.

"How's it going?" I asked.

"Shitty," he said. "Don't even ask."

We rode the elevator together down to the garage. "Is L.A. the ugliest city in the world?" he asked. "Or is it just my imagination?"

"This is paradise," I told him. "Only someone has to give you the key."

He seemed to like that. I watched him wander through the bowels of the garage toward a red Ferrari. He was half singing, "*Someone* has to give you the key, but where is she . . . where is she?" I guess he was writing a new hit song.

I walked out of the garage onto Sunset and turned west past a few billboards announcing fabulous new movies. I jogged to the other side of the street at a break in the traffic. At this point I still was unsure if I would see Zoe or pass on by. I told myself that I still had a choice, though my feet knew I was lying. They took me straight to the restaurant where Zoe was waiting.

Sushi on Sunset was a hole-in-the-wall kind of place. I found Zoe sitting at the counter speaking Japanese to a dashing young samurai chef who was wearing regulation white pajamas and a black sash around his forehead. From the way he was looking at Zoe, I had a feeling he would commit seppuku on the spot if she should only ask him.

Zoe turned my way and her face glowed with a smile.

"This is my brother Jonno," she said to the young Japanese. "Jonno, this is Kenichi."

"Komban wa," said Kenichi, with a military nod.

"We'll go to a table now. We'll leave our dinner entirely to you, Kenichi, if you don't mind."

"Hai! Doomo arigato!"

"Doo itashimashite," said my sister Zoe.

She led the way. I had a choice whether to sit down next to her or across the table where I could look at her. I sat across the table. She was wearing jeans and a shimmering green print blouse with long sleeves and a simple necklace of silver and highly polished stones. Despite her casual dress, I could tell the waitress was not fooled. Neither was Kenichi the sushi chef. Zoe looked like money all the way.

"So you speak Japanese," I said. "Your accomplishments always leave me a little breathless."

"I've spent years in the Orient, Jonno. I'm a natural mimic, I guess."

"You're a natural something," I told her. She lowered her eyes while I stared at her, taking her in, the whole picture of my sister Zoe. "Somehow I always imagined you in Paris all this time," I said.

"I keep a place there, a very old house in Montmartre with a courtyard and a little garden. I love it, but I'm hardly ever there."

"You prefer the mysterious East, do you?"

"I like to travel. My interest in tantric yoga drew me to Tibet."

I grinned at her. "I tried to get into Tibet once from northern India. But they turned me back at the border. That's the story of my life, Zoe, to be so close to paradise but never to arrive."

Zoe studied me with severe interest. I found her radiantly beautiful. Her eyes were full of a cool intelligence that could cut a man in half. There were small crow's-feet about the corners of her eyes and mouth—lines from past laughter and sunlight, the only sign of age I could find. Her beauty was almost more than I could bear.

"So what do you think, Zoe?" I asked. "Do I look decadent? Do I look old? Do I look like I drink too much? Am I what you expected to find after all these years?"

She measured her words carefully. "I can see you've been unhappy. It's in your face. But you still have that little boy smile. And there's a quality in you that seems to be yearning for goodness. No, you don't look decadent, Jonno. You just look like you've been through hell."

I forced myself to keep smiling but I was breaking up inside. The waitress came over with two wooden trays that had the ginger and wasabe. She also brought hot towels which she served to us with tongs. The waitress did this very well, she even wore a kimono, but she was a blond California girl, just another actress playing a part.

"So what brought you back to the land of make-believe?" I asked my sister Zoe.

"Didn't I tell you? I'm arranging an exhibit of my photographs of Tibet. Frankly, I need the money. Keeping a house in Paris and traveling around the world becomes an expensive habit."

"You could always play in a piano bar," I told her mockingly.

She shook her head. "About ten years ago I gave up the piano. I decided I wasn't good enough."

"You're good enough, Zoe. Believe me."

"No. I realized I'd never be a really first-class musician, not up there with the very best. And it didn't seem worth doing if I was only going to be second-rate. It almost seemed a sacrilege. What about you, Jonno?"

I shrugged. "Oh, I play for tips. I'm a regular human juke box. I'm not proud, Zoe, and I never aimed as high as you did."

"Then you won't have so far to fall," said my sister.

Food began to arrive, funny bits and pieces of octopus, raw tuna, and a lot of things I couldn't begin to recognize. Kenichi brought it to us personally, smiling and bowing like crazy. I think this was supposed to be a great honor. I like sushi, but I probably use a lot more of the hot green horseradish than a purist would approve of, and I hate how it's become so faddish.

"So you've been back two weeks," I said. "And you avoided the family. . . . I can't imagine why."

She smiled. "Oh, I was preparing myself. I'm a real coward, Jonno."

"I don't believe that for a second."

"Honest, I wanted to see Dad, I really did. But I had been gone so long, nearly a decade. I was getting used to things gradually. And then he was dead."

"Yes," I said. "And then he was dead."

We ate sushi in silence pondering our father's mortality while pieces of seaweed and raw fish slithered down our throats. Zoe could manage the whole thing with chopsticks, but I used my fingers.

"I ran into Carl though, quite by accident on the beach at Malibu," said Zoe. "Did he tell you?"

"No, he didn't. When was this?"

"Just a few days before Dad was killed. Carl invited me to see Harmony House, his shelter for the homeless."

"Wait a second," I interrupted. "Carl *knew* you were in California?"

"Yes, I just told you."

"Well, that's strange. We were talking about you at the big family powwow and everyone was wondering how we could reach you in Tibet to tell you about Dad. You think Carl would have mentioned seeing you."

"I asked him not to, Jonno. Like I said, coming from Lhasa to Los Angeles was a rather major culture shock. I wasn't quite ready for the family yet."

"Did you go to Carl's shelter?"

"Sure. Harmony House is an amazing place, and I'm glad to see Carl doing such good work. Actually, Dad came to see the shelter too—in the morning before I did. By the time I arrived in the afternoon, Carl was very upset. Apparently he and Dad had a big fight."

I was finding this surprising. "So you and Dad went to Carl's shelter on the same day. What day was this?"

"It was Tuesday . . . Tuesday of the week before Dad was killed."

"But Dad was killed on Wednesday. So you're telling me he and Carl had a big fight the day before he was killed? Jesus! What the hell were they fighting about?"

"Look, Jonno, I don't know why they quarreled. Carl didn't want to talk about it, and frankly I didn't want to discuss Dad either." Zoe gave me a funny look. "It seemed best to keep things a bit impersonal."

"Sure," I said. "I can understand that."

We let it drop, Zoe and I. This was dangerous ground, talking about Carl and Dad and our very crazy family. We were treading carefully with one another. It was curious seeing Zoe after all this time. Somehow it felt natural, like we'd never been apart, but there was a gulf too, like we were utter strangers. We went on to talk about different things, impersonal things, safe things, mostly travel and places we had each gone to in the long years: Greece and Brazil, Macchu Picchu and the pyramids.

Zoe had wonderful travel stories. She had trekked through jungles, crossed vast deserts and climbed tall mountains. I tried to resist her, but she was fascinating. She never spoke a false note. Zoe had become the sort of person who was as comfortable around a campfire in the Himalayas as she was in the best restaurants of Paris. She spoke six languages; she was completely natural; she was utterly sophisticated. As for myself, I had reached an age where intelligence was as much an aphrodisiac as a pretty face. I was beginning to want this evening to never end.

When dinner was over, Zoe and I fought over who would pay the check. I won by being more aggressive, but she insisted on paying the tip. We wandered out of the restaurant onto the Strip and we turned and looked at each other.

"Well, Zoe, so here we are. Middle aged," I said. "Who would have ever thought it was possible?"

"Thirty-six isn't middle age, Jonno. You've got a way to go."

"Do I? I feel like I'm a hundred."

"You look good," she said. "And I'm glad to see it."

"You look good too," I told her. "And it scares me to death."

She had the grace to smile. "Oh, Jonno!" she said. "I guess what we did was crazy."

"It was worse than crazy," I told her. "It was a crime."

We hesitated. I could feel the heat of her pulling me like a magnet. I kept my hands in my pockets and tried to look quite the ironic modern man.

"Do you want to walk some place, have a cappuccino?" she asked.

I shook my head. "I think I'd better go," I told her. "I think I'd better get used to seeing you again in little doses."

She reached out and took my hand. "I've always been sorry I hurt you so much. I want you to know that, Jonno. Over the years I've woken up in strange lands in the middle of the night, and I've thought about you and what we did, and it always cut me like a knife."

"Hey, we were just kids," I told her quickly. "What the hell."

My face was burning. I wanted her so much I could hardly breathe. She stepped closer and kissed me quickly, almost like Myra had earlier in the day, but Zoe kissed me full on the lips. For a moment it felt just like old times, the way Zoe had always felt when we kissed. Then Zoe turned one way on Sunset Boulevard, and I turned the other, and we walked apart from each other like strangers.

It had grown dark. The cars passed by with their headlights and snatches of songs on a hundred radios and tape decks. Crossing the road back to my hotel I could barely see through my tears.

20

I was bothered by what Zoe had told me about Carl, that Carl and Dad had a fight the day before Dad was murdered. It bothered me in a peripheral sort of way I couldn't quite shake off. So after dinner with Zoe, I walked back to the garage on the ground floor of the Chateau Marmont, I got my rusty '65 Buick LeSabre out from between a Porsche and a BMW and I went out in search of my older brother.

The big old Buick started up with a reassuring shudder and roar. The muffler was coming apart so people could hear me coming a block away, but there were four new tires and a tank full of gas. Earlier in the week Albert had urged me to take my father's Jaguar convertible from the driveway at home so I could make a better appearance. Fuck that, I said. As an ex-rich kid, I found it desirable to come on like a low-rider sleaze. It was an obscure form of redemption. My '65 Buick told the world this kid might have grown up with a butler, but he could handle himself on the hard streets. He was a tough motherfucker. You just had to look past the face streaked with tears.

I pulled out onto Sunset Boulevard going east, cutting in front of a Mercedes Benz that was flying an American flag. I joined the flow of Volvos and BMWs and Toyotas down Sunset, took a left by Hollywood High School and then used the side streets to make my way to Hollywood Boulevard, that famous street of footprints and broken dreams. The prostitutes were out in force, and the hustlers and winos and junkies, and a few terrified tourists from the Midwest searching desperately for glamour. I realized I didn't have the slightest idea where I would find Carl's shelter for the homeless, and it made me laugh. I was a lousy detective.

Then I had an idea. I pulled over into a no-parking zone and asked a ragged young man who was sitting on the sidewalk begging loose change. The guy knew all about Carl Sangor and the shelter's location. He even gave me advice as to when meals were served and when I could take a shower. Probably he figured anyone driving a car as old as mine was in need of some charitable assistance.

So I drove to the Pantages Theater and made a left turn near where some homeboys were being hassled by a cop. I found the side street where Carl ran his shelter. The place looked like it had once been a small apartment complex, the kind of ugly stucco structure they used to put up in Southern California before World War II. There were small windows and thick squat walls and a lot of vaguely arabesque moldings covered over with ancient layers of paint. Above the front door was a cheerfully hand-painted sign that said this was Harmony House.

Inside the door, I was surprised to find an old Indian sitting behind a desk. I guess Native American is the appropriate title these days. Carl always had a thing about oppressed minorities. Without much prompting the Native American told me his name was Thomas Running Deer and that he had come to Hollywood twenty years ago to be in the movies, but that was a tough proposition, and Carl had eventually rescued him from the streets. I told him my name was Jonathan Sangor and that Carl and I came from the same tribe, and could I please see him. Thomas Running Deer picked up a telephone, and in a moment Carl came walking down the hall beaming at me.

"I knew you'd come, Jonno," he said opening up his arms to take me in. "You can stay here if you want. I have a few extra beds."

I had to tell him I was grateful for the offer but I was set up at the Chateau Marmont and it would be hard to move all my things,

my toothbrush and underpants and stuff. Carl kept grinning like
crazy. He seemed really happy to see me here.

The first thing he did was give me a grand tour of Harmony
House. He took me through dorms for single men and dorms for
single women, rooms for families, a kitchen-dining area on the
ground floor, and a communal meeting room with plastic chairs, a
ratty old sofa, a card table and a television set. I kept telling Carl
how impressed I was, but my real feeling was more like the place
was drab, drab, drab. Everywhere I looked I saw the broken rejects
of America, those who had failed at the good life or who had never
had a chance.

I met a woman with long stringy hair and a sunburnt face who
told me she was Marilyn Monroe; I met a tiny leprechaun of an
old man who patiently described his bowel movements for the last
three days; and a young girl and her boyfriend who had dirty
ravaged faces and needle marks on their arms; and a man with
scabs over his face and hands who spoke in a stutter; and more.
And the children. They were the worst of all in this freak show of
failure, because the children looked absolutely normal, like children anywhere, and they didn't belong here at all except for an
accident of birth.

As we walked around, I couldn't help but notice that Carl looked
prematurely old, a drab middle-aged man with a pinched face and
sallow complexion and a pronounced stoop to his shoulders. His
body was too thin and didn't quite fill out his clothing. He wore
baggy olive-green corduroy pants and a white long-sleeve shirt that
looked like it came from the Salvation Army. The sleeves of the
shirt were not quite long enough for his arms, and with his rimless
glasses perched on his nose, he reminded me of an angry bald
eagle about to go extinct. I was frightened for him.

As we went on our grand tour, Carl gave me his rap: "We serve
two meals a day here, Jonno—breakfast and dinner. . . . I'm trying
to start a school for the children. It's shameful, totally disgusting
and immoral, of course, that in the United States one out of every
five children lives below the poverty level. . . . Did you know,
Jonno, that the state of California spends twenty-four thousand
dollars a year for each prisoner in one of our many penitentiaries,
but only four thousand a year for the education of a child in public

school? . . . Can you believe *that* for priorities? Basically, the best hope these children have is to be arrested, for God's sake!"

"It makes me sick, Carl," I told him.

"It makes *me* want to go to the barricades," he said angrily. "I just couldn't live with it, Jonno. I know Harmony House is only a drop in the bucket. I can feed and give beds to a maximum of fifty people a night, which is nothing, goddamn *nothing* in the face of our enormous national tragedy. But I had to do *something*, you see. I felt I couldn't exist as a moral human being unless I tried to make a difference."

After the tour, Carl and I came to his small office, a sad dark room cluttered with an old wooden desk, an ancient electric typewriter, metal filing cabinets, and a few ratty chairs.

"Glass of vino?" he offered.

"Sure."

Carl brought out a half gallon of Gallo Hearty Burgundy and filled up two plastic Dixie cups. It was all strictly egalitarian. We sat down facing each other on the ratty chairs.

"Chin chin," he said, raising his plastic cup.

"Mud in your eye," I told him. And then I added: "By the way, I had dinner with Zoe tonight."

His eyes sharpened, focused on me like a gun. "Ah-ha," he said. "I guess you want to know why I didn't tell you I'd seen her. . . . I wanted to, Jonno. But I thought it was up to Zoe to announce herself or not, depending on when she was ready."

"She said Dad came here too, on the day before he was killed. She said you and Dad had a fight."

Carl nodded, playing with his Dixie cup of wine. "Yes, yes . . . Dad and I had a fight," he said vaguely. "I should have told the cops about it, but frankly I was embarrassed, Jonno. It all seems so petty . . . so very vulgar."

"What did you fight about, Carl?"

He gave me a cagey look. "You think I killed him, maybe?"

"Of course not."

"Well, I might have. I've sure been strapped for money. Sometimes I found myself wishing I could hurry up the old inheritance. Did you ever wish that, Jonno?"

I shrugged. "Sure. Every now and then. It's only human."

"I don't care about money for *me*," Carl said peevishly. "You see how simply I live. But do you have any idea how much it costs to keep a shelter like this going? The city helps a little, I have a few private donors and a small endowment from a charitable fund. I bust my balls, really, trying to make people see that this is important, that we can't just let whole families fucking *die* on the streets. But this year, you know, we're suffering from charity burnout. The rich people felt guilty for a few years, so they gave. Now they don't even want to know about it. . . ."

"Carl," I interrupted, "I know all this."

"Well, you asked me what Dad and I fought about. It was money," he said in disgust. "You see, I have a balloon payment due next month on this building. Either I come up with half a million dollars or Harmony House closes. Can you believe it?"

"So you went to Dad?" I nearly laughed, the whole thing was so absurd: Carl, the revolutionary, going to Dad the capitalist pig for money. Carl didn't seem too happy about it either.

"I didn't go to him," he said bitterly. "He came to me. I invited him here to see the shelter and meet some of the people who are counting on me to survive. I wanted him to meet his victims. . . ."

"Come on, Carl!"

"No, I mean it. The poor people in this country are the victims of the insane greed of the rich. I asked . . . I begged, I *pleaded* for five hundred thousand dollars to take care of my balloon payment. I said, "Let it be a tax deductible gift—you rich people just *love* saving on your goddamn taxes! Let it be an advance on my inheritance . . . let it be *anything*, but just give me the money, please God, so I don't have to send these tragic and desperate people back to the streets!' "

Carl was getting pretty impassioned. I poured us some more wine hoping it might keep him from going off on an extended rap about all the social injustice in the world.

"So what did Dad say?"

"*He said no!*" boomed Carl in a voice as terrible as any Old Testament prophet. "He said I was a bad investment. He said I was wasting my life feeling guilty and that I'd better get on the ball and make a career for myself before it was too late."

"Well, you know Dad. That was the way he thought."

Carl glared at me with sudden hatred. "He said the people here *stank*. He actually said that. He said it was their own fault they were poor. And I told him he was already rotting in hell for his greed and indifference. I told him even his children hated him, and to get out of my fucking building and never come back . . . and the next day when I heard he'd been murdered, I did a little jig around my office and then I got a few bottles of champagne and I made a toast with some of my friends here and we celebrated long into the night, little brother. Now we could make our balloon payment and stay open after all."

"Well," I shrugged, "it's fun to come from such a rich and happy family."

Carl's mouth was open to unleash a new flood of invective, but suddenly he caught himself and laughed.

"Oh, Jesus! . . . Sorry to go on like that, Jonno. I guess I get a bit emotional. . . . Here, let's have some more wine and talk about old times."

Carl did the honors this time and poured out a new round of Gallo Hearty Burgundy. He confided he was able to buy a gallon of this stuff at Thrifty for $4.99. I guess I was supposed to be impressed, but somehow I couldn't quite share his enthusiasm.

We sat back in our chairs. We looked at each other and smiled and didn't quite know what to say to one another. There were no old times that either one of us wanted to talk about particularly. "So who killed Dad?" I asked after a while.

He grinned. "Who do *you* think?"

"Maybe it's Trisha," I suggested. "A real classic. Pretty young thing marries a rich old guy. Maybe she has a lover on the side, an accomplice. So they knock off the old fuck for the inheritance."

"Well, it's possible," Carl said. "But unlikely. Personally, I imagine it's someone closer to home, don't you?"

"Sure," I said. "I think it's David."

Carl laughed. "No you don't. You'd *like* it to be David, but that's not the same thing at all."

"So who do I think it is?" I challenged, starting to get a little angry.

"Zoe," he said, raising his glass in a kind of salute. "You think it's Zoe, don't you?"

I didn't answer. I just drank my wine.

"Listen to me, Jonno. If she's guilty, don't try to take the rap for her."

"Christ, you think I'd do that? Even for Zoe?"

"Oh, I know you, Jonno! I *know* the way you feel about her, but let me tell you a big secret. She's not worth it."

Carl was polishing off the wine pretty quickly. His cup was empty, but mine was not. He refilled his cup, drank it down in one swig, and poured himself another. I could see he was getting drunk, and it surprised me somehow.

"Yeah, a big secret," he said. "And you know *why* she's not worth it? She puts on a good show, but she's just a shallow little bitch like all the other women."

"Carl, I really don't want to hear this. . . ."

"Of course, you don't want to hear this. After all, *you're* in love with your sister! Big deal. She even fucked you too. Jesus, when I was a kid I would lie in my bed and I could hear you guys screwing and moaning in the next room. But here's the funny part, you see—*I* loved her too. But I was only the smart one, while you were the pretty one. It was no surprise she should choose you, kid. No surprise at all, for a shallow little bitch."

I stood up because I couldn't bear this conversation. Carl stood up too. He faced me with his pinched, angry face that was flushed with wine.

"Let's just forget this," I suggested.

"Hell with that! I loved her too. But I was ugly, covered with old scars. Look at this and tell me if I'm ugly!" Carl ripped open the front of his shirt, sending buttons flying across his desk, and he showed me the scars still on his chest from the many skin grafts performed a lifetime ago after our mother Corina Norman set his bedroom on fire.

"Oh, Jesus," I said. I felt sick with pity for my brother.

"Yeah, quite a sight," he said. "Maybe I should be a movie star. Whad'ya think? Hey, I can be just like Marco Mallory, Jonno. Remember *him*?"

"Jesus!" I said again. I never really knew Carl felt this way. "I wish it had been me that got burnt," I told him. "I swear to God. I never told you, but Mom came into my room first that night. I wish it had been me."

Carl collapsed back into his chair, and he buried his face in his hands with a sob. "Oh, shit. Forgive me, Jonno. I think I'm going crazy. All this stuff. I haven't really thought about it for years. But when someone dies . . . when your father dies, everything comes up like old vomit."

"It's okay, Carl," I told him.

"It's not okay," he said heavily. "It's not okay at all. But what the hell, I keep busy. I try to make the world a better place. You and me, we got a lot to make up for, Jonno. A lot of shit under the bridge . . ."

He was slurring his words. It bothered me because I was supposed to be the drunk of the family, not Carl. He was supposed to be the rock.

Carl had another glass of wine, but I got out of there. He was so drunk I wasn't even sure he heard me say goodbye. I went out past the woman with the long stringy hair, the junkies and the rejects, the man with the scabs over his face who spoke in a stutter, and the Indian who had come to Hollywood to be in the movies but ended up on the street.

I escaped from my brother's private hell.

21

I was beginning to realize some unpleasant truths about myself. I knew I was no saint, but I had considered myself a guy whose saving grace was an ability to look at life without illusions. And now I was shocked to discover that like most people I had spent a lifetime perfecting the art of selective vision. When I was a kid, it had been inconvenient for me to believe Carl was in love with Zoe, even though he had as much as told me so from the very beginning. So, clever me, I blocked it out.

And it was the same with Rags. I guess deep inside I always knew he was gay, even though he talked about girls all the time, "the babes" as he called them, and at one period he even dated some fabulous looking women, using his family name to score. But I knew, and so did everyone else, though none of us wanted to acknowledge that Rags was gay, so we all collectively turned our backs on the hard truth. And in doing so, we turned our backs on Rags. We all said we loved him—he was our lovable family clown— but we didn't give him diddleyshit when he needed us most.

I got worked up thinking about Rags and I decided to visit him the following afternoon. I called Albert to get the address of the AIDS hospice in Santa Monica where Rags now resided. I was

158

frankly terrified of going to such a place, but I reminded myself how much Rags had done for me when I was little, taking me to Disneyland and all that. I thought about all the good times before Gretchen, before Zoe, and I worked myself up into a fine state of guilt. Then, before I could chicken out, I drove the Buick to Santa Monica, clear to the ocean, to where my oldest brother was dying.

It was a muggy afternoon, dense and still. Santa Monica had changed a lot since I used to live in L.A. In the seventies it had been a place for poor hippies and retired folks on a budget and wild-eyed junkies, but now it had become self-consciously chic and expensive. I guess they call this "gentrification," raising the rents and pushing all the poor people toward distant ghettos so the rich can practice their selective vision and not be confronted by human misery. I'm not the only person on this planet with blinders on, not by a long shot.

I drove down a street of clothing boutiques, antique stores, and trendy nouvelle Italian restaurants where they probably covered your veal scaloppine with a small slice of avocado or an artichoke heart and then tripled the price accordingly. The people on the sidewalk seemed young, healthy, and thin. I drove past an exercise club and a place where they sold expensive sports cars. And then, on a side street, lurking in the heart of the good life, I came to a drowsy building of vaguely Spanish architecture that had a sign on the front that told me this was the Santa Monica AIDS Hospice. In the valley of pleasure lay the shadow of death.

I found my brother Rags out back in the communal garden. He was on his hands and knees pulling up weeds in a tomato patch. This surprised me, since I had never thought of Rags as exactly a back-to-nature type.

"Hey, look at you. Getting down and dirty with the vegetables!" I said merrily. I found myself speaking in the kind of fake-happy voice you use with the terminally ill.

Rags flashed me the palest possible smile and stood up creakily from the ground. He was dressed in a shapeless blue jogging suit that had mud stains on the knees. He looked like a scarecrow that had seen better days.

"French intensive," he said, pointing with a gaunt finger at rows of zucchini, tomatoes, lettuce, spinach, and beans. "That's the method we use here. It blows my mind the yield we get from a small plot of land. . . . This time of year we supply all the vegetables for the entire community."

"Well, that's great," I said, summoning up some enthusiasm.

"Good soil, good plants," Rags said.

"Probably just like raising children," I commented.

Rags gave me a wary look and then made a wobbly journey toward a metal garden chair a few feet away. He sat down and closed his eyes to recover from the effort. His face was emaciated and wrinkled, his head completely bald, but I thought there was something strangely beautiful about him. He had that unearthly glow I've seen sometimes with very old people when their physical body seems more spirit than substance.

"So why'd you come here, Jonno?" he asked, still looking at his garden. It wasn't a particularly friendly remark, and I was taken aback.

"Hey, I wanted to know how you're doing."

"How I am doing?" Rags said sarcastically. "Well, there are good days, and there are bad days. Sometimes I feel I could go out dancing all night on the town. Other days I can barely get out of bed."

I pulled up a second chair and sat next to him. We were close enough to the ocean so that there was a chill in the air and Rags angled his face to catch the warm rays of sunlight coming into the back garden. Two guys came by to pick some lettuce for lunch and Rags introduced me to them. Their names were Allen and Byron and they gazed at me sadly as if they knew some great secret that I did not. Rags didn't speak for some time. He seemed a thousand miles away.

"So, they treat you okay here?" I asked.

"Better than okay. This is a real community," Rags said. "Everyone is so supportive and loving to each other. It's something I've never experienced before. I used to hate myself, Jonno. I never knew there were so many people exactly like me and that we could help one another."

Rags went on about the joys of being a terminal member of the Santa Monica AIDS Hospice. He spoke with the enthusiasm of a recent convert and I was glad he had found something to believe in. It blew my mind, really, how AIDS had brought the gay community together. Some of the guys I had seen strolling about this hospice with their gentle sad smiles looked like they could all join hands and get on the bus and sing "We Shall Overcome" all the way to the afterlife. I felt strangely left out, almost envious.

"Well, at least you're in a good place," I said trying hopelessly to make conversation. "And the tomatoes, Rags. They're fucking terrific, they really are."

He turned my way. "You don't understand a thing, Jonno. You probably never will."

I didn't know if he was speaking about the French intensive, or having AIDS, or something I had missed altogether in my childhood and would never find.

"Tell me," I said. "What don't I understand?"

"Ah, it doesn't matter. It's too damn late."

"Hey, it's not too late," I told him, wanting to believe this myself. "I mean, I could die before you. I could walk out of here and get run over by a truck. But it's *never* too late, Rags."

He was grinning to himself, shaking his emaciated head. "You know, when you were young, Jonno, oh, you were the golden boy with sunlight in your face! I just wanted to be with you all the time, but then Zoe came along and everything changed."

"But we all loved you, Rags," I told him. "For Carl and me, you were the best older brother ever."

"Until Zoe came along," he repeated with a knowing nod of his head. I couldn't refute him. "But it's okay, Jonno. I understand. You were straight, you and Carl, and Zoe turned you both into dogs in heat. But me, I didn't know what the fuck *I* was until Albert brought me out of the closet. Thank God for that."

"What do you mean, Albert brought you out of the closet? What did he do? Talk to you about things?"

Rags laughed raucously, throwing back his head. "Oh, God, Jonno! You're such an innocent. You really are! Albert didn't *talk* with me, for chrissake, he *fucked* me."

"Jesus! When you were a kid?"

"No, of course not. I was twenty-two years old and miserable. *You* were the kid, Jonno. You were only twelve and you had fallen for Zoe and Albert took pity on me. He knew just what I needed at just the right time. He gave me my life," Rags said chuckling. "And then the gift he gave took my life away, I guess. How's that for an irony?"

I didn't know what to say. To tell the truth, I was a little shocked.
I had always known Albert was gay, of course, but I had taken it
as an article of faith he would never touch one of us.

"I can see this bothers you. Thinking of me and Albert in the
sack. You think it's perverted maybe? An unnatural act?"

"No, not really . . . except Albert was almost like a parent to us.
It makes it almost like . . ."

"Almost like incest?" said Rags with a cold smile. "Like you and
Zoe?"

I felt trapped, tangled in the past, confused beyond even my
usual level of confusion. I was beginning to see that the past wasn't
something solid you could put your feet on. It was quicksand in
which a person could drown.

"Well, well, so here you are. My little brother Jonno," said Rags,
looking at me with a kind of distant malice. "I can't tell you how
many times I've fantasized about seeing you again, and all the
things I would say to you. But, oh, I can see you've got troubles
of your own. Big troubles. You think maybe the cops are going to
charge you with murder, Jonno?"

"Who knows?" I told him miserably. "Sometimes I think maybe
it *was* me. I mean, maybe I blacked out and did the whole thing
in some psychotic trance."

"Oh, don't give me that bullshit! You and I both know who killed
Dad."

"I don't know," I said, shaking my head. "I really don't."

"Sure you do. There's just one person in this family who's ca-
pable of something like that. You *know*, for chrissake, so why don't
you just admit it."

"It's not Zoe," I said adamantly, shaking my head.

"Oh, of course not!" Rags agreed viciously. "She's a little angel,
isn't she? Like fucking butter wouldn't melt in her mouth."

"Rags, you just don't understand her."

"Oh, don't give me that crap. It makes me sick how that cunt
ruined your life."

I was getting an overwhelmed feeling. It was bad enough that
Carl seemed to think Zoe was guilty, but Rags and Carl together
. . . It made my head feel like it was in a vise being squeezed from
both sides.

"Come on, she's your sister too," I said helplessly. "And Zoe

wouldn't kill Dad. I mean, I can't see Zoe flying back from a lamasery in Tibet, for chrissake, just to knock Dad over the head
with his Oscar and set the place on fire. It just doesn't make sense
after all this time."

Rags was staring at me with cold reptilian eyes. "Jesus, she still
has you by the balls, Jonno. If you weren't so horny for her, you'd
see what a manipulating bitch she is."

"You're only jealous of her," I said in a blind heat, "because you
wanted to fuck me yourself."

He smiled. "Oh, yes! Little brother's hit it on the head. I was
jealous all right. I wanted to fuck you myself."

"Hey, I'm sorry. Look, I don't want to fight with you, Rags. You
know how I love you."

"Sure," he said, staring at his tomatoes. "That's why you went
away for sixteen years. You and Dad were the original disappearing
act. You know, you're just like him, Jonno. No wonder he left you
his movie studio."

Just like my father! I couldn't believe Rags could say such a
thing about me. I knew I had to make this right. I moved my chair
closer and tried to speak in a very reasonable tone.

"Look, Rags, maybe we can start all over again. I don't know
about the past. I mean, our childhood was crazy and we can never
change that. But what I'm saying is, I'll come visit you every day.
We can talk. We can make up for all the shit that's happened.
You're my brother, Rags, and I want to be close to you again."

But while I was talking, I could see Rags had tuned me out.
Finally he stood up and began his unsteady wobble back toward
the plants. "Son of a bitch!" he swore. "I don't fucking believe it!"

"What's the matter?" I asked in alarm.

"Son of a fucking *bitch!*"

I came up alongside him and Rags took hold of my arm as he
lowered himself onto his knees. I was surprised at the strength in
his claw-like hand as he clung onto me. Finally he let go and
reached into the thick green foliage and broke off a bright red
tomato that was nearly as big as a grapefruit.

"I was going to pick this guy tomorrow," he said. "But now look
at him! A fucking worm!"

Sure enough, the skin of the giant tomato was spoiled by the
scab of a worm hole. I wasn't sure how Rags had spotted this

imperfection from his garden chair, but maybe he had some kind
of psychic connection with his plants.

"Man, you sweat, you work, you do everything you can—and
what happens? Some parasite gets into your vegetables! I just can't
believe this, Jonno. I guess I should have picked him yesterday,
but I thought, one more day, one more luscious day of sunlight.
And now he's ruined. . . ."

I tried to humor him and say the tomato would still make a
dynamite sauce over some nice pasta. The Rags I used to know
would have laughed and made some goofy joke about all this, but
the new Rags was inconsolable with his loss. I saw I had lost him.

The two young men I had met earlier came out. They had a
group discussion over how to deal with pests and insects. The
AIDS hospice was a self-contained universe and had no place for
me. I was only an intruder upon the land of the dying, an unwel-
come reminder of the outside world.

I felt suddenly lonely. For a moment I saw myself with more
clarity than I liked: I was thirty-six years old and I had fucked up
a lot of things in my life, but I had always imagined there was
time, plenty of time, to make amends at some distant point in the
future. Now I knew I had been fooling myself. There was no time
at all. My brother Rags was dying and he hardly even glanced my
way when I said goodbye.

22

There were several messages waiting for me back at the hotel from my youngest sister Opera, leaving her private number in her dressing room. When I called back she invited me to lunch the following day at the studio where she did her series. She said she wanted to show me off to her friends, her wandering brother who had finally returned.

I only hesitated a moment. It had nothing to do with Opera, but the place where she wanted to meet: Everest Pictures, Dad's cast-off empire where my brother David was still CEO, forty-eight percent of which was possibly mine, as long as I didn't blow it and go to the gas chamber. I had so many conflicting emotions about this place it was hard to imagine digesting lunch there. But for Opera I'd try. After my sessions with Carl and Rags, I was belatedly trying to be a better brother.

So the next day I put on my cleanest jeans and drove the Buick over Laurel Canyon to the San Fernando Valley. I came to the great mud-colored complex surrounded by high walls; from this mud dreams were born. On the wall near the main gate I saw a huge billboard of my sister, Opera Sangor, and her TV family from "Life in the Fast Lane." It really tickled me. At the gate, there was a beery looking security guard with gray hair and suspicious eyes. He was the St. Peter of this particular paradise, keeping the unworthy from entering. He studied my old car with grave reservations.

"I'm here to see Opera Sangor," I told him. And then I added, "I'm her brother, Jonathan."

St. Peter's suspicious face broke into a grin. "Jonathan Sangor! Well, bless my soul! I was so sorry to hear about your father's passing."

So the guardian of the gate opened the barricade and let me through, and he gave me some fairly complicated directions as how to find Stage 22 and where to park. I made my way down narrow streets bordered with sound stages, past actors in makeup and technicians moving scenery and heavy lights. I tried to tell myself that I was the principal owner of all this glory, but my imagination couldn't make such a leap. I felt more like a kid in an old car, a barely tolerated guest.

Stage 22 was a big dark cavernous place, big enough to house a jumbo jet or two. Beneath the high ceiling and the bright lights stood what was supposed to be a typical American home in which there lived a typical American family where everybody was young and healthy and cute. The house had no roof and no fourth wall and it was probably a good thing that no one in this all-American family ever had to go to the bathroom. "Life in the Fast Lane" was taped in front of a live studio audience. A grandstand had been set up against the wall and several hundred people were being told when to laugh and when to clap by a young man who danced about like a cheerleader.

I've always hated television, but I was really thrilled to see my little sister in front of the three cameras saying her lines. I sat in the grandstand and watched for about half an hour as Opera did a scene in the roofless kitchen where she seemed to be advising a very yuppie-looking black teenager about his love life. The audience laughed like crazy whenever they were told to do so, and what the hell, so did I.

When there was a break, Opera came hurrying past the cameras and cable and crew to where I was sitting.

"God, it's *fabulous* you're here. I'm off for the rest of the day, isn't that great? I thought you could meet my friends and then we

can have lunch and after that we can do *anything* at all. Maybe
we can drive down to the beach or go shopping or even see a
movie. Or if you think of something different, that's okay too."

She was a very energetic little sister. She took my hand and led
me forcibly past the cameras into the inner group. I met directors,
assistant directors, a makeup lady, two teenage girls, the yuppie
black actor, and a few people I only had a hurried glimpse of.
Opera seemed to like everyone, and everyone liked her. I tried to
be on my best behavior so I wouldn't embarrass her. I grinned
inanely and avoided four letter words. All the people I met were
incredibly friendly to me, and I thought this was the damndest
thing. Hollywood had become a swell place in my absence. But
then I realized that Opera had informed them all that I would be
the new owner of this rather major Hollywood studio, so everyone
was probably just kissing ass.

It was all kind of a blur of smiling faces, and then Opera led me
to her dressing room, which was a large trailer with clothes scattered everywhere and two kittens climbing up on the furniture.

"So Jonno, don't you *love* it? Isn't everyone fabulously nice?"

"Sure they are," I said. Then I added delicately, "They seem to
keep you pretty busy here. Does that leave you any time to play?"

Opera, who had just turned fifteen, puckered up her lips
thoughtfully. "I don't know, I never really thought about it." Then
she brightened considerably and said, "Hey, I gotta show you
George!"

George turned out to be a pink golf cart with peace symbols
painted all over it. This was Opera's personal golf cart to get around
the studio and she took me on a wild ride careening down the
narrow streets toward the commissary, nearly running down two
guys from outer space who were coming out of Stage 12.

"Someday I'll take you for a ride in my Beamer," she told me.

"Someday," I agreed cautiously.

Fortunately everyone seemed to know Opera and they got out
of the way of George the Speeding Golf Cart. We came to a shud-
dering halt in front of the commissary, scraping the paint of a Jag
convertible.

"Whoopee," I said.

She laughed. Opera was a girl who seemed to be laughing nearly
all the time. We made our way into the commissary to her regular

table near the front window, and Opera ordered a large green salad because she said she had to keep her weight down. I went for a tuna sandwich named after a dead star. While we waited for the food, my little sister lowered her voice dramatically and told me how she was trying to end an affair with a film director who was thirty-five years old and married with two kids. She said she was tired of him and the whole affair, and that his wife was one of her best friends and that sneaking around had been fun at first but now had become kind of boring.

I felt I should say a few wise words about how she was fifteen and shouldn't be hanging out with a thirty-five-year-old guy, married or not. But then I remembered my own childhood and I didn't want to be a hypocrite. I mean, when I was a kid, I was screwing my sister and blackmailing the movie star next door, while Rags was meanwhile screwing the butler, and God knows what Carl was up to—and look how well *we* had turned out. David was another story, of course, but then *he* had tried to be an upstanding citizen, which was scary on a whole other dimension.

Opera chatted on like a bright little bird. Then, while I was munching on my tuna sandwich, she started talking about Zoe.

"Jonno, tell me the truth—if you were a guy . . . I mean, you *are* a guy, but if Zoe weren't your sister—wouldn't you like absolutely fall in love with her?"

"We-ell, maybe," I admitted. "But she's a little intense, you know. That definitely puts some guys off."

"Oh, I know, I know! You probably wouldn't guess this but some guys think *I'm* too intense," Opera confided. "But Zoe, I mean, she's gorgeous and she's brilliant and there's something about her . . . something . . . well, I don't know quite how to put it."

"I think I know what you mean. Knowing Zoe is like standing in a puddle and putting your finger in an electric socket."

"Oh, Jonno, it isn't like that at all! Anyway, you'll never guess. She's invited me to travel with her back to China after her exhibit is over. I haven't told my mother yet. I mean, my mother would absolutely shit a brick if I left the series. But I'm really tempted, Jonno. I mean, Hollywood is so incredibly bor-ring, and the idea of traveling with Zoe . . . well, it has a *definite* allure. But you gotta tell me what she was like as a little kid, Jonno. Was she fabulous or what?"

"Sure," I said. "Zoe was fabulous."

Opera tugged at my arm. "But you gotta tell me *stories* about her. So I can *visualize* what she was like."

"Honey, it was a long time ago. Maybe it's best to let the past be."

Opera puckered up her lips. "Oh, Jonno!" she pouted. "I thought you were going to be nice to me."

I guess my little sister was awfully spoiled, but I felt for her. The poor kid was lonely, clutching out for family ties. So I started telling her about Zoe.

"Well, honey, you have to understand I didn't meet Zoe until she was thirteen, so I can't tell you if she was a cute baby or anything, but I bet she was. Dad led a double life, you know. He had Zoe and David stashed away in Paris and me, Carl, and Rags in California, and then the first time I met her I was twelve years old and Zoe . . . and Zoe . . ."

I had been launching forth gaily as if this were a funny story, but suddenly I couldn't go on. Opera was looking at me with very big eyes, waiting for me to continue, and I knew I didn't want to tell her any bullshit. She deserved something more.

"Look, Opera, the truth is it was pretty crazy back then. I'm not sure you really want to know about this."

"I *do* want to know. You gotta tell me. You absolutely must."

"Well, everybody else in the family knows this, so I guess you might as well know too. Zoe and I . . . well, to be perfectly honest, we were lovers."

"*Lovers?*" My little sister was staring at me with her mouth open. "You mean, you screwed . . . you *screwed* your own sister, Jonno?"

"I was in love with her," I admitted. "Things just got a little out of hand. I guess we didn't have any sense of there being any natural limits."

To my surprise, Opera was delighted. "God!" she cried. "What a *fabulous* story! So how long did this incredible romance go on?"

"Until I was fifteen. Then one day Zoe ended it, just like that. She said it wasn't right. Pretty soon after that Dad sent me away to boarding school in Ojai, and one night I burned down the dormitory and after that I was put into this place near San Diego for disturbed adolescents for about six months. So you see, it was all pretty weird and you didn't miss a lot by being born afterward."

"Oh, I think it's incredibly romantic! At least you guys *did* things. I mean *nothing* like that ever happens to me. Did Zoe come and visit you all the time? In the loony bin, I mean."

"No. When Dad sent me to Ojai, he sent Zoe to a boarding school in Switzerland. Maybe he suspected something and wanted to split us up, I don't really know. That same year Carl went back East to start at Columbia and even David was gone, up north in Palo Alto, at Stanford. So the family pretty much split up. After all the things that happened, I guess we were happy enough not to see each other."

"Gee," said Opera. There was a dreamy look in her eyes. "I bet you're still in love with Zoe, aren't you? I bet the memory of her has like totally *haunted* you for the rest of your life!"

I took my little sister's hand and tried to smile.

"Jesus!" she said. "I sure wish *I* could have a tragic love affair. I mean, *my* affairs are only pathetic. Did I ever tell you I got pregnant, for chrissake, the very first time I screwed? It was my acting coach and he got scared and ran off to England so he wouldn't be prosecuted for seducing a minor. He didn't exactly turn out to be a knight in shining armor."

"Love is a thorny deal," I told her.

Opera and I shook our heads a little over our plates.

"You know, you might think I'm being crazy," she said, "But sometimes I have the weirdest feeling something *really* terrible happened back then when you guys were kids. Some big dark secret no one's ever been willing to tell me about."

"Well, I told you about Zoe and me. . . ."

"No, there's something else. I just *sense* it. It's like sometimes I walk into a room and everyone stops talking. *Something* happened, didn't it, Jonno?"

I was all set to lie, but I looked at her and I just couldn't do it. So I nodded. She stared at me, trying to figure it out.

"So tell me," she insisted. "I mean, it couldn't be worse than you and Zoe. . . . Is it?"

I nodded again.

"Worse than that? Boy!" said Opera, very impressed. "Now you *have* to tell me, Jonno."

"But I can't."

"But why can't you?" She was looking very disappointed, almost angry. But then she brightened. "Well, *I* have a secret too. A very *big* secret. So I'll make a deal with you, Jonno. You tell me your secret, and I'll tell you mine."

I laughed. "I don't know. Maybe your secret's not as deep and dark and nasty as mine."

"Oh, it's pretty deep and dark and nasty," said Opera, lowering her voice and moving closer. She whispered in my ear: "Maybe I know who killed Dad."

I regarded her closely, meeting her bright shining eyes. "Really?" I asked.

"Yup," she said.

"Both Carl and Rags think they know too," I mentioned. "They think it's Zoe."

Opera seemed shocked. "It's not *Zoe*, for chrissake? How can they say that? Zoe would *never* do something like that. So is it a deal?" she asked. "Your secret for mine?"

I didn't answer for a long moment. We kept gauging each other with a kind of half smile on our lips. I was curious what she might say. "Okay," I said finally, "But you have to go first."

"You won't chicken out and not tell me?"

"I promise," I said.

Opera moved her hair very close to mine and lowered her voice." "Maybe it was David," she said coyly.

"How do you know?"

"I was sitting in Dad's office at Cal-Star about four days before he was killed. I told you about the film with the girl and the whale—*My Best Friend*—well, I was there to discuss the director. You see, at the time I wanted to give the job to this son-of-a-bitch boyfriend of mine, the one who was married, so I was trying to convince Dad he was the best director in town. Then right in the middle of our conversation Dad's secretary interrupts and says David's on the phone, and will he take the call. So Dad winks at me and says, 'Listen to this,' and then he puts David on the speaker phone so I can hear the entire conversation."

"Did David know you were in the room?"

"No way. David was furious. You see, *My Best Friend* was originally a novel that Dad had optioned back when he was still at

Everest, before he left to go to Cal-Star. You know all about *that* sleazoid drama, I guess. Anyway, David was screaming that since Dad was still at Everest when he took the option, Everest owned the property, not Dad. David said he planned to make the picture himself and that he would sue Cal-Star back into the Stone Age if Dad tried to go into production."

"So what did Dad say to that?"

"He laughed. He was really confident, you know, smiling at me the whole time like the phone call with David was a real lark. He told David sure, he knew Everest held the rights for *My Best Friend* and that's why he had decided he was going to have to take control of his old studio again at the shareholders meeting next week. David said, 'Bullshit, you can't manage that. You don't control enough shares to call the shots.' And Dad laughed and said that maybe he didn't have enough shares on his own, but he and Albert did together. But Dad said for David not to worry about having a job. He said there would always be a job at Everest for David in the mail room. Can you believe it? I could tell David was really taken aback, that he didn't know a thing about Albert's shares."

"David was angry?" I asked. "How angry?"

"Well, he was silent for a moment. Then he said. 'Try it, Alex, and you're dead meat.' Then he hung up."

"So that's it? That's the big secret?"

"Of *course* that's it! Isn't it enough? I mean, fucking David tells Dad you're dead meat, and a few days later Dad is dead. What more do you want?"

"Well, it's a motive," I admitted. "But a lot of people make threats when they're angry. It doesn't mean David actually did it."

"I'm just trying to be helpful, Jonno," said my little sister with a sly smile. "Personally, I think David's a real shit."

"Yeah," I agreed heavily. I wasn't sure if my little sister's information was important or not. Like Opera, I wanted to believe David was the killer, but I didn't think her story exactly turned the key on his jail cell. It was an interesting angle though, and I would certainly mention it to Myra. I doubt if any father and son had mixed it up like this over control of a movie studio since Daryl Zanuck had fired his son Richard Zanuck from Twentieth Century-Fox.

"Okay, now it's your turn!" Opera cried gleefully. I guess this was a big game for her, show and tell. I hesitated, but she kept working at me. "You gotta, you gotta, you gotta!" she said. "I mean, I'll never be your friend again if you don't tell me."

This was serious. "Well, okay, there was this one time . . . Are you *sure* you want to know about this, Opera?"

"Jonno, I'm going to *strangle* you if you don't tell me."

"Okay, here it is. Zoe, Carl, Rags, David, and I—about the only thing we all did together—we murdered our maid. We got away with it too. We worked it out so nobody ever knew what we did."

Opera stared at me for what seemed a long time.

"You're telling me you murdered your maid?" she asked.

"That's it," I said. "We were terrible children. Regular brats."

Her mouth was slightly open, like when I told her about me and Zoe. Then she laughed and punched me playfully on the arm. "*You!*" she said. "And I almost believed you for a second! It's a good thing I like guys who tell me fabulous lies!"

23

I think God was looking down and He said to Himself, Jonathan Sangor is having a far too easy time of it hobnobbing about Tinsel Town with his relatives, so He threw me a complication.

I spent the afternoon with Opera going to different shopping malls, from Beverly Center to Century City. This was not precisely my idea of a good time, but I was trying to be the perfect older brother and make up for years of neglect. Opera wore a big straw hat and enormous dark glasses, but people still recognized her and from time to time I had to save her from mobs of adoring fans, most of whom were under the age of twelve.

Opera bought three sweaters, ten compact discs, a silk blouse, a slithery sexy cocktail dress, two pairs of shoes, a box of Godiva chocolate, a telephone shaped like a banana, and an umbrella that had a map of the world on it, even though it was ninety degrees outside and rain did not seem imminent. She also bought me a leather bombardier jacket that cost $699 despite many protestations on my part. I bought her a pair of silver earrings using the Platinum American Express card Albert had arranged for me; the card was in the name of Songbirds, Inc., one of Dad's companies. I had access to the goodies of the world through this credit card, but I still didn't have a cent of my own.

174

Opera got a kick out of riding in my old Buick. Toward evening I dropped her off at her home on Foothill Drive in the flats of Beverly Hills. She invited me for dinner and a round of parties afterward, but I declined and said old people like me had to get their rest. Then I drove through the heavy traffic on Sunset Boulevard back toward the Chateau Marmont Hotel.

And this is where God threw me His curve ball.

I was pulling in the narrow alley toward the hotel garage when I nearly collided with a red Ferrari coming out. In the Ferrari was the English rock star I had met in the elevator and there was a blond girl by his side. The alley wasn't big enough for both of us and one of us had to be polite and pull back to let the other pass. I could tell by the way he was sitting there that it wasn't going to be him.

Well, I'm a nice guy in certain situations. Sure, I considered ramming his Ferrari with my Buick to see which one of us was more macho, but it occurred to me this could be used as a mark against me in some future courtroom battle. So I did the humble, wise thing. I put the old car in reverse and backed out into the side street. With a roar of its mighty engine, the Ferrari lurched impatiently forward and came up alongside me.

"Hey, mate, that's a bloody dinosaur you're driving," the rock star shouted through his window. "It's a good thing I like you. You gave me an idea for a tune."

I hardly heard him. I was staring at the blond girl in the passenger's seat, and she was staring right back at me in an equal measure of surprise. It was Kismet, my ex-girlfriend from Petaluma. Kismet, the world's klutziest waitress. It was so wildly improbable to see her coming out of the Chateau Marmont Hotel in a red Ferrari in the company of an English rock star that it took my brain a second or two to register the image my retina was trying to send me. Then the Ferrari gunned forward onto the side street and disappeared.

I sat there a moment in shock. Then I shrugged my shoulders. "Oh, well," I said. Then I drove the rest of the way into the garage and parked by a concrete pillar. As I was locking up I heard girlish feet running my way on the pavement.

"Jonno! It's *me!*"

"Jesus, that's really *you*, Kismet? I thought maybe it was just some Hollywood groupie who had taken over your body."

Something I said caused her to burst into tears. Kismet was wearing a T-shirt that said TOBY'S FEED BARN, denim shorts, and Birkenstock sandals. It really was her, I could tell by the sandals. She lurched into my arms and got my shoulder wet.

"Oh, God, I just had a horrible experience. I can't tell you how much I hate this *horrible* city!"

"There, there," I said. "You'd better tell me all about it."

I ushered her upstairs to my suite, sharing the elevator with two movie types who were talking about a sunset shot they wanted through a certain lens. They probably wouldn't have noticed Kismet and me if we had died in front of their eyes.

"Oh, Jonno! Are you mad I'm here?"

"Mad's not quite the word. Try curious."

"I *had* to come, I was so worried about you, sweetie. That lady cop, Sergeant Fisher, she talked to me for hours and hours after you left that night and she told me all about who you really were and everything. I mean at first I was *really* mad at you for telling me all those lies about how your parents ran a hardware store—it made me feel like such an idiot—but then I realized you were in a lot of trouble and you might need me. So I took the bus down to Hollywood . . . and . . . and it's been *horrible*, Jonno. My God! I can't imagine how anyone *lives* in this place!"

I got Kismet into my suite, forced a shot of cognac through her lips, sat her down on the couch, and gradually got the story out of her between a few cloudbursts of tears.

The first bad thing that had happened to Kismet in Hollywood was that she put her backpack near a locker in the bus station and then went to a newsstand to get some change. When she returned, the backpack was gone. She said she didn't mind losing the clothes so much, but she had lost her dream journal too, in which she had recorded some real whoppers since I had been gone. Then two men approached her and tried to offer her a job in porno movies, and after that a businessman offered her fifty bucks for a blow job. This was a harsh landscape for a country girl. Everywhere she looked there were hustlers and perverts giving her the eye. So she retreated to the snack bar but was dismayed to find not a single thing on the menu for an organically minded health-food vegetarian. She settled for a bag of potato chips but burst into tears when she read the list of ingredients on the package.

At the end of her wits, she found a phone booth and dialed 911 and was eventually patched through to Sergeant Myra Fisher. Myra told her to sit near the ticket counter, clutch her handbag closely to her breast, and neither look at nor talk to another human being until she arrived. Myra came just in time to rescue Kismet from the circling sharks and bought her breakfast at the Source, a faddish health food place on the Strip. But Myra had a lot on her mind and couldn't babysit forever, so she sent Kismet my way, dropping her off at the Chateau Marmont.

Alas, Kismet wasn't in safe water yet, not by a long shot. While she was waiting for me in the hotel lobby, the famous personality who owned the red Ferrari had wandered down to the lobby to check his mail. He happened to observe the attractive young girl sitting scrunched up at the end of a very long sofa looking a bit miserable and lost. He went over to see if he could be of any assistance. Kismet was gaga to see an actual living legend, and he seemed so nice and helpful, almost like an ordinary person. He listened with great interest to her tales of woe, how she had survived the Hollywood bus station. She almost felt she knew him. After all, she had grown up listening to his records. So it seemed okay to accept his kind invitation to wait for me up in his hotel suite. She would be much more comfortable there. She could even take a bath, he said. She could relax and put her feet up.

Ah, well.

The English rock star got her high on marijuana, played his new album for her, flattered and cajoled. Somehow she just couldn't quite say no when he carried her off into his bed for an afternoon of fun and frolic. "I was just so *overwhelmed*, Jonno! I mean, it was like nothing was *real* anymore. Oh, do you hate me? I feel so incredibly . . . I don't even know if there's a *word* for what I feel. It's like *Alice in Wonderland*, and I just fell down the rabbit hole."

"It's okay," I told her. "Los Angeles is like that. Anyone would feel overwhelmed."

"But not anyone would get laid by some *total* stranger just *hours* after getting into town! I mean, I feel like a . . ."

"Shh," I said. "Don't call yourself bad names."

"Oh, Jonno! Is it okay I'm here? Now that you're rich and famous, maybe you don't want to know me anymore?"

I told her I wasn't exactly rich and famous yet, I was poor and infamous, and there was a vast difference. I also told her not to be too hard on herself about the guy in the Ferrari. We all make mistakes, and believe me, I'd made a few mistakes of my own over the years. Then I got Kismet to take a shower and I tucked her into my bed because she had spent all of last night sitting up in a Greyhound bus, and with everything that had happened so far in Hollywood she was feeling totally exhausted. She cried herself to sleep.

Outside on Sunset Boulevard night had fallen and the city lay stretched out at my feet, glowing with a million little lights. I sat for a while in my darkened hotel room sipping cognac and staring out the window and listening to Kismet's regular breathing. Far across town, the beams of two searchlights criss-crossed the sky.

I picked up the phone and dialed Myra's number at home. After a few rings, another lady answered, probably her live-in friend, Carol. When I asked for Detective Sergeant Fisher she passed the phone to Myra.

"Thanks a lot!" I said.

"Somehow I thought you'd be calling, Jonno. Did you and Kismet have a tearful reunion?"

"You bet," I said, and I told her about the British rock star.

"Sorry about that," Myra said. "I thought she'd be safer in the lobby of the Chateau Marmont than at the Hollywood bus station."

"She just got taken by a more sophisticated hustler," I responded. "Anyway, she'll live."

"You got a lot of women on your hands, kid. What are you going to do with her?"

"I don't know. Maybe I'll take her to Disneyland tomorrow and then put her on the return bus to Petaluma."

"Jonno, don't forget the memorial for your father tomorrow. I think you should attend."

"For chrissake, Myra, are you my mother or are you a cop?"

"Jonno, I wouldn't be your mother for all the tinsel in lotusland. But I still think you should go to the memorial. It's only right."

The memorial in question was a big formal tribute and shindig to be held at David's house in Bel Air. Albert had mentioned it and so had Opera. The whole occasion sounded terrifically phony and I wasn't certain I'd get a very warm reception at David's home.

"Take Kismet," Myra suggested.

"What?"

"I mean it. It'll make a good impression to show up with a fresh-faced country girl. And David won't be able to throw you out of his house so easy. You should dress in a nice conservative suit and be very humble and mournful."

"You're kidding!" I said.

"I'm serious. If I have to arrest you again, you're going to need all the help you can get. If you skip that memorial it's going to look like you don't care your father's dead. Besides, I'd like you to nose around David's house a little. I'm curious about his general lifestyle and if it looks like he's living beyond his means. I'm also curious if he has a snub-nosed .38 revolver in his bedside table or in his office desk or some cute place like that. Now I sure as hell don't want to encourage you to break the law, my dear, but if you just *happened* to find such a gun you might accidentally drop it in your coat pocket and kinda forget it's there and then bring it to me, quick as a little bunny rabbit."

"Why don't you get a search warrant and go through his house yourself?"

"Because with what I got there's no judge in the state of California that would sign a warrant for me."

"What *do* you got?"

"Absolutely nothing," she said.

"Then what's this business about a .38? I thought Dad was killed with Best Picture of 1972."

"Sorry, but I can't tell you about the gun. It's a secret. Official police business."

I thought about this a moment and then I decided I would profit from the tactics of my little sister Opera. "Look, I got a secret too, Myra. I could tell you something very interesting about David, for instance. What do you say we get very confidential here and maybe you tell me your secret and I'll tell you mine. We can whisper sweet nothings over the phone."

She giggled. "Oh, you make it sound so deliciously dirty. I'm tempted, but no deal, sweetie pie. If you know something about

David you'll tell me anyway. In this case, darling, I don't need to prime the pump."

"Oh, come on, Myra. My pump hasn't been primed so long the damn thing's rusty. Can't you give it just a teeny little yank?"

"Try that line on Kismet, sugar plum, and it might get you someplace. Now what do you know about David?"

"Myra, you're just too good for me," I said. And I told her what Opera had told me, about the conversation she had overheard between Dad and David in Dad's office, and how if Dad had lived there was a chance David might have been demoted from CEO down the long slide of success clear to the mail room. Myra made me tell the story twice so that she was sure she had all the details.

"Well, I don't know," she said. "It gives David a good motive. But of course you *all* have good motives, even Opera, with the money you're all set to inherit. Until now, you simply had the biggest motive, Jonno, because you stood to inherit the most."

"Thanks. But if David thought he might lose his job . . ."

"Sure," said Myra. "Right now I'd say that you and David are running neck and neck in the motive department. Only David's a very respected member of the Hollywood community, a college graduate, a family man, and you're an itinerant piano player with a history of mental illness and rash deeds. And he has an alibi for the night of the murder, whereas you do not."

"What's his alibi?"

"He was asleep in bed with his wife."

"Oh, gimme a break!"

"It's a better alibi than yours, Jonathan Sangor. Not only that, but I couldn't shake the kid who works in the gas station in Brentwood. He identified your photograph out of a stack of fifty pictures of different guys, and he swears you bought a gallon of gas in a metal can about ten o'clock the night of the murder."

"But you told me the fire was set with propane, not gas."

"Sure, but this makes you a very serious liar, Jonno. You claim you were camping in the Sierras, but this kid comes along and says he saw you in West L.A. It's strong stuff, Jonno. Frankly my boss is suggesting we bring you in and make a formal charge. This is a sensational case and there's a lot of pressure for results."

"Great!" I said. "Maybe I should just slit my wrists and save the taxpayers the money for the trial."

"Jonno, don't even *joke* about that. Listen, I'm going to tell you about the .38 we were discussing, just because I'm nice. But don't quote me, okay? I like being a sheriff. It suits my gung ho lesbian image."

"Myra, I'm the very soul of discretion."

"Bullshit, but you need me in a big way. Now, first of all you gotta know how the fire was set. It was both very tricky and very simple, which is a winning combination when it comes to crime. Now pay attention. The way we picture this, the perp knocked your old man over the head with the Oscar and then picked up a table lamp and set the thing on its side on the floor. Then the guy very carefully broke the outer skin of the light bulb so that the filament remained intact. Do you get the picture? Now this is the clever part—the perp plugged the lamp into a small electric timer, the kind people buy to turn on their lights when they're not home in order to fool burglars. Probably the timer was set to go off in ten or fifteen minutes, just long enough so the perp would be gone when it went off."

"I don't get it," I said. "I mean, so what? The lamp will turn on in ten or fifteen minutes but with the broken bulb nothing happens."

"Not exactly *nothing*. Something will happen," Myra said. "This is where the propane comes in. The way we figure it, the perp brought along a small canister, maybe the kind you buy for camp stoves, and after the lamp was set up the guy opened up the valve and let out the entire contents of gas into the room. Now propane gas is heavier than air and it would settle on the floor near the broken lamp. You see how this works? All the perp has to do is put the empty metal canister in his backpack or briefcase or whatever, shimmy down the tree from your old bedroom window and then get the hell out of there, climbing the old horse trail you kids used to play on up to where he left his car on Mulholland Drive. A few minutes later, the timer turns on the broken light, which gives one small flash, just enough to ignite the propane, and in a second the whole bedroom's on fire.

"It was clever," she continued. "We were stumped for a while, we couldn't figure out how the hell the fire was set, but we found pieces of the timer and this made us suspicious. One of our lab people came up with the idea of making a gas chromatography test on the room, and they discovered very small traces of propane. And that's how we put it all together."

While she was talking, I remembered how a long time ago Carl had been very interested in homemade bombs that might speed the downfall of capitalism. But Carl had proved totally inept as a bomb maker. And anyway, he wouldn't do something like that. Not to Dad. I couldn't believe it.

"You still there, snookums?"

"Sure. I was thinking someone went to a lot of trouble to set that fire. Personally, I would have just used a match."

"Yeah. And you would have still been on the property when the fire engines arrived. You'd better stick to piano playing, Jonno."

"So what about the .38?"

"Oh, yeah. Exactly a week before the murder, someone broke into a hardware store on Fairfax and stole a bunch of timers like the one we're talking about. This was a dumb move. The guy was being too clever this time, it would have been better to just walk into the store and buy the son of a bitch with cash. A silent alarm was set off and a patrol car was dispatched. A figure in dark clothes and a ski cap was seen leaving the building. Shots were exchanged before the burglar got away and one of the officers took a .38 slug in his leg. We recovered the slug and we'll be able to identify the gun from which it was fired if we ever find the damn thing. So there it is. What we have here is a fine example of science and law enforcement techniques going hand in hand."

"Well, la-di-da," I told her. "And if this burglary took place a week before the murder, I got a fine alibi. All kinds of people saw me up in Northern California at that time."

"Yeah, this will do wonders for you, kid. But of course it's all just a theory. I mean there's nothing to connect the stolen timers in the hardware store to the timer that was used to start the fire in your father's bedroom except wishful thinking."

"Oh," I said.

"But if you find the .38, and the striations inside the barrel match the slug from the officer's leg, who knows, you might even grow up to be a wise old man, Jonno."

It seemed a slim hope. I hung up the phone and sat for a long while watching Kismet sleep. Then I made up a bed for myself on the couch. I didn't want her to wake in the depths of the night and think I was the sort of guy to take advantage of innocence so freshly arrived from the country.

24

I woke up on the couch with Southern California sunlight streaming into the room. This was the day of my father's big shindig
memorial. According to Opera everybody in the movie industry
was going to be there. It depressed the hell out of me. Actually, I
wouldn't have minded some kind of memorial for my father.
Maybe all the people who knew him, who loved or hated him,
could gather at the beach and build a bonfire and we could all get
righteously drunk and tell each other stories of Alexander Sangor's
driving ambition, how this man bypassed every human virtue in
his frenzied rush at success.

But a sanctimonious gathering at David's fancy house in Bel Air?
Gimme a break! I could imagine people drinking Perrier and saying a lot of hypocritical nonsense to one another, and making deals
on the side, for in Hollywood no event, not even a funeral, is
entirely devoid of business.

I hated it. I spent the entire day under the gathering shadow of
my father's memorial, and ended up doing something fairly foolish:
I started drinking. I poured a shot of Courvoisier into my morning
coffee while I watched Kismet going back and forth to the bathroom wrapped in a big towel. The liquor gave me a buzz. It was

like suddenly I could see everything in perspective, me and Kismet and Zoe, Rags and Carl and David and Opera and my father: nothing but a big joke. And really a very funny joke at that. I was surprised I had ever taken the whole seedy drama so seriously.

I had a second cup of coffee with a second shot of cognac, and that's when I had my big bright idea for the day. I decided I was going to turn my klutzy Kismet into a real Hollywood glamour puss. It seemed like a fun project and since she had bothered to take the bus down here, why not go all the way? I took my coffee into the bathroom where Kismet stood naked in front of the mirror drying her hair with a hotel blow dryer. She flashed me a worried smile. I smiled back encouragingly. She had nice breasts, long legs, a lovely figure and face. All she lacked was poise, sophistication, intelligence, and a proper wardrobe.

"You know, my dear, I've decided we're going to play Pygmalion, you and I."

"Is that like a card game?" she asked nervously.

"A little," I told her. "You certainly have to learn how to bluff."

I spent some time reassuring Kismet I wasn't really angry or hurt about the English rock star. Things like that just happened sometimes, I said. She wanted to drag me back to bed to cement our new understanding, but I told Kismet we simply had too much to do and that carnal love would have to wait. At the moment I was only interested in major transformations.

I called the concierge downstairs and arranged to hire a limousine—a long white one with tinted windows, TV, phone, and well-stocked bar. There are times when it is psychologically necessary to leave one's rusty old Buick in the garage, and this definitely seemed such a time. Kismet dressed in her cut-off jeans and TOBY'S FEED BARN T-shirt, and I bundled her into the limo and told the driver to head toward Beverly Hills.

Kismet had never been in a limousine before and she really got a kick out of it, trying out the TV set and all the dials and buttons. She asked if she could use the phone, and I said sure, that was what it was there for. So she dialed her parents' dope plantation up in Mendocino County and got her little sister, Sinsemilla. "You'll *never* guess where I am!" she cried. "God, I'm in *Hollywood*! In a *limousine* . . . and like I'm talking to you on a *car* phone!"

Kismet kept squeezing my leg. She had to tell Sinsemilla how this piano player she was dating had inherited this movie studio, more or less—well, *that* was a long story—but everything was just like taking psychedelics, a real crazy dream. She wanted to say hello to her mom and dad, but they were out working on the back forty. When she hung up, Kismet grinned at me like a little girl and I felt just like Santa Claus.

The limousine left us off on Rodeo Drive and trailed behind us as we went in and out of places like Nina Ricci, Sonia Rykiel, Lina Lee, and Ralph Lauren. Kismet was timid at first. She kept saying things like, "My God, these sweatpants cost *seven hundred dollars!* . . . We can't . . . Oh, Jonno, look at those shoes!"

We bought, bought, bought. I think the little guy with the helmet on my American Express card was getting bruised from being slid so many times through the machine. At last I took Kismet to the mysterious Red Door that marked the domain of Elizabeth Arden. I went in myself for a few minutes and chatted with a very glamorous older lady who reminded me of a madam of an expensive bordello in Paris I once visited in my dissolute youth. Then I left Kismet in the madam's care and I walked outside and stretched out in the back seat of the limousine with a glass of Dom Perignon. Frankly, I was having a great time.

As it happened, the chauffeur was an attractive young woman named Claire who kept glancing at me in her rearview mirror.

"I hope I'm not being nosy," Claire said. "But did you guys win the lottery or something?"

"A bit like that," I admitted. "Mostly it's a psychic thing. We decided to visualize abundance and let our material chakra float its way to a new level. If you see what I mean."

"Oh, yes I do," said Claire enthusiastically. "It's like you have to experience inner wealth before you can find outer wealth. That's such an empowering thought, a real validation of my own feelings. You're really an inspiration to me, Mr. Sangor."

"You can call me Jonno," I said.

Claire confessed she wasn't a chauffeur full time. Surprise, surprise, she was really an actress. She told me about her acting classes and auditions and things like that, which aspiring actresses tend to talk about, and I invited her to have a glass of champagne. At first she said no, she couldn't do that, she might lose her job and then how would she pay for her acting lessons? But I swore I would never tell and I handed her a glass of Dom Perignon over the divider.

Kismet took a long time in Elizabeth Arden, more than two and a half hours. Claire and I finished off the champagne and then I walked to Jurgensen's Market and bought two six-packs of beer— Bud, in cans, no less, really plebeian stuff. I took the beer back to the limo and Claire got in the backseat with me and we both proceeded to get fairly blottoed.

We were laughing about something when I happened to notice a very elegant young woman standing on the sidewalk peering in the window at us. The lady had exotic blond hair comprised of a thousand little ringlets. She had a sultry mouth, a cool stare. Frankly, for a moment I thought it was Kim Basinger. But it was Kismet, goddess from the North. Claire quickly jumped out of the backseat and opened the door for Kismet and then she returned to her own proper place in the front of the limousine. I knew the operation with Kismet had been a complete success when I tried to kiss her and she offered me her cheek instead and said: "Careful, you'll mess my make-make."

"Well, well," I said. "Not even Sinsemilla would recognize you now!"

"Jonno, you seem a little . . . I mean, you smell kinda like . . ."

"The King of Beers? It was a long wait, sweetheart, and Claire and I got a tad thirsty."

"Oh, Jonno. I feel so bad when you drink. It's really not at all good for your health."

"I know," I assured her. "I'm in mourning, you see. But don't let it worry you, because tomorrow . . . tomorrow, I'm going to jog and be a vegetarian and even start meditating again. . . . A whole new leaf, Kismet. Maybe even a whole new tree."

She radiated her new beauty and glamour my way. It was incredible what Elizabeth Arden had done. Then Claire started up the long white limousine with the tinted windows and the TV and the car phone and the bar, and we lurched unsteadily back toward the Chateau Marmont.

25

David's house in Bel Air was one of those westside monstrosities that looked a lot more like a department store than a private home. The outer façade was white from top to bottom, very cold and impersonal, a series of cubes on different levels with strangely shaped windows that made me think of a colony for alienated ants. Frankly, David's house baffled me. There were slanting smoked-glass ceilings and roofs going off in all kinds of weird directions, and I wouldn't have lived there for a million dollars.

"Wow!" said Kismet as we made our way up an impressive red-brick driveway to a courtyard in front of the house. I had intended to arrive here in the limousine, but unfortunately our chauffeur Claire had become sick and had gone home. The young just don't have the same stamina for self-abuse as us older folk. So there was nothing for it but to pull the old Buick out of the garage and toodle over to Bel Air on our own.

For some reason, Kismet insisted on driving. In front of David's house, two valet parking attendants gave our car a wary looking over and for a moment I thought they were going to give us a hard time. But when they saw Kismet emerge from the driver's seat in a drop-dead black cocktail dress and high heels with starlight in her eyes, they could hardly take their eyes off her. The dress shimmered and clung to her like a second skin. It intimated lovely secrets. One of the guys handed me a claim check, a playing card, a black one-eyed jack.

Kismet took my arm and I guided her past a sign that indicated that anyone would be shot dead who entered this happy home without permission.

"Don't be nervous," I told her. "You look fine."

"I'm not nervous," she told me, and I realized it was true. *I* was on edge. Clothes make the woman, and Kismet suddenly had a brand new wiggle in her walk I had never seen before.

The night was dry and warm and there were pink and blue palm trees swaying gently in the breeze, lit from below by colored spotlights. I tried to tell Kismet how pink and blue palm trees crystalized a lot of feelings I had always had about Southern California.

"Jonno . . . don't drink too much, okay?"

"I'll be good," I told her. "But it's a Greek legend that you can't cross the river Styx unless you're stoned."

This temporarily stumped her and we entered David's house holding hands. The inside atrium was two and a half stories high, and beneath the vast skylights there was a jungle of plants and fragrant flowers. This was the indoor-outdoor look in a big way. Set among the plants were white sofas and armchairs and ornate coffee tables inlaid with gold. At one end of the living room stood a big stone fireplace; at the other end there was a small waterfall and indoor pool with fat multicolored fish darting about.

Then I saw David. He wore a white linen suit with a paisley tie that was retro-styled to the sixties. David had a bandage on his nose, which made him look pretty silly. The bandage had an elastic band around the back of his head to keep it in place. My brother glared at me like an angry owl, and then he shrugged and came over my way.

"Pax," he said, offering his hand. "At least for tonight. What do you say, Jonno?"

"Sure," I told him. "I'm only here to mourn the dead." I introduced Kismet and he introduced his wife, Christina Dorn, the famous actress. Christina wore a green dress and reminded me of a very large tropical parrot. I made chitchat with her about her kids, my niece and nephew presumably, while David put on a terrific amount of charm for Kismet, asking if she was an actress.

"You know, this young lady could be great on screen," David said in my direction over her shoulder. "She has a very natural look."

This showed, of course, what David knew about being natural. Kismet looked like a girl who had just spent thousands of dollars on Rodeo Drive and two and a half hours in Elizabeth Arden.

"Have you ever done any acting?" he was asking her.

"Well, I was First Fairie in *Midsummer Night's Dream* . . . in the eighth grade."

"No kidding? First Fairie's a *terrific* part. 'Over hill, over dale . . .'"

"That's Puck's speech, darling," said his wife, interrupting.

"Is it?" grinned David, "Well, fuck Puck!" he said merrily, and all of the sudden I knew I wasn't the only person who had been drinking.

David asked if he could "borrow" Kismet for a moment and introduce her to a producer friend of his who was looking for a "very natural young woman who has real chemistry with horses." I told Kismet this could be her big chance, and she went off with David with a bedazzled smile that made her look like the queen of the prom. This left me alone with Christina Dorn.

"What an asshole," she said watching her husband disappear across the room. "Was he like this as a kid?"

"Worse," I told her. "Zoe used to say it was because he was so insecure about being a bastard the first fifteen years of his life."

Christina laughed. She was a handsome woman with a smoky voice, the kind of woman whose age was a shrouded mystery, though if I had to guess I would say forty. She looked me over with shrewd blue eyes.

"Everyone says you're the cocksman of the family, Jonno."

"No, not at all," I replied. "When I was young, I was too sincere, and now that I'm old the game has lost its bite."

"Maybe you haven't been nibbled in the right place?" she suggested.

I grinned. To my surprise, I quite liked David's wife. "Listen, Christina," I said in a low voice. "By any chance does David have a .38 snub-nosed revolver? I mean, in any of his drawers or anything. Maybe in the medicine chest or laundry hamper?"

"Why, no. If David had a gun, he'd probably end up shooting his dick off. If he *had* a dick," she added.

I laughed uproariously. What a clever woman, what a charming marriage! Christina and I had a drink together and then she introduced me to a few of her friends. I met a director, an agent, and an actor with a deep masculine voice. Everyone said what a great guy my dad was, and how the industry was going to be hard pressed to replace him.

Somewhere in all this revelry, I got separated from my new friend Christina. She said, "Let's do lunch together sometime soon," and then she disappeared with the actor with the deep masculine voice.

I was getting pretty sloshed. The funny thing was, every now and then I actually thought about Dad. I could *see* him, almost feel his presence nearby. And it hurt like hell. I'm not sure if it was exactly love so much as a lost connection. For better or worse, Dad had defined my life: I felt like a puppet whose controlling wires had been abruptly cut. I was on my own, and my drink was empty.

I noticed Albert standing by himself with a glass of champagne in his hand and a pensive look on his brow. He was wearing a dark suit elegantly flared at the waist. I went over to him, snagging a glass of champagne from a roving waiter on the way.

"Well, well, Jonno?" Albert said sternly. "How's the family frog?"

"Not quite a prince yet. Nor sure I want to be. Look, can I ask you something? Maybe this isn't any of my business, but it's been bothering me. It's about you and Rags."

"He told you," Albert said.

"Yeah, he told me. And it's not that I think it's *wrong* exactly. It's just that I always thought that me and Carl and Rags were off-limits."

Albert gazed at me without expression. "So you think it was improper for me to press my sexual preference on innocent young Rags?"

"No, not *improper*, Albert. I was just surprised, that's all. It seems out of character somehow."

Albert smiled in a sad, misty way. "Oh, Jonno! I felt so tremendously sorry for him! You have no idea what that poor kid was going through. Rags didn't know he was gay, but *I* knew. Oh, I knew all the signs. And he was so in love with you, Jonno, but you dumped him for Zoe. And he was all in the dark . . . all in the dark," he repeated. Albert took a delicate sip of his champagne and glanced around the room. "So I helped guide him to what he was supposed to be. Rags wasn't a duck, you see. He was a swan."

"Jesus," I said. I really didn't know what to say. Once again I felt I had missed some essential part of my own drama because my attention had been someplace else. "Somehow it's like we're all little animals for you, isn't it, Albert? I'm a frog. Rags is a swan. What's Carl?"

"A wolverine."

"How about David?"

"A jackal."

"Do you have one for Opera?"

"Of course. She's a pussycat."

"And Zoe?" I inquired with some hesitation.

He turned to me and his smile faded.

"Zoe? You know what she is, Jonno. She's a killer."

26

I escaped from Albert by saying I was going in search of one of the smoked-salmon sandwiches I had seen making the rounds of the room and then I never returned. It was a standard cocktail party ploy, guerrilla warfare in the social trenches.

I was feeling uneasy about the fact that Albert had seduced Rags so many years ago, though I wasn't sure why. I don't normally think of myself as a homophobe. Live and let live, I always say, and make love to the reindeer if it turns you on. But when it came to my brother, Rags, I didn't know. What Albert had done seemed exploitive somehow, because Albert had so much power over us. And I had always believed in Albert as the final judge, the only one of us who wasn't corrupt and could be counted upon to do the right thing.

I had to sort it out. I realized I was angry about what he had said about Zoe, though Carl and Rags had said pretty much the same thing. I told myself Albert was just being a grouchy old queer. He was jealous. He didn't like women and he always believed Zoe had split our happy family asunder. He wasn't moved as I was by fabulously sexy Botticelli angels who might redeem your life with a single kiss.

Oh, Zoe! Standing in a roomful of Hollywood strangers, I conjured up an image of her, the first time I ever saw her, the day she appeared at La Chanson d'Or at the age of thirteen in her pleated skirt and knee socks with a look of tearful innocence on her face.

Could innocence kill? I wondered.

You bet! came the answer, loud and clear. Innocence was like a truck full of dynamite careening down the highway without a driver in the cab.

I avoided the smoked-salmon sandwiches but had myself another glass of champagne. I saw Carl and Opera across the crowded room. Opera waved at me enthusiastically and Carl flashed a pale ironic smile that seemed to say: "Well, it's pretty crazy, but what the hell."

I made funny faces at them and beat my chest like Tarzan from behind one of the indoor trees and then I moved away in another direction. I passed from the main atrium into a kind of enormous den and saw my brother Rags in his wheelchair, being pushed by the very healthy looking blond giant I had seen the first afternoon I had arrived at home. I think the blond giant was named Ken or Keith, or something like that. I did a vague about-face as if I hadn't seen them, but they saw me and my show of make-believe was probably not very convincing. The mood I was in, I sought the comfort of strangers.

I wandered into the dining room. There was a long table laden with food; turkeys and trays of raw oysters, bowls of cracked crab and prawns on ice, stuff like that. Raw vegetables and dip. No red meat because this was the new healthy Hollywood where everyone planned to live to a hundred. At the side of the room, near a big plate-glass window overlooking the swimming pool, a bartender was serving drinks. I switched from champagne and started hitting the scotch and water. A lot of the unpleasant things that were to happen to me on this night happened because I was so drunk. This was Jonathan Sangor's last great binge. And what a binge it was!

The house seemed to pulse and pull around me and go in and out of focus. I met a screenwriter who was as lit as I was. We gravitated toward each other like celestial bodies weaving too closely in the night. We became fabulous friends almost instantly.

I think his name was Marty, or Mernie, or maybe even Muffy. Something that began with an M.

He told me all about his most recent divorce and a movie he had written that was getting absolutely fucked by some asshole director who didn't comprehend the subtleties of his work. The poor guy wasn't in good shape; his tie was askew, his hair was standing up in a funny way on his head, and he had red beady eyes. Eventually he began to depress me and our new friendship foundered in shallow waters. I wandered off.

Around this time the speeches began in the main atrium. Someone I didn't know stood in front of the indoor waterfall and spoke about what a decent and loving person Alexander Sangor had been. Then David got up and proceeded to recite "O Captain! My Captain!" by Walt Whitman:

> Oh Captain! my Captain! our fearful trip is done!
> The ship has weather'd every wrack,
> The prize we sought is won . . .

Honest to God, I'm a great fan of Walt Whitman, but this was too much. I retreated by myself back into the dining room. I snatched a bottle of Johnny Walker Black Label from the unattended bar and carried it through a door to a library with a pool table in the middle. I took off my shoes and then Johnny Walker and I climbed up onto the cool green velvet of the table. I stretched out onto my back and lay with my head between the cue ball and the eight ball, staring up at a ceiling of acoustic tile.

I heard footsteps, and then a voice I would recognize if it followed me all the way to hell. "Oh, Jonno! You're going to feel terrible tomorrow."

Her accent seemed more British than French these days, and less American than ever. "I feel terrible now," I told her. "Why wait until tomorrow?"

Zoe kicked off her shoes and climbed onto the pool table with me. She made it seem like a very elegant place to sit. I hadn't seen her earlier. She was wearing a black dress that might have been suitable for mourning except it was cut well above the knee. She wore nylon stockings and a diamond pendant on a silver chain around her neck. She even had a new hairstyle for the occasion, a lot of little curls like Kismet's. Maybe they had been behind the Red Door at the same time. Zoe took the Johnny Walker out of my hand and raised the bottle to her lips and took a swallow.

"Ugh," she said. "I hate the taste of hard liquor."

"So do I," I told her.

"I met your girlfriend. Kristie?"

"Kismet," I said. "Like the old musical comedy."

"She's lovely, Jonno. A very sweet person."

"Yeah," I said. "She's sweet all right. But I'm going to toughen her up. To survive in this world you need an iron jockstrap. Metaphorically speaking, of course."

"Jonno . . ."

"No listen, I'm glad you met her. You see Kismet's the name of the game, she's the story of my life. It's fate," I said with a big drunken leer. "But seriously, Zoe, after you taught me the Exact Right Spot, women threw themselves at me all the time. I mean, hell, you even taught me to play the piano and that was the clincher. So the women came and the women went. Sweet women, sour women, young, and old. But they all had one thing in common. They always went away unhappy. And do you know *why* they went away unhappy?"

I had risen with the wings of speech until I was propped up on one elbow and I could look at Zoe better. "You're drunk," she said.

"Damn right," I told her. "They went away unhappy because every time I've ever made love to any lady over these long, long years, every time I was inside someone and looked into her eyes and we did the dance fantastic, every time, Zoe, I was always pretending it was you."

She was very close to me. So close her face blurred.

"Jonno, what happened between us was a long time ago. We were children."

"Yeah," I said lying back exhausted on the pool table. "Little innocent children. But I loved you, Zoe. I loved you more than anything. And the punchline of this joke is I've never been able to love anybody since."

Zoe took another swig of the Johnny Walker, but her eyes never left my face.

"This kind of obsessive love, Jonno, it's not a good thing."

I giggled. "You got it, doctor! So do you have any medicine that will cure me? Maybe I should learn to meditate, whad'ya think? Or I could join a nunnery?"

She smiled. "I don't think a nunnery would be helpful in your particular condition."

I closed my eyes and attempted to create some poetry for the occasion. "Oh, Captain, my Captain, my sister sure was fun . . . I loved to kiss her ruby lips, she certainly was no nun . . . But now my goose is really cooked, my ship is sinking fast . . . And here my sister sits so near, a gorgeous piece of ass."

"Oh, Jonno, *honestly!*" I started going off into a second stanza but Zoe put her hand over my mouth to stifle the creative muse. "What am I going to do with you?" she wondered. I suppose it was what you'd call a rhetorical question, but I had some more concrete ideas. I took her hand captive in my own and I kissed the fleshy part of the palm and then I did something crude. I brought her hand down between my legs and pressed it over the bulge of my pants upon my cock. Zoe didn't encourage me, but she didn't take her hand away either. For a drunk guy, I was coming back to consciousness in a big way. I was hard as a rock.

"You think this is going to solve anything?" she asked skeptically.

"Sure it will. A hair of the dog, sort of thing. Maybe I'll find you're not as good as I remember."

I saw a wicked naughty-girl smile on her face I remembered from the old days. "You've grown, Jonno," she said, feeling the outline of my cock.

"Oh, I'm a big boy now, Zoe."

She laughed, and while she laughed I pulled her down to me and kissed her.

"This is all wrong," she whispered.

"You bet it is," I said. And then we began kissing for real, kissing our way through all the dark years of separation. I was her mirror image, I knew exactly what to do. Everything about her was familiar, the smell of her hair, the taste of her tongue. She was as hot as I was. She was panting a little and we began tearing at each other's clothing, reaching with our hands and reeling in our senses.

I couldn't stand it that she was wearing clothes. Somehow I got the black dress over her head and pulled down her nylons and bikini panties and she was left with just her diamond necklace and earrings and her bra down somewhere around her waist.

"This is crazy," she said.

"Who cares?" I answered.

I rolled over on top of her. She ripped my shirt open and my pants were down around my knees, and I entered her with a long sigh. It was like slipping into a warm bath after being out in the cold. "I love you," I said, and I said it again and again until I was out of breath. The pool table was hard against my knees, but Zoe and I had always made love in strange places and this was just like we were kids again.

Oh, I was deep in the perfect clover. I heard the sound of Zoe's orgasm well up in her throat like she was giving birth, and there was a cry coming from my own throat that was hardly human. And then I heard the door open behind us and a man said, "Holy shit!"

I was beyond caring. Frankly, I was coming like the Hoover Dam suddenly let loose and there was no way to reverse the tide of nature.

"Jonno!" screamed someone new. It was Kismet.

"Go away," I said. "Can't you see I'm busy?"

"I'm sorry, but you cannot fuck *my* sister in *my* house on *my* pool table!" said a voice I recognized as David's.

"Oh, leave them alone," said a new voice coming into the room. It was David's wife Christina. I was beginning to feel like the turkey on display at Thanksgiving. "Personally, I think they look rather *fabulous* together," said Christina thoughtfully.

"But they're ruining my pool table!" David screamed. "And this is *supposed* to be Dad's memorial!"

Now that the dam had been breeched, and the floods were subsiding, this was beginning to strike me as pretty funny. I rolled off my sister Zoe and lay on my back on the pool table laughing my head off. Zoe was laughing too. For a moment David, Kismet, and Christina were staring at us, each with various expressions of incredulity on their faces. Then Kismet burst into tears and fled, and David followed her looking very upset and put out. "This is the last straw!" he said as he made his exit.

"Mm, you guys want a threesome sometime, you let me know," said Christina, and she gave us a wink and then she too departed. Zoe climbed down from the pool table and began searching for her clothes. She was laughing, but the laughter gradually stopped.

"Well?" she said. "I hope you're satisfied. Was it worth it?"

"You bet," I told her. "And don't try to tell me it wasn't good for you."

"Oh, Jonno, of *course* it was good," she said angrily. "That's not the point. I should never have let this happen. We're too damn close. It's like making love to myself . . . and Christ, I'm not even taking birth control right now. What if I get pregnant?"

I thought about this a moment. "We'll run away together to Bora Bora, the three of us. Someplace where even if Junior is born with a tail he can swing from tree to tree."

She looked exasperated. She did not laugh. "Oh-oh," she said. "Get dressed, Jonno. David's coming back."

And he was. David came storming into the room like an angry little Napoleon. "I want you out of my house! Out of my house!" he cried. "This is absolutely shocking, an *insult* to our father. *I'll* take care of Kismet. That poor girl doesn't want to see you again, ever."

I stood up from the pool table, but the solid floor did not feel so solid, particularly since my pants were down around my ankles. Suddenly I saw stars. David had just connected an uppercut to my chin and I reeled backward onto the pool table.

"Leave him alone!" Zoe screamed.

"Then *you*, my dear. *You* come with me! It's time we had a serious talk, Zoe," David said imperiously. It was almost like he thought he was our father or something.

"Are you okay, Jonno?" Zoe asked.

"Euphoric."

"I'll be back," she said. Then David and Zoe left the room. Frankly, I was surprised she followed him so meekly, but then David always had some kind of control over her I never understood.

I decided not to wait for her. I was filled with a romantic notion that when I saw Zoe next it had to be on my own turf, not David's. I lay on the pool table and struggled back into my pants. They seemed to be the kind of pants that were easier to get down than up. The bottle of Johnny Walker was still on the table and I took a last long swallow and then tried to slink off the green velvet onto the floor. The room began to swim around and around in a funny way. With exaggerated steps I moved carefully, one step after another, out of the room, down a hall, and through the dining room to the atrium. They say drunk men can't get an erection, but I *still* was hard, I swear to God. A lady I did not recognize gave me a very strange look, and then her glance settled midsection on my body and she said, "Oh, my God."

I grinned at her and kept going, moving through the atrium, past the trees and the artificial ponds and people, toward the front door. A crowd moved aside for me and I felt like Moses parting the Red Sea. I walked in a more or less straight line out into the night.

"Black one-eyed jack," I said to the parking valet, pleased as hell I could remember. The face of the valet separated into two parts, a mouth and a forehead which began to swirl around like a kaleidoscope. I had to stop looking at him so I wouldn't get dizzy.

"Sir, perhaps you shouldn't drive. Why don't you let me call a taxi for you. Or maybe one of your friends . . ."

"Get me my goddamn car!" I said. "Fucking Buick LeSabre, 1965. A fine vintage automobile."

He tried to convince me I was in no shape to drive, but I made a scene. I said I would sue the damn valet company, if there *was* such a thing as a valet company. Finally the Buick appeared in the courtyard, and the guy reluctantly held the door open for me.

I think I started the car and tried to drive, but I didn't get far. I slumped forward, my head falling against the steering wheel, and I had the best sleep I can remember in years.

It was a pity I woke up in hell.

27

I realized everything was wrong even before I opened my eyes. It wasn't only that my head throbbed, and my tongue was like a cactus. There were other troubling signs as well, such as the fact that my cheek lay against hard gravel rather than against a nice soft pillow, and that my left hand found itself grasping hold of something that felt suspiciously like long grass.

From nearby I heard a dry crackling sound I couldn't quite identify. I felt a blast of heat against my forehead and suddenly the crackling sound made an awful sense. I opened my eyes and it took only a moment to comprehend my situation. I was lying on my side in the open country, with the diffuse gray light of early dawn in the sky. There was long dry grass near my nose, and a dusty oak tree a few feet away. And I felt scorching heat coming at me from very nearby.

Fire!

The long grass was on fire only a dozen feet from my head, sending up a white nearly invisible flame into the morning sky. I leaped to my feet and fought off the haze of my hangover with the stronger potion of primal fear.

There was not a house in sight and I had no idea where I was or how I got there. I seemed to be in a canyon of sorts, bone dry this time of year at the end of the long summer. It was a world of dead grass, scruffy brush, a few dusty manzanita and oak trees.

I could see an advancing line of flame maybe a dozen feet long moving unevenly. Then I saw something at the base of an oak tree that made my heart skip a beat. It was a discarded gasoline can toppled over on its side. I picked up the can to discover it was empty. I had a pretty good suspicion the Chevron attendant in Brentwood who had supposedly identified me would say this was identical to the can I had filled with gas.

The reality hit my scotch-soaked brain in disagreeable waves. I stepped backward, tripping over a root. I fell on my ass, and picked myself up and scrambled up a small hill to the top of a dusty knoll. I saw my Buick sitting at the end of a dirt road. The keys were in the ignition, but when I tried to start the car the engine would not turn over. I pulled the latch to release the hood but stopped myself from sticking my head into the engine. I was running out of time and I knew it would be useless. The distributor cap would be missing or the gas line cut. There were hundreds of ways to disable an old crate like mine.

The fire was spreading, and I could now see a big plume of white smoke rising into the early dawn. I began jogging torturously along the dirt road up a small incline to a meadow. My head felt like broken glass and every jog was like trotting on some psycho-sadistic horse. I forced my legs forward and at the top of the meadow I recognized where I was. I was back in my childhood, in a canyon below Mulholland Drive less than a quarter mile from La Chanson d'Or. We kids had played in this meadow years ago, setting off firecrackers and throwing baseballs and doing the innocent things that children do. I was surprised the land was still undeveloped, but the L.A. hills were like that. There were strange pockets of rural neglect hidden away in the land of plenty, pockets where time stood still. I wondered which of my brothers or sisters had brought me here in my drunken stupor. It had to be one of them. To tell the truth, I was a little surprised someone in my family hated me so much.

I was out of breath. I proceeded at a slower pace along the curve of the overgrown road toward a line of oak trees. That's when I saw an early morning jogger coming my way from the direction of

the trees. It was a woman and she had a dog jogging alongside her
on a leash.

"Hey!" I cried. "Hey, over here!"

The lady stopped and looked me over and did not seem to like
what she saw. Then her eyes shifted and she noticed the smoke
rising up from behind me. I must have looked like hell, but I
couldn't understand why she seemed so frightened of me. I mean,
hell, I was dirty and hungover and unshaved, but not exactly Jack
the Ripper. Then I figured it out. I was still carrying the empty
gasoline can. I dropped the can to the ground.

"Look, I didn't do this. We gotta call the fire department," I
said. But when I tried to move in her direction, she let her dog
loose on me, a vicious black ball of fur that went straight for my
ankle. Sharp teeth sank down into my right calf and I screamed in
pain. "Fucking dog! Get the bastard off me!" I shrieked.

Fortunately it was a small dog and with a single energetic kick
I was able to send it sailing through the air a few feet toward its
mistress. The dog yelped and ran away, and the lady jogger did
likewise, sprinting for all she was worth back down the dirt road
toward the trees, with the nasty little dog hot on her heels trying
to keep up. I guess she was glad they were both in such good
shape.

"I didn't set the fire!" I yelled after her. "Honest!" But the lady
did not return, and it took me only a moment to see how bad this
was going to look. I would be the fall guy all around, blamed for
the fire and for my father's murder, and probably any other un-
solved crime they could throw at me. Being an ex-rich kid, I did
not have a finely tuned sense of survival, but I knew I had to get
out of there fast.

I ran as fast as I could manage along the dirt road until I came
to a small residential road that came snaking down into the canyon
from Mulholland Drive. I came to a sweet blue house that had a
lot of flowers in the front yard and a Volvo station wagon in the
driveway. The house was quiet in its early morning slumber. There
were signs that children lived here, bicycles and baseball gloves
abandoned in the grass. All the inhabitants seemed asleep and
there was no sign of a dog. I crept up the driveway feeling like
the boogeyman. Very conveniently, the owners of the Volvo had
left a magnetic Hide-A-Key underneath the chassis by the front

left wheel. It was the first place I looked, and I took it as a sign from heaven that this Volvo was destined to be mine.

I drove fast along the road away from the fire. I kept expecting to hear a siren coming up behind me and see a flashing red light in my rearview mirror, but I was lucky. I reached Mulholland and drove east until I hit Laurel Canyon and then I made a left turn toward the San Fernando Valley. I didn't relax until I had managed to lose myself in the thick morning traffic on the Ventura Freeway.

Later in the morning, I heard on the car radio that twenty acres in the hills of Coldwater Canyon were ablaze, and that ten homes had already been destroyed. A few hours later, the figure was revised upward to a hundred acres and twenty homes, and the fire was still raging out of control.

Then came the Santa Ana winds. This was the annual California nightmare, the hills on fire in dry September. Only this fire was no accident, and by the afternoon the radio and everybody else was screaming for the blood of the demented arsonist whose name and photograph were being broadcast over all the airwaves: yours truly, Jonathan Sangor. Rich kid on the run.

Part Four

28

Some of the best things in my life and some of the worst things have happened to me riding in the back of limousines.

In the spring of 1968, when I was twelve years old, my sister Zoe persuaded me to join the Bel Air School choir with her. We were going to perform Bach's *Magnificat* on graduation day, and Zoe said this was a very important piece of music that everyone should know. So Zoe and I would stay after school for rehearsals, and our chauffeur Speedo had to come for us each afternoon to bring us home. I loved riding in the back of the long Cadillac with Zoe, the world drifting by so softly outside. But I wasn't that wild about being in the school choir, particularly since I still had a fairly high voice and Miss Cunningham, the music teacher, put me in with the altos.

I guess I was Zoe's experiment, her Frankenstein of the New Age. I was supposed to be a kid who could play the piano superbly, commit felonious crimes upon the neighborhood, meditate, sing Bach, roll a joint one-handed, and perform cunnilingus with deadly accuracy. A Renaissance man à la 1968.

Personally, I was dubious, particularly about the choir part, but at least Zoe was in the alto section too, generally standing in front of me and a little to the left so I could see her face in profile, watch her smooth throat and the swell of her breast as the music came gushing forth. I was the ultimate Zoe watcher, of course, and this Bach choir brought out her angelic best. With her music book in hand, her eyes half closed in concentration, frankly I wouldn't have been at all surprised to see wings sprout suddenly from her shoulder blades.

And then, when the rehearsals were finished, we would find our long black chariot waiting in the school driveway. Our Filipino chauffeur, Speedo, generally had a baseball game going on the AM radio and he kept the window up between the front seat and the back so he could smoke his foul little cigars. And this left Zoe and me gloriously to ourselves.

It was time in limbo. When I was tired, Zoe would let me stretch out with my head on her lap. I remember the feel of her school uniform against my cheek. She wore a light blue wool skirt, slightly scratchy, and if I was lucky and she was in the right kind of mood, the skirt would ride upward on her thighs and I'd find my cheek resting against the warm smoothness of her bare upper leg. And if I turned the right way, my nose might nestle against her white cotton panties and I would envelop myself in the warm musky smell of girl. I was content simply to lie there in my sleepy euphoria.

If I felt I could get away with it, I'd let my tongue come out and rest against her inner thigh. I used to imagine I was an abalone clinging to bare girl leg. Sometimes the cunning abalone foot made a small pilgrimage to higher ground, sneaking in under the elastic band of her panties. Zoe kept an algebra book opened on my head so that Speedo wouldn't see what we were doing in case he looked in the rearview mirror. To tell the truth, I have spent my entire life getting sexually aroused by even the opening strains of the Bach *Magnificat*, and I have seldom ridden in a limousine without an erection.

These were the delights of my wicked childhood. I think I could have ridden forever in the back of my father's limousine with my head nestled in my sister's lap. But Zoe had more complicated desires. Just when I'd be getting absolutely comfortable, lulled almost to sleep, she would make me sit up and discuss her plan to blackmail Marco Mallory, our movie-star neighbor. Frankly, I didn't know why we were doing it. I liked Marco Mallory. I admired his swashbuckling ways. But Zoe was set on it and I went along, and pretty soon it became the sort of thing that took on its own momentum.

We took our time. We plotted and planned and eventually we had it all worked out. Since it was all basically make-believe, the original pay-off figure of twenty-five thousand dollars gradually became sixty thousand dollars. When Zoe discussed the blackmail, I saw how her face changed, becoming cold and hard as marble. It frightened me to see this transformation. I sensed she was planning some great revenge upon the world, but I had no idea of the motive from which this revenge was born. It seemed formless, some kind of abstract hatred. Or maybe Zoe was just practicing her basic superiority, making the world dance to her tune. I don't know. It was beyond my adolescent comprehension. I only knew my sister's body, her lovely outward form, but what was ticking inside remained a mystery to me. When I once asked her why we were blackmailing Marco, she said it was "an experiment in existentialism." Whatever the hell *that* meant! Frankly, I was afraid to ask, lest she add a cram course in philosophy to my piano practice and everything else.

I just figured I'd better go along or I might lose her.

29

On a dark night a few weeks after school ended, in late June, a number of events converged and Zoe thought it was time to make our move. Our father was in Yugoslavia where his biggest client of the moment was making a movie about ancient China; my stepmother Michelle was in London on a shopping spree; and we knew exactly where Marco Mallory was going to be: at the Pantages Theater in Hollywood attending the gala premiere of his new movie, *Kiss of the Pirate*.

Zoe and I waited for Gretchen to turn off the downstairs lights and disappear into her room for the night. Around ten o'clock, Zoe slipped into my bedroom from the hall. She was dressed in black tights, a black T-shirt, and a black beret, with her long blond hair tied up in a tight bun. She looked just like a beatnik. There was a green book bag over her shoulder with the blackmail package inside containing sample photos and our demand for sixty grand.

"Zoe, you're sure this is a good idea?" I asked one last time.

"Are you afraid?"

"Of course not," I lied.

So I swung out my bedroom window onto the oak tree and used the broad branches as a ladder to the ground. Zoe followed after

210

me, a lithe shadow in the night. We made our way quickly over
the lawn and past the swimming pool, crawling like commandos
past Gretchen's window. At last we came to the hedge, and the
hole that passed through to Casa Monte Carlo, the estate on the
other side. It was so dark I had to feel ahead like a blind man as
I sought the rotten part of the fence with my hands. Zoe followed
close behind, holding on to my leg so she wouldn't lose me. This
was one area of expertise where I was better than Zoe. When it
came to crawling around in the dirt and going through hedges and
things like that, I really was unbeatable. Zoe had a flashlight in
her book bag, but we had already decided we would not risk using
it except for an absolute emergency.

As we stood on the Marco Mallory side of the hedge, we tried
to get our bearings. It was too dark to see the Rodin statue of the
naked woman or even the grape arbor. The darkness seemed so
thick that I had a momentary image of Zoe and me in the womb
together, that we were twins. I liked this thought and tried to tell
her about it, but she said we should concentrate on the business
at hand. I inched forward and Zoe followed holding on to my belt.
Then we came around a line of bushes into the warm lights of the
big Mediterranean villa and we could see again. The upstairs of
the big house was dark but all the downstairs lights were ablaze.

"I thought there wasn't going to be anyone here," I whispered.

"He has servants, naturally," Zoe whispered back. "It's okay,
Jonno. His bedroom is dark, and that's where you're going."

Zoe and I had made a brief survey here a week before, a kind
of trial run in which we had sat in the bushes one night smooching
a little and watching the routine of the household. We had discovered the position of Marco Mallory's bedroom on the second
floor. He had French windows opening out upon a small ornamental balcony, and there was a convenient cypress tree nearby
against the house. Zoe and I studied the dark windows in silence
and then she handed me the book bag with the manila envelope
inside. All of a sudden my mouth felt so dry I could barely swallow.

"Good luck," she said, and she gave me a quick kiss on the
mouth. How could I turn back now? I was her Lancelot off to do
a heroic deed. All I had to do was climb up the cypress tree to
the little balcony, swing over the wrought-iron rail, open the
French doors and leave the blackmail package on Marco's bed. It

was simple. This was supposed to scare Marco to death, make him think we could get in and out of his inner sanctum any time we liked, and he would obviously pay us sixty thousand dollars without question. Only one problem. It was *I* who was scared to death.

"*Go on!*" Zoe said.

"I'm going," I told her. Zoe waited for me by Marco's swimming pool. She sat rather coolly on the diving board and watched my progress.

My heart thumped so loud I was afraid I would wake the neighborhood. I wondered what would happen if I had a heart attack and died, if Zoe would grieve for me. Zoe and I had been over this in conversation a dozen times. She had told me the tree to Marco Mallory's bedroom was the easiest tree on God's green planet. I had never tried to climb a cypress before and it turned out to be as dense and scratchy as a bush, about the hardest tree I had ever found. I only wished it was an oak or a maple or an elm, because I was dynamite on those trees. But frankly, with the damn cypress I hardly even knew where to get started.

The thing was like a giant pricker. I finally made my way up the tree by sheer willpower, tearing my T-shirt, holding on to Zoe's green book bag with my teeth, scrambling up the branches. Somehow I managed to do it, I don't know how.

I hoisted myself onto the ornamental balcony. I didn't know if the French doors to the bedroom would be locked or if an alarm would sound the moment I touched the handle, but neither turned out to be the case. The door swung open easily, and I found myself in a darkened room in which I could just make out the main features. I was confronted by a humongous orgy-sized bed with mirrors on the ceiling and all kinds of hanging drapery that smelled vaguely of marijuana. With trembling fingers I opened the book bag, found the manila envelope, and placed it in the middle of the giant bed. Then I heard a big booming voice downstairs. It was Marco. I didn't know what the hell he was doing here, but it didn't look too good for me. Marco was walking up the stairs and talking to someone.

For a moment I just froze. Then some instinct took over and I swung over the balcony and jumped toward the cypress tree, hoping for the best. It was like grabbing hold of a porcupine. I let go and tumbled the last five feet to the ground and lay there in agony.

I was crying. My hands were covered with blood and there was the taste of blood in my mouth. Then Zoe was there at my side helping me to my feet.

"I think I've broken something," I said. "*Everything* maybe."

"You're all right," she whispered in a very definite way. Above our heads the light went on in Marco's bedroom and I heard him say, "What the hell is this?"

Zoe took my bloody hand and yanked me into a shadow of the house. We heard someone step out onto the narrow balcony. "I don't see anyone, Marco." It was a woman's voice. "Maybe you should call the police."

The lady stepped back inside and Zoe and I dashed toward the darkness of the formal gardens. I tripped over a potted plant and went sprawling. I had stopped crying for a moment, but I started up again in a big way. This was just too hard. Zoe came back for me. "You can make it, Jonno," she told me. And she pulled me to my feet somehow and held on to my hand and led me into the darkness.

We got lost in the formal gardens and couldn't find the grape arbor or the Rodin. Everything was starting to go wrong.

"Give me the flashlight," she said.

"Oh, shit," I answered.

It was so dark I couldn't even see her face, though she was standing right next to me.

"*Where's the flashlight, Jonno?*"

"Look, Zoe, I heard Marco coming up the stairs and I sort of panicked."

"You left the flashlight in the room?"

"The whole book bag," I told her miserably. "Everything."

She was silent a second. I thought maybe she was going to leave me there in the dark. Then she said, "We won't worry about it now. Come on, let's get out of here."

She took my hand and eventually she was able to find the Rodin, and from that point I was able to find the hole. We crawled back through to our side of the hedge, and I managed to cut myself a few more times on some low hanging branches because I was too scared and exhausted to watch where I was going. Zoe kept me moving. We climbed up the oak tree to my bedroom and then she led me to her room where she got me undressed and into her bathtub, carefully pressing the washrag against all my scratches and cuts.

There was so much blood Zoe got undressed too so she wouldn't ruin her clothes.

"They're just superficial cuts, Jonno. You're going to be all right," she kept saying, and her voice was so soothing I finally stopped crying.

"Look, I'm bleeding too," she told me. She had a shallow cut on her arm, and she put it right next to a cut on my cheek so our blood would intermingle. She told me we were now blood brother and blood sister. Sangor and Sangor. But we were that already, I suppose.

When the bleeding stopped she led me to her bed and the pleasures therein, but I didn't enjoy it too much. Not that night. I kept visualizing the manila envelope on Marco Mallory's bed and I knew I had started something that could not be stopped.

It was my first taste of the bitter knowledge that some things you did lasted forever and could not be taken back. I mark my emergence into adulthood from that moment, and it was all pretty much downhill from there.

30

It was summer and I was supposed to be having a good time—long languid days around the swimming pool and riding my bicycle around the neighborhood, that sort of thing. But I was worried. I kept hearing seven dangling words: "Maybe you should call the police, Marco."

But *had* he? That was the question. I had grown up watching shows like "Dragnet" and I knew the police had uncanny means of zeroing in upon the guilty. At this very moment, the green book bag could be in some gleaming laboratory with a team of scientists examining every fiber. I kept thinking about reform school. I just hoped they would put Zoe and me in the same cell.

My days were uneasy, my nights a torment of tossed sheets not even Zoe's occasional presence could ease. I waited day after day for something terrible to happen. I remember one day Rags played hooky from work and took me to the beach in his new Mustang convertible (he had wrecked the MG a while ago), and all of a sudden a cop started coming after us on the Pacific Coast Highway. I nearly had a heart attack. But it turned out it was only Rags's speeding, going seventy in a forty-five-mile-an-hour zone. It was his fifth speeding ticket that year, and Dad was giving a lot of money to various police charities to keep Rags on the road.

"You look white as a ghost," said Rags when the cop was gone. This was the first time I had gone anywhere with him in months and I was probably not great company.

"Just go a little slower, okay?" I said grumpily. Rags grinned at me through weird psychedelic sunglasses. It was a good thing the cop hadn't searched his trunk because there was half a kilo of Panama Red where the spare tire should have been. Rags was going through a fairly wild period, wrecking cars every six months, and selling dope to all of Dad's racier clients at the agency. My whole family was turning into outlaws.

Then there was Carl. Carl was trying to make a bomb to blow up an army induction center that was sending American soldiers to Vietnam. He had all kinds of apparatus set up in his closet, flasks and glass tubing and strange things with wires coming out the sides. Probably it was a good thing Carl was not such a hot chemist. I mean, he was a genius when it came to philosophy, but he couldn't do a thing with his hands. So he never got anything to explode.

A few days after I left the blackmail note on Marco Mallory's bed, Carl came over to me in the living room. I had been practicing the piano, which was about the only thing that made me forget reform school and the cops who might be ringing our doorbell any moment. When Carl came down from upstairs, I was going through the Hanon exercises, the whole book. Now the top speed for these exercises is to make a quarter note equal to 120 on the metronome, but I had set my metronome to 150 and I was going like a bat out of hell. Even at normal speed Hanon starts sounding pretty demented when you're doing things like chromatic runs in opposite directions, but at the speed I was playing, it really sounded insane.

"Jonno! For chrissake, stop! You're driving me nuts! I can't read, I can't do anything!" Carl cried.

I stopped playing and sat on the bench while the metronome kept ticking like a clock gone berserk. Carl came over and picked it up with a thoughtful expression on his face. "Do you think something like this could be turned on at a distance?" he wondered. "Say from a hundred yards away?"

I shook my head. I was at an age where it was beginning to bother me how nuts my family had become. Carl picked up the metronome, examined it from every angle and then put it back on the piano with a sigh. "I guess not," he said. "And the thing is, I really need some sort of timer. It's the only thing hanging me up."

About a month before, every alarm clock in the house had mysteriously disappeared, and I suddenly had a very good idea where they had gone. I didn't say anything though. I had enough troubles of my own. Carl was looking at me sharply.

"You know, you look like shit, Jonno. How did you get all cut up?"

"I fell from a tree," I told him.

He continued to stare at me. "Look, why don't you come up to my room. I want to talk with you," he said after a moment.

I closed the piano and followed Carl upstairs. Carl's room was next to mine and it was always a real mess. There were stacks of books and old copies of the *New Republic* and the *Progressive* piled high on every surface. The room smelled awful from overflowing ashtrays and pipe smoke since Carl hated fresh air and never opened his windows.

He filled a meerschaum pipe with Balkan-Sobranie tobacco and sent pungent clouds of smoke billowing in my direction. As for me, at the age of twelve I was into Lucky Strikes in the small packages with the red bull's-eye on the front. So I lit a Lucky and pretty soon Carl's bedroom was so thick we could barely breathe.

"So what's going on?" he asked.

"Whad'ya mean what's going on?"

"Jonno, don't shit me. *Something's* up with you and Zoe. I heard you two climb back in your window after midnight the other night and you were crying. I mean, don't tell me if it's none of my business, but somehow I have the feeling you're in some kind of deep trouble. Am I right or am I wrong?"

Carl stared at me through his glasses in his very owlish way, and I ended up telling him everything. About the photographs, at least, and the blackmail—not about Zoe and me. The suspense of waiting to be arrested was just too much. I had to tell someone or go nuts. And my brother Carl was the kind of person you told things to. He puffed on his pipe and listened carefully. I found myself feeling extremely relieved to pass on my great secret and let him decide what to do with it. From the expression on his face, he was surprised, but not entirely shocked.

"So when's Marco supposed to come up with the money?" he asked finally.

"This Saturday night. Oh, Christ, and that's only three days from now!" I moaned. "God, I'm fucked. Absolutely totally fucked!"

"You're letting yourself get carried away, Jonno. Where does Marco deliver the cash?"

"You know that little park at the top of Coldwater and Mulholland? There's a big tree and a picnic table right by it. He's supposed to leave the whole thing, sixty grand in used twenty-dollar bills, in a garbage bag beneath the picnic table at midnight."

"And how does he get the negatives?"

"They'll be waiting for him at the same spot, in an envelope beneath the table."

"So what keeps him from just taking the negatives and keeping his money?"

"In the blackmail note we mentioned there would be a sniper with a high-powered rifle keeping him in the crosshairs at every moment. If he tries to double-cross us, he doesn't get out of there alive."

Carl grinned. "A sniper at *night*?"

I shrugged. Actually, this had been one of my small contributions to Zoe's plan. "He has a special infrared sight, you see. I saw it in a movie once."

Carl shook his head. "Hmm, I don't know about that part. But go on. What are you threatening if he just doesn't show up?"

"The pictures will be mailed out to all the scandal sheets. Particularly the ones where Gretchen's giving it to him up the ass. It'll ruin him. I mean, Marco will never be able to swing down from a chandelier and rescue some virgin again."

"But if these pictures are sent around, it'll hurt Michelle almost as much as Marco. Doesn't Zoe care about that part?"

"She says it serves her mother right for being such a slut. I don't know, Carl. It all seems pretty crazy. And after I left that damn book bag in his bedroom, I'm hoping we can just forget the whole thing."

"What was in the book bag?"

"Only the flashlight."

"Zoe didn't have her name on the bag? Anything like that?"

"No, but chrissake Carl, the flashlight has our fingerprints all over it. And the book bag. I mean the cops these days, they have these incredibly sophisticated machines, they can probably analyze the fibers and pick up the oils from our skin or something. And maybe from the oils they can tell what we look like and where we live, even what school we go to."

Carl was smiling. "Don't let them fool you, kid. The cops only want you to *believe* they can do all that shit, it's how they keep the proletariat in line, you see. But it's all nonsense of course. Besides, Marco's not going to the cops. If he does, he'll have to say what the blackmail is all about and he can't afford that."

"So you think this is going to *work*?" I asked in surprise.

"Why not? Making money in this society is all a big con game anyway. Marco's con is that he's some kind of superhuman stud. The moment it gets around that he likes his sex up the old wazoo, well, the con is over and so is his career."

"But he's still a real good actor," I put in, because I was personally a very big fan of Marco Mallory. "What does his sex life have to do with anything?"

Carl smiled patiently. "Jonno, face it, the guy's not exactly Laurence Olivier. Marco's success depends on a very fragile aura of public perception. If you change that perception, the whole thing evaporates."

"But sixty thousand dollars!" I objected.

"He makes that much in two weeks. It's nothing to him," Carl said. "And frankly, I think Zoe should be commended for trying to spread the wealth around a bit. It's obscene, Jonno, how much some greedy bastards make in this society while other people are totally starving."

I was blown away. I had expected Carl to be shocked at our blackmail scheme. "So you think it's *okay* to do this?"

"From a moral standpoint? Damn right! Any way you can attack the system, the quicker it will fall. And when it goes, Jonno, it'll just keel over and die."

Carl went on about how corrupt the system was and how it had to be destroyed before the new order could come to pass. Then he got to specifics: "So what are you going to do with the cash?"

"The sixty grand? Fuck if *I* know. I mean, that's another crazy part of this whole deal. Even if we pull it off, what are we going to do? Put it in our piggy banks?"

"Zoe hasn't thought this aspect through, hm?"

"Carl, I don't think Zoe gives a shit about the money. I don't know how to put it. It's like she's proving something to herself, that she can pull this off. That she has power over people."

"You know, Jonno, money in itself is not evil. What's evil is the way people hoard it and do such selfish things with it. Sixty thousand dollars could do some real good in this world. I'll have to talk with Zoe."

"Oh, *God*, you can't do that! She'll kill me, Carl, I wasn't supposed to tell anyone about this."

"Relax," Carl said in his most calming manner. "I'll pretend I wrung it out of you. I'll take care of it, Jonno. I'm not putting Zoe down, but I can see you guys need me here."

I paced anxiously over to Carl's bedroom window and threw it open to a serene blue summer day that had nothing whatsoever to do with me. I used to love summer. Now I had a feeling of paradise lost. "I think I'm going to be the first kid ever to get ulcers," I complained.

Carl pulled the window shut. Maybe he was afraid some of our pipe and cigarette smoke would escape. "Jonno, I'm telling you, *relax*. Go play the piano or something."

So that's what I did, but I certainly couldn't relax. Things were getting crazier by the minute. And if it wasn't bad enough Carl was included in the deal, all of a sudden Rags was in as well. This was turning into a real Sangor family circus.

31

The reason Rags was brought in was because theoretically Rags was an adult. He was twenty-three years old and this meant he had access to some things that the rest of us did not. In particular, he could open bank accounts and invest our sixty thousand dollars in various clever ways.

I had a sense of intrigue going on behind my back. Carl went to Zoe's room almost directly after he had talked with me. He remained with her for nearly three hours, and I was so nervous I sat at the baby grand in the living room playing the entire book of Chopin preludes over and over again, starting with number one, Agitato in C Major, and ending with number 24, Allegro Appassionato in F. I got so I could play them at about twice their normal speed, and I bet poor Frédéric Chopin was turning over in his grave.

Then Zoe and Carl came out of her room. They had agreed upon what Carl described as a "long-term agenda." I think Zoe and Carl had somehow inherited my father's chromosomes for the grandiose, whereas I had been given only Corina Norman's sex drive. Zoe and Carl planned to pull off a little deal like we were doing with Marco Mallory every few months or so, finding a fresh victim

221

each time. They estimated we might rake in sixty grand or so from
each caper, and we would invest this money in various enterprises,
maybe even finance a movie or a rock album. Within five or six
years, we would have millions of dollars squirreled away, and then
we could split it up and do whatever we wanted.

The way they spoke, you would think this was going to be the
simplest thing in the world. Personally, I was of a more pessimistic
bent. My attitude was forget the grandiose and concentrate on
pleasures closer to home. I guess I've always been a very down-
to-earth guy. As far as I'm concerned, if you can't fuck it, or eat
it—why bother?

"So what if these investments go bust?" I asked, with a very
reasonable expression on my face. "I mean, sometimes people lose
money."

"Jonno, Jonno! Money is only an abstract thought," Carl patiently explained. "As long as you keep that in mind, you never
run any risk of losing it. How can you lose something that doesn't
exist?"

This stumped me. Carl was already spending his imaginary loot
in his mind, talking about how he might buy land in Oregon and
create a perfect community that would serve as a model for the
rest of the world. He was thinking big all right. He wanted to use
money "as a seed that would eventually destroy itself, and then
we could all live in a world without money." I didn't know what
the hell he was talking about, but I soon learned that Rags was
somehow the key to all this glory. Rags could set up holding and
umbrella companies. He could diversify and multiply and all kinds
of things. And he could do all this because he was twenty-three
years old.

I hardly knew what to say. After all, Carl and Zoe were older
than I was and they were both very brainy, whereas I was more
your average sex-maniac kid. Still, there seemed a very basic flaw
in their thinking. Rags might have been twenty-three years old in
a literal sense, at least his body had gone spinning around the sun
twenty-three times, but mentally it was an entirely different matter. I think somewhere around the tenth solar revolution Rags's
brain had jumped ship. I mean, Rags was really goofy.

You have to picture the way Rags was at this time. In 1968, a
kind of Sergeant Pepper look had settled upon L.A., but Rags took

his fashion statement a few steps further. He wore all kinds of weird dark glasses all the time. One pair had pink frames shaped like hearts, another had eyeballs painted on the lenses, and there was one where the frames glowed in iridescent colors, powered by a little battery he kept in his pocket.

At a time when everybody was growing their hair long, Rags kept his tightly cropped. He would dress in different styles, sometimes for a month at a time. For a while, he went around like a jockey, complete with a little cap on his head and tight jodhpurs, bright shirt, and a number seven on his back. Then the next month he would become an Indian or a spaceman, and once he even started going around in drag as Zsa Zsa Gabor, but Dad came home for a few days and put a stop to that in a hurry. The psychedelic era of the late sixties had freed Rags to be a real freak.

And that was just the way he dressed. I've already mentioned how he was wrecking expensive sports cars, about one every six months. It's amazing he never got killed. I guess this was shortly before Albert seduced him and brought him out of the closet because Rags was still dating girls at the time. He was not reluctant to use his family name with aspiring actresses who thought it wouldn't be a bad idea to cozy up to the son of Alexander Sangor. I don't think Rags wanted to score in a sexual way. He just wanted pretty women around him so he could make a good impression. And he was running around town like crazy going to all the wild places, the Daisy, the Whiskey A Go Go, dropping acid and wrecking cars and usually showing up for work the next day sometime in the early afternoon.

A real happy-go-lucky guy. One of the girls broke her neck in one of his auto wrecks and she nearly died. Rags and the girl were stoned on Quaaludes and they missed a curve on Mulholland and drove his MG through a fence right into someone's swimming pool. This was when Dad bought him the Mustang convertible, mistakenly thinking an American car might slow him down.

So this was Rags in 1968, the person Carl and Zoe planned to trust as our banker. To complete the picture, he still had the really nerdy chuckle he had developed as a little kid when my mother Corina Norman used to torment him. I mean, Rags would wreck a car, nearly kill some poor girl, and then stand before you dressed as a spaceman laughing his goofy laugh. It was enough to drive you insane. Rags just didn't take anything seriously. I loved him, but it was getting so I could only take him in very brief doses.

Rags came home in the late afternoon while I was in the pool swimming laps. I had decided I was too scrawny and needed to build myself up to face the hard life awaiting me in reform school. I was on lap sixty-seven when I got tired and turned over to float on my back, and that's when I saw Carl, Zoe, and Rags on the roof of our house smoking a big waterpipe. I had a feeling they should leave the dope alone right then. I mean, these were people whose imaginations really did not need any more stimulation. I drifted to the shallow end and tried to hear what they were saying, but the words did not carry nearly as far as the faint aroma of marijuana. I saw Rags nod a few times rather somberly. To my surprise, he wasn't laughing.

Later that night I was lying in bed with a book on my stomach, just about to turn off the light when Rags came into my room without knocking. He plopped down on the bed near my feet. He was unshaved and wearing Superman pajamas and Arabian slippers that curled up at the toe. I have no idea where he managed to find outfits like these. He looked a real mess. His face was pale, bloated, fish-like. I was shocked to see him so close up in the unflattering wash of my reading lamp. A person can burn the candle at both ends, but a day comes when all of a sudden the drugs and excess and late nights begin to show.

"So what'cha doin'?" he asked.

"What does it look like I'm doing? I'm reading a book."

I was in an irritable mood. Rags didn't help when he grabbed the book out of my hands, examined the title and said, "Jesus H. Christ. This is the shit Zoe has you doing, I guess."

Actually, it was a standard music textbook, *Harmony* by Walter Piston, that Zoe had given to me for Valentine's Day. She assured me I'd be totally lost in later life unless I had the skill to instantly arrange four-part harmonies. Rags thumbed through the book with a disgusted expression on his face and then tossed it back on my bed.

"Why the hell does Zoe make you do this shit?"

"Look, Rags, music theory is the one perfect thing in a *very* goddamn imperfect universe," I assured him, quoting Zoe verbatim. "I mean, face it, you probably don't even know what the hell key you're in half the time."

Rags shook his head. "*Key* I'm in? What the hell are you talking about?"

"Everyone has their own natural key. I'm B-flat, for instance," I said. And then I blushed and added: "Zoe's C Minor, which is very rare."

Rags shook his head mournfully. "So how do you know what key you're in, for chrissake?"

I didn't tell him that what you do is smoke a little hashish and then stand naked in a bathtub with tile walls all around and chant the mystic syllable *om* while someone with a tuning fork puts his or her ear to your bare stomach. At least, this is how Zoe and I had done it. I told Rags only that you had to study music diligently for a very long time.

He kept shaking his head and saying, "Jesus!" I could tell he wanted something from me, but I tried to ignore him, burying myself back in my textbook. Rags picked up a comic book from my collection of pre-Zoe days and he began to read it, all slouched over sitting on the foot of my bed.

"You know, it really kills me Donald Duck doesn't wear any pants," he said finally, apparently his big thought for the evening. "I mean, where's his goddamn duck dick, for chrissake?"

"Look, Rags, this is fascinating and all, but I think I'm going to have an early night here. . . ."

"Yeah," he said aimlessly, tossing the comic to the floor. "I guess so."

But Rags didn't stand up from my bed. He wasn't going anyplace. He just sat there with his terrible posture, slouching over, and staring gloomily at the rug. I hated feeling so cold about him, but God, what a dork!

"And besides Donald Duck, something else that *really* kills me is Zoe," he said finally. "I mean, is she for real about this Marco Mallory business or what?"

"Of course she's for real," I said defensively. And then I suddenly had a very good idea. "Look, Rags, why don't you just tell Zoe the whole thing's impossible. You can make up some reason you can't get involved. Tell her we're all going to end up in jail if we go through with this. And why the hell do kids like us need money anyway? You can tell her, Rags," I almost pleaded. "Maybe she'll listen to you. I mean, you're an adult, kind of."

Rags didn't look at me. He seemed to slouch over so low his chest was nearly touching his knees. I'm not sure I had ever seen him depressed before.

"Yeah," he said. "It's a bitch all right."

I was beginning to feel hopeful. If Rags refused to help invest the money, maybe Zoe and Carl would forget the whole thing.

"Come on, Rags. You *gotta* talk with her," I said, pushing my book off the bed and moving closer to him. But then I got a shock. Rags was crying, and I couldn't remember ever seeing him cry before.

"Oh, man, I'm really in for it this time. I *really* fucked up," he said.

He put his head against my shoulder and I could feel the wetness of his tears going through my T-shirt as well as the scratchy stubble of his unshaved chin. I was becoming alarmed. "What's wrong?" I asked.

"What's *wrong?* I'll tell you what's wrong. I'm about to get fired from the agency."

"Come on! How the hell could you get fired from the agency? I mean, Dad owns the damn place, and anyway, he's in Yugoslavia."

"Yeah, but he's going to fire me as soon as he comes back. And that's not all. He's going to kick me out of the goddamn house and then where the hell am I going to be? I mean, it's not like I know how to support myself or anything."

"But what did you *do*, Rags? You wreck another car or what?"

He gave me a very furtive look. "I stole money from the office. About three grand from petty cash, and then I put another ten grand or so on the company American Express card."

"Jeez, that's terrible," I said. "But you know Dad'll forgive you. He always does. He'll just make you promise not to do it again."

Rags gave a very melodramatic sigh. "Yeah, but that's the thing, you see. This isn't the first time. He already made me promise. Last time he said if I ever did it again, he'd have to fire me and give me the big boot into the cold world. He said he wouldn't have any other choice. Everybody else at the office, they know about it, you see. Dad said the morale in the place would get too bad unless he took action."

I was quiet for a moment. All of us kids had gotten away with some serious shit, but I had a sense Rags might be right. If Dad thought his business was threatened, he would be ruthless.

"So how many times did you steal?" I asked.

"I don't know. Three times. Maybe four."

"But *why* Rags? Why did you do it?"

"Look, how the hell do *I* know why I do anything?" he said irritably. "I just *do* things, okay? So don't give me a hard time, Jonno. You're just a little kid and you don't realize how much money you need out there. If you're going to make an impression, I mean. You take people out to dinner and to clubs and stuff, and you gotta be able to pick up the check. Otherwise they won't like you anymore. You dig what I'm telling you, Jonno?"

I was flabbergasted. I had never taken anyone to dinner or a club, but this didn't quite seem right.

"Can't you go dutch or something?" I asked. "Or maybe if you're broke, just go to someone's house and watch TV?"

He laughed his goofy nerdy laugh, the first time I had heard it that night.

"I'm serious," I said. "And hell, why not let the other people pick up the check sometimes?"

"Not if your name is Sangor!" Rags cried with a sudden anguish that surprised me. "When your father is Alexander Sangor *you* gotta be the one that pays! Don't you understand? They hate us, Jonno. They're envious as hell. But you can have the whole world sucking up to you as long as you can pick up the goddamn check." Rags collapsed back onto the foot of my bed. "And for that you need goddamn money," he told me in a toneless voice. "And Dad only pays me a goddamn three hundred and fifty bucks a week."

I really didn't know what to say. Frankly, three hundred and fifty dollars a week seemed a lot of money for an office boy who never did any work and lived at home in Coldwater Canyon, all expenses paid. But I was only twelve, so what did I know?

"So you see, I gotta do this," Rags said.

"Gotta do what?"

"This blackmail thing. I mean, it's my last chance. It'll mean I can pay back the petty cash before Dad returns, and maybe even take care of the American Express bill. Otherwise, I'm totally fucked."

I felt terrible. For a moment I had imagined Rags was going to help me get out of this whole blackmail nightmare, but now I saw it was the other way around. I was the one who had to help Rags.

"So what I wanted to ask you, Jonno, is, don't let Zoe fink out on me, okay?"

"She's not going to fink out on you," I told him unhappily. "Zoe never finks out on anybody."

"You mean that? I thought maybe she might decide to include me out. She might think I'm not up to my end—but I am, I swear to God. I won't let you guys down. As a matter of fact, I have all kinds of ideas about investing."

Rags wiped the tears from his eyes and started talking a mile a minute about some movie studio that was about to go public, and how we could get in on the ground floor of a really killer deal. I started to get a very big headache just listening to him, and it depressed me so much I wanted to bury my head under the pillow and totally disappear from the human race. What I did finally was yawn and say I was really zonked and had to get some sleep. Rags turned out the lights, and when we were both in the dark he stood waiting by the door.

"Look, I need that money so bad I'd just about kill for it, I swear to God," he said. "You can't let me down, Jonno. You, Zoe, Carl, and those dirty pictures are my salvation."

I didn't say anything. I just lay there in the dark.

"It's not only paying Dad back," he said. "With money of my own, I could tell people to fuck off. Don't you understand? I'm tired of being the big clown, stupid old Rags, everybody's flunky. You're just a kid, Jonno, but I know you're incredibly smart and you can understand these things."

"I'm not smart," I assured him.

"Sure, you are. You think Zoe and Carl have all the smarts in this family, but that's not true. You're better than all of us. To tell the truth, I even love to hear you play the goddamn piano." Rags was silent and for a moment in the darkness I thought he had left my bedroom. Then he said softly, "I love you, Jonno." I didn't answer and finally I heard him leave.

I cried myself to sleep.

32

I trust you are beginning to get a full and torrid picture of my wacky family: My beautiful sister Zoe, with her advanced ideas about incest and larceny. My revolutionary brother Carl, making bombs in the closet. My goofy brother Rags, wrecking sports cars and stealing from the company till. Me, of course, the only sane person anywhere in sight. And last of all, David. Before I can go any further and relate the great blackmail fiasco that was going to overtake our lives, I must explain a few things about my least favorite brother.

On the surface, I guess David was what the world might consider "normal," particularly in comparison to the rest of us. David liked football and baseball and all-American things. He wasn't the sort to smoke dope, or fall in love with his sister, or overthrow the government, or wear weird sunglasses. This was a guy who at the age of sixteen was already thinking ahead to where he might go to college and what he was going to do for a living.

Poor David. He lusted after normalcy. He hated how eccentric the rest of us were. Maybe he never got over being illegitimate and knowing his mother was only Dad's secret mistress, and that there was another family, a legitimate family, far away in California.

Eventually, of course, Dad married Michelle and brought Zoe and David to America, but for David the damage had already been done. He grew up believing himself to be an outcast and wishing fiercely to be utterly respectable and just like everybody else.

I have to stretch my imagination to understand David, because he was so unlike me and Carl and Rags and Zoe. Being respectable had no attraction for the rest of us. To tell the truth, I'm not sure we even knew what respectable meant. We grew up on our small island of wealth with no real reference point to the outside world. I think the very rich have this in common with the very poor: They do whatever they want and don't particularly care what the neighbors have to say about it. Probably this is why, in my own life, I have passed with so little culture shock back and forth between mansions and slums. There is only one social group I've personally had trouble relating to, and unfortunately it is this social group to which David aspired: the middle class.

So at school, David joined the football team and dressed and talked like everybody else, and liked the same music and movies and cars. He was desperate to fit in, I guess. Too desperate, because he tried too hard and it was all wrong, just some strange fantasy in his head, and the other kids at school sensed it was wrong and he was very unpopular as a result.

What David didn't understand was that normal kids in Southern California—kids who really did fit in—were extremely laid back. But David was all hyped up. He was bossy, he was a braggart, he even took politics too far, mistakenly believing a good all-American boy should be rabidly right wing. The Harvard School was an extremely Republican sort of place, but David went beyond even the usual right-wing hysteria of the time. I mean, for David, Richard Nixon was a flaming liberal. He started to write letters to the school newspaper about how the United Nations was a communist front, and at one point he even took up a collection to help support the twilight of white supremacy in Rhodesia, the African nation which was soon to become Zimbabwe.

It was pretty crazy, and you can imagine the dinner-table conversations between David and Carl. It kept us all on our toes to have both a neo-Nazi and a Marxist revolutionary in our midst, and there were times I thought David and Carl were about to attack each other with their knives and forks. Basically, David had only one friend in the entire world: our maid, Gretchen.

It was a very bizarre relationship, Gretchen and David. I've already mentioned how David spoke German and how Gretchen began to favor him at mealtimes, making him special apple strudels and things like that. They shared something else as well. Coming from East Germany and escaping over the Berlin Wall, Gretchen was every bit as virulently anticommunist as David. I guess this gave them a lot to talk about. But I think the main thing that drew them together was the fact that she was lonely too, disliked in our household just as David was. David started disappearing into Gretchen's living quarters off the kitchen for long stretches at a time. Carl, Rags, and I thought this was pretty funny and of course we speculated endlessly about what they were up to in her room.

"They *have* to be fucking," Rags declared.

"Of course they're fucking," Carl agreed. "It's typical upper-class decadence. Young man takes advantage of the serving girl. It's terrible this kind of exploitation still goes on."

Personally, I wasn't so sure David was exploiting Gretchen. I suspected it was the other way around. Sometimes I would see David coming out of Gretchen's room and he would look really miserable, and I had a notion that Gretchen had figured out some way to control him for her own purposes. I guess she was out to better her position in the world, and maybe she thought it was to her advantage to have some sort of liaison with the master's son.

Of course, I'm only speculating. Gretchen was dark and witchy and cunningly seductive in her own way. Her sex appeal was like something secretive buried beneath a rock. It didn't appeal to me, but still, she had managed to seduce Marco Mallory, and even Michelle. So why not David?

A few days after I had left the blackmail note in Marco Mallory's bedroom, I walked into my bedroom and I was surprised to find David going through my drawers. He looked startled and guilty.

"What the hell are you doing?" I cried. I didn't like him being in my room and I was about to start slugging.

"Calm down. Honest, this isn't what it looks like. I'm . . . well, to tell the truth, I'm looking for a little mari-gucci," he said nervously. "I thought you might have a stash somewhere."

"Mari-*gucci*?" I demanded. No one half-way cool ever called it that. "For chrissake, you don't even smoke the stuff, David."

"Sure I do," he told me. "I just keep a low profile about it, that's all. Look, Jonno, I would have asked you but I didn't know you were home and quite honestly I was having an attack."

"An *attack*?"

"You know. For a fix."

I laughed. The thought of David smoking dope was ridiculous enough, but he had all the terminology wrong as well. I was about to call him a liar, but then I had a fun idea.

"Well, okay. Let's get stoned," I suggested. "I mean, you should have told me you were an addict, David. I would have helped you out before."

"You mean, get stoned right now?"

"Of course, right now. If you need a fix, David, hell, probably you can't wait another second more."

I thought he would back down and maybe tell me what it was he was really looking for in my drawers, but to my surprise he said nervously, "Well, okay."

"So do you want to shoot up or smoke the stuff?" I asked.

"Well, I don't know. What do *you* usually do?"

I got my stash out from between my mattress and box spring and I took David out on the roof and showed him just exactly how us hippie degenerates turned on. I rolled us a very fat joint of primo Panama Red. David tried to take a puff without inhaling, but I showed him how to suck the smoke down into his lungs and keep it there for a while. It seemed very bizarre doing this with David. He coughed and sputtered, but I offered him another puff and then another, and he went along with it. A big four-engine airplane droned overhead flying toward the ocean. David looked up into the sky and said, "Wow. I never heard an airplane so loud before. I feel a little . . . weird."

"Maybe you've had an overdose," I said.

"My God! You think so?"

"It happens all the time," I assured him. "Does your mouth feel dry?"

"Oh, yes. Is that a sign . . ."

"Yeah, definitely an overdose," I said. "But you'll probably snap out of it in a few weeks."

David started to shiver although it was about ninety degrees outside. He told me he didn't feel so well and maybe he'd better go to his room and lie down. I had to give him a steadying hand to get him back inside the window from the roof.

"You sure you don't want to smoke a little more?" I asked.

His eyes looked at me in sheer terror. He left my room like he couldn't get away fast enough. I laughed and then I decided to follow him, just for the hell of it. I peered out into the hall in time to see him going down the stairs. After a moment, I followed. When I reached the bottom of the stairs, there was no sign of David, but I had a pretty good idea where he had gone. I tiptoed through the empty dining room and stopped by the closed door to the kitchen. I could hear David and Gretchen talking on the other side.

"Oh, you foolish boy, you smell of drugs!" she was saying.

"I had to do it. Jonno came in just while I was going through his stuff. What was I supposed to tell him?"

"Did you find anything?"

"No."

"You are certain of this, David? You are not holding back?"

"No, no! I promise you. Why would I hold back?"

I heard the two of them move from the kitchen into Gretchen's room. My curiosity had been aroused in a big way and I decided to do a little more spying. So I went back through the dining room into the living room and walked out one of the sliding glass doors to the backyard. As soon as I got around the house toward Gretchen's bedroom window, I crept into the flower beds and crawled closer on my hands and knees until I was hidden below her window sill. The window was open a crack, but I was able to hear only fragments of conversation.

"It is your sister who will have them," I heard Gretchen say. "This is where you must look."

David muttered something I couldn't make out. And then I heard his voice, loud and clear: "Why should I get involved with this anyway? It doesn't have a thing to do with me."

"Oh, you will do this for me, my little one. You will do this because I tell you to. . . ."

"I won't!"

"Oh, yes you will! Otherwise, I will be forced to be very unkind
to you, David. *Very* unkind."

I didn't hear anything for a while. It blew my mind to hear
Gretchen ordering him about. I couldn't imagine why David put
up with it. I stayed kneeling on the ground for a long time wishing
they would keep talking. Then I started hearing strange sounds,
little gasps of pain. After this went on for a while, I screwed up
my courage to take a peek. The curtains were drawn but I was
able to see through a crack of the material. I was confronted by
about the strangest sight I had ever seen.

Gretchen was naked except for black leather boots and a metal
chain around her waist. David had his pants pulled down and he
was kneeling on the bed with his ass up in the air and Gretchen
was whipping him with a small leather riding crop. Each time she
hit, David gave out little gasps of pleasure and pain.

I could hardly believe my eyes. I couldn't bear to watch for very
long, and I crept away along the flower bed and back inside the
sliding glass door. I went looking for Zoe and found her working
in her darkroom. I was full of big news.

"Listen, we gotta call this whole thing off. Gretchen knows
everything. She's told David to search through your things. I'm
sure she's looking for the blackmail negatives."

I told Zoe all about what happened and she listened without any
great show of interest while continuing to examine a contact sheet
through a magnifying glass.

"Well, I expected this, of course," she said unconcerned. "But
don't worry, Jonno. The negatives are hidden where no one will
find them."

"But she *knows*!" I cried. "And we can't go through with this
now!"

Zoe at last put down her contact sheet and looked at me. "Jonno,
she only suspects. Obviously, she is on intimate terms with Marco,
we've known that from the beginning. And obviously, he's told her
about the blackmail note. And more obviously still, she knows we
live next door and that I have a darkroom. Ergo, we are the logical
suspects and Marco has asked her to keep an eye on us."

"But if she knows, if she even suspects . . ."

"She can't do a thing," Zoe interrupted. "And neither can Marco.
We simply hold all the cards."

"But Zoe . . ."

"My dear, you worry too much. I have this all under control. You'll just have to trust me," she said. And Zoe drew me closer to her in the confined space of the darkroom and she kissed my lips.

So I shut up. I kept looking for ways out, but I needed Zoe, maybe just like David needed Gretchen. I guess this was a household of strange obsessions and the blackmail scheme seemed to move forward with a life of its own.

You can see how it was: me and my siblings, each of us involved for our separate reasons. We were crazy, we knew no limits. Being rich kids I guess we thought we could have anything we wanted and never pay the consequences. But we were poised on the edge of disaster, and when the disaster came, it was worse than I imagined.

33

I've always believed I would have had an easier childhood if I had grown up someplace where there weren't a lot of trees around. Trees have been my downfall again and again, going up and down them in my own monkey-like fashion to various forbidden adventures I would have done better to avoid. But of all the trees in this big green world, there is one tree above all others I should never have climbed: a tall, majestic oak with gnarly old limbs that stood at the very top of Coldwater Canyon, and from whose upper branches you could see an endless panorama of Los Angeles spread out to the west, and the flat sprawl of the San Fernando Valley to the east.

This was the mother of all oak trees, my personal Tree of Knowledge, and it grew in the small park off Mulholland Drive above the third picnic table to the left of the entrance. It was my job to climb to the very top branches of this monstrous beauty on the Saturday night of our blackmail caper, wait for Marco Mallory to arrive with sixty thousand dollars in used twenty-dollar bills in a plastic garbage bag, and then climb down and retrieve the money when the coast was clear.

I was unable to settle down to anything all day Saturday. Rags,

236

Carl, Zoe, and I had agreed to meet in my bedroom at ten o'clock
that night. Gretchen always disappeared into her room off the
kitchen before nine. She had her own television and sitting room,
and maybe a collection of shrunken heads to stare at for all I knew.
About nine-thirty I decided to check on her. I went downstairs to
get a glass of ice water. The kitchen was dark and there was a
yellow band of light creeping out from the bottom of her door. I
was more worried about David, who was lounging in the living
room watching television and eating chocolate ice cream out of the
carton. David and Rags were the only ones in our family who had
any interest in TV, but they never watched together.

David didn't even glance my way as I walked past him to the
kitchen and back. He looked like a drugged-out zombie sucking
on his spoon, washed in the reflected light and inane noise of a
cop show, tense music and cars squealing around, and lots of shots
being fired. I hoped the show would keep David occupied so he
wouldn't realize that the rest of us had disappeared.

I was nervous as could be. My bedside clock ticking down from
twenty of ten to ten o'clock seemed to take a couple of hours. I
kept going to the bathroom and thinking I might throw up. Then
Carl drifted into my room, and in a moment Zoe and Rags. We
were all dressed in black, and anyone just looking at us would
know we were up to no good.

There's a scene in the play of *Peter Pan* where all the kids
disappear out of the nursery window, flying into the night on their
journey to never-never land. That's pretty much what I felt like
as I held open the window for Zoe, Carl, and Rags, and then finally
climbed down to the ground myself. We moved silently in single
file through the trees to the northernmost edge of our property to
where there was a rusty iron gate that was nearly overgrown with
brush and weeds. We slipped out the gate into the open countryside and began to climb the twisty old horse trail toward the top
of the hill.

It was a velvety night. There was a crescent moon in the sky
and fat twinkly stars and a smell of wild mustard and the pungent
brush that grows on the dry California hills. The trail snaked its
way past backyards and tennis courts and even past someone's
secret marijuana patch. We didn't want anyone later to remember
seeing us on this trail so there were places we crawled on our

hands and knees to avoid the rear windows of houses, even though they probably couldn't see us in the dark. It felt like we were kids playing cops and robbers, all a big game. I nearly had a bad accident because I was paying attention to the crack of Zoe's ass in her tight jeans ahead of me instead of to the path. I tumbled down into a thorny bush and gave a sharp cry of pain.

"Quiet back there," Rags said. He was having lots of fun playing commando. Carl and Zoe had to haul me out of the bush and they had some stern words for me, how I should pay more attention. They were all really getting into the big adrenaline rush of a mock-military operation.

We kept moving up the trail until we came to Mulholland Drive. We hid in the bushes until a line of cars passed and then when it was quiet we heard two people screwing in a van parked about fifty feet away. Mulholland Drive is a real lover's lane. It was nuts. I mean, they were really going at it, huffing and puffing and moaning into the night. Rags was smirking like crazy. For me it added just one more ridiculous touch to the whole event.

When we couldn't see any headlights coming up the road, we made a dash to the other side and then made our way cautiously to the park near where Coldwater and Mulholland intersected. It was a few minutes past eleven o'clock, nearly an hour until the drop. We hid in the brush and tried to see if Marco had set up any kind of ambush for us. Down the road the girl in the van had an orgasm that probably woke up half of Hollywood.

"I think the coast is clear," Carl whispered.

"It's up to you now, Jonno," Zoe said. I felt her give me a look that seemed to burn through the darkness. She couldn't kiss me because there were others around, but she squeezed my hand as she handed me the manila envelope that contained the negatives we were going to exchange for money.

"Too much, dude," said Rags, putting a hand on my shoulder.

"Break a leg," said Carl.

So it was up to me. It didn't seem fair, since I was the only one who thought this was a lousy idea and we would all be better off home in bed. But life isn't fair. I'd discovered that a long time ago.

Zoe, Carl, and Rags spread out around the perimeter of the park, each of them finding a separate hiding place. I walked by myself into the tall trees, spooked by every shadow, expecting a hand on my shoulder or a knife in my back at any moment. The trees cast weird nighttime shadows over the ground. I found the picnic table and put the manila envelope on the ground underneath, glad to be rid of it. Then I looked toward the sky.

The great oak tree had wide branches that spiraled upward almost like a staircase. It seemed to invite me for a climb into the dark heavens. So I did it. I climbed up that Tree of Knowledge all the way to the very top. And then I waited for something to happen.

The funny thing was, I loved it up there. I was high above all the troubles of the world. I couldn't see Zoe or Rags or Carl. I couldn't even see the picnic table below me where the money would be left. Up in the high branches, there was an erratic breeze blowing that sent me swaying gently to and fro.

Far below me, spread at my feet, there were millions of twinkly lights and I had a kind of mystical thought as I gazed upon the distant city: I tried to imagine how many people were fucking at that exact moment in all the little houses with all the twinkly lights. There must have been millions of people out there—young people, old people, fat and thin, lovely, and not so lovely—all of them sticking it in and out and getting it on. It was a stupendous image and I would never be able to look out upon Los Angeles at night in quite the same way again. It dwarfed my own self-importance somehow, and made my own little drama with Zoe seem very small. We were just one small drop of sperm in the great ocean of sex.

I got caught up in this mind-boggling thought and almost forgot what I was doing up there at the top of a tree. I looked at the radium dial of my wristwatch and saw it was five minutes past midnight. I felt a flood of relief. Marco simply wouldn't show up. Maybe he never took our dumb blackmail note seriously in the first place. I decided I would wait a few minutes and then climb down and pretend to be very disappointed.

But then I saw the headlights of a car coming up from Coldwater Canyon. The car crossed Mulholland and pulled into the entrance to the park. I heard a door open and close. My heart was pounding and I wished I had taken a pee earlier because suddenly I really had to go. A stiff breeze came up and my tree and I started swaying back and forth like we were on an amusement park ride. I held on for dear life.

I heard footsteps come to the base of the tree, and then the footsteps went away again. The car door opened and closed, the car started up, backed into the road and drove away, back toward where it had come, down Coldwater.

I waited. Zoe, Carl, and Rags each had a flashlight and they were supposed to signal me when the coast was clear. But the foliage was so dense I couldn't see the ground. It was like I was on another planet from everyone else. After five minutes I still didn't see a signal, but I decided to chance climbing down. Among other things, I *really* had to pee now.

So I made my way slowly down the staircase of branches, careful not to lose my footing in the dark. I swung down the last few feet, lowered myself to the picnic table and jumped to the ground.

And there it was, underneath the table where I had left the manila envelope: a plastic garbage bag with a wire tie around the top and a nice little fat bulge to it. It was like magic. I was grinning from ear to ear. It reminded me of when I was very little and I would leave a tooth under my pillow and Albert would play tooth fairy, exchanging my tooth for a crisp ten-dollar bill while I slept. This whole blackmail thing was turning out just like that.

I picked up the garbage bag and then everything started going wrong. A hand came out of the darkness, out of nowhere. It was a very strong grown-up hand, and it picked me up off the ground and held me dangling helplessly. I was about to scream, but another hand covered my mouth.

"Well, well, what do we have here? A little thief, I believe!" said a bass voice. It was Marco Mallory. I was so scared, my bladder let loose. I peed my pants. Marco carried me to the entrance of the park and in a moment a long dark limousine came gliding our way with the headlights turned off. He bundled me into the back seat, and the limousine took off on a ride I will never forget.

34

Marco Mallory turned on the ceiling light in the back of the limousine. He was rakishly handsome with wavy black hair and a face that seemed etched in granite. It was hard to believe a human being could be so handsome. He was studying me, the scared kid in his car. I remember thinking he had the kind of perfect nose you tend to see only on Greek statues. But right then, what impressed me most about Marco Mallory was that he was holding a small silver-plated revolver whose barrel was pointed about a quarter inch above the crown of my nose.

"You peed your pants," he remarked.

"Sorry," I told him. Actually, it was extremely embarrassing being in the presence of a world-famous movie star with a big dark stain around my zipper. "I had to go for the longest time, but I was stuck up that damn tree," I added. I didn't want him to think I was a retard.

The limo was carrying us down Coldwater Canyon. It was different from my father's Caddy. There was wood paneling and the softest leather I had ever sat on. This was my first ride in a Rolls-Royce. It was also the first time anyone had ever pointed a gun at me, and I was getting a little cross-eyed looking at it.

"So your name is Donno," he said. "I remember seeing you at a party once."

"Jonno," I corrected.

"And you like to take dirty pictures of people and then blackmail them. Is that your angle, kid?"

"Well, I don't *like* to do it," I told him. "But sure, that's my angle."

"And you want sixty grand? It's pretty damn ballsy of you, kid."

"Well, that's me," I said. "A real ballsy kid."

He laughed, a big booming masculine laugh that filled up the car. But the gun never wavered from the point above my nose. "No one will believe this," he said. "*No* one." Then, while he kept the gun very steady, he managed to open the manila envelope I had left under the picnic table. With his free hand he brought out a strip of negatives and held them up to the ceiling light. Marco was a very suave guy. He could do several things at once with astonishing grace.

"Well, well," he said. "So you think this is worth sixty grand?"

"Sure," I said. "It's what these pictures can do to your career that makes them so expensive."

He gave me a long hard look. "These are all the negatives? Every one?"

"Hey, we may rob, but we don't cheat," I said with bravado. And then I wanted to bite my tongue, because I didn't mean to use the word *we*. I also realized I should have pretended I had some negatives in reserve as a bargaining chip. Marco smiled but he didn't say anything.

The Rolls pulled up to a huge wrought-iron gate which began to swing open magically. I had never arrived at Casa Monte Carlo by the main entrance. This was definitely a more impressive way to get there than climbing through a hole in the hedge. From the front, the Mediterranean villa resembled a huge palace from a kid's storybook. The driver came to a stop alongside a massive front door, and then he got out and came around to open the car door for Marco. Only the driver was not a *he*, it was a *she*. And not just any she either. The driver was Gretchen.

"Oh, I do think you're in over your head, Master Jonno," said Gretchen with a malicious smile.

"Thank you, Gretchen," said Marco. "You can go home now."

"But Mr. Mallory . . ."

"That's quite all right, my dear. I think this lad and I have a few matters to discuss. You should go home and get your beauty rest, Gretchen."

"But Mr. Mallory, you may find this young man quite a handful. He looks innocent, but he's very sly and deceitful."

"Oh, I can see that, Gretchen. I can see that indeed. But you go home and I'll call you if I need you."

She seemed reluctant to leave, but Marco had definitely given her her marching orders. Gretchen gave me a kind of "I told you so" look, and she started walking down the long driveway to get back to La Chanson d'Or. Marco waved me out of the limo with his gun and held me by the collar of my shirt and guided me inside the house.

The house was huge and filled with giant vases and medieval armor and all sorts of strange delightful things. There was a stuffed tiger in the main foyer, and a multicolored parrot in a cage. I had a glimpse of a living room that was about as large as a football field. There was a pipe organ and a stone fireplace at one end that seemed big enough to roast a few oxen. The whole place looked like a set for a silent movie. And there wasn't a soul around. It was just me and Marco and the silver-plated revolver.

"I gave the servants the night off," he said. "Just so we could take care of this business in private. Let's go upstairs, I think."

Marco kept just enough pressure on the back of my shirt to guide me where he wished me to go. The staircase was humongous, like everything at Casa Monte Carlo. It rose to a landing half-way up and then two branches went off to the right and left. Marco pushed me along the stairs to the right and then down a long hallway to his bedroom, which I had seen before briefly in the dark. He switched on a glittering crystal chandelier. There was a bear rug on the floor by the bed with all its canopies and mirrors. Closer to the door there was a sitting room arrangement around a small stone fireplace. The room contained leather sofas and heavy masculine armchairs. A stuffed rhinoceros head with glassy eyes and a single horn rested on the mantlepiece.

"I bagged that monster in East Africa when I was doing *Revenge of the Zulu*. Lousy picture, but at least I got some hunting in."

"Hey, I thought *Revenge of The Zulu* was fabulous," I told him.

"How old were you when you saw it?"

"Eight or nine," I said.

"Yeah, well that's just it. You had to be eight or nine to like that flick. Look, would you mind taking those pants off, Jonno? Frankly I can't stand the smell of pee. Here, let me get you something."

Marco Mallory opened up a closet that was bigger than my entire bedroom at home. There must have been three hundred suits on various hangers. He picked out a glittering silk robe and threw it at me. "Go change in the bathroom, kid. Clean yourself up a little."

I took the silk robe into the bathroom. There was a deep marble tub in which you could bathe with all your friends. There were also drawings on the walls of people having sex in just about every conceivable position. The bathroom had the first bidet I had ever seen and I was very curious about it. I didn't know exactly how the thing worked but I sensed it had something to do with sex. The bathroom also had a window and I could see a branch of a tree outside. It hit me that I could probably get out the window and escape, but I had the strongest feeling that I was in the middle of a story and I wanted to see how it was going to end.

That's nuts! I told myself in no uncertain terms. *The guy has a gun, so get your ass out that window.* But another part of my brain, the part that always gets me into trouble, was telling me: *Sure he has a gun, but it's Marco Mallory, the most fabulous movie star on planet Earth, and this house is really unbelievable.*

I mean, when would I ever get a chance to see a house like this again?

He called to me through the bathroom door. "Hey, Jonno, I'm making myself a drink. You want a beer or something?"

"Okay," I said. "A beer sounds fine."

"Heinekin, Becks, or Guinness Stout?"

"Guinness Stout," I said. And I was trapped by my own greed for experience and my endless curiosity. I wasn't going out that window for anything.

35

I sank way down into a leather armchair with my feet up on an embroidered hassock that had hundreds of little mirrors sewn into the material. There were lots of mirrors in Marco Mallory's bedroom, small and otherwise.

Marco made a fire in the stone fireplace and then closed the opening with a door of insulated glass since it was summer and he didn't want any of the heat to escape into the room. After he made the fire, he turned up the air conditioning. I guess it sounds crazy, but this is Southern California in a nutshell. Sometimes our great nation must go to war just so L.A. can continue to waste energy so prodigiously. The rhinoceros head gazed down upon me from above the mantle with a kind of sad ironic leer of the doomed.

"How's the Guinness?" Marco asked.

"It tastes like a loaf of bread."

He laughed, indicating I had said something clever. "In Ireland they drink the stuff at room temperature, but I can't stand it that way. Have you ever been in Ireland, Jonno?"

"Not recently," I said. And then I admitted the truth. "Not ever."

Marco was sitting in the armchair next to mine, staring moodily into the fire through the glass. "Your father travels a lot. Doesn't he ever take you with him?"

"Well, he's busy, you know. A lot of his clients are real nervous types and I guess he has to travel around with them and hold their hands."

"Fucking agents," said Marco vaguely. "Hey, I'm sorry. I don't mean to insult your old man, but agents—they're taking over the industry. Guys like Lew Wasserman and your father. It gets to me."

"That's all right," I told him.

"It's just Hollywood used to be a lot more fun. You could show up on the set bombed out of your mind three hours late, propped up by a blonde on either side of you, and no one would give a shit. But now with men like your father taking over . . . it's all business. Agents and lawyers. Pretty soon it will be like they won't have to make movies at all anymore, they can just make deals and get rich. You understand what I'm talking about?"

"Sure," I said. "But the money . . ."

"It's *not* the money, Jonno," he interrupted with a gesture like he was swatting away a fly. "It's *never* the money. It's the romance, and don't you ever forget that. Have you ever been in love?" he added, which seemed to me a wild change of subject.

"Well, sure," I said.

"Then you know what I'm talking about. So if you want the sixty thousand dollars, it's yours. I don't give a shit about money, kid. What I'm concerned about is glory. Here, let me get you another beer."

I was feeling pretty comfortable, I have to admit, stretched out in front of the fire in a fine silk robe. Marco picked another Guinness from a small refrigerator near his bed, and he poured himself a new scotch and water.

"So what are you going to do when you grow up, Jonno?"

"Hell if I know," I told him.

"Well, you got a great puss, kid. You could always be in the movies."

"But I can't act worth shit," I admitted.

Marco thought this was a riot. "Can't act!" he cried. "You don't have to *act*. All you gotta do is *pretend*. And from what I've seen of you, you got that department down real good."

"You think so, Marco?"

"Sure, I do! It's obvious you're a lad of many talents. And I say this to you as one who knows. And frankly, it doesn't hurt a bit that you look exactly like your mother."

"I *hate* looking like my mother," I told him.

Marco got angry at me. "*Never* say that again, kid. I'm telling you for your own good. In her prime, Corina Norman was maybe the greatest piece of ass of all time."

"Were you and my mother . . ."

"Oh, yeah . . . *yeah!* You kidding? We made that picture together in '52. *Dime Store Goddess*. And look, I *always* have an affair with my leading lady. It's my trademark almost. I mean, why be a movie star if you can't fuck the leading lady? In a way, Jonno, I could almost be your father. That's why it hurts a little that the way I get to meet you, you're trying to put the squeeze on me."

I was starting to feel real bad about it myself. I liked Marco Mallory. I liked him a lot. "Look," I said. "Why don't we just forget the money. I mean, now that we're sitting around shooting the breeze like this, it just doesn't seem right."

"No, I guess not," said Marco. "But, of course, your accomplices might not feel the same way. Your sister, Zoe, for instance."

I was unhappy. I didn't want to say anything to give Zoe away, though Gretchen must have told him pretty much everything about my family situation. Marco was looking at me with new interest.

"I saw her once. You and Zoe were getting on the school bus together. She's a very pretty girl, Jonno."

"Yes," I said, staring at my hands. "Zoe is very pretty."

"Beautiful, in fact," said Marco, "And believe it or not, that's not a word I often throw about. Your sister Zoe, well, she has a beautiful other-worldly quality to her. That's why I'm wondering, well, frankly, Jonno, I'm wondering why she has it in for me."

"Oh, it's not *you*, Marco," I assured him. "It's her mother, Michelle, she hates. And the thing about the sixty grand—it's kinda just to prove we can do it. It's a very existential sort of thing, you see," I added, hoping to sound very intelligent.

"Oh, I see. Existential," Marco said thoughtfully. "Well that explains it then. Kinda like climbing a mountain because it's there. I guess your sister is a philosopher."

I felt miserable. I hadn't meant to talk about Zoe, but now that I had started it was hard to stop.

"Zoe's really a wonderful person. She's just very, very intense, you see. But there's something almost angelic about her. I know that sounds sort of corny."

"No, no. Not at all. That's just what I thought to myself when I saw her get on the school bus. A goddamn angel. But these photos, Jonno! My God! I've seen a lot of things in my life, but a young girl like that creeps into my backyard and takes photographs like I've never seen before—it really sends me for a loop."

"Listen, I'll talk to her. You have the negatives now. It's all over. I mean, with Zoe, you gotta understand . . ."

"Jonno, Jonno, I *do* understand," Marco said. "What I understand is you love your sister and you want to protect her. It's only natural."

"Well, it's not *completely* natural," I admitted sheepishly.

"Ah, I think I'm beginning to see the writing on the wall. I can tell you're a romantic, like me, Jonno. You're after the big hot rush. Look, I have to confess something. I came from a big family, and to tell the truth I had sex with some of my sisters, cousins, even my aunt once. Frankly it never bothered me, not a bit. You see, people like us, big Technicolor people, we can live a few steps beyond the normal rules."

"You did that? I mean you went to bed with . . ."

"My whole damn family practically. We were horny as rabbits and we were so poor we lived mostly in one room. So who's to say it's not natural? Human beings are weak, Jonno. We all need a little pleasure and love."

I hesitated only a moment, and then I started telling Marco Mallory all about Zoe and me. I've wondered about this for years, because I had never told another living soul about my relationship with Zoe. Even Carl and Rags and the rest of the family, they might have guessed what was going on, but they never heard a word from me. But there was something about Marco. Maybe it was because I really did believe he was above the normal rules, and he wouldn't be shocked. He was the biggest, grandest person I ever met and I felt he would understand.

So I spoke nonstop for about an hour, and he just listened, nodding occasionally, and sometimes getting up to get me another beer. I told him about the first time I ever saw Zoe and how I fell in love and how I was obsessed with her, and afraid for her as well. And I also told him my deepest worry, the really crazy part: that when all was said and done, despite the fact that we had commingled our blood and joined our bodies, I didn't understand her, not one damn bit. She was a total, absolute, utter mystery to me, and it was tearing me apart inside.

"Well, that's love," said Marco with a languid shake of his handsome head. "Are you religious, kid? I am, deeply religious in my own way . . . and there are some women, you see, it's like loving God, and it always has to be a mystery. That's the whole banana, Jonno."

"The whole banana!" I repeated awestruck. And I could see he was right. Loving Zoe was like looking up at the stars at night and wondering about the beginning and the end of the universe. It was both torture and it was sublime.

We talked long into the night. Marco Mallory was a very charming guy. Before I met him, I had the mistaken idea that charm meant someone who was very witty and told lots of amusing stories, and stuff like that. But that was ass-backward, and I learned something from Marco I remembered the rest of my life: real charm, the kind that is impossible to resist, comes from being interested in other people, in looking at them the way Marco looked at me, and making *them* feel witty and fabulous and incredibly special. Marco made me feel that I was his equal, and at the age of twelve this was a gift I will never forget.

Around four in the morning we both were getting pretty sloshed. He stood up to get us another round and all of a sudden he turned pale as a ghost and clutched hold of the mantlepiece to keep himself from falling.

"Jesus, what's wrong?" I cried.

"It's okay . . . okay," he said, slinking back down into his chair. I couldn't believe the transformation. From a man who a few minutes before had appeared to be in his absolute prime, Marco now looked old and sick and frail. I know now that at four o'clock in the morning, this kind of change can happen to the best of us, but at the age of twelve to see my idol in this new light was a shock. It was like the fine granite features of his face had turned into a gaunt death mask. In this revealing moment I even saw that the wavy black hair was not his own. It was dyed, or maybe it was a wig, but it definitely did not fit with the rest of him. In fact, the entire handsome figure of Marco Mallory was nothing but a mirage and I had been allowed momentarily to see the truth underneath. Then he seemed to recover, but he stayed seated and never went to get us another round of drinks.

"Well, fuck me, I'd better get some rest. I can't stay up all night the way I used to. You'd better go home now, Jonno. But tomorrow night . . . tomorrow night I want you to send me your sister Zoe."

I was startled. "Zoe! Gee, I don't know, Marco. I don't know if she'll come."

He turned to me with his gaunt, handsome deathly face. "Convince her, kid. Tell her I don't have horns. Tell her I'm a sick old man. Tell her that you and she can have all the money you want, because from now on it's like you two are my children. But I want to put this blackmail thing behind us. So promise me. And send me your sister Zoe."

I left Casa Monte Carlo thinking Zoe and Marco Mallory were my two favorite people on earth, but I was worried as hell about what would happen when they met.

36

It seemed unnatural to leave Casa Monte Carlo by the front gate.
Rags was waiting for me outside, half asleep with his back up
against a tree. He opened his eyes wide when I pushed the electric
switch that made the big iron gate swing open.

"I've been worried sick about you," he said. "I was trying to get
the others to storm the place and rescue you, but Zoe said we
should wait a few hours and see what happened."

"Well, thanks for nothing," I said irritably. Rags and I started
to walk side by side up Coldwater Canyon to our own driveway.
The eastern sky was showing the first hint of gray dawn.

"Why did you come down from the damn tree, Jonno? You were
supposed to wait until we flashed you the all-clear."

"I couldn't see diddleyshit from up there," I complained. "I
thought maybe you *did* flash the all-clear."

"What a goddamn mess! Did he torture you or anything?"

"For chrissake, do I *look* like I've been tortured?"

Rags was trying not to ask, but he was obviously very concerned
about getting the money. I felt strangely reluctant to discuss Marco
and everything that had happened.

Back in my bedroom, I found Zoe asleep on top of my bed, and

251

Carl asleep on my floor. They both opened their eyes groggily when I came in.

"Well, what happened?" Zoe asked.

I shrugged. "We talked. Nothing special."

"Nothing special?" Carl cried. "Did you get knocked on the head or what? We've been worried sick about you!"

"Yeah, that's why you came and rescued me."

"Jonno, we didn't know if he had called the police," Carl explained patiently, "For all we knew he even had a gun."

"He did have a gun," I said. And Carl was about to ask a whole bunch more questions, but Zoe stopped him.

"We're all tired and this isn't getting us anywhere," she said. "Carl, why don't you go back to your room and get some sleep. I'll talk with Jonno a few minutes, and then we'll all call it a night."

Carl seemed about to object, but then he sighed and did what Zoe told him. When we were alone, Zoe just looked at me for the longest time.

"You smell like a brewery," she said finally.

"Well, we hoisted a few. What the hell."

"It sounds quite pleasant."

"He's a nice guy, Zoe."

I tried to tell her all about him, what a relaxed and perceptive person he was. And hell, if he wanted to be a movie star and get it on with two women at a time, what harm was there in it? In a way, the world had a big need for some Technicolor heroes who could do whatever they damn well pleased. I told Zoe all this, but I don't think I did it very well. In the end, I guess it was just one of those situations where you had to be there.

"I think he snowed you, Jonno. By any chance did you discuss sixty thousand dollars and an envelope of negatives?"

"Look, he doesn't care about money. He says we can have all the money we want. And I believe him. I mean, Marco's a very existential sort of guy."

"Jonno! Don't use words you don't even know what they mean."

"I'm *getting* the meaning of that word in a big way," I assured her. "It means everything's bullshit, right? So you might as well have a good time and do whatever the fuck you want. Zoe, I'm not dumb and I can see these things for myself sometimes."

"Did I ever say you were dumb, Jonno?"

I sat down next to her on my bed. I was exhausted. This had been a long night and the very last thing I wanted to do was fight with Zoe. "Look, I'm sorry. I'm feeling kinda strung out. Marco asked if you would go see him. He says he wants to give us money and put the blackmail thing behind us. He wants to be our friend, Zoe."

"He wants to see me, does he?" said Zoe with a kind of far-away smile on her face. "Do you think I should go, Jonno?"

I was so tired I stretched out on the bed. "I don't know," I told her with a very big sigh. As much as I liked Marco, there was still something that made me nervous about Zoe going to see him alone. My nervousness had to do with the fact that Marco was such a terrific womanizer. "I don't know at all," I said miserably.

She put a cool hand on my forehead. "I'll go. I can take care of myself. You go to sleep now, Jonno. Close your big lovely eyes and drift away."

37

Our father telephoned from Transylvania that afternoon. Frankly, I don't have the slightest idea what he was doing there. He said he just wanted to see how things were going back in good old California. Rags was at the office, but Carl, David, Zoe, and I each picked up the phones in our separate bedrooms and we bullshitted for a few minutes about how everything was great. He told us to be good kids and mind Gretchen. We said, sure thing, Dad. You bet. He told us he loved us and then he hung up.

The first thing I thought when Dad had hung up the phone was a betrayal: I said to myself, if Marco Mallory were my father he would have taken me with him. To Transylvania or wherever the hell he was. Then I immediately felt guilty.

It was a funky day. I was tired from not getting much sleep. Everyone in the house avoided one another. When we met on the stairs or in the kitchen our eyes did not meet. Even Gretchen looked the other way. I guess we all had our schemes and dreams and secrets.

That night I went into Zoe's room just a short while before she was set to leave for Casa Monte Carlo. I had a small hunting knife with a deer-horn handle I had bought when I was nine years old

and going through a Davy Crockett phase. As much as I admired
Marco, I wanted Zoe to take the knife along for protection. Just in
case, I told her.

"Jonno, do I strike you as some blushing maid in distress?" she
asked.

"Well, no-o . . . not exactly."

"Then relax. I can take care of myself. It's *him* you should worry
about if he thinks he can get away with stealing those negatives
from us. I have backups, you know. Some negatives I didn't include."

"Really?"

"Of course, Jonno. And I don't entirely believe his rap about
how we are going to be like his children from now on. Your problem, my dear, is you are extremely gullible."

Zoe refused my offer to walk her next door to Casa Monte Carlo
and wait in the bushes within earshot just in case she needed me.
She left me with a platonic kiss on my cheek. I went back to my
room and began my vigil. I couldn't get into anything. I couldn't
read. I couldn't even take a shower. The problem was, I had convinced myself that Marco Mallory and I were actually a great deal
alike, and if I was in love with Zoe, then why wouldn't he be as
well? And Marco wasn't exactly the sort of rival one could take for
granted. As each minute passed, and Zoe did not return, I began
to feel deeply, horribly, miserably jealous.

About eleven-thirty, when Zoe had been gone a little more than
an hour, Carl and Rags wandered into my room.

"She's not back yet," Carl said.

"Hell, Zoe can take care of herself," I said weakly.

Rags sat down on my bed and started reading my old comic
books. "This is just like last night," he mentioned. "Only then we
were waiting for you."

A dissolute twenty minutes passed, the three of us slouching
about my room, none of us saying much. Then Carl threw down
my textboook on music harmony that he had been glancing
through and he said, "I'm worried."

"So am I," I agreed. "Why don't we just go over there and see
if we hear anything. I mean, it can't hurt."

Carl and I started moving out my window, glad to be doing
something that seemed like action. Rags told us we were crazy,

but he followed along too. We shinnied down my tree, though it
was mostly out of habit since at this point there didn't seem much
use in keeping anything secret from David and Gretchen. We
jogged quickly to the hole in the hedge and even before we
climbed through I could hear a deep rumbling bass sound that
bothered me. When we got to the other side I realized it was
music, and by the time we reached the grape arbor I could even
identify what music it was: Beethoven's Symphony Number Three,
the *Eroica* in E-flat Major. Marco must have had a stupendous
stereo system, for Casa Monte Carlo was totally vibrating with Beethoven's thunder. Somehow it scared me to death.

I started running toward the house and Carl and Rags ran behind
me. Every light seemed ablaze in the entire place, top and bottom,
and the rollicking music made it seem like a fiesta was going on.
I didn't care about secrecy anymore. I ran up to a big French
window and peered into the living room, but I couldn't see anything but furniture and carpets. I tried to open the door, but it
was locked. The first movement of the symphony was building to
a climax and I was starting to feel crazy with dread and jealousy,
because I knew the *Eroica* was one of Zoe's favorites. Maybe
Marco had put it on his stereo to impress her. Maybe Zoe had
asked for it.

Rags and Carl were gathered around me, all of us trying to see
what was happening inside. I decided I would climb up the cypress
tree to Marco's bedroom. I hated even thinking what I would find
there. Rags and Carl said they weren't keen on trying to climb a
weird tree and they'd keep looking for an open window on the
ground floor. I hardly heard them.

One thing about Beethoven symphonies, there are plenty of
dynamics. Even the loudest, most grand and climactic section will
suddenly die to the softest whisper. And it was in the lull of one
of these symphonic whispers that I heard Zoe scream. It made me
nuts. I went up that cypress tree like it was a stepladder, and I
swung myself onto the narrow balcony and looked through the
French door into Marco's bedroom. What I saw there made me
feel sick.

Zoe was in the middle of the room and her clothes were torn.
Her blouse had been almost ripped off and since she seldom wore
a bra one of her breasts was showing through. She looked like a

savage thing, a jungle cat caught in a corner. Marco was only a few feet away and he was totally naked, brown all over. He was laughing, taunting Zoe, playing with her. There was nothing but a coffee table between them. I saw Marco feint to the right and Zoe started going around the table to get away from him, but then he reversed directions and came at her the other way. He almost got her, but then Zoe reversed as well. I have no idea how long this cat and mouse game had been going on. I had a sense that Marco could have simply stepped over the coffee table and grabbed her, but that wouldn't have been his idea of fun.

I was beyond anger, I was ready to kill or die. I tugged on the French door and when it did not open I slammed my elbow through a pane of glass and then reached in and opened the door from inside.

"Well, it's my friend Sir Galahad!" cried Marco happily. "Oh, the more the merrier. Maybe I'll have you together, a brother and sister sandwich!"

I charged him, my head lowered like a goat. I wasn't exactly sure what I was doing. Marco neatly grabbed my shoulders and spun me around by my own velocity and slammed me into a wall full of books. For a second I couldn't see anything but bright flashes. I nearly blacked out. When I staggered to my feet, Marco was still playing his circle dance with Zoe, laughing and having a great time. I threw a book at him, the only weapon I could find. It bounced harmlessly off his hairy back. I picked up a vase and threw that at him too. The vase broke against his shoulders with a lot of noise and that got his attention.

"Jonno! That was Ming dynasty, kid. Couldn't you have thrown something a bit less expensive?"

The guy was totally nuts, a real maniac. But while he was jesting with me, he should have been paying attention to Zoe. My sister picked up the coffee table and threw it at his unguarded back. It had enough weight to knock Marco face-first onto the floor.

Zoe ran around him and took my hand. "Come on," she said. We ran as fast as our legs could carry us out the bedroom door, down the hall, and halfway down the grand double staircase to the ground floor. But then a really dumb thing happened. I don't know where they came from, but Rags and Carl were coming up the stairs just as Zoe and I were barreling down. We were going so

fast, Zoe and I, we simply couldn't stop. So we crashed right into
them and with our momentum all four of us rolled to the bottom
and we lay in a tangle of arms and legs.

Then we heard a pistol shot, which got our attention in a big
way. Marco was standing at the head of the stairs, still naked as
he was born, and he had just fired a shot into his ceiling.

"Well, children," said Marco. "Sweet children, innocent children. I believe your collective goose is cooked."

Then Marco Mallory did something I'll remember for the rest
of my life. It was an incredibly foolish thing, and a wonderful thing
as well. He stepped up onto the wooden balustrade and stood
balanced for just one moment, and then he leapt out into empty
space toward the mammoth crystal chandelier that hung over the
foyer.

Carl, Rags, Zoe, and I watched in sheer terror and awe. Marco
managed to grab hold of the bottom part of the chandelier and he
rode it like a pendulum from wall to wall, back and forth above
our heads. At just the right moment he let go so that he landed
on a small sofa, and with one bounce he rebounded to the floor.

"Voilà!" he cried grandly. It was amazing, but he somehow still
had the gun in his hand, and he pointed it our way. "I used to do
that better, you know, when I was young. I began my movie career
as a stunt man."

Frankly, I wasn't sure whether to clap or cry. I knew now what
Marco had meant when he said he was in this life for glory, not
for the cash. As far as I was concerned, swinging down like that
had been about the most glorious act I had ever witnessed. The
chandelier was still creaking above his head. We were speechless,
even Zoe.

And then he turned pale like he had the night before. A strangled cry came to his lips, his eyes rolled upward to the still-swing-
ing chandelier, and he collapsed on the floor. We heard him choking for a moment and then he was still.

"He's dead," Carl told us, bending over the body. Somehow I
knew that even before Carl pronounced the words. I think Marco
Mallory was the ultimate Hollywood man. He could not tell fact
from fantasy, and even though I hated him for what he tried to do
to Zoe, I loved him as well, and I felt strangely honored he had
performed his last swashbuckling feat for us.

"Wow," said Rags. "The dude must have been tripping on *something*."

We got out of there and ran back to our house through the hole in the hedge, and then up the tree to my bedroom window. Unfortunately, Gretchen and David were waiting for us in my bedroom, and our evening was not done yet. Not by a long shot.

38

"Ah, so what do we have here?" cried Gretchen in triumph as we came in the window one by one. "Just like little fairies flying in from the night."

I was out of breath from running and Gretchen was about the last person I wanted to see. She was standing in the center of my room dressed in her crisp white maid's uniform. David was sitting unhappily on my bed. He didn't look like he wanted to be there at all. Zoe started speaking to David in French. I don't know what she was saying, but it made David look even more miserable than before.

"And what have we been doing, my children?" Gretchen asked.

"We're not *your* children," I said nastily. "*We* know what you are. You'd probably spread your legs for the garbage collector if you thought it would help you get ahead."

She stepped closer to me, half smiling, and then slapped me across the face. She had a heavy ring on one finger and that hurt the most. For a second the world faded in and out.

"Hey, don'cha hit my brother!" I heard Rags say.

"Now you listen to me, you devils. Your father left me here in charge, and he has a great deal of faith in my judgment. So you will do as I say."

260

"Go fuck yourself," I said. "We don't have to do what you say at all."

Gretchen raised her hand to slap me a second time, but Zoe stepped between us and said very softly: "If you hit my brother again, I'm going to kill you."

Gretchen smiled ironically. "Aha! The pervert sister has a pretty story to tell, I bet. And wouldn't your father like to know about all your unnatural behavior?"

I was about to kick Gretchen in the shin, but Zoe sensed my anger and stood in my way. Gretchen was staring at Zoe and not paying any attention to me at all.

"And how did you tear your shirt, my dear?" Gretchen asked her. "I think I should telephone Mr. Mallory and see if everything's all right."

"You'll probably wake him up," I said quickly. "He'll be angry as hell."

"Oh, I don't think so. Mr. Mallory is a person who adores the night."

Gretchen used my phone and dialed a number quickly. She held the receiver to her ear and I could imagine the telephone ringing in the big dead house. Finally she put the receiver back on the cradle.

"How very peculiar. And I know he planned to spend the evening at home. I do believe we should investigate."

"All right," said Zoe. "Let's all go together."

I think Carl, Rags, and I were equally surprised. I had no idea what Zoe was up to.

"Yes, let's go right now," said Gretchen. "Perhaps you've stolen something from him. You all look so guilty, like real little thieves. Come along, David, you don't want to miss this. We'll turn this into a family occasion."

"Hell with that. I'm not going anywhere," David said stubbornly.

"Oh, yes you are. Otherwise I might have to tell your little secrets, and you wouldn't like that, would you?"

Zoe said something to David in French, but Gretchen interrupted. "It's rude to speak in a language the rest of us don't understand. Why don't you speak in English?"

"I was only telling David he should do what you say. After all, Gretchen, our father left you in charge."

"Yes, that's right. I am in charge."

It seemed crazy to me, but we all started filing out of my bedroom and down the hall. Carl went first, then Rags, me, and Zoe. Gretchen followed after us and David came reluctantly in the rear.

We made quite a gloomy procession. "Hell with this!" said Rags to Carl. "*I* sure don't want to go back to that house."

"Let's just do what Zoe says," Carl suggested quietly.

Zoe started speaking French to David again. All my life I've wondered exactly what she told him, but I don't expect I'll ever know.

"I thought we were all going to speak the same fine language," Gretchen pointed out. She was halfway down the stairs, and Zoe, Rags, Carl, and I were at the bottom. David hadn't started down the stairs yet. He stopped stubbornly on the top.

"I'm not going," he told her. "This has nothing to do with me."

Gretchen turned with a smile and began walking back to the top of the stairs. "Oh, then shall we tell your little secrets? How you wet the bed sometimes when you have bad dreams?"

"Shut up," he said.

"That's something only your maid would know, isn't it? And the dirty pictures you keep in your closet."

"Shut up."

"And the very strange things you like to do with women."

"Shut up! Shut up!"

Gretchen stood two steps from the top of the stairs, but she seriously misjudged her power over David.

"You will do *exactly* as I tell you, and you will do it now," she commanded.

But what David did was entirely something else. His palms jerked forward and he shoved Gretchen with a sharp desperate jab as though he couldn't stand to be near her a moment longer. The jab was so violent with distaste that Gretchen flew backward the distance of five or six steps, landed on her back, and then slid the rest of the way down the stairs to fall in a heap on the bottom. I turned my head so I wouldn't have to see her.

"Oh, God, what if she's dead?" said Rags.

"Of course she's dead," Carl said, looking first at Zoe and then at David.

"Two in one night!" Rags said. He gave his goofy nerdy laugh. I think his nerves were strained to the breaking point, like mine.

"So what now?" Carl asked Zoe.

"We carry her over to Casa Monte Carlo, of course."

It took me a while to get the picture, what she had in mind, and when I got it, I wasn't sure whether to be impressed by how clever she was or merely terrified.

My beautiful Zoe had figured out how we could get away with murder.

So we carried Gretchen through the hole in the hedge to Casa Monte Carlo. It was hell getting her there because a limp body is like a formless sack of flour that resists all sense of forward motion. We had to push and tug, but we sure as hell didn't want to carry her out onto Coldwater Canyon Boulevard where the police might see us.

Then we hoisted her on our shoulders and carried her past the Rodin statue and the grape arbor, past the swimming pool and in the French door that Carl and Rags had found earlier. The late Marco Mallory was where we had left him, on the floor of the foyer where he had made his last big splash. We carried Gretchen past Marco up the great staircase and onto Marco's bed. Then we took off all her clothes and threw them carelessly over a chair. It wasn't pleasant work.

When that was done, we went downstairs for Marco and carried him to his big canopied bed and put him next to Gretchen where his sightless eyes looked up into the mirrors overhead. Rags got a bit artistic at this point and arranged Gretchen's arms so they wrapped rather lovingly around Marco. While Rags was doing that, Zoe started searching through the bedside tables and immediately found a treasure trove of drugs: grass, hash, cocaine, uppers, downers, you name it. She put a bar of hash in the ashtray on the bedside table, and alongside of it a half-finished bottle of Johnny Walker.

It was quite simple. Marco and Gretchen were going to die smoking in bed. It happens all the time.

At the last minute, I thought of a problem. "The window," I said. "I broke the window pane coming in here to rescue Zoe."

"Don't worry," said Zoe, "It's going to burn so hot in here all the windows will explode."

Zoe lit one of Marco's cigarettes. He smoked English Ovals. She took one puff and then passed it to David, who took a puff and passed it to Carl, and so on until the cigarette had made its way around to all of us. I knew we were making a very solemn vow.

Zoe was the one who put it into words: "None of us will ever speak about what happened here tonight, not ever. Not even to each other. It doesn't matter that David was the one to shove Gretchen. What we're about to do makes us all equally responsible. Do we all understand that?"

We nodded solemnly.

"All for one, and one for all," she said. And we repeated this in unison, and we all put our hands together and for that moment we were more of a family than I think we ever were before or after. I was even one with David.

Then Zoe held the end of the burning cigarette to the lace canopy. The material smoldered and Zoe blew on it until there was a flame. The flame gobbled up the curtain like a hungry beast and in a moment the whole bed was on fire. Somehow it seemed a fitting end for Marco Mallory, a real Viking funeral.

We were surprised how fast the fire spread and we had to get out fast. But we were running down the hall, getting away, when something truly horrible happened. I heard Gretchen scream. She had not been dead after all, but only unconscious, and she had awakened at the last moment to find herself in a burning hell.

I stopped and turned. I thought maybe I had only imagined it, but then I heard her scream again. It was an unbearable sound. I started running back toward Marco's bedroom, knowing I had to rescue her somehow. I couldn't leave her there to die, not like that, not to be burned alive, but I didn't get far when a blast of heat forced me to stop in my tracks. Then Zoe was by my side holding on to my arm.

"We've got to run, Jonno! Run!" she cried.

"But she's alive, Zoe! I heard her scream."

"It's too late," she said. And I knew Zoe was right. It was too late to change what we had done. So Zoe took my hand and yanked me out of there, out of the burning house and back through the hedge for the very last time, and up to our rooms.

And that's how we got away with murder. We each lay in our separate beds and after a while we heard the sirens coming our way, and then there was a commotion and the reflection of emergency lights through the trees, and a distant scramble of radios relaying garbled messages.

The beautiful old house, Casa Monte Carlo, burned all the way to the ground. Eventually, Gretchen was identified only by her dental work. When our father came home, Zoe felt compelled to give him one of the photographs of Gretchen, Marco, and Michelle in their orgiastic ritual in the pavilion by the swimming pool. The photograph seemed to explain what Gretchen was doing in Marco's bed. A few months later, Michelle Cordell and my father were divorced. Her children, Zoe and David, remained in America, but Michelle returned to Paris where she involved herself in a fairly wild scene at the end of a wild decade. She was killed in a car crash in the south of Spain in 1971.

So that's what happened, and though for months I waited in dread and horror, neither the police nor the fire inspectors ever came to ask us kids if we had any knowledge of what had occurred next door.

As for Zoe, Carl, Rags, David, and me, we never spoke about it and after enough time had passed it was like it had never happened. I was young, the years erase unbearable memories, and soon it seemed a very distant dream. But throughout my life, at odd intervals, I wake sometimes in the middle of the night, in strange rooms, and I hear Gretchen's final desperate scream chasing after me. And then I know that what happened was real and that my brothers and I, and even my lovely sister Zoe, are truly of the damned.

Part Five

39

I drove my stolen Volvo station wagon to Santa Monica and parked in a public lot near the beach. I was careful to feed the meter three dollars of quarters for three hours of time. It was a hungry machine but I didn't want to get busted by a meter maid. When I was done, I had exactly eighty-three cents to my name, as well as a Platinum American Express card I knew I dared no longer use.

Plastic to plastic, dust to dust. Broke I came unto this city, and broke I would leave, probably feet first. It seemed a fitting end for a rich kid.

I walked toward the Santa Monica Pier, crossing the Pacific Coast Highway on a narrow pedestrian overpass. It was a hot Sunday morning, hot even for September, and September is usually the sizzling time of year in Southern California. I was unshaved, deeply hung over and I was wearing the filthy slacks and filthy white shirt I had slept in the night before on the hard ground. Basically, I fit right into the Santa Monica scene, where people were either driving BMWs or looked just like me. It was a great disguise being a red-eyed bum. There were so many of me I was invisible.

I took off my shoes and waded in the surf. The beach was packed with colored towels and umbrellas and human beings of every description and lots of ice chests full of beer. To the east I noticed white-gray clouds of smoke drifting across the sky, and with a shock I realized this was *my* smoke, my fire. I felt vulnerable, like everyone on the beach would know I was guilty just by looking at me. But the crowd was not concerned with fires raging out of control, only with suntans and sandwiches and keeping the kids from throwing sand in everyone's eyes.

I had a great longing to strip naked and dive into the cool surf, and maybe even do a James Mason and make the long swim to eternity. Instead, I walked up the steps to the pier and found a phone booth near the carousel. I started to dial Detective Sergeant Myra Fisher's home number, which I kept on a card in my wallet, but then I stopped and hung up fast. Fortunately I had been raised on the movies and I knew how these things worked. Myra would say to herself, What's that sound in the background? Well, fuck me purple, it's the calliope of a carousel. And where is there such a carousel in this fine city? On the Santa Monica pier, of course! And with just that brief lapse of care and concentration, Jonathan Sangor, master criminal, would become a great gone goose.

So I walked clear to the end of the pier where there was a phone booth near a place that rented fishing poles. I only hoped the seagulls wouldn't give me away. Myra answered on the third ring.

"Is this Wing Fat Chinese restaurant?" I asked. "I would like to place a take-out order, please. Two egg rolls, sweet and sour love, and a fortune cookie where everyone lives happily ever after and the rent never comes due."

"Jonno!" she said with a heavy sigh. I can't imagine how she knew it was me. "Where are you?"

"The Shadow never tells."

"Jonno, I can't help you anymore. It's gone beyond my control. You have to turn yourself in."

"But I'm innocent, Myra. At least I think so."

"What happened last night?"

"Well, I got drunk as a skunk at Dad's memorial. I really fucked up. If I remember correctly, I was screwing my sister Zoe on a pool table when a bunch of people came in and told me this was desperately inappropriate behavior at such a solemn occasion. And then I drank some more and got in my car and passed out. When

I came to, I was in the hills above Coldwater Canyon and everything was on fire. I got out of there fast."

"But you *think* you're innocent, is that your story?"

"Look, Myra, I can't imagine how I could have set that fire when
I couldn't even walk. But I was blacked out in dreamland. So who
knows? Maybe I'm a crazy lunatic and just don't remember when
I do bad things."

"Come in, Jonno. This isn't a game anymore. Give yourself up
or you're going to get killed."

"I don't know . . . I just don't know," I told her.

"Jonno, I have to warn you, in about twenty seconds I'm going
to have a fix on the number you're calling from."

"Bye, Myra."

"Jonno, don't go. Let me help you. You can come over to my
place, and I'll make you brunch and then I'll take you in so soft
and easy you'll hardly even notice. . . ."

I let the phone slip down on the hook and I felt more sad and
lonely than before I had made the call. It blew my mind that she
had warned me about getting a fix on my number. I felt a surge
of love for Myra Fisher, just as I had felt love for Marco Mallory
and, of course, a reckless love for Zoe. It seemed I had a great
attraction to people and things that wished to destroy me.

I wandered back down the pier thinking about Zoe. I wondered
if it meant anything to her that we had made love last night, or
whether these days Zoe put out for all the guys on pool tables.
Basically the adult Zoe was even more of a mystery to me than
the teenage Zoe had been.

I tried to stop thinking about her. I knew it was urgently important I concentrate on figuring out who had killed my father and
then set me up for the arson rap of the decade. But could it have
been Zoe? For me, everything always came back to Zoe. I could
imagine her killing Dad, but I couldn't see her trying to set me
up for the fall. I must mean something to her. Didn't I?

I walked with my back to the ocean toward what passed in
California as solid land. I had some ideas where to begin my investigation, but meanwhile all the smells of fried food and greasy
hamburgers on the pier were awakening my hunger. After my
phone call to Myra, I now had fifty-eight cents in my pocket. I
couldn't even afford a cappuccino.

I came to a snack bar halfway down the pier. I watched a very blond and hygienically sexless yuppie mother hand a hot dog to a little boy with freckles. Then she turned her back to him while she put ketchup on another hot dog for a slightly older girl.

I only hesitated an instant. I grabbed the hot dog out of the kid's hands and took off down the pier in a run. I heard him burst into tears behind me. I was the worst kind of criminal. Totally ruthless.

40

I thrive on chaos. My address book consists of assorted scraps of paper, napkins, and matchbook covers stuffed into every nook and cranny of my wallet. I had my little sister Opera's home number in Beverly Hills on a Tampax wrapper she had torn off from her purse.

The phone rang four times and then a machine came on. I heard jungle drums and something that sounded like Tarzan beating his chest and then a voice that said, "Love you madly. And don't forget to beep beep!"

They shouldn't let teenagers have telephones, let alone answering machines.

"Opera," I said sternly. "This is your elder brother, Jonathan. I won't tell you my exact location at the moment for reasons you might appreciate if you turn on your TV news . . ."

"Jonno!" she cried breathlessly coming on the phone. "I'm screening calls 'cause there's some guy I'm avoiding. Is that really you?"

"Let me pinch myself and see if I'm real. Ouch. Yes, I hurt therefore I am. Look, I have a couple of favors to ask, but if you don't want to get involved I'll understand. Frankly, if I had a choice I'd stay clear of me myself."

"Damn you, you know I'll do *any*thing for you. Now what do you need?"

"For starters, money. A few hundred dollars to tide me over. And I need a car. I seem to remember you have a BMW you're not quite yet allowed to drive. I'll try not to wreck it or anything."

Opera was great. She kept saying yes, yes, this was the first unboring thing anyone had asked of her in years. And it really didn't matter if I wrecked the Beamer anyway because what she decided she *really* wanted was a Lamborghini.

"So you want to come here and pick it up?" she asked.

"I guess so. I'll have to get to Beverly Hills somehow. I've been driving about in a stolen Volvo, but I think I'd better ditch the thing. Is your mother back from Europe?"

"You kidding? They're about to show the fall collections in Milan, and she wouldn't miss that for the world. Why don't I just drive to where you are and get you?"

"You mean you *drive*? My dear, you don't have a license."

"Don't be an old fart, Jonno. Anyway, it's not fair if *you* get to steal Volvos and run around with half of Los Angeles looking for you, and then you won't let me do anything fun."

I guess she had a point. I certainly didn't want to be an old fart. I told her I'd meet her at the Third Street Mall in Santa Monica around five o'clock. I wasn't sure if anyone had thought of tapping Opera's phone yet, but if they had and they followed her, the Third Street Mall was crowded with enough tourists and Hollywood phonies and panhandlers that I could probably melt into the crowd.

I hung up the phone. It was about one o'clock, which gave me four hours for my next project. I walked up Santa Monica Boulevard away from the beach toward the hospice where Rags spent his days dying of complications due to AIDS. I didn't quite remember the name of the side street, but I recognized my way past a few Italian restaurants, an exercise club for the trendy, and a store selling gourmet fat-free ice cream.

From the outside, the AIDS hospice had a drowsy Spanish feeling. It seemed to be a place where time stood still. I passed by the front door a few times trying to look like a normal everyday window shopper deciding between exercise, Italian food, or death. Peeking inside the front door of the hospice, I could see the main reception area and the official looking person at the desk. What bothered me was that the official looking person was wearing a uniform. This was an entrance which seemed closed to a mere heterosexual arsonist bound for the gas chamber.

I had an idea. I walked down a short cul-de-sac to the side of the building where there was a tall adobe wall that had spikes and broken glass on top to discourage uninvited guests. A nice friendly maple grew alongside the wall, and a branch dropped conveniently over the other side into the communal garden. It had been years since I had climbed a tree and I couldn't resist. It appealed to the little boy locked within the breast of the man.

I was definitely out of practice. I managed to hang from the lowest branch while my feet climbed up the trunk, and eventually I got a leg up. The second branch nearly ruined my sex life for all time, but probably this would not be a major loss to humanity. By the third branch I could look over the garden wall. I was in luck. My brother was in the garden on his hands and knees tending his prize tomatoes. There were a few other guys in pajamas sitting in deck chairs reading books. I lowered myself to the other side.

"Hey!" came a voice. "You're not allowed to come in like that."

It was a man gardening. "I want to see my brother, Rags. Hey Rags, it's me."

My brother glanced up from his tomatoes, and shook his head like he really wasn't pleased to see me.

"Shall I call the office, Ragnar?" asked the other man.

"No, it's okay," Rags said. But he kept pulling out weeds and he didn't look at me. I went over and stood above him and watched him work. The other man, the gardener, gave me a dirty look but eventually he moved away from us and got involved in the corn.

"You know, I never figured you for the type that would end up putzing around in the dirt," I said.

"Well, what type *am* I?" Rags asked sullenly, still showing me his back.

"I don't know. I guess you've been through a lot of changes, bro. Remember your psychedelic phase? All those weird sunglasses you used to wear? I remember there was a girl who came into the agency, an actress, and you put about a thousand micrograms of acid on the sugar cube in her coffee. You were pretty wild, Rags."

He turned and looked at me now. "We were all pretty wild back then. But eventually *most* of us grow up, Jonno."

I did a little play-acting, pretending a spear had been thrown into my breast and I made a great show of getting it out. "Oh, that hurt! It really did. And you're right, Rags, I'm a very immature person. But look, the reason I swung over the wall, I'm hoping you can help me. Last night at the big shindig, I guess I got pretty whacked. The last thing I remember, I got in my car and passed out. I was wondering if you can help me fill in a few blanks."

Rags sighed and looked real put out. "Help me up," he ordered. "Help me into my goddamn chair at least."

I gave him my arm, which he clung onto ferociously with his emaciated hand. He used me as a crutch to traverse a dozen feet or so to his wheelchair and then he sat down like all his energy was sapped.

"I just can't *believe* the fuss you caused last night," he said irritably. "Everybody in town's going to be talking about it for months. I mean, screwing on the pool table and not even locking the door! What are you, an *animal* or something?"

"Okay, I'm a bad boy," I said. "I told you, I was drunk."

"And then that sister of ours. She doesn't even have *that* excuse. Well, I tell you, I've *had* it with Zoe, I really have. I mean, that girl is absolutely crazy, she'll do *anything*."

"Well, I guess she would," I said with a smile. "Look, Rags, what the hell happened last night? After I passed out, I mean."

"Jonno, I know you're in trouble, but you don't have any right barging in here asking all these questions. I'm not very strong, you know. I just can't take any more emotional upheavals. I've suffered a lot in my life, and basically I just want my family to leave me alone."

"Oh, Rags . . . Rags! I came to you because I need you. You're my brother, for chrissake and I'm really in a jam."

"You don't think *I'm* in a jam? I'm *dying*, for chrissake! I mean, I just don't believe how selfish you are."

"You're right, of course. I'm selfish. I'm a lousy son of a bitch. But you were there last night, you must have some idea what happened. I mean, I was passed out in the driveway and *someone* must have been called out from the house to deal with me."

He didn't say anything for the longest time. I thought maybe I had lost him and he was contemplating his tomatoes again. "You didn't pass out in the driveway, Jonno. Don't you remember? You drove about a quarter mile up Stone Canyon Road. You passed out in someone *else's* driveway."

"Jesus! I actually *drove* in that condition?"

"Not far," he said dryly. "The Bel Air Patrol found you and they called David when they checked the license and discovered your last name was Sangor. Carl and David and Zoe, they all set out together in David's Jag to pick you up."

"All of them together? And then they brought me back to the house?"

"I wasn't there. Keith and I left. I'd had it. Honestly, Keith thinks it's just sinful what my family puts me through. He insisted on driving me back to the hospice so I could get some rest."

Rags stared at me maliciously. "But I *do* know who drove you home last night," he said. "Carl phoned this morning and told me everything. He's the only one of you who bothers to stay in touch. He calls me every Sunday morning to see how I'm getting on. Carl cares."

"We all do," I told him unhappily. "It's just Carl takes the time to be thoughtful and the rest of us don't. So who drove me home, Rags?"

"Who do you think? Who is it who *always* takes you for a goddamn ride? Only you're too dumb to see what she's doing to you."

"Zoe?"

"Of course Zoe. Like I said, Carl, David, and Zoe all set out together when the Bel Air Patrol called. David and Carl got you pulled over into the passenger's seat and then Zoe got in your Buick and she *said* she was going to drive you back to the Chateau Marmont and have a few bellboys haul you upstairs. Now what she actually *did*, that may be another matter completely."

I was drifting off into my private purgatory. *Zoe!* Rags was going on about how she had always been crazy, what with her Catholicism and her sex and her fanatic ways. Rags said that she destroyed me, that I might have amounted to something if it had not been for Zoe, and it really broke his goddamn heart.

It broke my goddamn heart too, but I didn't want to stay and listen. So I did my ape-man routine, jumped up onto the over-hanging limb, and I got away over the garden wall the same way I had arrived.

I kept saying to myself, Zoe . . . Zoe! I hope to God it wasn't you.

41

Opera was late getting to me at the Third Street Mall. The area is not a mall in the usual sense, but simply a street that is closed to automobiles, which is a very radical idea in Southern California, almost an insurrection. You see pedestrians wandering around nervously with ice-cream cones from store to store, kiosk to kiosk, looking like they expect the traffic to begin at any moment and mow them down. I waited on a bench listening to some street musicians, a group of Indians from Peru who were playing bamboo panpipes and drums and guitars. The music jogged along like llamas winding their way up a high Andes pass. I closed my eyes and wished I was in South America.

When I opened my eyes, I saw Opera walking my way in her celebrity disguise, enormous dark glasses and a Mexican sombrero. She wasn't exactly inconspicuous.

"Sorry I'm late. Some lady cop came to see me asking if I'd heard from you. I said no, of course. I said we hardly even *know* each other and you'd *never* come to me."

"I hope you didn't lay it on too thick. Myra Fisher is a very smart cop. Were you careful driving here?"

"Jonno! I waited forty-five minutes after she left, and then I circled around Beverly Hills before I got on the freeway."

279

Opera took my arm and we walked toward the public garage where she had parked her silver BMW. I had to keep her from going into stores and buying things, reminding her this was not a shopping trip.

We found her Beamer and I had an argument convincing my little sister that I was going to be the one to drive, not her. I was glad the thing had tinted windows, that made me feel less exposed to prying eyes.

"Hey, where are you going?" she asked. I had just hung a left from Seventh Street up Santa Monica Boulevard toward Beverly Hills.

"I'm taking you home."

"No way! Look, there's a party tonight at my girlfriend's house in Malibu. I thought maybe we could go together."

"Honey pie, I'm not exactly in my party clothes. And even if I were . . ."

"Jonno, I have this all figured out. My friend is Christy Lawrence. You've heard of her, haven't you? She has this gigantic old place in the Malibu Colony, and you can stay there and no one will find you, ever."

From what I could gather, Christy Lawrence was seventeen years old and fabulously wealthy. She had so many houses and cars and friends that she could hardly keep track of any of them. One stray fugitive sleeping in one of her bedrooms would go totally unnoticed in such a setting. The best part was that her entire crowd was under the age of twenty-one, no one read a newspaper, not ever, and they certainly didn't watch anything boring like the TV news. So no one would recognize me or have even the slightest idea who I was. It sounded like a fun bunch of kids. I guess all they did was ride around in limousines to each other's houses and party all the time.

"I mean, where were you planning to sleep tonight?" my little sister pressed.

"I thought maybe under the Santa Monica Pier. Or in the back seat of your Beamer. Maybe I won't sleep at all. First I gotta see Zoe somehow."

"What are you going to do? Go to the Century Plaza? You'll get picked up in no time, Jonno. Look, I'll call Christy and you can hide out in Malibu and then I'll get in touch with Zoe and have her come to the beach. It's really the best way."

Somehow she convinced me. Being a fugitive was probably making me weak in the brain. Opera called her friend Christy Lawrence on the car phone and said she had a *very* famous friend who was *very* shy, and that this unnamed friend needed to avoid his fourth wife for a few days and was looking for a discreet place to hide.

So it was arranged. Opera gave me the big Mexican sombrero and the oversized sunglasses, and I could have been Robert Redford for all anyone knew. I drove us down the Pacific Coast Highway to the Malibu Colony and, once there, to a big Cape Cod house that was painted gray with white trim. The servants were expecting us. We went in a backdoor from the garage and Opera took me to an attic room with a slanting roof on the third floor. Opera said she had spent a week in this room herself once when she had run away from home.

The room had a telephone and a television set. Opera used the phone to call Zoe at the Century Plaza Hotel. From Opera's end of the conversation, it sounded like Zoe had been about to leave for dinner with some people who owned an art gallery.

"I think you should cancel," Opera said. "Say you've got a sudden headache or something. There's someone here who wants to see you."

I could almost hear Zoe making calculations. Opera nodded at me and whispered, "She's going to do it." Then she spoke into the receiver. "Okay . . . good. . . . Why don't you meet me at Wolfgang Puck's new restaurant in Malibu. You know it? All right . . . around eight."

Opera hung up the phone triumphantly. "I'll order take-out in advance. Wolfie's absolutely one of my best friends ever and they'll do anything for me there."

I had stretched out on the big double bed with the TV on to the local news that seemed to stretch on forever this time of evening. Between a rape, a gangland killing, and the weather, I saw aerial footage of the terrible fire ravaging the hills around Coldwater Canyon. Five square miles had been evacuated, many homes had been lost, and the search was still on for the suspected arsonist,

Jonathan Sangor, a disturbed person from a "privileged Hollywood background" whose photograph was shown repeatedly on the air.

I was too exhausted to care. I fell asleep with the image of the fire raging in my mind, thinking of Zoe, waiting for her to come and save me from this purgatory.

42

I woke up to the smell of food in the attic bedroom. Zoe was standing at the foot of the bed bearing gifts: Styrofoam containers and a bottle of wine underneath one arm. The TV was still on, but there was a game show on the tube. Outside the window, night had fallen upon Malibu Beach. I could hear the restless ocean breaking against the sand.

"Opera left it up to the chef," Zoe was saying, setting the styrofoam containers down on a low table. "I believe we have wild boar topped with fresh crayfish and a port-wine sauce, a Caesar salad for two, and a bottle of California zinfandel. Cakebread Cellars, '87. Was that a good year?"

"I don't know. I think I missed it taking drugs."

Zoe smiled. "Don't try to impress me with your decadence, Jonno. You're a virgin at heart."

"Ha!" I said. "Where's Opera?"

"Downstairs with her friends. She's being discreet and leaving us unchaperoned."

I gave Zoe a lingering lusty look, head to foot. She looked a lot more tempting than the food. To my surprise she blushed and told me I looked like a dirty old man and I'd better take a shower before anything else. My bedroom hideaway had its own private bathroom, complete with razor, toothbrush, and everything a person might need who was too drunk to return home after a party, or who was running from the police. Zoe had seen me naked enough times, so there wasn't any need for false modesty. We talked through the open door as I shaved.

"Guess what? Your girlfriend's staying with me at the Century Plaza."

"Kismet? You must be kidding."

"I invited her. Partly to keep David from getting his hooks into her. Anyway, I thought she might be lost at the Chateau by herself. I was sorry for her. She thinks you're angry at her because she had sex with some British rock star."

"Do her a favor, Zoe, and send her home to Petaluma. I'd appreciate it if you'd give her a little money. I'll pay you back when I can."

"Too late, my dear. Tomorrow some director's giving her a screen test."

"Well, at least that's one crime of which I'm innocent," I said wiping the shaving soap from my face. I came back into the room in a white terrycloth robe I had found hanging on the bathroom door. Zoe had dinner spread out on the low table, and two bathroom glasses half full of zinfandel. We ate sitting on the floor.

"So here we are," I said. "You and me."

She cocked an eyebrow at me. "Eat your dinner, Jonno."

"I'd much rather eat you," I said, giving her my best Big Bad Wolf imitation. "You appeal to me more than wild boar. I want to put that up front, even before we lay our cards on the table, Zoe."

"Are we laying our cards on the table, Jonno?"

"You bet we are. It's a little late for playing games. So I want to tell you in the beginning that when I fell in love with you when I was twelve years old, it was for keeps. There's nothing you could do that would make me not love you. But I want to know the truth."

"The truth about what?"

"Let's start with last night," I suggested. "You, Carl, and David went together in David's car to find me after I passed out in someone's driveway. You got in my car and said you'd drive me back to the Chateau. Now, since I didn't wake up in the Chateau but on some burning hillside, I'd like to know where you took me."

Zoe took a delicate sip of zinfandel. "Are you going to believe what I tell you?"

"Zoe, I'm in your hands. If you set me up, that's okay. If you killed Dad, as far as I'm concerned, that's okay too. I'm not a very judgmental person. If you want me to take the rap for you, I'll do that too. I'm an easy sort of guy."

"You'd go to prison for me?" she asked. "What if it's the gas chamber, Jonno?"

"Look, I'm putting my cards on the table. I'm not sure if this is a good thing or a bad thing, but this is how it is. I'll die for you, Zoe, if you want me to. It really isn't a big thing. I'm dead without you anyway. My entire adult life has been nothing but a long empty waste, so just tell me what you want me to do."

I think I was going to go on in this vein and make a speech about how much I loved her, but suddenly Zoe was in my arms and she was kissing me, and I could feel her tears against my cheek. "Oh Jonno, God help us," she said.

"But I want to know the truth," I reminded her, kissing her mouth.

When I let her speak again, she said: "It's simple. David and Carl turned around in the Jaguar and went back to David's house. I was about to drive you and your Buick to the Chateau but you woke up and started getting amorous again. Don't you remember?"

"No. I *do* remember the pool table though."

She smiled ruefully. "Well, I'm glad of that, my dear, because we're never going to live that down."

"In the car, when I woke up and started getting amorous, did we . . ."

Zoe laughed, showing her fine teeth, throwing her head back, tossing her golden hair. "Sweetheart," she said, "you were out to lunch. You were babbling, crazy. I was worried about you, you were so drunk. You kept trying to take off my clothes."

"Was I obnoxious?"

"You were *extremely* obnoxious. And I was afraid to drive with you hanging all over me, so I gave up on getting you back to your hotel. I decided it was best to simply get you back to David's,

which was only half a block away. And that's where you spent the
night. Or at least, that's where I left you."

"At David's? I seem to remember I was never to step into his
house again, that sort of thing."

"You didn't *step* into his house, my dear. You were carried. His
wife Christina and I managed to drag you to the guest house and
put you to bed. I do believe Christina quite has the hots for your
body, in case you ever desire a stray adventure."

I pulled her closer to me. "I'm through with stray adventures,
Zoe. Did David know you brought me there?"

"I didn't see him at all. The guest house is behind his tennis
court."

"What happened to my car?"

"I left your Buick in David's driveway. I don't know, maybe he
saw it and figured out where you were. I wasn't really thinking of
hiding you, Jonno, so much as getting you somewhere you
wouldn't hurt yourself. As soon as you were tucked in, I drove my
rental car back to the Century Plaza. To tell you the truth, after
what happened on the pool table, *I* wasn't particularly anxious to
return to the party and chat."

Wolfgang Puck, of course, is a world famous restaurateur, but
Zoe and I had ignored his food. We stretched out together on the
floor, and I ran my fingers through her hair.

From what Zoe told me, I realized the mad arsonist could still
be me. My memory of the night was imperfect and clearly missing
large chunks. I didn't recall driving away from David's house and
passing out farther up Stone Canyon Road, and I didn't remember
waking up with Zoe in the car and getting amorous. So why
couldn't I have woken up in the middle of the night and decided
to drive back to Coldwater Canyon and set the hills ablaze?

Anything was possible. Maybe I was the best suspect of all. Then
I remembered something from last night.

"Look, after the pool table, when David was real pissed and all,
he took you out of the room, saying he wanted to talk with you. I
guess that's when I made my exit. What did he say to you?"

"Oh, he gave me a big lecture. How I was ruining my life. Now
that he's a grown-up and become very pompous, David thinks he
has to act like an older brother and protect me from all my dark
urges."

I laughed and pulled her closer. "And do you get these dark urges often?" I asked.

"Often enough," she said. "As a matter of fact, I'm rather experiencing a dark urge right now."

I picked Zoe up and carried her to bed. She stopped as I was getting on top of her, holding me off momentarily with her arms. "There's really no future in this," she whispered.

"No future at all," I agreed. So we took the present by storm for everything it could give us.

43

Waking up in the morning with Zoe in my arms was the best part of it. When we were kids, one of us would have to return to our own room by dawn so we would appear to be an innocent brother and sister. Just in case anyone cared. Now we stretched out indolently together with the waves breaking outside and the ocean still a steel gray. Zoe climbed on top of me and rode me lazily while the sun rose.

"Do you love me, Zoe?" I was still inside of her. I just wanted to hear her say it.

"You're my other half," she said. "You're my obsession."

"Yes, but do you love me?"

She laughed at my persistence and bent over me and kissed me so that her golden hair fell about my face and made a little tent.

"If we lived in a primitive tribe, we'd be stoned to death for what we're doing. But I'd get stoned with you any time, darling."

"Oh, Zoe!"

"All right, I love you. Why do you have to have everything put into words, Jonno?"

"Because I'm insecure. Will you marry me?"

She laughed and slid off me and lay with her head on my chest.

288

I felt her become sad. "I'm married to you in spirit and true blood, and a lifetime of sin," she said. "I'm afraid that'll have to do, my darling brother."

I didn't have any glib response. I lay in silence feeling the enormity of our love and the weight of what I suppose most people would call our great transgression. I felt a surge of bitterness toward a world which would condemn our love.

"I don't know if you read about this, Zoe, but in the Gulf War when the American troops started crossing into Kuwait, the tanks and trucks just went over the Iraqi trenches and they buried thousands of people alive . . . buried them *alive*, for chrissake! And this was all supposed to be very moral stuff, it made America feel good about itself again, and people in L.A. could keep on driving the freeways and wasting gas like always. And what I'm trying to tell you is, fuck them, Zoe. Fuck those dirty hypocritical bastards, fuck George Bush, fuck America. And if I want to make love to my sister, I'm goddamn going to do it, because I don't *like* what the rest of the world calls morality. Do you hear me? I'm proud to be your lover and I don't give a shit who knows it."

She sat up in a kind of lotus position on the bed and she picked up one of my hands and started playing with my fingers. "Oh, Jonno. I think that was lovely what you just said. But it still doesn't change the fact that some taboos are very old and can't be broken, lest they break you. No, listen to me, darling. War is *not* a taboo, whether you like it or not. Human beings have been burying each other alive throughout the millennia, and then afterward they beat their chests and throw great banquets and brag about the noble deeds they have done. It's primitive maybe, but civilizations grow and thrive on such things. But incest is something else. It's a crack in the very structure of things. And my darling, it has brought down houses more royal than our own. That's why it's taboo. It's a sin against the species, Jonno."

I laughed, because I didn't believe in sin, not the way Zoe did. I was a modern man and thought I could do as I pleased. "So what else is taboo?" I asked with a light smile, putting my hand on her bare breast.

"Patricide," she told me. "That's the greatest taboo of all."

This took the light smile off my lips in a hurry. Zoe was looking at me in an unfathomable way and I wanted to come out and simply ask her the big, big question but I wasn't certain I was brave enough for the answer. Zoe and I were staring at each other with a hundred undercurrents and innuendos and questions when there was a knock on our door.

"It's me, Opera," came a voice. Frankly, I was glad for the interruption. Zoe threw on a shirt and let Opera in. Our little sister looked at me in the bed and then at Zoe.

"Are you shocked?" I asked.

"You guys," she said. And her face burst into a very big grin. "No, I'm not shocked. Life is too short and you gotta take love where you find it."

My sentiments exactly. Opera's presence made everything light and fun again, but it was Monday morning and she had to be at work at the studio. I offered to drive her since I had her car, but she said a limo was already waiting for her outside and she had only come to say goodbye.

Zoe left me too. She said she had some photographs she had to mount. I wanted to get together that night, but she put a finger to my mouth and said, "Careful, Jonno. Don't fool yourself and start making plans."

So I was left with a Mexican sombrero, a pair of oversized sunglasses, a silver BMW, five hundred dollars in cash Opera had slipped me, and an attic room in a house of teenage millionaires. I told myself things could be worse, but I slipped into a funk anyway without Zoe or any promise that she would see me. I started wondering what I was going to do in search of innocence and redemption.

I decided I would go see Carl.

44

I was surprised to find a hazy day outside, a shroud of white clouds. Then I realized those were not clouds overhead, but smoke that was blocking the sun. I drove on the Santa Monica Freeway to Hollywood to avoid going anywhere near the fire.

Driving the BMW felt like being inside an expensive coffin. I didn't like it, and I longed for the comforting James Dean feeling of cruising in my old Buick. I kept thinking about Zoe and that last number she ran about patricide, and taboos against the species, and sins that could bring down a royal house. It was heavy stuff, but I was no philosopher. I had more practical concerns, like whether or not Zoe had murdered our old man.

Was she the killer?

It was driving me nuts. I kept changing my mind about it. One minute I'd be totally convinced my sister was the killer. The next moment I was astonished I could even imagine such a thing about my darling Zoe. But all that talk about taboos made me wary. I mean, Zoe *broke* taboos in a very big way. It was her modus operandi. So she might make a good case that incest was a crack in the structure of civilization, but when it got right down to the facts, when I was twelve and Zoe was thirteen, she seduced me.

291

She was the crack in the structure of civilization, *she* was the cause of the fall of the royal house. Sweet, lovely, deadly Zoe.

So I went back and forth as my car radio played the pop hits. Incest. Patricide. And will you still love me tomorrow? As a witness for the defense, I said to myself that Zoe had no motive to murder our father. Sure, there was her inheritance, a couple of mil, but Zoe lived on a grander scale than mere money.

And then as a witness for the prosecution, I remembered how she had attempted to blackmail Marco Mallory with hardly a furrow on her angelic brow. And then there was that long ago night when David had shoved Gretchen Krieger down the stairs of our house, and right before Zoe had been talking to David so calm and cool in French. I would have given my inheritance to know what it was she said to him. Were they discussing escargot, or was she telling him to give Gretchen that little push to hell?

Whatever she told him, when Gretchen hit the bottom of our stairs, Zoe already had it all figured out exactly how to get rid of two inconvenient bodies and never get caught. While the rest of us were numb with shock, Zoe's mind had been working like a cold little computer, figuring out all the deadly details.

I thought about all this so intently I missed my freeway exit and it took me an extra half hour to get to Hollywood. By the time I reached Hollywood Boulevard, my inner pendulum had swung back and forth from innocence, to guilt, to a wait-and-see attitude. Hell, maybe Carl was guilty. Maybe he had knocked off the old man to hurry up his inheritance so he could meet the balloon payment on his precious shelter for the homeless. I started fantasizing about how I might stick Carl for the murder, and then Zoe and I could sail free and easy to South America where we could live happily ever after. And then, of course, I started feeling guilty at the selfish tricks my mind was playing. Poor Carl. Here I was trying to nail him and he was the only one of us who ever had tried to do some good in the world.

And, in fact, I found my brother Carl right in the middle of doing good deeds on Hollywood Boulevard. I was driving along and just happened to glance out my tinted window and there he was, kneeling on the sidewalk next to a ragged woman with an emaciated baby in her arms who had set up housekeeping on the marker of some long forgotten star. Carl was talking quietly, patiently, his face grave with concern. I pulled into a red zone and lowered the electric window by the curb.

"Hey, bro!" I cried.

Carl looked from the ragged woman toward the silver BMW. It took him a moment to see who had called him, and when he saw it was me, his face filled with a few extra shades of concern. He came over and leaned in my car.

"Are you crazy coming here? The cops have been all over my shelter thinking maybe I might be in touch with you."

"Sorry about that," I said.

"Jesus," he said looking at me and shaking his head. "How did you get this fucking Beamer? Oh, no, don't tell me! You've turned our baby sister into an accessory-after-the-fact!"

"A *what*? Look, Carl, I just want to talk."

"Hold on," he said. He returned to the lady and the baby on the sidewalk. He wrote something on a page in a notebook and handed it to her. Probably it was the address of his shelter. Then he pulled out his wallet and gave her some money, I don't know how much. I guess Carl was the patron saint of Hollywood Boulevard. When St. Carl had finished his good deeds, he slipped in the passenger side of Opera's glitzy Beamer and I started driving.

He seemed irritable and out of sorts. We drove along for a while without talking, each of us staring straight ahead. I got off Hollywood and headed past a triple-X adult theater toward Sunset.

"So where are we going?" Carl asked. "Why did you come here, Jonno?"

"I thought we'd just drive around in circles a while. Come on, Carl, it's *me*. Your brother, Jonno. Can't you give me a few minutes of your time?"

"Jonno, I'm sorry if I'm out of sorts. I know you're in trouble and I'm glad you've come to me. It's just I'm under a lot of pressure myself trying to keep the shelter open. If I get messed up with some criminal investigation, it could be bad for my people."

"*Your* people," I repeated. I started heading down Vermont toward Wilshire. "You really identify with your people, don't you? The homeless, the downtrodden, the babbling crazies."

I guess I struck some nerve. Carl came on angry. "You think we're any better? Just because our father was a ruthless son of a bitch who didn't stop at anything to get what he wanted? I mean,

this was a guy who didn't even blink when he drove his first wife
to suicide. I guess that makes us real aristocracy, huh? But as far
as I'm concerned, I'll stay with the honest people on the streets."

There was something about Carl's attitude that annoyed me.
"I'm not thinking about Dad," I said. "I'm thinking about you."

"What about me?"

"Well, how come you never got married, Carl? You live such a
bleak Salvation Army life. I bet there's some Joan of Arc out there
who would love to get her hands on a dude like you. You could
have a little boy martyr and a little girl martyr and maybe you
could all run a nice soup kitchen together."

I had not come here to fight with him, but it was like neither
of us could stop. Carl flashed me a cold superior smile that was
nasty as could be.

"Ah, methinks the real Jonathan Sangor is coming out at last,"
said Carl. "The disenfranchised aristocrat. The pretty boy with a
broken heart. You know what I think? I think you're a snob, Jonno.
Maybe a more subtle snob than Albert or David. You pretend to
be very hip and streetwise, but I know what you want."

"Oh, yeah? What do I want?"

"You're so fucking adolescent, that's what kills me. It's like
you're still twelve years old, for chrissake. Basically, what you want
is to be Marco Mallory."

"Fuck you," I said.

"No, fuck *you*, Jonno. That asshole was your hero. You want to
live in an enormous house and be a big movie star and fuck every
woman on planet Earth. But your problem, Jonno, is you just
couldn't get it together. You didn't have the talent or the guts to
make your selfish little dream come true."

For a second I was so mad I was about to pull over and slug
him, but I forced myself to chill out. We drove two blocks in
silence. I hated having so much bad feeling between Carl and me.
I tried to start over again with a reasonable tone of voice.

"Look, Carl," I said, "I'm trying to figure out who killed Dad
and then went around doing things to make it look like it was me.
This new thing, setting fire to half of Los Angeles—I'm pretty sure
I didn't do it."

"*Pretty* sure?"

"Well, you know. I was blotto in extremis. So I'm trying to

retrace everything that happened that night. I guess I passed out in my car a few blocks from David's house, and then you, David, and Zoe set out to pick me up."

"Well?"

"I understand Zoe got out and said she was going to drive me and my car back to the Chateau Marmont. Is that what happened?"

"Yeah, that's right. Only I guess you woke up and started getting rowdy and she ended up putting you in David's guest house for the night."

"You actually *saw* me in the guest house?"

"No. Frankly, I had my fill of fun and games with the rich folk in Bel Air. David dropped me back at his house and I didn't even bother to go inside. I got my own car, and drove back to the shelter."

"So how did you know about Zoe putting me in the guest house?"

"She told me. She called me this morning."

"She *called* you?" Somehow this surprised me. "What else did she say?"

"She said she spent the night with you. Don't be so surprised, Jonno. You may be her goddamn lover, but I'm the guy she confides in." He turned to me with a twisted smile. "Somehow, I've always felt that between the two of us, we add up to what Zoe's looking for."

I think he was getting even with me, taunting me, letting me know he had part of Zoe that I would never have. It was a strange image, like Zoe had split herself in two: I got her body, but Carl got her mind. To be perfectly honest, I wasn't sure which of us had got the better deal. It was as much frustration for me as I'm sure it was for him. All my life I had hated possessing her but never knowing what was going on inside.

I asked the next question very carefully: "Carl, when I came to you the other day, you said you thought Zoe was the one. The killer, I mean. Do you still think that?"

Carl looked away. "What difference does it make?"

"It makes a difference," I assured him. "I've been going back and forth about it, Carl. It's driving me crazy. Somehow I think it's her. She's the only one of us with the balls to *do* something like that. But the way I see it, she doesn't have a motive."

"You don't think so?"

"No, I don't. There's the inheritance, of course, but I don't see Zoe killing for money. And there's the anger. I know she used to be angry at Dad when she felt abandoned as a kid, back in the days when he was keeping separate families in L.A. and Paris. But that's a long time ago. I mean, if Zoe was going to kill Dad, there would have to be some very big reason for it, and as far as I can see, it's just not there."

"There's a motive," Carl said icily. "You just don't know about it, Jonno."

"What don't I know?"

"You don't know anything," he told me contemptuously. "You only fucked her, Jonno. But she told all her secrets to me."

I pulled over to the curb because I couldn't drive anymore. My hands were shaking and I started wishing I still smoked cigarettes.

"Tell me," I said.

"No, *you* tell me."

"What the hell are you talking about, Carl?"

He flashed me a ghastly smile. "You tell me your half and I'll tell you mine. Maybe between the two of us we can put Zoe together into a whole person. All the king's horses, and all the king's men . . . so what do you say, little brother?"

"I don't know what you're talking about."

"Sure you do. I want you to tell me what it was like to fuck her, Jonno. I want to know all the details. Did she suck your dick? Did you come in her mouth?"

"Oh, Jesus!" I cried. "Carl, please, this is too horrible . . ."

"Sure, it's horrible. But I want to know what I was missing all those years, and if you tell me your part, I'll tell you mine. And that's my deal, take it or leave it."

I was staring at Carl like I'd never seen him before. I couldn't believe we were having this conversation. "She killed Dad?" I asked.

"Who the hell knows? But Zoe has a very big secret, little brother, and I'll tell you all about it. So what was she like, Jonno? Was she good?"

"Go to hell," I said.

He grinned at me and taunted in a child-like voice: "Then I'm not going to tell you, and you'll never know."

I hated this. "Jesus, Carl! It was nothing unusual. We made love like people do. What do you want to know the details for?"

"Because you were there, and I was not. I want to pretend I was there, Jonno. I want to be able to close my eyes at night and reminisce what it was like making love with Zoe."

It was a devil's bargain. The horrible part was I wanted to know Carl's secret as much as he wanted to know mine. It really killed me that she had confided in him but never me. It killed me that I never knew what was going on inside her beautiful head. So I was as much of a Peeping Tom as Carl was. I knew what we were doing was sick, was wrong, but I couldn't help myself either. I had to know.

So, in the end I told him. I could see he was getting some horrible pleasure from my account. He was getting aroused. A few times I begged him to let me stop, but he said go on, go on. And he kept prying, and asking, and squeezing out the disembodied erotic details.

"Enough," I said finally. "Now you tell me your end. Why would Zoe kill Dad?"

Carl smiled maliciously. "Because you weren't the only one getting into her pants, little brother. Dad was too."

I felt a kind of ocean roar in my ears. "Bullshit," I said.

"Oh, yeah? Was Zoe a virgin the first time you guys got it on?"

"No, but I always figured . . ."

"You figured what? Maybe some nice young man in Paris? It was Dad, for chrissake. He started molesting her when she was five years old, and he kept at it until she was eighteen, nineteen, long after she stopped doing it with you."

I shook my head. "No. This is a lie. I would have known."

"Sure you would. You were just the pretty boy, Jonno. She didn't tell you anything at all."

I kept shaking my head like a zombie. "I would have *sensed* something," I said.

"Oh, yeah? Well, what did you sense? Did you think Zoe was the girl next door? Did you think she was as normal as apple pie? Christ, Jonno, you're so stupid I can't stand it. Why do you think Dad even married Michelle Cordell in the first place? You think he was suddenly in love with his French mistress? It was so he could have Zoe around. Michelle was threatening to leave him, for chrissake, and then he wouldn't have his lovely daughter. So you see, you, me, and Dad, we were *all* in love with her."

"This is bullshit," I said furiously. "A lot of lies. You're just making these things up because you're jealous, Carl. You're a pathetic son of a bitch living a secondhand life."

He laughed. "Oh, go to hell, Jonno. You asked and I'm telling you. Zoe used to come into my room crying all the time whenever Dad was back from Europe, which, thank God, was not that often. Poor little Zoe didn't know what to do when big lustful Daddy came into her room at night. But knowing Zoe, she wasn't such a victim as she pretended. You know, and I know, that Zoe used sex to get her way. Hell, I bet she was nearly as seductive at age five as age fifteen. Maybe she thought that by seducing Daddy he would actually stick around a while. What do you think, Jonno?"

"I think you're crazy. And even if I did believe you, she wouldn't kill him suddenly years later. It just doesn't make sense!"

"Jonno, it took her all these years to realize how he had ruined her life. Look, I see this all the time on the streets. Victims of incest, they hardly know what's happening to them when they're kids. Some of them even like it. It's *attention*, for chrissake. But then they grow up and they forget and then they remember again, sometimes only in dreams. And then it suddenly comes back to them exactly what happened, and they see how the long shadow of this thing has ruined everything, and a great anger comes over them, all the anger they couldn't dare express as children. And this is what happened to Zoe. She waited until she was an adult, and then she had her revenge."

"No, I don't believe any of this. She would have *told* me."

"My God, she was trying to *protect* you, Jonno! She didn't want you to hate your father. She was afraid you'd kill him."

"No, *you* killed him," I cried. "*You* were in love with Zoe and you wanted to punish the bastard yourself."

Carl threw back his head and laughed. "Oh, Christ! You can lead a horse to water, but I swear! It's all so sordid and typical. I used to hear Zoe talk about incest as some kind of royal thing, a curse of the oh-too-refined aristocracy. But there's nothing royal about it. It's only greed and moral idiocy. And then she turned around and abused you, Jonno, just like she was being abused herself. You think it was love? Hell, she was just passing on the curse. It's a textbook case, sordid as they come."

"You lying bastard!" I got out of the car and stepped around to his side and pulled him out. "You killed Dad, I know you did. You wanted that money for your horrible dreary shelter and he wouldn't give it to you, so you killed him."

Carl and I were on the sidewalk. He took a swing at me. He was never a very physical person and I could see the punch coming a mile away. I blocked it neatly, and then I slugged him hard enough in the stomach to make him bend over and fall down on his knees. His chin was a tempting target, and I wound up to hit him again, but then I couldn't stand it. I couldn't stand myself. I couldn't stand Zoe. I couldn't stand Carl. And I couldn't stand that maybe I had *not* murdered my father, because if that bastard had been messing with Zoe, I sure wished I had.

In rage and frustration, I kicked the side of Opera's BMW with all my might. It was not a clever thing to do. I think I broke my foot and I set off the car alarm on the BMW, which started wailing like an air-raid siren. Already people were looking at us from a corner delicatessen and a shop that sold picture frames. I had a feeling the cops would be coming soon.

"Stupid bastard," Carl said, massaging his stomach where I had hit him.

"I don't want to fight with you, Carl. Just tell me one thing. This thing about Dad and Zoe, it's really true?"

"It's what she told me, Jonno. Now you'd better get out of here before the cops come."

There was something that held me, even though the damn car alarm was beginning to sound like the start of World War III.

"Look, I'm sorry, Carl," I said. "I'm sorry about the whole damn thing."

"Oh, go fuck yourself, Jonno. Now beat it while you still can."

So I turned and ran, leaving my brother on his knees, like he was praying to some distant god on the dirty sidewalk.

45

I ran three blocks up some long straight street with low dreary buildings whose name I didn't know. I ducked into a bar where a few tough looking women were playing pool. The bartender was a lady with a tattoo on her forearm and she stared at me with little affection. It didn't take a genius to conclude I had sought refuge in a lesbian dive. I was limping because my foot hurt so badly from kicking Opera's car. I ordered a soda water with a hit of grenadine and a cherry.

"A Shirley Temple?" asked the lady bartender, her voice rising in an amazed question mark.

"Please," I said. And as if this wasn't bad enough, I paid for the thing with one of the hundred dollar bills I got from Opera.

"Either you're the ballsiest guy I ever met, mister, coming in here like this," she said, "or you're just some utter wimp."

"Let me know if you figure it out," I told her.

The lady kept shaking her head and muttering to herself as she made my change. I think I was the kind of guy who confirmed her choice of a different sexual orientation. I took my change to a phone booth in the back of the bar. I desperately wanted to reach Zoe. My hand was shaking as I put the quarter in the slot and asked information for the Century Plaza Hotel. Information used to be free back in the days when gas station attendants cleaned your windshield. Now I had to put in another quarter to dial the hotel.

"I'd like to speak with Zoe Sangor," I told the operator.

"Who shall I say is calling."

"Tell her it's Mr. Fred Chopin," I said.

In a moment I heard a woman's voice, but it wasn't Zoe's. "Hello?" It was Kismet.

"Is Zoe there, please?"

"*Jonno!* I thought you were supposed to be a Mr. Fred Something."

"I'm on the run, Kismet. It's an alias," I explained.

"Oh . . . well, Zoe isn't here," she said. I noticed her voice had grown chilly. "Jonno, I'm glad you've called. I really think we should have a talk. I just don't think I can go on seeing you anymore. I mean, I don't want to hurt you, and I hope that one day we can be friends. . . ."

"Kismet, don't worry about it. Really. Now where did Zoe go?"

"She went to lunch at some French restaurant."

"Who did she go with, do you know?"

"Jonno, I have to tell you, there's another man."

"With Zoe?"

"No, with *me!* I mean, Christ, who are we talking about? That's the whole problem, Jonno, you just treat me like I could be someone else, like I'm some kind of klutzy idiot who can't do anything right, but Howard . . . Howard treats me like I'm important."

"Who's Howard?"

"Howard Kramer. You know, the director. He made *Freak Show Two* and *Three*, but not *Four*, which was terrible. . . ."

"Kismet, this is swell. I'm glad for you, but can you tell me who Zoe is having lunch with?"

"Some person named Rip . . . or maybe Robert. It began with an R."

"Rags?"

"That's right."

This threw me for a loop. The last time I saw Rags he didn't exactly look like he was in good enough shape to go to a French restaurant and sit around with Zoe poking at some duck à l'orange. Kismet kept talking about her new boyfriend, Howard Kramer, and how he had convinced her she had a "certain quality," like a young Goldie Hawn. And she was sorry about her and me, it was sad but sometimes these things happened and people had to move on to new possibilities.

It was all background noise in my ear.

"Kismet," I said, "are you sure it was Rags?"

"Who?"

"*Rags!*"

"Oh, yeah. He's your brother in the wheelchair. I even met him. He stayed the night at David's house . . . the night of the memorial. He and his friend Kevin."

"Keith," I said. "But you must be mistaken. Rags told me he went back to Santa Monica fairly early, not long after I left."

"Oh, no, that's not true. Rags was feeling really weak and they decided to stay in one of the spare rooms upstairs and go back to the hospice in the morning. I know, because, well, that's the night I met Howard, and we stayed in a room next door. You see, Howard's getting a divorce right now, and he *really* wanted to take me home to his big mansion in Brentwood but . . ."

"Did you see Rags in the morning, or his friend Keith?"

"No, Jonno, I didn't. But then Howard had to be at Fox and we got up very early, so I imagine he and his friend were still asleep."

I was taking this in, that Rags had lied to me, and I was trying to figure out what it meant. Kismet was going on about Howard and how as soon as the divorce was final they were going to live together and make really serious movies full of social content, not at all like *Freakshow Two* and *Three*, which Howard had done only to establish a name for himself in the industry.

"Kismet, do yourself a favor and get on the bus back to Petaluma."

"Oh, Jonno! You can see why we can't be together. You just don't give me the same kind of inner validation like Howard does."

"Yeah. Well, I wish you lots of luck, honey. But if things go wrong and I'm not in San Quentin, you can always give me a call if you're in a jam. Okay? Or Zoe, if she's not in San Quentin in an adjoining gas chamber, I'm sure she'll give you some bus fare north."

"Jonno! You see what you're doing? You're undermining my sense of inner-worth by planting the possibility of failure!"

"You're well rid of me," I admitted. "Now, about Rags and Zoe—did he call her, or was it the other way around?"

"He called," she pouted. "About midmorning."

"And he suggested lunch at a French restaurant? Can you try to remember the name?"

"The Something Door, I heard her say. Something like that."

I tried to think if I could remember a restaurant with a name like the Something Door. It didn't ring a bell, but for me that didn't mean much. In a city like L.A. trendy little restaurants came and went too fast for reckoning, and I wasn't the type to even try.

"Anyway, Jonno, I think Zoe is an incredible person, and I guess I can see . . . I mean, it's a little *weird* . . . but, well, you know, it's important to take a sophisticated attitude . . . and I wish you luck too. That's what I'm trying to say."

"But are you sure Zoe said it was a restaurant?"

"Jonno, I don't know. She only said the name. It *sounded* like a restaurant."

It hit me then like an electric shock. I put the phone back onto the receiver. For reasons I could barely comprehend, Zoe was meeting Rags at the house of our childhood in the middle of a raging fire. She was going to La Chanson d'Or.

46

I called a taxi. When it came it was a big American station wagon painted yellow. The driver was a baby-faced man who drove like a captain piloting an aircraft carrier through heavy seas. He had a compass attached to his dashboard, he wore aviator glasses, a hat with a black plastic brim, and there were pencils and pens neatly arranged in a plastic holder in his pocket, neat as little soldiers on parade. I guess in the naked city everyone lives their own fantasy. The radio was on to an easy-listening station where all the songs sounded like they had gone through a food processor and had lyrics like Hallmark cards.

I told him to take me to the top of Coldwater and Mulholland. He turned around and I saw my own reflection in his dark glasses. "Can't," he said. "That area's closed off due to the big blaze. You must be from out of town."

I told him he was right, I had just flown in from China. I asked him to drive up Laurel Canyon to Mulholland and then go west as far as he could until he hit the fire lines. He nodded and said, "Aye aye, skipper."

The traffic was slow and it seemed to take a long time to get anywhere. I thought I was going to go crazy with impatience. The driver started telling me all about an accident he had passed on the freeway the night before where there had been bloody bodies all over the road. I kept thinking about Rags and Zoe . . . Zoe and Rags . . . wondering why he had asked her to meet him at La Chanson d'Or. I didn't know what it meant, but I didn't like it at all.

We drove up Laurel Canyon and then made a left on Mulholland. The baby-faced driver was a fund of unasked for information. He said the fire was mostly contained but it was still burning in some parts of the hills. One hundred and thirty seven homes had been damaged or destroyed. One old lady had a heart attack and died. There were rumors that an ex-president of the United States who lived in Bel Air had gone to his ranch up the coast just to get away from the smoke. It was a darn shame, he told me, when the actions of one cowardly psychopath could disturb the well-earned rest of an ex-president of the United States.

I was looking out the window at the view of the city stretched out at my feet and for a moment it reminded me of being up high in the giant oak tree on the night when Marco Mallory came for the blackmail negatives. I realized the taxi had stopped. I turned to the driver and was surprised to see him turned around my way with a long-barreled revolver pointed at me. It was a real cowboy gun, about the biggest revolver I had ever seen.

"All right, put your hands where I can see them. I know who you are. I've seen your picture on television."

I put my hands up. We were pulled off into someone's driveway. There wasn't anyone else around. The driver kept staring at me like this was the big moment of his life, and he might never get to hold a gun on a psychopathic killer-arsonist again.

"What were you planning to do? Burn a few more houses? Kill another old lady?"

"Sure," I said. "Old ladies are my specialty. I like to roast 'em like marshmallows."

"I know all about you. You were raised with all the advantages. You had the finest things money could buy, but it wasn't enough for you, was it? You had to go out looking for thrills and perversions."

The guy went on like this for a while. He really hated me and had me all figured out. He said I was a cancer on society. Maybe he was right. I kept looking at the big pistol in his hands and I tried to stay very still. All the time I was wondering if Zoe was in a burning house with Rags, or maybe the house was no longer there and neither of them had managed to get beyond the fire lines. It was frustrating not knowing. I wanted to kill the baby-faced taxi driver.

He used his two-way radio to call his dispatcher. "Charlie Five-Oh to Mother One. Hey, you'll never guess what I got here in the back of my cab. It's the arsonist who started the big blaze, Jonathan Sangor, himself."

He kept jabbing the long barrel of the gun at me for emphasis as he spoke to his dispatcher. That was his undoing. At the long end of his jab, I brought my left hand up from my lap and brushed the barrel aside. The gun fired. There was an explosion in the car like a bomb going off, but the bullet missed me and shattered the back window. I was all over him, getting one arm around his neck and trying to wrestle the gun out of his hand with the other. I jerked his gun arm down against the back of the front seat and I heard a sickening crack as his arm broke. The gun fell harmlessly into the backseat.

"Don't kill me, don't kill me, please," he pleaded.

"Get out of here, you dumb fuck," I told him.

The driver opened his door and started making a run for it. He was overweight and he sort of waddled down Mulholland scream-ing in pain. It was a pathetic sight. I took the gun from the backseat and stepped around to the front and got in behind the wheel. The first thing I did was turn off the easy-listening radio station. I can't stand that kind of music. Then I took off fast up Mulholland with the gun in my lap knowing it was too late to be cautious. Whatever happened now, this was Jonathan Sangor's last stand.

The station wagon did not exactly handle like a sports car, and my last stand almost came sooner than expected on one of the sharp curves of Mulholland. I slowed down a little. I wanted to get there. The road snaked its way along the backbone of the Hollywood Hills, past closed gateways that led to expensive houses. I could smell smoke in the air, but I had no idea when I would reach the fire lines. Then I came around a curve and there it was: a police cruiser with flashing lights on its roof was stopping traffic close to the intersection with Coldwater Canyon Drive. Behind the cruiser I saw a fire truck and from somewhere down in the canyon there was a great plume of black smoke. The officer by the police cruiser started waving at me to stop. I began to slow down so he wouldn't get nervous.

I knew this countryside. I knew it so well it had filled my adult dreams and followed me over the years. To my right was the small park where Marco Mallory had picked me up off my feet and scared me into peeing my pants. To my left, somewhere between two houses, was the old horse trail. I slammed on the brakes of the big station wagon and dove out the door into the thick hillside brush. I took the cowboy revolver along with me for good luck.

"Hey! Stop! You can't go there!" the cop cried.

I was swallowed in the brush before he even had a good look at me. Everything seemed more overgrown than I remembered from my childhood, but the path was still there. Probably it had been kept intact by a new generation of local kids. For a while I thought I was lost because there were several new houses to confuse me, but then I saw a familiar tennis court and after that the trail became more pronounced.

I passed the charred ruins of a once-proud home, and a little farther along there were three more houses that had been destroyed. The fire had passed by in an erratic path, devastating some houses and then jumping farther along, leaving other structures curiously untouched. I heard a helicopter overhead and I hid beneath the branches of an oak tree. Halfway down the trail, I came to the fire itself. A great eucalyptus tree was burning like a giant torch, and beyond that I saw a sprawling Hollywood-style farmhouse in flames. I heard the shouts of firemen not far away and the rumble of heavy equipment. The heat blasted against my face. I couldn't stay there. I backed up from the path and made a detour up the hill through a deserted backyard, and then down again into the canyon.

Then I heard a voice from the sky. And the voice said, "Jonathan Sangor . . . Jonathan Sangor . . . come out into the open with your hands in the air . . . you cannot escape."

It was like the voice of God, a loudspeaker on a helicopter passing overhead. The smoke was so thick I knew they couldn't see me. Despite the fire and the voice from the sky, I felt protected here in the bosom of my childhood land.

Deep in my soul I knew I would find La Chanson d'Or still standing. A childhood home lingers in the imagination and dies a hard death. I came in through the back gate, which swung open on a rusty old hinge, and I stood beneath a tree that was being strangled by vines. This part of the property had always been seldom used. Everything was overgrown, decayed, but I could tell someone had been here before me. I followed the trampled grass until I came to the meditation studio, and then I walked on toward the big pretentious house with its Gone With the Wind façade.

There was a crackling sound of burning wood, and when I came out from under the trees I saw the garage was on fire, as well as the apartments Albert and, at one time, Speedo had called home. As I watched, a maple tree between the main house and the garage erupted into flames. At this rate La Chanson d'Or would not be standing long.

I ran over the open ground past the swimming pool and I heard a helicopter beating overhead. I felt like a rabbit running from an eagle in the sky. I heard a gun shot, the long, hard crack of a rifle. At first I thought the helicopter was shooting at me, but then I saw Rags sitting in his wheelchair in the open doorway of the kitchen with a rifle raised to his shoulder. He was taking aim at the sky. He fired again, two more times. The helicopter dived away toward the safety of the smoke.

Rags was laughing, having a great time.

"Are you crazy?" I called out at him.

He saw me now for the first time and his rifle swung my way.

"Drop your gun, Jonno."

"Where's Zoe?"

"Oh, she's inside with Keith. Still chasing the women, are you? You shouldn't have come here, Jonno. Now drop the gun."

I did as he told me and I walked toward where he was sitting in the open door. He backed up in his wheelchair to let me in.

"Close the door, Jonno. Those helicopters are going to be back. All they're going to find, though, are a few barbecued bones and one ex-mansion."

"Oh, Rags," I said sadly. "I'm sorry it had to be you. You killed Dad, you crazy bastard."

He grinned at me. "You think I could manage that from my wheelchair?"

"There's always your friend Keith," I said. "It's the same thing. He acted as your arms and legs."

"Oh, Jonno, you got it all wrong. Right now I'm just playing housekeeper, cleaning up the Sangor family mess."

"What are you talking about?"

"I was going to leave you out of this, due to my past feelings for you. But since you're here, I think you should come on into the dining room. Zoe's already arrived and so has David. We're just waiting for Opera and Carl, and then we'll have the naming of the names. I think it's going to surprise you who killed Dad."

"Rags, look, we gotta get out of here. The garage is already on fire and the house is going to go any minute."

"Oh, we're all going to fry, Jonno. That's the whole point. I'm doing the world a big favor. Albert's already gone, making the long journey to hell. He was all tied up in his apartment when I set it on fire. I thought I'd give nature a little helping hand."

"Oh, Jesus, you killed Albert?"

"Well, in a way you could say he killed me first. So now we're even."

47

I did not feel my usual sunny optimism. With the fire raging all around us, and Albert already dead, and Rags and his blond giant Keith armed with rifles, I couldn't imagine how this was going to come out well.

Zoe and David were sitting in the dining room at the long mahogany table beneath the crystal chandelier. Zoe gave me a wary smile and I joined the group. David scowled and looked away. Rags sat down at his old place and I might almost have expected Gretchen to come out of the kitchen with a serving platter of cow's tongue, except for the presence of Keith who stood guarding us with a rifle.

"Carl and Opera will be here any minute," Rags said.

"That's impossible," I told him. "No one can get in here. I just barely made it myself down the old trail, and I bet Opera doesn't know that back way."

"Oh, Carl will get her here, don't you worry. They're coming together. They wouldn't miss this for anything. I made up a very convincing story, you see, to gather the old clan together. You can see how I snared David and Zoe here. Like rabbits in a trap. You know what I used for bait?"

"Tell me, Rags. What did you use for bait?" I said to humor him.

"Greed," he replied. "I told them that Albert had stayed behind when the rest of the canyon was evacuated, which was perfectly true, by the way. The old fart just couldn't bear to leave the scene of his servitude. So I phoned David and Zoe and Carl and Opera, and I said Albert was going through Dad's papers trying to put things in boxes to save them from the fire. And, lo and behold, he came across a previously undiscovered codicil to Dad's will dated just a week before his death. And in this codicil, you, Jonno, were disinherited. You can see what this would mean for the rest of us. The stock in the studio, which is worth nearly half a billion dollars, would now come to us. Me and Zoe and Opera and Carl and David. Hell, we all love you, Jonno, but half a billion dollars! It wakens the appetites even of the best of us, and we are not the best, Jonno. We are rotten. We're like little apples who have fallen to the ground and have already begun to smell."

"Speak for yourself," I said.

"Oh, I'll let you be the judge. After you've heard my story. But right now I'm telling you how I've gathered the tribe. You see, I told everyone on the phone, there's only one problem about this interesting new codicil that makes us all so immensely wealthy. Albert. Albert likes Jonno best, our handsome golden boy, our wandering youth. Albert thinks Jonno should have the studio, not the rest of us. In fact, I said I was afraid our faithful butler might leave this piece of paper behind to burn unless we immediately showed up en masse and convinced him to do his impartial duty. Are you getting the picture, Jonno?"

"You got quite an imagination, Rags. I guess I've underestimated you all these years. I used to think you were the original goofball."

Rags smiled and without warning he let loose his nerdy chuckle that started in the back of his throat and ended in his nose. "Like that?" he asked. "Oh, I was goofy all right. That was my disguise. It used to protect me from all the pain of your goddamn sadistic mother, and then, later, the pain of knowing I was secretly gay. It was the kind of disguise I even came to believe myself, until one day I realized it wasn't me at all, it was just a convenient skin that no longer had a purpose."

We heard voices from the kitchen. "Albert! Rags! Where are you?"

It was Carl.

"Get out of here, Carl!" I screamed.

I was too late. Keith, who seemed to be the strong silent type, made a quick move through the dining-room door and came back leading Opera and Carl in front of his pointed rifle. The newcomers looked at the rest of us sitting calmly around the dining room table with surprise.

Carl said urgently. "The eastern wing of the house is already on fire."

"But Rags doesn't plan for us to get out," Zoe said. It was the first word I'd heard from her.

Carl and Opera sat down at the table and Keith took up his position leaning against the side buffet, guarding with his gun. I wasn't sure how Rags had won his loyalty, but being burned alive in this house seemed to hold no terrors for him. I scratched my head suddenly, curious to see how fast he could move. The barrel on the rifle had swung my way even before my hand touched my hair, and he relaxed only when he had concluded my movement was not a threat. Zoe was looking at me intently. I wished I could read her mind. Knowing Zoe, she had probably figured out a way out of here.

"I think we should discuss a deal here," David said in his best boardroom manner. "Under the circumstances, I'm sure Jonno could be persuaded to a six-way split of the studio stock, and, of course, I'll agree to drop my legal maneuvering. That way we can share equally. It will be like a new beginning, we can be a family again. But we've got to get out of here, Rags. This minute. Because time is running out."

"Oh, I've known that for nearly a year now," Rags said. "So there's nothing you can offer me to make a deal, David, because you don't have anything I want."

"Rags, you're really being a shit about this," Opera said. "And if you don't let us out of here right away, I'm going to start to get really mad."

No one paid any attention to our little sister. I heard the sound of flames not far away, and little wisps of smoke were creeping into the dining room.

"Well, which one of us is the killer, Rags?" I asked. If time was running out I wanted to know that much at least.

"It isn't one of us," he told me. And just when I was beginning to relax, he added, "No, it isn't *one* of us at all."

And all of a sudden I got it. I looked around the table at my brothers and sisters and I felt a nauseating wave of understanding. It was just like before. A group effort. The family that kills together . . .

"*All* of you?" I whispered.

"Pretty much," Rags said.

"Tell him the truth, Rags," Zoe insisted.

Rags shrugged. "Well, all of us, Jonno, except you and Zoe. You were up in the idyllic north and Zoe was in Tibet. You were with us in spirit, so we thought you wouldn't mind if we proceeded without you."

"Tell him everything, Rags," Zoe urged. "I want Jonno to know the truth."

"Okay. Zoe actually returned to fabulous L.A., and Carl tried to include her in. But she said she didn't want any part of it."

"Then why is Zoe here at this table?" I demanded. "She's not one of your rotten apples, Rags, so let her go."

"She's here because I hate her. Because she came and broke up our family—you and me and Carl. And anyway, she's not that fucking innocent. She knew we were going to kill him and she didn't do a thing to stop us. It's Zoe all the way. She gets her inheritance, she gets everything she wants, and she still gets to act like a goddamn angel."

"I promised Carl I wouldn't tell anyone or try to stop you," Zoe said. "And when I promise something, I do it."

"Oh, isn't that fantastic?" Rags said sarcastically. "But you're going to burn with the rest of us, darling, I can goddamn assure you of *that*."

I was having trouble absorbing all this. If I was understanding this right, Zoe and I were the only ones not involved in the killing. I kept looking around the table.

"But *why*?" I asked. "Why did you kill him?"

"Oh, we all had our reasons. All of us. You were poking around, Jonno. I'm sure you even figured out what these reasons are. Take David. He was about to lose his job at the studio if Dad took power again, which was likely. And Carl. He needed the money to make the balloon payment on his shelter in Hollywood."

"I gave him a chance, Jonno," Carl interrupted. His voice was high-pitched, full of anguish. "I invited him to the shelter the day before we were set to kill him, like I told you. I *pleaded* with him for the money, and all he had to do was give it to me and he would still be alive. But he laughed at me and he was so arrogant, and it made me remember . . ."

We heard the sound of a rafter falling somewhere in the house. We all looked at each other around the table.

"It made you remember what, Carl."

"It made me remember our mother, Jonno. The monstrous Corina Norman. How could he marry someone like that and then go off and leave her in charge? Oh, he pretended to love us, but he never even came back from overseas when Mom nearly burned me to death when she was drunk. The bastard didn't even want to know how the fire started. I tried to tell him once, but he thought I was making it up. So fuck him. All that money he had, I knew I could put it to a good use."

"But killing your own father, Carl! And you, Opera! I just can't believe you were part of this insanity."

Rags laughed. "*She* did it, Jonno. She was young and agile, so she got elected. She climbed in your bedroom window and bashed the old man over the head with the Oscar and then left the little propane bomb that Carl dreamed up."

"But why, Opera?" I pleaded.

She shrugged. "He was really being a shit, Jonno. That movie I told you about, about the girl and the whale, he decided he wasn't going to give me the lead after all. There's this other girl, Tracy Carlson—he was going to give the part to her. But if he was dead, you see, David promised I'd get to play it after all."

"Jesus. You killed him for a part in a movie," I said.

"Jonno! You've been away, you don't know what it's like in this town." My little sister seemed to smell smoke and she stopped for a moment with a look of anxiety on her face. But I guess the perils of Hollywood were more interesting to her than a mere fire. "I mean, I'm a *television* star, Jonno. Big fucking deal. I've done a few features that did this-way that-way at the box office, but nothing that was going to guarantee that the network wouldn't cancel me next season and I would go the way of ninety-nine percent of all child actors who you never hear from again. Fuck that. This picture will *make* my career. I'll never have to worry again. I mean, what do you want from me? You want me to turn into 'Leave It to Beaver' or something?"

It was incredible. Opera was still the same very likable young girl as always. She was a sweetheart. But her sense of morality was about as thin as a piece of paper. Maybe it wasn't her fault, growing up in this town with a pushy stage mother who was always away in Europe. I don't know. Maybe this was none of our faults. Maybe people who grew up with mothers like Corina Norman and fathers like Alexander Sangor were simply doomed to be dangerous moral imbeciles with no sense of the real world under their feet. I was beginning to think Rags was right after all. We all deserved to burn up here along with the terrible old house.

"So Opera whacked the old man over the head, Carl made the bomb. Who broke into the damn hardware store and stole the timers?"

"That was Carl also," said Rags. "Amazing, huh? He finally figured out how to make something explode."

"And what did you do, Rags? Why did you get involved with this?"

"I thought it up. Me and David," Rags said.

"For the money?"

"Naw. Where I'm going, money won't help much. I did it to make amends. When I die, I want to feel I'm wiping the slate clean. I want to leave the world a better place with a few less villains."

I kept shaking my head. This was all so wild. "So who drove me out to that field when I was drunk? Who set this fire?" I asked.

"That was David, of course. It was his little pet project, something he was doing on his own. You see, it came as a shock that after we killed Dad and then opened the will it turned out his entire holdings in the studio were going to you. David had the idea that if you got blamed for the murder, the stock in the studio would revert to the estate, so he was planting a few little bits of evidence to help the police along. When you conked out at the memorial, he saw a great chance to improvise."

"And this final little bonfire gathering?"

"Well, when David improvised, I thought I might too. Somehow it seemed a fitting end for all of us to die together in this house. Only you weren't supposed to be here, Jonno. You crashed the wrong party, I'm afraid."

"And Keith," I asked, looking at the blond giant with the gun. "You're the only outsider here. What about you?"

Keith stared at me moodily, but didn't speak.

"Keith darling gave me the disease," Rags said. "He's a carrier of the HIV virus. It's not his fault, he's healthy as a horse, he didn't even know he had it. But most likely he'll get as sick as I am one day soon, and we simply decided to join our fates together. Why wait for death when you can grab it by the horns?"

"That's right." Those were the only two words I ever heard Keith say. And then the staircase collapsed in the next room and the dining-room door burst open and there was a flash of heat like a bomb going off in our faces, a great whoosh of flame.

I heard screaming all around me. The big crystal chandelier over the dining-room table came crashing down. There was heat and smoke and confusion and I saw David for a second with a burning rafter falling down on his head.

I was on the floor dazed and uncertain. I don't know how Zoe got to me, but she was there beside me using her hands to swat at the legs of my pants which were on fire. I knew there was no way out of this, but then I had the craziest thought: If I were Marco Mallory, I said to myself, I would save the woman I love and get us out of here alive.

"Stay low," I told her. "We can breathe better near the floor." There was so much smoke it was hard to see, but I told Zoe to hold on to the back of my pants, the way she did so many years ago when we were sneaking into Casa Monte Carlo in the dark. The entire ceiling was starting to cave in. I could hear the wood cracking and beginning to separate. I put my arms around Zoe and told her to run with me and we went crashing through the swinging door into the kitchen just as the entire dining room collapsed behind us.

Zoe was coughing. She could barely breathe. She said we were going to die. But I knew that deep in my soul I was a swashbuckling hero. It was just that I'd never had a chance before, but this was my big moment, and I was going to save her. I picked Zoe up in my arms and carried her out the kitchen door. But the entire world was on fire, the trees, the grass, everything. There was no safety out of doors.

"I love you, Zoe," I said. I held her as close to me as I could and I made a run across a field of flames. We were burning. Zoe and I. We were on fire, our hair, our clothes. But I just kept going and I jumped with Zoe through the burning air, a great final leap of faith and love . . . and we landed with a splash in the swimming pool.

I held her in the water. I was sobbing. Her beautiful golden hair had burned and she seemed just barely alive, but her arms were around me. I held on to Zoe while the world burned around us and finally some men came, men from another world. They wore silver suits and glass shields over their faces and tanks on their backs. They came to carry us away.

Epilogue

The studio jet heads south from LAX on my regular Thursday night run to Peru. As a movie mogul, I have my eccentricities I suppose, one of which is that I always take a three-day weekend to my ranch in the Peruvian Andes, leaving Thursday night and returning to Hollywood first thing Monday. Advanced technology has created a decentralized world where this is possible. A lot of my friends commute to Hollywood from up north in Marin County, and places like Utah and Santa Fe. It seems like no one who can afford it actually lives in L.A. anymore. Peru is just a little bit farther afield than most of the show biz crowd is willing to go, but I like that. In a sense, that's the whole point.

I bought the Gulfstream twin-engine jet two years ago from an ex-dictator of a Third World country who was trying to pay his hotel bills in Palm Beach, Florida. So I got a deal on the thing, and, what the hell, I was able to charge it off to taxes. I have an office in the tail section, with telephones and FAX machines that I can use to communicate anywhere in the world.

Moviemaking is an uncertain occupation and I have found it prudent to diversify. A year ago I started a dog food company. I call the stuff "Yuppie Puppy." It's organic all-natural low-fat dog

318

food and it's doing a pretty good business in grocery stores all around the country despite the fact it is twice as expensive as anything else on the market. Americans spend more on dog food than most countries spend on human food, so it is basically a low-risk venture that absorbs the chanciness of some of my other schemes.

Kismet, who is one of my biggest stars at the moment, did a real cute commercial where a yuppie mom comes home and has dinner with her yuppie puppy, complete with designer pasta and imported water. Kismet has become quite a comedienne. Somehow the qualities that made her a terrible waitress, work in her favor in this new setting to make the entire country laugh.

So Kismet and I are fairly good friends and we peck each other on the cheek when we meet at various industry functions. There are no bad feelings. As for the studio, I guess I have my own particular slant. My company policy is: "Less violence, more tits 'n' ass." I get a lot of flak on this issue because America, after all, loves violence and despises sex. It comes with our puritanical heritage. But I keep at it. My philosophy is, what can be more family oriented than tits 'n' ass? I mean, where do families *come* from, for chrissake? But it's not always easy to be a visionary.

My other company policy is that any screenwriter gets fired on the spot if he or she tries to insert a car chase into any of my pictures. As far as I am concerned, there have been enough car chases in enough movies and TV shows and I feel it is high time to move on to new areas of entertainment. I had a famous screenwriter quit over this point. He came storming into my office one day screaming, "What the hell are we going to show people for a hundred and twenty minutes if we can't show 'em cars running around bashing into things?" And I answered with my old standby, "Show 'em tits 'n' ass."

A lot of people hate me, and I'm sure they sneer behind my back. Some of my recent movies have raised what is usually called "the painful issue of censorship." A few days ago, I gave a speech at the Screen Directors Guild, and I said basically, "Guys, gimme a break. In Indiana Jones movies, people get cut in half, decapitated, mauled by wild animals, pushed out of airplanes, and generally someone comes to a gory end about every thirty seconds, and these pictures get rated PG. I show a few human genitalia and everyone's screaming for censorship. Frankly, I think the country's sick."

So that's my big controversial issue right now. I've found that life is never easy, not even when you have tons of money. Some Christian groups have sworn to kill me, and the other day a very moral person tried to send a bomb in a package to the studio. Fortunately, a few years back I was able to hire Myra Fisher, ex-Special Investigator for the L.A. County Sheriff's Department, as head of studio security. I have great confidence in Myra's ability to keep me alive, and sometimes when I'm in L.A., she and her girlfriend Carol cook me fabulously high-cholesterol dinners.

I guess life is pretty good. I do my best, anyway. I've set up a Carl Sangor Memorial Foundation that runs a half-dozen shelters for the homeless in Los Angeles. And the Ragnar Sangor Foundation recently purchased the exercise club next door to the Santa Monica AIDS Hospice, knocked the thing down, plowed the earth, and created a Ragnar Sangor Memorial Vegetable Garden and Tomato Grove. I don't have any bitterness toward my brothers and sisters. I feel what we did wasn't entirely our fault, but was due mostly to our strange upbringing. Even David. Hell, I named the new commissary at the studio after him. And there is also an Opera Sangor Foundation which each year scouts the nation's high school drama classes and awards scholarships to a hundred talented teen-age actors.

I wish I could do more. I love the memory of my brothers and sisters, and when I think of them I experience great pain. Generally, at these moments there is a foggy far-away look in my eye, and my secretaries and various assistants know it is best to leave me alone.

The best part of my week comes on Thursday night when the company jet picks me up and flies me through the sparkling night sky clear to the Southern Hemisphere. It's a nine-hour flight. I have a stateroom on the plane and a nice double bed, so I generally sleep pretty well. In the morning the stewardess wakes me up with a glass of fresh-squeezed orange juice and a cup of coffee, and I can sit in bed and look out the window at the high snow-covered peaks of the Andes.

The jet comes down in Cuzco, the old Inca capital nestled in a high valley on the top of the world. Going through customs is never a problem since I give all the guards a hefty cash incentive each time one of them has a birthday. In Los Angeles, I try to look the part of a bigshot. I go about in limousines and expensive Italian suits, but as soon as I hit Cuzco I get out the blue jeans and sneakers and T-shirts and I feel my whole body relax. I have an old four-wheel-drive Chevy pickup truck waiting for me at the airport, and I drive over the torturous mountain roads into the Urubamba Valley about halfway between Cuzco and Macchu Picchu. This is where I have my ranch.

The mountains of Peru can be dangerous, but each year I donate ten percent of my personal income to the Shining Path, so I am a welcome and well-protected guest here. The head of the local guerrilla outfit is a stern and handsome lad who calls himself Manco Capac the Second. The original Manco Capac, of course, was the legendary founder of the Incas, so this is a grandiose name which stirs some consternation in the bureaucracies of Lima. Actually, Manco Capac II is a sweet kid. His real name is Roberto Saunders and he reminds me a little of Carl. The world has become so conservative these days, frankly I feel it's the duty of the rich to adopt a Maoist guerilla or two lest they become totally extinct.

About once a month, I invite Roberto and a few of his top lieutenants to my house for dinner. It gives me a chance to ask how the overthrow of the government is progressing, and usually after dinner I show them a new Hollywood movie in my projection room. Deep in my heart, I know the reason Manco Capac II leaves me in peace has nothing to do with the ten percent of my income, nor the pleasures of my table, nor the movies I show. Roberto Saunders is in love with my sister Zoe. Fortunately he is very shy. Whenever Zoe is in the room, he simply becomes a bit more fanatically stiff and polite and chivalrous.

Zoe and I own nearly five thousand acres here, and the Urubamba River cuts savagely through our land, rushing down from the fabulous rain forests beyond Macchu Picchu. We live as brother and sister, and in this part of the world it is not considered strange for families like ours to remain together. Zoe is raising llamas on our land. Right now she has about a thousand or so, a whole herd. Or maybe it's a flock, I've never been entirely certain.

I really get a kick out of Zoe's llamas. They look like creatures Dr. Seuss might have dreamed up. I love their long necks, their fat furry bodies and their gentle eyes. I have no idea what Zoe plans to do with all these animals, and the size of the herd or flock is increasing all the time. Like the old days, Zoe tends to get a little carried away with her projects. Sometimes I have returned from Hollywood to find a sick llama in our living room and Zoe feeding the animal with a baby bottle. I don't mind. Everything Zoe does is okay with me.

And so we have come, Zoe and I, to this far corner of the planet in order to be left alone. When Zoe's hair grew back after the fire, it came back ashen-gray, nearly white, and so she finally looks her age. I'm awfully glad about that. Among other things, when we go to Cuzco, or make an occasional shopping trip to Paris, men don't look at her in quite the same way . . . though if you look at her through my eyes, she's just as lovely, maybe even more so, than before.

The fire left its mark on me as well. I have a scar along the side of my face, and I am no longer such a pretty boy. I like the scar. I wear it proudly. I feel it gives me an advantage in business because people are a little afraid of me. Sometimes I look in the mirror and I pretend it's a sword cut I got in some duel, and then I start thinking about Marco Mallory and the past and how I was able to rescue Zoe and me from the fire. Like Zoe's, my hair is also gray. Time marches on. Neither of us is exactly a kid anymore.

So Zoe and I live with painful memories, but also a strange contentment. We keep separate bedrooms so as not to shock the servants, but there is a connecting door which we often use. Basically, I think of us as man and wife. The only thing Zoe won't let us do is have children. Being into animal husbandry, she's frightened about what such close interbreeding might bring. I've often told her, "Zoe, so our kids have a chromosome missing, maybe two. So what? It could be an advantage in a world such as ours." But Zoe remains firm on this point. She says we're too happy, and this is unnatural enough. She doesn't want to risk the wrath of the gods with any more hubris.

Personally, I'd like to have children with Zoe, lots of children, and it's a disappointment for me. But miracles come from strange places. This summer my brother David's widow, Christina Dorn, sent down her children, my niece and nephew, to stay with us for their entire vacation. Christina's a wicked old girl, but she has a